TWILIGHT AT MAC'S PLACE

TWILIGHT AT MAC'S PLACE

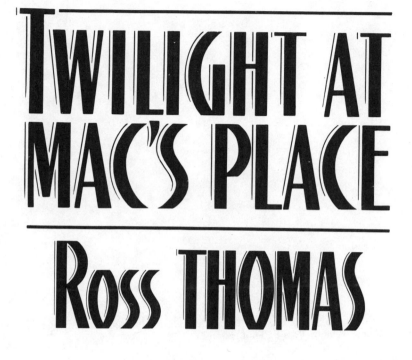

Ross Thomas

THE MYSTERIOUS PRESS
New York · Tokyo · Sweden · Milan
Published by Warner Books

Mysterious Press books are published by
Warner Books, Inc., 666 Fifth Avenue, New York, NY 10103.

A Time Warner Company

Printed in the United States of America
First printing: November 1990

10 9 8 7 6 5 4 3 2 1

Library of Congress Cataloging in Publication Data

Thomas, Ross, 1926–
    Twilight at Mac's Place / Ross Thomas.
        p.   cm.
    ISBN 0-89296-214-3
    I. Title.
    PS3570.H58T9   1990
    813'.54—dc20

                                                            90-43904
                                                              CIP

To Roberta Kent

TWILIGHT AT MAC'S PLACE

One

Shortly after the death of the failed Quaker, Steadfast Haynes, the Central Intelligence Agency received a telephoned blackmail threat that was so carefully veiled and politely murmured it could have been misinterpreted as the work of some harmless crank.

But it wasn't misinterpreted. And it was solely because of this vague threat to reveal what Haynes had really done while serving as an occasional agency hire in Africa, the Middle East, Central America and Southeast Asia that the Department of Defense, after much grumbling, gave in to CIA pressure and ordered the Army to bury him at Arlington National Cemetery with standard military honors.

Steadfast Haynes was 57 when he died at 11:32 P.M. on January 19, the night before the inauguration of the nation's forty-first President. He died in bed on the fourth floor of the Hay-Adams Hotel in a $185-a-night room that commanded a fine view of the White House. He died quietly, even discreetly, much as he had lived, and the 33-year-old woman who lay next to him when he died was a former

Agence France-Presse correspondent and old friend who knew just whom to call and what to do.

Her first call was to Paris and lasted a little more than four minutes. Her second call was to the front desk to notify the hotel that Haynes was dead. Her third call was to the robbery and homicide division of the Los Angeles Police Department.

After this third call was finally transferred to Sergeant Virgil Stroud, she identified herself and, speaking in tones both formal and slightly accented, asked for Detective Granville Haynes in order to inform him of his father's death.

"That's not bad," Sergeant Stroud said.

"Sorry?"

"I mean we had one guy call yesterday, maybe the day before, that had to talk to Granny because he was Granny's identical twin and dying of leukemia and needed a bone marrow transplant."

After a moment of hesitation, she said, "There is no twin brother."

"Yeah. I know. But you'd be surprised what people will say to get to him." This time it was Sergeant Stroud who hesitated. "Or maybe you wouldn't. Be surprised."

"Something's happened to him—is that it?"

"That's it all right. He won the lottery three weeks ago and quit us the next day."

"I still need his home telephone number."

Sergeant Stroud used a chuckle to say goodbye and end the call.

When the Los Angeles Police Department was robbed by fortune of Granville Haynes's services, it was also robbed of its only homicide detective with a master's degree in Old French from the University of Virginia, where he had written his thesis on the three major humanistic aspects of Rabelais's *Gargantua and Pantagruel*.

After making detective, Haynes frequently had been assigned to the occasional rich folks homicides in Bel Air,

Brentwood and even as far west as Pacific Palisades, where, it was felt, the usually wealthy and often influential relatives of the victims would be reassured by his competent demeanor and soothed by his faultless manners, which some mistook for diffidence.

Haynes had spent an odd childhood on the French and Italian Rivieras among the very rich and, consequently, was not only knowledgeable but also chary of their curious folkways and taboos. This knowledge, effortlessly acquired as a child, later enabled him to move among them as one of the nearly anointed—almost as if once long ago they had given him a temporary guest membership that nobody had ever remembered to cancel.

Haynes had acquired his false passport into the land of the rich without any encouragement—or discouragement, for that matter—from his father, who had made it a rule never to give his son unasked-for advice, except once, back in 1974, when Steadfast Haynes, then 43, had delivered a brief homily in Washington. The occasion had been his son's eighteenth birthday and the homily had dealt with the basic economic benefits of inflation.

"Inflation," the older Haynes had said, "means that if you borrow ten bucks today, you just might be able to pay it back next year or the year after that with ten quarters, ten dimes or even ten nickels."

The homicide detective and three other Californians (a journeyman pool cleaner in Santa Barbara, a dentist in Modesto and a waitress in Eureka) had hit the state Lotto for a little more than $1 million each with six numbers, 3 11 13 19 32 45, that had been picked for Haynes by a computer. The gross amount of each check he and the other three winners would receive for the next twenty years was approximately $58,000.

But once all taxes were withheld, the net came to $39,979, which sum, Haynes quickly decided, was enough to let him abandon one of his two careers. So, after almost ten years on

3

the force, seven of them in homicide, he had abandoned police work and turned instead to full-time acting.

It was nearly 4 A.M. in Washington and 1 A.M. in Los Angeles before the former Agence France-Presse correspondent pried Haynes's new and unlisted telephone number out of a reluctant GTE with lies, threats, tears and, finally, help from the French consulate. After Haynes answered his ringing phone with a sleepy but polite hello, the former correspondent used a carefully thought out twenty-three-word paragraph to identify herself and tell him his father was dead.

The brief silence that followed was ended by Haynes with a series of questions of no more than five or six words each that asked about cause, time and place of death. Once satisfied that he had most of the pertinent information, another silence began. Haynes also ended this one when he asked whether his father had ever said anything to her about wanting a particular kind of funeral.

She replied that although Steadfast Haynes had never once talked to her about dying, she thought it might be possible to have him buried in Arlington National Cemetery with some form of military ceremony. Haynes said he thought his father would have appreciated the irony of that, if not the occasion. There was yet another silence, longer this time, and during it Haynes thought he could sense the woman's long-distance smile just before she offered, providing he approved, to arrange the interment at Arlington.

After he gave his approval they ended the call and Haynes went over to the cracked-leather armchair by the living room window of his one-bedroom apartment in Ocean Park. He sat in the chair, staring out in the direction of the Pacific Ocean, his view blocked by the pale yellow monster house across the street that had been built on speculation six months ago but still hadn't sold because of its exorbitant price.

As he sat, trying to summon up images of the near stranger who had been his father, Haynes found himself murmuring the lines he would deliver later that day during the filming of a one-hour television cop show in Burbank. He was to play Cal, a very minor thug, who died early on, and whose only lines were "Forget it!" and "I'm outta here!"

The son of Steadfast Haynes continued to sit in the cracked-leather chair, staring out at the moonlit yellow house, running blurred images of his father through his mind and chanting the two lines aloud. They were, he discovered, almost as good as a mantra and far more comforting than prayer.

An autopsy revealed the cause of Steadfast Haynes's death to have been a massive cerebral hemorrhage. It also revealed a slightly fatty liver and a mild case of emphysema, neither of which surprised the son, who knew that his father, from 15 on, had smoked at least a package of cigarettes a day and drunk as much alcohol as he wished for nearly as long.

After flying into Washington, Haynes soon learned, again with no surprise, that there were only a dozen or so persons in the capital and its metastasizing suburbs who, unless pressed, would even admit to having known the late Steadfast Haynes. Nor did most of them really care that he was dead—although there were two former U.S. government supergrades who might have paid their respects, except both were under Federal indictment and far too worried about their own fates to mourn for anyone else.

Still, there was one man at the Central Intelligence Agency who remembered Steadfast Haynes with a measure of admiration, if not affection, from their days together in Laos. Now 67 years old, the man had retired two years ago as the agency's senior Burma analyst. Of necessity, he temporarily had been called back from retirement after the recent political upheaval in Burma—soon to be renamed

Myanmar—and after, as he put it, "They found out they didn't have anyone who really knew fuck all about the place."

The aging analyst, correctly suspecting he would either be asked or ordered to go, had volunteered to sacrifice a lunch hour and attend the Arlington ceremony as the agency's unofficial observer, if not mourner.

The only true mourners at the grave of Steadfast Haynes were his son, the woman who once had been an Agence France-Presse correspondent, and Tinker Burns, the 66-year-old ex-French Foreign Legionnaire, who had flown in from Paris on the Concorde.

Two

Holding a dove-gray Borsalino homburg in his left hand, Tinker Burns stepped out of the rear of the hired chauffeur-driven Lincoln limousine just as the army bugler began playing "Taps" over the grave of Steadfast Haynes.

Burns snapped to attention and quickly transferred the hat to his right hand so he could hold it over his heart. The homburg went nicely with the dark gray double-breasted suit that had a faint chalk stripe and must have cost at least 9,000 French francs. Burns also wore a white shirt, so carefully ironed and starched it glistened, and a plain tie whose color could have been either black or the deepest navy blue. A black band, which Granville Haynes somehow knew to be silk, was worn just above the elbow on the suit's right sleeve and testified to Burns's status as an official mourner.

The big gray Lincoln, a special pass displayed on its windshield, had crunched to a stop on some loose gravel in the asphalt roadway. The sound of the crunching gravel had caused Granville Haynes to turn from the flag-covered casket. Turning with him were Isabelle Gelinet, the former

Agence France-Presse correspondent, and Gilbert Undean, the recycled Burma analyst.

Once "Taps" was over, Tinker Burns's enormous feet, shod in gleaming black wingtips, carried him from limousine to grave at the Legion's official slow-march pace of eighty-eight steps per minute. Burns marched at attention, which is how Granville Haynes seemed to recall he did almost everything, with head high, chin tucked, shoulders back and arms swinging just as the Legion long ago had decided they should swing.

Burns now wore his hair longer, Haynes noticed. Hair that once had been kept at a maximum length of three quarters of an inch was now one and a half inches long on top but still far less than that at the back and sides. It was a different color, too. Instead of being a shiny tar black, it was now a shiny lard white.

There were also some new lines, Haynes saw. Creases really. But those merry green eyes still sparkled, or maybe even glittered, although not enough to spoil the solemn expression that Haynes knew was meant to portray sorrow, perhaps even grief, and had been carefully applied to the long brown face that had spent too much time under too many tropical suns.

Tinker Burns was almost halfway to the gravesite when the Army sergeant stepped over to present Haynes with the U.S. flag that had covered the casket and was now folded into the prescribed triangle. After the sergeant stepped back and saluted smartly, Haynes murmured his thanks and looked at Isabelle Gelinet, turning the look into a silent offer that she refused with an almost imperceptible headshake.

Haynes turned again and waited for Tinker Burns to come to a halt before offering him the folded flag. "You take it, Tinker," Haynes said. "You knew him longer than I did."

Burns tucked the homburg against his left side with an elbow and used both hands to accept the flag reverently. He stared down at it for several seconds, as if to certify its

8

provenance, looked up at Haynes and said, "Not longer, Granny; just better."

After performing a slow-time about-face, which left him facing the Lincoln, Burns nodded at the uniformed chauffeur, who was leaning against a front fender. The chauffeur hurried over, relieved Burns of the flag and hurried back to the Lincoln.

Still facing away from the others, Tinker Burns bowed his head—in plot, if not in prayer, Haynes thought—looked up finally, turned and said, "I'm going to miss the shit out of Steady."

"It was good of you to come," Haynes said.

Burns sighed and looked at the former Agence France-Presse correspondent, who wore a navy-blue dress under her unbuttoned oyster-white trench coat that had a plaid lining.

"*Ça va*, Isabelle?" Burns said.

She shrugged. "*Ça va*, Tinker."

Burns let his green gaze wander over to the tall thin elderly man with the posture of a crooked stick. Because the weather was unseasonably warm for late January, the man wore only a brown herringbone jacket, gray flannel trousers, scuffed brown loafers that may not have been polished in years, if ever, and a purple tie.

Haynes had wondered whether the tie was the nearest thing to mourning wear the man's closet had to offer. Or maybe, he thought, somewhat cheered, he just doesn't give a damn what he wears.

Tinker Burns finished his own brief inspection, gave the man a charming smile and said, "Don't think we've met, friend. I'm Tinker Burns. You by any chance the official representative of a grateful government?"

"Gilbert Undean," the man said. "I knew Steady in Laos."

"That a fact? Who you with now?"

"I'm sort of retired."

"Sort of?"

"They called me back. Temporarily."

9

Burns nodded twice, as if confirming expected news. "Believe somebody did tell me they were running short of experts on that part of the world, especially after the dust-up in Burma."

Undean frowned. "Who's running short?"

"Langley. Who else?"

"Don't think I mentioned them. Don't think I said damn all about Burma."

"Just a hunch, Mr. Undean. I figured that if you knew something about Laos, since that's where you knew Steady, then you probably knew right smart about Burma, since it's just across the fence. And I also had a hunch that Langley, as caring and sentimental as always, would've sent someone from the old days to represent it at the grave of a fallen comrade."

Tinker Burns smiled again, a bit quizzically this time, as if in anticipation of Undean's reply. But when the reply turned out to be only an indifferent stare, Burns said, "Why don't the four of us take the afternoon off, Mr. Undean, and go have us a long wet lunch somewhere on me and hear all about you and Steady during the Vientiane follies?"

"Thanks," Undean said, "but I wouldn't much care to eat with anyone who'd want to listen to that old crap."

Before Tinker Burns could respond, Haynes quickly went over to shake hands with Undean and said, "Thank you very much for coming."

"Volunteered before I got sent," Undean said, bending forward to examine Haynes more closely. "Thing I remember best about Steady is how well he did it and how easy he made it all look."

"A matter of style?"

"Or nerve." He peered even more closely at Haynes through thick bifocals. "You sure look like him—or at least how I think he used to look almost twenty years ago." Undean paused, opened his mouth as if to say something

10

else, clamped it shut instead, nodded goodbye, turned and walked away.

"What kind of report you think Brother Undean'll turn in?" Tinker Burns asked, once the analyst was out of earshot.

Still staring at Undean's back, Haynes said, "'How I Alone Swelled the Crowd at Steady Haynes's Grave by Twenty-five Percent.'"

Burns chuckled and made a quick survey of the cemetery slope with its rows of matching white headstones. "When I was fixing up my pass and getting directions, they told me they were burying Steady not far from where they'd buried two other great Americans, Lee Marvin and John Mitchell. How'd you get 'em to plant him here?"

"Isabelle arranged it," Haynes said.

Burns looked at her. "Blackmail?"

"What else?" she said.

"They know it was you?"

"Of course."

Burns shook his great head in appreciation, chuckled again and said, "Well, it by God deserves a great lunch and all we can drink."

Without waiting for their acceptance of his invitation, which he obviously took for granted, Burns asked Gelinet whether she had a car. After she nodded, Haynes volunteered he had come by taxi.

"Then you ride with me, Granny, and Isabelle can meet us there."

"Where?" she asked.

"What about Mac's Place?" Tinker Burns said. "If it's still in business."

.

Three

The man with the courtly air and the bald head turned from the seventh-floor window at 1:13 P.M. and dropped into his high-backed leather chair with a sigh just as Gilbert Undean finished the last of his egg salad sandwich on whole-wheat toast.

The man in the high-backed chair was Hamilton Keyes, who had sent down for the sandwich after learning that Undean had not yet eaten. After Undean licked a trace of mayonnaise from the left corner of his mouth, carefully folded the unused paper napkin and stuck it down into the right-hand pocket of his brown herringbone jacket for possible future use, Hamilton Keyes said, "Steady was never in any branch of the service, you know."

"Wrong," Undean said. "He was in Korea in fifty and fifty-one."

"But not in the service," said Keyes, leaning back in the leather chair and resting his feet on one corner of the 137-year-old rosewood desk his rich wife had given him as a fifteenth wedding anniversary present. He had given her a copy of the 1915 Woodberry Society edition of *The Collected*

12

Poems of Rupert Brooke, numbered (No. 27) and signed by George Edward Woodberry himself. Keyes had acquired the copy at a Georgetown garage sale (where it had been called an estate sale) for $3.50 after realizing it was worth between five and seven hundred dollars.

"We talking about the same Steadfast Haynes?" Undean said.

Keyes smiled slightly and nodded. A careerist, Keyes only recently had realized he had gone as high as he would ever go in the agency. The realization had come not as a shock, or even as a disappointment, but rather as a curious kind of relief, and he now took an almost morbid interest in the progressive atrophy of his ambition.

Undean said, "Well, if he wasn't in the Army in Korea, what the fuck was he doing there?"

"He was a C.O."

"Different Steady Haynes then," said Undean, who had known the courtly man since 1962, when, fresh out of Brown with a full head of hair and even then a certain mannered courtliness, Hamilton Keyes had joined the agency as a probationer.

"Steady was with the American Friends Service Committee," Keyes said. "The Quakers. He drove an ambulance or carried a stretcher or passed out doughnuts. Something humanitarian. He was attached to the Seventh Division when the Chinese hordes overran it on Thanksgiving Day in nineteen fifty. It *was* Thanksgiving, wasn't it?"

"Around in there," Undean agreed. "He get captured?"

"No, but during the retreat he hooked up with six GIs, all that was left of a rifle company, who were hell-bent on surrendering. Steady argued against it. The ringleader, or lead surrenderer, I suppose one might call him, aimed his piece at Steady and told him to shut up."

"And?"

"And Steady, of course, refused. The ringleader shot at him and missed, probably on purpose. Our Quaker friend snatched a submachinegun, a Thompson, I believe, from the hands of one of the other GIs." Keyes looked doubtful for a moment. "They did use Thompsons in Korea, didn't they?"

"Must've."

"At any rate, Steady promised to shoot the first fucker who tried to surrender. The ringleader fired again and this time the round grazed Steady's left arm just above the elbow. Steady shot him dead. After that he led the remaining five down to Hungnam, where they were evacuated."

"Leaving his faith behind," Undean said.

"He may not have lost it completely until after the five he led to safety preferred murder charges against him, which was their way of thanking him for saving their lives. The Army couldn't decide whether to shoot Steady or give him a medal. So they shipped him back to the States and forgot him."

"That must've been when he went back to school," Undean said. "The University of Pennsylvania."

"Where we tried to recruit him just before graduation in nineteen fifty-five."

"Tried?"

"They say he laughed at us. Well, smiled anyway. He told our recruiters that if he ever went into the hearts-and-minds business, it would be for money, not country. So he landed a job with one of the big New York ad agencies and made such an impression that three years later they transferred him to their Paris office."

"This was when?" Undean asked.

"Fifty-eight, I believe. In late fifty-nine, the ad agency's Paris office was approached by representatives of the Belgian government. The Belgians were concerned that there might be something of a mess in the Congo after independence— nothing to fret about, you understand—but they still thought an American ad agency might be useful in putting the best face on it. The ad agency's Paris office, for various reasons, said no thanks. So our friend Steady quit, made his own presentation to the Belgians in his quite serviceable French and landed the account. And that's how he wound up in the Congo during the troubles of the early sixties."

"And where he met Tinker Burns," Undean said.

"Apparently. Had you ever run into Burns during your travels?"

"I'd heard the stories about him, but today's the first time I ever met him."

"And your immediate impression?"

"White hair. Stiff neck. Smart mouth."

"Then he hasn't really changed," Keyes said. "Except for the hair." His right palm made an exploratory pass over his own bald head. "Tinker's used to be coal black."

"He really at Dien Bien Phu like everybody says?" Undean asked. "Or is that just more bullshit?"

"There were four of them with the Legion there. Four Americans, I mean. Tinker was the only one to survive."

"How long was he in?" Undean said.

"The Legion? Ten years. From forty-six to fifty-six. Before that he was a paratrooper with the Eighty-second Airborne. A battlefield commission made him a second lieutenant. When he left the Legion after ten years, he was a captain, which, for an American, I understand, is quite extraordinary."

"Why the fuck would he join the Legion?"

Hamilton Keyes smiled. "If you'd accepted his invitation to lunch, Gilbert, you could've asked him. He might even have told you." Keyes paused. "Like some coffee?"

"Yeah. I would. Thanks."

Keyes picked up his telephone and asked for two coffees. They waited in silence until a young man brought them in on a tray. After the young man left without speaking, Undean took a sip, put his cup down and said, "If Steady wasn't ever in any branch of the service, why bury him at Arlington?"

"The woman who was at the graveside services thought it would be nice if we did."

15

"Isabelle Gelinet."

"Pretty name, isn't it?" said Keyes. "Mlle Gelinet quit her job at AF-P a few years ago and moved in with Steady at that place of his in Virginia."

"The farm near Berryville?"

Keyes nodded.

"Heard it was part of his divorce settlement from that rich widow he married."

"I see you've kept up with the gossip, Gilbert."

"I'm retired, not deaf."

"In any event, Gelinet moved in, ostensibly to help Steady write his memoirs."

"I'll buy a copy."

Keyes chose to ignore the comment. "The day after Steady died, the day of the inauguration, in fact, Gelinet called us. Her call was finally routed to me at home because Steady, there at the very end, had been one of mine. She refused to identify herself, but I'm sure she didn't care that I could easily guess who was calling."

"What'd she want?"

"She wanted him buried at Arlington with a bugler blowing 'Taps' over his grave. That was the last forthright statement she made. The rest was all hints and verbal nudges, the gist of them being that unless we agreed to bury him at Arlington, the manuscript of his memoirs would be expressed that same day to a most reputable literary agent in New York. I hinted back that if this indeed were to happen, we might be forced to take legal remedies. She said we were more than welcome to try and hung up."

The courtly man stopped talking, looked somewhere past Undean's left shoulder and added, "So we buried him at Arlington."

"And sent me to count the house."

"You were the only one left who had the slightest reason to go—except for me."

16

Undean frowned. "What happened to your legal remedies?"

Keyes shrugged.

"A bluff, right? And after she called it, you caved in."

When Keyes only stared at him, saying nothing, revealing nothing, Undean smiled sourly and said, "It doesn't scan. You've stopped plenty of others from publishing. You even stopped two or three guys so hard they went bankrupt. So why not Steady?"

"Because one, he's dead, and two, he never worked for us."

"Number two is bullshit."

"Not this time, Gilbert. You see, we never had a contract with Steady. He would never sign anything, never endorse any check of ours or even set up an offshore account we could move his funds into. From the very first—there in the Congo—he insisted on being paid all fees and expenses in either Swiss francs or gold. So how could we stop a dead man, who we couldn't even prove had ever worked for us, from publishing his memoirs, which we hadn't even read? And that's why we caved in, as you so nicely put it, and buried him at Arlington."

When Undean made no reply, Keyes picked up his cup and drank the rest of his now tepid coffee. As he put the cup down, he said, "What did you make of his son, Granville?"

"I thought he was nice and polite, maybe too polite for this day and age, and I think you just threw the switch."

"To sidetrack you?"

Undean nodded. "What're you really going to do about them?"

"Who?"

"His memoirs."

"Oh. Those. Well, nothing more than we've already done, which is to pay a plot of what?—hallowed ground?—to prevent them from being published. Of course, I wouldn't really worry if they were published because I'm sure they're nothing more than the same old thrice-regurgitated public

17

domain rogue elephant stuff. Warmed-over old hat, to mix yet another metaphor. At best, a slow read on a long flight."

"I know better," Undean said. "And if I know better, you damn sure do."

Hamilton Keyes favored Undean with another polite but empty stare.

"Want some advice?" Undean said.

"Not really."

"Buy 'em," Undean said. "Buy the memoirs and all the rights thereto. It'll save you one hell of a lot of grief and money in the long run."

The courtly man rose with a smile that was neither warm nor cold. A room-temperature smile, Undean decided. A smile of dismissal.

"It's been awfully nice chatting with you again, Gilbert," Keyes said as he came around the rosewood desk, waited for Undean to rise, put a comforting hand on the old man's shoulder and gently guided him to the door.

Four

After nearly a generation it could still be found at the same location a few blocks north of K Street and a little less than that west of Connecticut Avenue. Because it had endured so long in Washington, where restaurants often have the life span of a mayfly, many thought of Mac's Place as either an undesignated landmark or, if they were under 30, a quaint and curious monument to the sixties.

That it still existed at all was largely because of a firm of prospering criminal defense lawyers who occasionally dabbled in real estate. In 1987 they had formed a syndicate to buy the land beneath Mac's Place and much of that on either side of it.

The syndicate had then erected a seven-story office building over and around the restaurant, taking great pains to preserve its unprepossessing façade and excellent kitchen. When asked, the lawyers always justified the extravagant preservation by saying, "We needed a nice place close by to eat lunch."

Long before the advent of either salad bars or nouvelle cuisine, and long, long before the fading craze for something

19

called plain American cookery, which usually meant meat loaf redux, it was possible to find a restaurant, chop house or bar & grill very much like Mac's Place in almost any American city. They were often long narrow quiet rooms with a slightly foreign, melancholy air that offered generous drinks, swift monosyllabic service and a varied menu that on Thursdays might even include spit-roasted sweetbreads.

Largely through inertia, Mac's Place had managed to preserve a similar atmosphere. It was, as Michael Padillo, its co-owner, once said, "The sort of place you go when you have to meet someone and explain why you won't be getting the divorce after all."

It was 1:22 P.M. when Tinker Burns escorted Isabelle Gelinet and Granville Haynes into Mac's Place, where they stood blinking and waiting for their eyes to adjust to the perpetual twilight. Glancing around, Haynes noticed the lunch crowd was beginning to disperse.

Herr Horst, the 74-year-old maître d' with the enviable posture of a martinet, gathered up three menus and slowly advanced on the new customers, much as if he were leading a procession of bishops. When he was a few feet away from Tinker Burns, whom he hadn't seen in three years, Herr Horst stopped and greeted him with the single abrupt nod that regular patrons had named The Whiplasher. "Three for lunch, Mr. Burns?"

"Three."

"Still prefer to be seated with your back to the wall?"

"Old habits, good or bad, die hard."

"But as Proust noted, they also fill up time. This way, please."

After he had seated them at a banquette, handed out the menus and complimented Gelinet by name on what he called her frock, Herr Horst, as even Padillo called him, examined Granville Haynes and said, "We haven't had the pleasure of your custom, Mr. Haynes, since September of nineteen seventy-four when you and your father dined with us. It was your eighteenth birthday, as I recall, and you were off the next day to the university at Charlottesville." Herr Horst paused, dropped his voice to a somber note and added, "I was extremely saddened to learn of his death."

"You're very kind," said Haynes.

Still studying his menu, Tinker Burns said, "You ever think of maybe taking that memory act of yours on the road with some carnival?"

"Not recently," Herr Horst said.

Burns looked up. "The McCorkle around?"

"Alas, no."

"What about Padillo?"

"I'll tell him you're here."

"Don't bother."

Herr Horst's lips twitched, as if he were considering a smile. "But he would be desolate were he not told."

After the maître d' turned and marched slowly away, still leading his invisible procession, a waiter hurried over to take their drink orders. Burns wanted a martini, straight up; Gelinet, a vermouth; and Haynes, a bottle of Beck's. Arriving with the waiter and the drinks was Michael Padillo.

Haynes couldn't remember Padillo from that seemingly endless birthday dinner of more than fourteen years ago. Yet there was something about him that he found oddly familiar.

Recalling the long-ago birthday dinner, Haynes discovered he could easily draw a mental picture of the man Tinker Burns had referred to as the McCorkle—a big man, well over six feet, who had stopped by their table to exchange pleasantries and quips with Steadfast Haynes. McCorkle had been wearing too many laugh lines around self-mocking eyes that were either hazel or brown. He also had a skeptical grin, most of his hair and the build of a middle-aged jock who had long since stopped bothering with the Canadian Air Force exercises. But the real reason you remember him so well, Haynes decided, is that he sent over two cognacs, which was the first time a publican ever bought you a drink.

21

Still watching Padillo, who was bowing over the hand of a smiling Isabelle Gelinet, Haynes found himself reverting to his abandoned role of homicide detective as he measured Padillo's height at a little less than six feet; weighed him in at 160 or 165; classified his nose as straight-long, his mouth as thin-wide; judged his complexion to be a light olive, his hair a gray-streaked dark brown.

Haynes wondered briefly whether Padillo was part Mexican or part Spanish but decided it didn't really matter because he'd never seen anyone with that many years move with so much athletic grace, which usually was the franchise of those who'd made a living from it on some playing field—or in rings where they send in either the bull or another middleweight.

What made Padillo so strangely familiar to Haynes were his eyes. Not their color, which on Haynes's private chart was coded as Gray-Green Cools #1, but rather their look of semi-devout fatalism. This look, he believed, was acquired only by those who at some risk have peered into the human abyss and aren't at all reassured by what they've seen.

Haynes had known old homicide badges, nearing their pensions, who had worn that same look. So had two poets, one young, one old, both women. And once, on the rooftop of a Wilshire Boulevard office building in Westwood, a 47-year-old psychiatrist had turned to gaze briefly at Haynes with that same look just before he turned yet again and stepped off the edge.

It was Isabelle Gelinet who introduced Padillo to Granville Haynes. After they shook hands, Padillo said he was very sorry about Steady's death. Haynes thanked him and asked whether they had been close friends.

"Close acquaintances," Padillo said.

"You knew Steady well enough to have shown up at Arlington," Tinker Burns said. "Either you or the McCorkle."

Padillo, still standing, examined the seated Burns as if for signs of moth and rust. "McCorkle's out of town and I no longer go to funerals."

"Then you must miss out on a lot of quiet satisfaction," Haynes said.

The small surprised smile Padillo gave him was that of a very minor prophet discovering his first disciple. It encouraged Haynes to say, "Join us for a drink?"

Padillo thought about it, agreed with a nod and glanced at a waiter, who hurried over with a chair. Once seated, Padillo resumed his inspection of Tinker Burns, nodded again, as if partially satisfied, and said, "That arms boutique of yours must be flourishing, Tinker."

"A steady, unseasonal demand," Burns said. "Much like the toilet paper business."

The waiter returned with a pale drink that could have been either plain ginger ale or a very weak Scotch and water. Padillo ignored it and looked at Gelinet. "Who showed, Isabelle?"

"We three—and a man from Langley. Gilbert Undean."

"They send him?"

"He said he'd known Steady in Laos and volunteered before he got sent." She shrugged. "But who can say?"

Padillo picked up his drink, tasted it and put it back down. "I heard Steady died of a stroke in the Hay-Adams the night before the inauguration. He wasn't in town for that, was he?"

"We were here for the North trial," she said. "Steady had booked us rooms for the next three months."

"Why so early?"

"He was trying to arrange for a permanent seat in the courtroom."

"Did he know North?" Granville Haynes asked.

"Not North," she said. "But he'd known Secord since the Congo and, of course, Albert Hakim." She paused. "And some of the others."

"Dear Albert," Tinker Burns said and, displaying a remarkable flair for mimicry, added, "'Just let us handle the money, Ollie, so you won't be burdened with all that tedious bookkeeping.'"

"Was he in on it, Tinker?" Haynes asked.

"Steady? Nah. Nowhere near it. And it's too bad in a way. If they'd've had Steady doing the retouch, Secord, Hakim, North and the others might be thinking about what they oughta say at Oslo when they got handed the peace prize."

Haynes turned to Padillo and said, "My old man and the truth were never more than nodding acquaintances."

"He was exactly what he claimed to be—a propagandist," Gelinet said. "And a superb one."

Haynes stared at her. "That's what I just said. What I don't understand is why he'd want to spend weeks or even months in some courtroom."

"It was to be the epilogue," she said.

"To what?"

"His memoirs. He thought the North verdict, however it goes, would serve as the perfect metaphor for an epilogue— although there won't be one now."

"No book or no epilogue?" Padillo said.

"No epilogue."

"But there will be a book?"

She shrugged.

"Who's in it?"

Isabelle Gelinet made a small but encompassing gesture that managed to capture the restaurant, Washington and half the world.

Padillo rose. "Then I'll have to buy a copy, won't I?"

Five

Standing at the very end of the long line, McCorkle rearranged his expression into one of terminal boredom and used a foot to shove his ancient one-suiter toward customs at Dulles International Airport. For years he had been convinced that a bored look, when combined with a suit and tie, made the perfect match to the U.S. Customs Service's profile of the innocent traveler.

Still looking bored, McCorkle watched two Federal dogs, both mutts, sniff out a pile of luggage for drugs. He continued to watch the dogs when a roving uniformed customs inspector appeared at his elbow and said, "Nice flight?"

"Not bad."

"Could I see your passport?"

McCorkle turned and began the search, slowly patting his pockets with no sign of panic. He finally removed the passport from his hip pocket, the last one left, and handed it over, trusting that his carefully unhurried search was another hallmark of innocence.

The inspector opened the passport and leafed through it. "Frankfurt, huh?"

"Frankfurt," McCorkle agreed.

"Business or pleasure?"

"Neither. My wife's brother died. We went to his funeral."

The inspector glanced around as if hoping to discover a Mrs. McCorkle. "She stayed on?"

"There was some family business to clear up."

"Your wife's first name, Mr. McCorkle?"

"Fredl."

"*Eine gute Deutsche Hausfrau, ja?*"

"Washington correspondent for a Frankfurt paper."

"You're kidding. Which one?"

After McCorkle told him, the inspector nodded approvingly and said, "The serious one."

"Profoundly so."

"And what do you do, Mr. McCorkle?" the inspector asked, his eyes pricing the five-year-old gray worsted Southwick suit McCorkle had bought on sale at Arthur Adler's.

"I run a saloon."

"In Washington?"

"Right."

"What's it called?"

"Mac's Place."

"Ate there once," the inspector said. "Not bad." He looked down at the passport again, read the name "Cyril McCorkle" aloud and looked up with a smile. "Bet everybody calls you Mac."

"You win."

The inspector bent down, marked the old suitcase with a piece of chalk, straightened and handed McCorkle a slip of paper that was the treasured *laissez-passer*. "Take the express line, Cyril," the inspector said. "And welcome home."

McCorkle later blamed his sunglasses for having caused the case of mistaken identity in front of Mac's Place just after he paid off the taxi, picked up his old suitcase and turned. Although his eyesight in recent years had gone from near perfect to good to the stage where he now needed reading glasses, McCorkle refused to wear prescription sunglasses because he couldn't remember, offhand, ever having read a book all the way through in the sunshine. And since he felt the need to blame something, he blamed the sunglasses for causing him to mistake the man who came out of Mac's Place for the late Steadfast Haynes.

"It was a quarter past three or a little earlier," he said as he later recounted the incident to Padillo. "And he was in the shade and the sun was just low enough to stab me right in the eyes. So when I looked away from the sun into the shade, there he was—same tennis-pro build, same walk that makes you wonder when he'll start tap-dancing and that same face."

"But a face at least twenty-five years younger," Padillo said.

"Not if you're half blind from the sun and looking into deep shade through dirty dark glasses. So what I saw were the same moves, height, build—plus a face that shade, sunglasses and memory were adding twenty-five years to."

"The world's most honest face," Padillo said.

"I always felt it was those flag-blue eyes."

"Plus the resolute chin and that most serene brow."

"But somehow you knew nobody could be as honest as Steady looked," McCorkle said. "So just before you started edging away from him, he'd grin that god-awful kid's grin that could melt rocks."

"And also make you want to believe everything he said."

"Another mistake," McCorkle said. "How big a tab did he run up?"

Padillo shrugged. "A few hundred dollars that we might as well eat." He paused, obviously curious. "So what'd you say to him?"

"Well, since I didn't know he was dead, I said, 'How the hell are you, Steady?'"

27

*   *   *

Granville Haynes said, "I'm afraid he's dead, Mr. McCorkle."

McCorkle put the old suitcase down, removed his dirty sunglasses, stared at Haynes and said, "When?"

"About a week ago. A stroke."

"Then you're . . . Granville, right?"

Haynes nodded. "We buried him earlier today. At Arlington."

"I'm very sorry," McCorkle said. "I didn't know. I would like to have been there."

"Thank you. Tinker Burns flew in. Isabelle Gelinet was there. And some guy from Langley."

"I know Padillo would've gone except—"

Haynes interrupted him with a smile. "He told me."

McCorkle found the smile to be an exact and uncanny replica of the one the late Steadfast Haynes had so successfully employed. "How long will you be in town?"

"A day or two. I have to see a lawyer whose office seems to be in this same building." He looked up. "They just built it over and around you, didn't they?"

"We were lucky," McCorkle said.

"The lawyer's name is Mott. Howard Mott. You know him?"

"He's one of our landlords."

"What's he like?"

"I don't know how he is on probate," McCorkle said, "but if I ever got in a real jam, he's the one I'd call."

Haynes smiled his inherited smile again. "Sounds like Steady's lawyer, doesn't it?"

Six

Mott, James, Lovelandy & Nathan specialized in the defense of white-collar criminals and had grown from two to fourteen partners in less than eight years. With offices that now occupied the top three floors of their seven-story building that crouched over Mac's Place, the firm was prospering almost indecently because of the bevy of frightened clients who had retained its costly services during the final years of the Reagan administration.

Howard Mott, one of the two founding partners, looked as if he had been assembled from mismatched parts by unskilled labor. He stood a bit under five-ten, had a long, long trunk supported by stubby legs and required custom shirts with thirty-seven-inch sleeves. For eyes he had a pair of shiny black vibrant things that glared out from deep inside the two small dark caves they dwelt in.

But most people, especially those in jury boxes, usually forgot what Mott looked like once he opened his mouth. He had a deep voice that would do anything: entreat, thunder, cajole, accuse, reason and even sing a remarkably bawdy parody of how they were hanging Michael Deaver in the morning.

Mott's principal asset, however, was his mind, which a respectable majority of the Washington legal fraternity, not all of them admirers, agreed was brilliant.

He lived in an old three-story house in Cleveland Park with his 36-year-old wife, Lydia, who was expecting their first child in July. Mott usually felt that he was as lucky as anyone deserves to be and it bothered him, although not very much, to discover he was almost envying the man who sat in the client's chair across the desk.

"I'm sorry I couldn't make the services," Mott said. "But I had to be in court all morning. And I'm very, very sorry that Steady's gone."

"Thank you," Granville Haynes said.

"You sure as hell look like him, don't you?"

"So I'm told."

"I've sometimes wondered how it would be to go through life with Steady's looks."

"It makes some people, especially women, mistrust you." Haynes paused, didn't quite smile and added, "At first."

"Then it's just like being ugly, isn't it?"

"I never quite thought of it like that, Mr. Mott."

After a deep sigh, Mott said, "Better call me Howard. When I'm through with what I have to say, you may want to go back to 'Mr. Mott.'"

"Bad news?"

Mott leaned back in his chair to study Haynes. "Depends upon your expectations."

"Nonexistent."

"That's fortunate because Steady died broke—or damn near."

Haynes said nothing.

"His principal assets consist of the farm near Berryville and a seventy-six Cadillac convertible with around forty-three thousand miles on it."

"Now comes the 'but,'" Haynes said.

"A realist, I see," Mott said with a small approving nod. "*But* the farm is only twenty acres and has a ramshackle 119-year-old house, a fair barn and two very fat mortgages. If sold, it might net twenty or even thirty thousand, once the two mortgages are paid off."

"He left it to me?"

"To Isabelle Gelinet."

"Good."

"You know her, I understand."

"Since I was three and she was four. Or maybe it was the other way around. We grew up together for a time. Playmates. In Nice. Then Steady married stepmother number two and we moved to Italy."

"Sounds like a strange childhood."

"Different anyway," Haynes said. "Does Isabelle know about the farm?"

"Not from me, but Steady might've told her."

"What about his debts?"

"Maybe two or three thousand around town and to American Express. Nothing major."

"I'll take care of them."

"No rush."

"How'd he live?" Haynes asked. "I mean he hadn't really worked at anything for two or three years, had he?"

Mott inspected the ceiling. "I'm trying to decide how circumspect I should be."

"As much as you like."

Mott brought his gaze back down. "We did Steady's taxes because he always said he wanted one-stop service. Our house CPA did them. Steady received a check for four thousand dollars every month from Burns Exports et Cie. in Paris. The check was always earmarked 'For Consultative Services.'"

Sounding more amused than surprised, Haynes said, "So old Tinker was carrying him."

31

"Out of what? Compassion? Moral obligation?"

"Tinker Burns? Not quite."

There was a silence caused by Mott waiting to hear what Haynes would say next, and by Haynes wondering whether he should say anything. Finally, he said, "Ever hear of a place in what used to be the Congo called Kilo Moto?"

"No," Mott said.

"It's known for its gold mines. In March of sixty-five it fell to Five Commando—Hoare's outfit."

"The mercenary they called Mad Mike?"

Haynes nodded. "Tinker was an officer, a captain, I think, in Five Commando when it took a town called Watsa and with it the gold mines of Kilo Moto."

"I didn't think the Congo mercenaries would accept Americans."

"They wouldn't," Haynes said. "But by then Tinker was no longer an American. After his first five-year hitch in the Legion was up, he had the option of becoming a French citizen and grabbed it."

A practiced listener, Mott only nodded.

"Steady was also back in the Congo then—doing good works for Mobutu Sese Seko, or the Supreme Guide, as he calls himself these days. Tinker and Steady had known each other before—from Nice in the late fifties. Some people think they met in Zaire but they didn't. Anyway, Tinker got word to Steady that he'd liberated thirty kilos of gold bars—"

"About sixty-six pounds," Mott said.

"Right. And if you're beginning to wonder how I know all this, it's because I heard it through a thin wall when I was thirteen and supposedly asleep. Tinker and Steady were on the other side of the wall and well into war stories and a bottle or two of Scotch."

"But if Tinker Burns and Five Commando were trying to dump Mobutu, why get in touch with Steady, who was, from what little I know, Mobutu's chief image polisher?"

"You really want to discuss ethics?"

32

"Sorry," Mott said.

"As I said, Tinker got word to Steady that he'd liberated the gold. He needed a way to get it from Zaire into Uganda, which is next door in case you're a little fuzzy on your African geography."

Mott again said nothing.

"Well, the CIA had hired some Cuban pilots to fly and fight for Mobutu. They were a hard-luck bunch who hadn't done all that well at the Bay of Pigs, which is where they'd last flown for the agency. Steady suborned one of the pilots—he was really quite good at suborning—and convinced him to 'borrow' a plane and fly to Watsa. There the pilot would secretly pick up a deserting officer from Five Commando. After he flew the deserter to Uganda for debriefing, the Cuban would be paid five thousand dollars. And that's how Steady Haynes got Tinker Burns out of the Congo with a knapsack containing sixty-six pounds of gold bars. And that's how Tinker acquired the capital to go into the arms business and possibly why Steady received that four thousand dollars every month."

"What happened to the Cuban pilot?"

"Who knows?"

Mott nodded thoughtfully, spun around in his chair and stared out of his corner window. His view was of some other buildings very much like his own. Over their rooftops he could watch the planes as they descended and rose at National Airport.

Still watching the planes, Mott said, "Did you know Steady's written a book?"

He spun back around just in time to see Haynes nod. "He and Isabelle. His memoirs—or autobiography."

"It's copyrighted, of course," Mott said.

"So?"

"He assigned the copyright to you in his will. Except for the old Caddy, it's your sole legacy."

"My own copyright. Imagine."

"Bear with me," Mott said. "Steady deposited a sealed copy of the manuscript with me two weeks ago when he made out his will just before he and Isabelle checked into the Hay-Adams. He said it was the only copy. Of the manuscript, not the will."

"The phrase 'only copy' has always bothered me."

"Me, too," Mott said. "But in this case it may be true." He paused, as if beginning a new paragraph, and said, "About thirty or thirty-five minutes before you walked through my door, I got a call from what I'll describe as a very well connected lawyer."

"Which means he's an ex-what?"

"An ex-U.S. senator with a client who, he says, wants very much to buy the copyright to an unpublished work by Steadfast Haynes. Meaning, of course, that the client wants to buy and control all rights—print, tape, film, stage and so forth—to Steady's manuscript. The senator wasn't authorized to divulge the name of his client, but he was authorized to make an offer."

"On something he hasn't even read," Haynes said.

"Exactly."

"How much?"

"One hundred thousand."

"Somebody wants to bury it deep."

"Apparently."

"Call him back and tell him the son and heir wants half a million firm and see what he says."

"He'll say no."

"Then tell him the son and heir's lined up some offshore development money and plans to write, direct and star in a feature based on his father's unpublished manuscript."

Mott stared at Haynes, not bothering to conceal the rapid reassessment his mind was making. "I thought you were a homicide cop."

"I was but now I'm an actor."

"I also believe you're serious."

34

"An actor's job is to make you believe."

"Steady could usually do that—make me believe almost anything. Note my stress on 'almost.'"

"Then obviously I've inherited not only a car and a copyright but also a talent."

"Take the hundred thousand," Mott said. "That's my best advice. If you try to squeeze them, you could be out a whole lot of money."

"I already have a whole lot of money," Haynes said.

"For some strange reason, I believe that, too."

Mott fished a small key from his pants pocket and used it to unlock the bottom right-hand drawer of his desk. From the deep drawer he removed a package wrapped in heavy brown paper that was bound with twine. The package was sealed in three places with red wax. Mott handed the package to Haynes, who read the hand-printed label that bore his dead father's name and Berryville, Virginia, address. The package also bore $3.61 worth of stamps. The words FIRST CLASS had been printed on the brown paper wrapping in red ink.

"He went to a lot of trouble to mail it to himself," Haynes said.

"Check the seals?"

"Unbroken."

"It's one of our enduring myths that to copyright something you've written you have to mail it to yourself," Mott said. "In fact, anything anyone writes is automatically copyrighted. If you want to announce it to the world, all you need to do is write the word 'copyright' on whatever you've written, followed by the year it was written and your name. Want to know anything else about copyrights?"

"That'll do," Haynes said.

"Then you might as well open it and take a look."

Borrowing a pair of scissors from Mott, Haynes cut the twine, broke the wax seals and removed the brown paper that concealed a Keebord stationery box. He lifted off the box's lid. Inside were what appeared to be three or four hundred sheets of 25 percent cotton bond. Haynes read the first page, which was the title page, and noticed that its letters had been formed by an electric typewriter, probably an IBM Wheelwriter. He handed the first page to Mott, who read it silently:

MERCENARY CALLING
by
Steadfast Haynes

At the bottom of the page was a line that read: "Copyright 1989 by Steadfast Haynes."

"You're sure it's valid—the copyright?" Haynes asked.

"Absolutely," Mott said.

Haynes read the second page and handed it to Mott. This page read:

> *These, in the day when heaven was falling,*
> *The hour when earth's foundations fled,*
> *Followed their mercenary calling*
> *And took their wages and are dead.*
> —A. E. Housman

While Mott was reading Housman, Haynes quickly leafed through the rest of the pages. Mott looked up from the lines of poetry to accept the manuscript's third page. It read: "For my son, Granville Haynes, with faint hope that he will find it of great profit."

When Haynes silently handed over the fourth page, Mott saw that it was numbered page one. Not quite halfway down the page and centered was: CHAPTER ONE. Below that was a sentence that read: "I have led an exceedingly interesting life and, looking back, have no regrets. Or almost none."

Mott looked up from the page, his eyes puzzled, his mouth opened by surprise. "That's it—the whole fucking thing?"

Haynes smiled and nodded. "Except for three hundred and eighty-odd blank pages, all carefully numbered. Of course, he might've written the rest in invisible ink. Maybe even lemon juice." He held a page up to the light from a window. "But I don't think so." He put the page down and looked at Mott. "You're sure about the copyright?"

"Of course I'm sure."

"Then let's see whether they still want to buy it."

"You're asking me to help perpetrate a fraud, right?"

"I didn't say I'd sell it to them. I said let's see whether they really want to buy it and, if so, how high they're willing to go."

After considering what he first thought of as the proposal, but redefined as the proposition, Mott said, "My curiosity is overwhelming my judgment."

"Then ask for five hundred thousand and see whether their initial bid's got any climb to it."

Before Mott could agree or argue, his telephone rang. He picked it up and said, "Yes," listened for a moment or two and said, "Put him through in fifteen seconds." As he waited, he nodded at Haynes, switched on the phone's speaker, glanced at his watch and let a tight confident smile spread across his face. When he spoke it was as if he were addressing someone sitting two feet to the left of Granville Haynes.

"Sorry to keep you waiting, Senator, but I was just discussing your offer with Mr. Haynes's son."

"And what does the boy say, Howie?" asked a voice that, although strained through the echoing speakerphone, was still full of pleasant southern ooze. Haynes thought the accent probably had originated somewhere between Natchez and Birmingham.

"He's quite willing to sell the copyright to his father's work, which, incidentally, is entitled *Mercenary Calling,* providing a more reasonable offer is made."

"A hundred thousand's awful reasonable down my way, Howie."

"Down your way, I'm sure it is. But young Mr. Haynes is from Los Angeles and quite confident he can arrange offshore development money that would enable him to produce, write, direct and even star in a feature film based on his father's work."

"The kid's an actor?"

"Not only that, but he bears a startling resemblance to Steady."

There was a long weary sigh over the speaker. "How much, Howie?"

"Five hundred thousand."

"Any wiggle room?"

"Maybe. But not much."

"Then I'll have to talk to my folks to see if they're even interested in making a counteroffer. But I won't be able to get back to you until Monday. Okay?"

"Monday's fine. And by the way, would you like me to make a Xerox copy for your people so they can be sure they're not buying a pig in a poke?"

The senator exploded over the speakerphone. "No copies, goddamnit! Not now. Not ever. You got that, Howie?"

"I merely assumed they'd want to read before buying."

When he replied, soothing syrup again flowed from the senator's mouth. "They don't want to read it, Howie. They just want to buy themselves a fucking copyright. That clear?"

"Perfectly," said Howard Mott.

Seven

After pleading executive stress, Padillo went for a swim in the Watergate pool and left McCorkle to interview a prospective waiter, whom he hired; anglicize the spelling of the menu's three dinner specials; and lend an unwilling ear to Tinker Burns, who had moved from banquette to bar after his two lunch guests left.

Burns had nearly finished his third cognac and a long involved gunrunning tale of how he and two American mercenaries had escaped from Enugu in eastern Nigeria in a hijacked DC-3 during the final days of the Biafran war. The names of the two mercenaries, Burns said, spelling them carefully, in case McCorkle wanted to write them down, were Guice and Spates.

"I never heard from old Spates again," he said. "But about a year ago I got a letter—well, a postcard really—from Guice in Tijuana, where he said he'd finally found a doctor who could cure his AIDS. You think that's possible?"

McCorkle was saved from answering when the restaurant's door opened and Granville Haynes entered. He stood for several moments, waiting for his eyes to adjust to the interior

39

gloom, his left hand clutching a brown paper grocery bag by its folded-over top.

"Hey, Granny," Burns called.

Haynes crossed to the bar, nodded at McCorkle, took a stool, placed the grocery bag on his lap and examined Burns. "Are you recently returned or still here?"

"Where would I go?"

"The National Gallery's nice."

"Already been."

"Today?"

"Nineteen—" Tinker Burns broke off to search his memory for the correct year, finally located it and said, "—seventy-nine, right before they junked Somoza, who I'd just done a little business with and never got paid for. But you're right. The Mellon's nice although I think the Louvre's a lot nicer. What're you drinking?"

"Beer. Where's Isabelle?"

"She left." Burns turned his head and called, "Hey, Karl."

Karl Triller, the fiftyish head bartender, had distanced himself as far as possible from his only paying customer. He sighed, put away his *Wall Street Journal,* moved down the bar to Tinker Burns, picked up a bottle of Rémy-Martin, poured an exact one and a half ounces into Burn's glass and said, "You just failed to make the cut, Tinker, so sip it."

Before Burns could protest, Triller turned to Haynes and said, "Beck's okay?"

"Fine."

As he poured the beer, Triller said, "You're Steady Haynes's son, aren't you?"

"Yes."

"I'm Karl Triller and I'm real sorry Steady died and wish I could've made it to the funeral or whatever it was. A few years ago, right after he broke up with your stepmother, Steady and I'd close the place up almost every night and go have dim sum or ribs at this Chinese joint up on Connecticut where he claimed all the embassy staff ate. The Chinese embassy."

"Which stepmother was this?" Haynes said.

"Letty Melon—spelled with one *l* instead of two like the Pittsburgh Mellons. Letty's only medium rich, if that."

"Then she would've been stepmother number four. The one I never met."

"Well, she and Steady weren't really married all that long. But he still took it pretty hard after they split and started drinking more than usual. I'll say this for Steady though: the more he drank, the more polite he got to everybody."

"The last egalitarian?"

Triller thought about that, shrugged and turned to Mc-Corkle. "You want anything now that I'm all the way down here?"

"No."

"Good," Triller said and headed back to the far end of the bar and his *Wall Street Journal*.

Haynes turned to McCorkle. "You have a minute?"

"Sure."

"It's private."

McCorkle got down from the stool. "Then let's go back to the office."

The office was a small room at the rear of the restaurant behind the kitchen. Before Mac's Place had been swallowed by the seven-story office building, the room had had a window and a view of the wall on the other side of the alley. The window had been bricked up and plastered over. In its place was a *trompe l'oeil* view of Washington as seen from the steps of the Jefferson Memorial. The painting had been a gift from Fredl McCorkle. Padillo always claimed he especially liked it because it was the only painting from that viewpoint that didn't have the cherry blossoms in bloom.

Another, earlier gift from Fredl to McCorkle and Padillo was the fine old partners desk, which dominated the small

41

office. McCorkle sat at the desk and Haynes on a brown leather couch that looked as if it had been designed to encourage long naps. The rest of the furniture included some chairs, a four-drawer steel filing cabinet, a Mosler safe manufactured the same year McCorkle's father was born, and a wall calendar still turned to December 1988.

"So," McCorkle said, took a small silverish square from his jacket pocket and started peeling it open. He removed an equally small square of something that looked very much like putty, eyed it with obvious loathing and popped it into his mouth.

"I know two-and-three-pack-a-day guys who switched to Nicorette gum," Haynes said. "They don't miss smoking at all. I also know junkies who don't miss heroin as long as they have an assured supply of methadone. Some of the guys on Nicorette go to two or three doctors for extra prescriptions because they're chewing thirty or forty pieces a day, which is about the same number of cigarettes they smoked. The main difference is that cigarettes cost about nine cents apiece in California but the nicotine gum costs them forty or forty-five cents a chew."

McCorkle, still chewing, said, "You preach a nice sermon."

He opened a desk drawer, took out a piece of blue Kleenex, spat the nicotine gum into it, wadded the tissue into a ball and dropped it in a wastebasket. After opening the desk's center drawer, he took out a pack of unfiltered Pall Malls, lit one, inhaled deeply, blew the smoke out and said, "I'm well aware of the surgeon general's opinion."

Haynes rose, crossed to the desk and placed the brown grocery bag on its top. McCorkle blew some smoke at the bag and said, "I'm fairly sure that's not eggs, bread and the milk."

"It's a manuscript."

"A novel?"

"A fairy story. Steady's memoirs."

"Well, he did live a full life. Does he tell all?"

"There seems to be some concern about that."

"And you want to do what—park it here for a day or so?"

Haynes agreed with a nod, then indicated the old safe. "Does that thing work?"

McCorkle rose, picked up the paper bag and went to the safe. He pulled its door open, placed the bag inside and closed the door, locking the safe and spinning its dial. "The combination's my birthday in case I get hit by a truck."

"And who else knows your birthday?"

"The IRS, the State Department, the Social Security folks, the Department of Motor Vehicles, the bank, the doctor, the dentist, my wife, two or three close friends and probably any reasonably clever thief who was hell-bent on opening it up."

Haynes nodded, as though satisfied, and asked, "Where can I find Isabelle?"

"You try the Hay-Adams?"

"She checked out."

"What about the farm in Berryville?"

"No answer although I'm not sure she's had time to get there yet."

"Is that where she was going?"

"I don't know."

McCorkle returned to the desk, sat down, picked up the telephone and tapped out a number from memory. Haynes guessed the call was answered two and a half rings later.

"It's McCorkle, Sid. I need our D.C. billing address for Gelinet, Isabelle."

He put the cigarette out in an ashtray, took a ballpoint pen and a scrap of paper from the middle drawer of the partners desk and wrote down the address.

"Phone number?"

McCorkle also wrote that down; thanked Sid, the accountant; hung up the telephone and handed the scrap of paper to Haynes. "Connecticut Avenue."

Haynes looked up from the address. "Thirty-eight hundred block?"

"You remember Washington?"

43

"It's been a while."

"Remember Taft Bridge on Connecticut—the one with the lions?"

Haynes nodded.

"It's a little more than a mile north of the lions on the right. Anything else?"

"I need a hotel."

"Cheap, moderate, expensive, what?"

"Different."

"Go to the Willard. You'll find it completely restored in brand-new Second Empire style with just a touch of Potomac baroque thrown in. There're also some old ladies sitting in its lobby who I'd swear were sitting there when I first came through Washington in nineteen fifty."

"I already like it," Haynes said.

"Want me to make you a reservation?"

"You're sure it's no trouble?"

"No trouble at all," McCorkle said, again picking up the telephone.

He was just putting it down a few minutes later when someone knocked twice at the door. Before McCorkle could say "Come in" or "Who's there?" the door opened and a yellow-haired woman of 21 or 22 swept in, wearing a belted camel's-hair polo coat and a smile that, for some reason, reminded Haynes of California sunshine on a smog-free day.

Her smile was aimed at McCorkle but vanished at the sight of Haynes. She frowned, gasped slightly—or pretended to—and said, "My God. The ghost of Steady Haynes."

"The son," Haynes said.

"I was very fond of Steady."

"As he must've been of you, whoever you are."

McCorkle sighed. "My daughter, Erika; Granville Haynes."

In only two long strides she was in front of Haynes, her right hand extended. Haynes discovered that the right hand of Erika McCorkle felt strong and dextrous, as if it could change a tire or sew a fine seam with equal proficiency. She was only a few inches shorter than Haynes, and her eyes, he noticed, were a far, far lighter blue than his own. They were, indeed, almost gray.

She held onto his hand just long enough to say, "I'm so very sorry about Steady and, God, you do look like him."

"You're very kind," Haynes said.

"I left at seven this morning," she said, turning to McCorkle. "I wanted to say goodbye to Steady at Arlington. But that piece of GM junk broke down again and by the time I got it fixed it was too late for Steady and too late to pick you up at Dulles. How's Mutti bearing up under all the relatives?"

"Nobly," McCorkle said. "How's school?"

"It's over. Done with."

"You quit?"

"Graduated."

McCorkle looked at Haynes. "Can this be June?"

He smiled. "For some perhaps."

"A diplomat," she said to Haynes and turned again to McCorkle. "My junior year?"

"At Heidelberg."

"Well, there's this very nice little man down in the basement of an administration building who, armed with nothing more than a Radio Shack computer, just happened to be running my midterm records through it and discovered I hadn't been given nearly enough credits for the Heidelberg year. In fact, I have more than I need for a degree. So I said *auf Wiedersehen* and told them to mail me the diploma."

McCorkle rose, went around the desk and gave his daughter a long hug. "I'm awfully damned proud of you."

"You're also off the fees and tuition hook."

"And now your mother can have her warm winter coat."

Her alarmingly sunny smile reappeared. "Where's Mike?"

"He went for a swim," McCorkle said. "Are you okay for dinner?"

"Of course. I only wish Mutti were here."

"We'll call her."

45

"Around ten. It'll be around three in the morning there. She'll love that."

His daughter went up on her toes to give McCorkle a quick kiss, turned to Haynes and said, "I'm glad we met. Steady spoke of you often."

"I have to be going, too," Haynes said.

"Can I give you a lift?"

He smiled then, the smile that McCorkle suspected could melt both rocks and female hearts. "If you're heading out Connecticut."

"Let's go," she said.

The sudden discomfort McCorkle felt as they left was in the region where his heart was supposed to be. For a moment he experienced a mild shortness of breath. The symptoms vanished as quickly as they came and McCorkle found himself hoping it was his first angina. If it weren't, then he knew he had just suffered his first serious attack of male parentitis.

Padillo entered the office twenty minutes later to find McCorkle sitting at the partners desk, glumly drinking Irish whiskey.

"Somebody else die?" Padillo said as he located a glass and poured himself a measure of Bushmills.

"Childhood," McCorkle said.

"Well, it couldn't last forever—not even yours."

"Erika's. They somehow messed up her college credits and discovered she had more than enough to graduate now instead of in June. We're celebrating tonight. You're invited."

"You're sure it's a celebration and not a memorial service?"

"You didn't see the smile," McCorkle said, once more staring into his glass.

"What smile?"

"The one Haynes gave her."

"Ah. That one."

"Exactly."

"Don't worry," Padillo said. "The Haynes kid is four or five times as smart as his old man ever was, which is very bright indeed, and maybe ten times as honest, which brings him up to about average. But if you really need something to brood about these long January nights, think on this: who does Granville Haynes remind you of—other than Steady? Take your time."

McCorkle continued to stare down into his drink. He was still staring down into it fifteen seconds later when he said, "Of you."

"And somebody else."

"Who?"

"Yourself," Padillo said.

McCorkle only grunted.

"Erika could do worse," Padillo said.

McCorkle finally looked up. "How?"

Eight

They scarcely talked until Erika McCorkle stopped her five-year-old Oldsmobile Cutlass for a red light at Connecticut and R. She indicated the venerable Schwartz drugstore on the intersection's northwest corner and said, "I used to hang out there when I was a real little kid."

"How little?" Haynes said.

"Six or seven. The world's two fastest soda jerks worked there. One had a bad leg; the other had terribly crossed eyes and both must've been well over forty. Pop sometimes took me there for what he said were the best ice cream sodas in town. We'd sit at the fountain and watch the two guys work. God, they were fast. I remember Pop kept telling them they were an endangered species. Think they're still there?"

"We could find out," Haynes said.

"You're serious?"

"Sure."

As the light changed to green, Erika McCorkle spotted an empty metered parking space just south of Larimer's market, raced a BMW for it and won. She stopped parallel with the car in front of the empty space, shifted into reverse, spun the steering wheel to the right, backed up, spun the steering wheel again, this time to the left, and shot the Cutlass into the empty space, its two right wheels coming to a stop no more than three inches from the curb.

Haynes dug into a pants pocket for some quarters to feed the meter. "Very smooth," he said.

"More slick than smooth."

They crossed Connecticut on the green light only to find themselves marooned on the center traffic island. "When you were hanging out with the sandwich and soda artists," Haynes said, "did you live around here?"

"My folks've always lived within a mile of Dupont Circle. It's because Pop likes to walk to work although lately he's been taking a lot of cabs."

"Nothing wrong with him, is there?"

"Yes," she said, stepping off the curb as the light changed. "He's lazy." She glanced at Haynes. "Known him long?"

"We talked once in nineteen seventy-four. It was my eighteenth birthday and Steady took me to dinner at Mac's Place. Your father stopped by the table and later sent over two cognacs that made me feel all grown-up."

"That makes you thirty-three then, doesn't it?" she said.

"Not until August."

There were no longer any soda jerks or a fountain for them to work behind in the Schwartz drugstore. The young Nigerian pharmacist in the rear told Haynes the fountain had been gone for at least ten years, maybe even twelve. The drugstore now seemed to concentrate on selling toiletries, discount vitamins, over-the-counter cure-alls, junk food and the occasional prescription.

They were in the drugstore just long enough for Haynes to question the young pharmacist. After they left, Erika Mc-Corkle stood on the corner, looking around and glowering, as if trying to will the neighborhood back into what it had been when she was 6 or 7.

"I'm not old enough to hate change," she said more to herself than to Haynes.

"You hate it most when you're five or six."

"Nothing changed when I was five or six."

"Then you obviously had a happy childhood."

"What I had were two older but remarkably well suited and reasonably well adjusted parents."

"Then you were also lucky," Haynes said. "Want some coffee?"

"The Junkanoo," she said. "The bastards tore down the Junkanoo."

"A nightclub, wasn't it?"

"Right over there," she said, pointing to a missing-tooth gap on the east side of Connecticut Avenue in the 1600 block. "I knew it closed. But now it's gone. It just—aw, fuck it. Let's get that coffee."

They found a small Greek restaurant up the street called the Odeon that seemed willing, if not anxious, to serve them. He drank his coffee with cream and sugar; she drank hers black. As he stirred the coffee, Haynes said, "You see much of Steady?"

"Not till I was seventeen. It was just after he and Letty split, and Steady was using Pop's place as a kind of headquarters. That was the summer before I went off to school and I was helping out, doing scut work mostly. Steady was there night and day, looking for somebody to talk to. When I wasn't busy, I listened. Sometimes he even talked about you, which must be what you're really interested in."

"Am I," Haynes said, somehow not making it a question.

"He could never understand why you became a cop."

"He never asked."

"I'll ask."

"Because I needed a job and they were willing to hire me."

"That's what I guessed, but Steady claimed it was a lot more complicated than that."

"Well, if you're a lapsed Quaker turned anarchist who

hires out to prop up rotten governments you despise, every-thing might seem complicated. Even getting out of bed."

"Did he know you despised him so much?"

"I never knew him well enough to despise him."

"He once told me he was worried that you'd never got over the death of your mother."

There was no trace of the inherited charm in Haynes's bleak smile. "That sounds too pat even for Steady."

"Why?"

"Because my mother died when I was three and I can't even remember her. Three months later, Steady married a French woman who was stepmother number one. She and I were very close. When I was nine, he divorced her and married an Italian and the three of us went to live in Italy. Stepmother number two and I became such good pals that she wanted me to go on living with her after Steady got the Mexican divorce. And I did."

"Then what?"

"Then I was thirteen and Steady brought me to the States and popped me into St. Alban's here. I still get birthday letters from stepmothers one and two, but I never did meet stepmother number four. What was she like?"

"Pretty and rather rich. Letty once told my mother that she married Steady because he could make her giggle. Not laugh. Giggle."

"'Giggles Ended, Wife Charges.'"

"Was she there?" Erika asked.

"At Arlington? No."

"Who was?"

"Some guy from the CIA. Me. Tinker Burns. And Isabelle Gelinet."

"Dear Isabelle," she said. "When I was thirteen I used to daydream about her drowning. Sometimes she drowned in the C and O Canal. Sometimes just below Great Falls. But the one I liked best was her drowning over and over in the yuckiest stretch of the Anacostia."

Haynes smiled. "Jealous?"

"Of her brains, looks, style and foreign correspondent job. What thirteen-year-old wouldn't be? But most of all I was jealous of her hopping into bed with Michael Padillo anytime she wanted to."

"You and Padillo? Dear me."

"I fell in love with him when I was five and wrote him all about it when I was six. I wrote it with a crayon. A blue one. Pop was my mailman. Padillo wrote back that we should wait awhile. I'm still waiting, but Isabelle didn't have to. And neither did about a hundred and one other bimbos."

"Still want her to drown?"

"I guess not."

"Just as well. She's a damn good swimmer."

"How do you know?"

"We used to go skinny-dipping together."

"When?"

"When she was seven and I was six. Or maybe vice versa. In Nice."

"I bet she was gorgeous even then."

"I always told her she was too fat."

Just past the Hilton Hotel where Reagan was shot, Connecticut Avenue began curving its way to the bridge that was guarded by the stone lions. A block or so before the bridge, Erika McCorkle flicked her left hand at an imposing gray stone apartment building that Haynes guessed to be sixty or seventy years old.

"Where my folks live," she said. "It's one of the city's first condos. They bought theirs in sixty-eight during the riots when Padillo convinced them that riots and revolutions are the best time to buy property and diamonds."

"Sounds like an oft-told family tale," Haynes said.

"It is—and sixty-eight must've been one weird year. Can you remember it?"

"Only the Italian version."

"What d'you remember most about the sixties?"

Haynes didn't reply for several seconds. "The music," he said. "And, in retrospect, the innocence."

It was 4:47 P.M. when Erika McCorkle parked next to a No Stopping, No Standing sign in front of the seven-story apartment building at 3801 Connecticut Avenue. Because the rush hour was nearing its peak, Connecticut Avenue had increased the number of lanes going north and Haynes had only a moment to thank her for the lift.

She gave the building a curious glance. "Who lives here?"

"Isabelle."

"Shit."

An irate driver behind the Cutlass started honking. Erika McCorkle gave him the finger.

"That can get you shot in L.A.," said Haynes as he climbed quickly out of the car. The irate driver honked again.

"Fuck off," Erika McCorkle snapped as Haynes slammed the door. The Cutlass sped away. Haynes watched it go, wondering whether her farewell had been aimed at him or the honker.

He turned to study the apartment building from the sidewalk. It was built of a brick that Haynes, for some reason, had always thought of as orphanage yellow. The only frill the architect had allowed was the white stone facing around the severe casement windows. A sign in front claimed that one-bedroom and studio apartments were available. Minimum maintenance, maximum rents, Haynes thought, and wondered whether Isabelle Gelinet, after moving in with his father at the Berryville farm, had kept her apartment as a bolthole.

After he reached the building entrance with its inch-thick glass door, Haynes noticed the intercom system to the left that featured the usual tiny speakerphone and the usual row of black buttons. He ran a finger down the buttons until it came to the inked-in name of I. Gelinet. He pushed the button and waited for the speaker to ask who he was. Instead, the buzzer sounded, unlocking the glass door.

Haynes made no move toward the door until the buzzer stopped. He then reached over to give the metal handle a tug. The door was locked. Haynes turned back to the intercom and again pushed the I. Gelinet button. Again, the speaker failed to ask his name or business. But when the unlocking buzzer sounded this time, Haynes went quickly through the glass door and into the lobby.

Unless four newspaper vending machines and rows of stainless-steel mailboxes counted, there was no furniture in the lobby. To the right of the mailboxes was a narrow reception cubicle with an almost chest-high counter that was guarded by a steel mesh screen. Safely behind the steel mesh was a three-sided brass stick with raised letters that read, MANAGER. But no manager was in sight.

Haynes crossed to the four newspaper vending machines that offered the *Washington Post*, the *New York Times*, the *Washington Times* and *USA Today*. Haynes bought a copy of the *New York Times* and rang for the elevator.

When he got out on the fourth floor, the news section of the *Times* was rolled into a tight cylinder that was one foot long and two inches thick.

Haynes went slowly down the corridor until he came to apartment 409. Standing well to the right of the door, he knocked on it with his left hand. When nothing happened, he knocked again. When there was still no response, he used his left hand to try the doorknob. It turned.

Haynes pushed the door open and found no lights on in the apartment. He took one slow step inside and was turning back to flick on the light switch when an arm wrapped itself around his neck in what he immediately diagnosed as an interesting variation on the chokehold he had been taught at the Los Angeles Police Academy. He also had been taught how to break it.

Haynes stamped down hard with his right heel, drove back

hard with his left elbow and connected both times. Behind him somebody's breath exploded. The chokehold loosened just enough for Haynes to tear himself away, whirl and thrust his pointless paper spear up as hard as possible, hoping for an eye.

But the light from the still open corridor door gave him a glimpse of his would-be strangler and made him deflect the thrust just enough to miss the left eye and smash the paper spear into Tinker Burns's nose. The resulting flow of blood was immediate and, Haynes felt, most gratifying.

"For Chrissake, Granny," said a snarling, bleeding Burns. "How the fuck'd I know it was you?"

Leaning forward to let the blood drip onto the carpet instead of his expensive gray suit, Burns plucked the silk display handkerchief from his outside breast pocket and applied it to his nose.

"Where's the kitchen?" Haynes said. "You might as well go bleed in the sink."

"Over there. One of those Pullman things."

The only light in the apartment came from the open corridor door. Haynes switched on a lamp, closed the door and steered Burns to the stainless-steel kitchen unit. Burns bent over the small sink, turned on the cold water, soaked his handkerchief and reapplied it to his nose. "I don't bleed long," he announced.

"Where's Isabelle?" Haynes said.

"For Chrissake, give me a second, will you?"

Burns stood up straight, threw his head back, stared at the ceiling for nearly half a minute, brought his head down, gently blew his nose into the wet handkerchief and inspected the results with obvious satisfaction.

Back at the sink again, Burns carefully rinsed out his bloody handkerchief, wrung it nearly dry, folded it carefully and tucked it away in a hip pocket. He then switched on the garbage disposal unit and let it and the cold water run for another thirty seconds.

55

It was only then that Tinker Burns turned to Haynes and said, "What'd you use?"

Haynes raised the *New York Times,* still in its semi-blunt-instrument form.

"Shit, I taught you that."

"I believe you did."

"Cute," Burns said, patted his pockets, found his cigarettes and lit one. "Come on."

As they crossed the studio apartment, heading toward a closed door, Haynes took note of the beige couch that probably folded out into a bed; the blond desk that held a personal computer; the round Formica-topped breakfast table just large enough for two; the small TV set and its attendant VCR; and a pair of old Air France posters that gave the otherwise monochromatic room its only touch of color.

Burns opened the door of what turned out to be the bathroom and switched on a light. Haynes followed him in. A green plastic shower curtain decorated with yellow daisies concealed the bathtub. Burns studied Haynes briefly, reached out, grasped the shower curtain and quickly pulled it back.

Isabelle Gelinet lay on her left side in the white tub. She was naked and her wrists were bound behind her with coat-hanger wire. Another coat hanger had been used to bind her ankles. Her left cheek rested on the bottom of the tub that was filled with water up to its overrun drain. Haynes knew Isabelle Gelinet was dead but wasn't at all sure she had drowned.

Nine

The 41-year-old homicide detective-sergeant from the Metropolitan Police Department was pretending he couldn't keep all the players straight. It was a useful stratagem that Haynes himself had sometimes used and he thought Detective-Sergeant Darius Pouncy was carrying it off nicely.

Pouncy was also carrying ten or fifteen more pounds than he needed on a six-foot-even frame that was clothed in a salt-and-pepper tweed suit, white shirt and quiet tie. On his dark brown face he wore a look of almost utter detachment. It was the look of a man who asks questions for a living and expects nothing in return but lies and evasions. Haynes had known Los Angeles detectives who had perfected that same look but couldn't recall any who'd worn salt-and-pepper tweed suits.

Pouncy had walked Haynes down to the end of the corridor to question him while another detective questioned Tinker Burns in the dead Isabelle Gelinet's apartment. Pouncy stood with his back to the narrow casement window, letting what little light there was fall on Haynes's face.

Looking up suddenly from notes he'd written on a small spiral pad, Pouncy said, "Granville Haynes. What do your friends call you? Granny?"

"Sometimes."

"You say you all went to your dad's funeral around noon today. You, Burns and Gelinet."

"It wasn't really a funeral. It was the interment."

"Burial."

"Yes."

"You all the only ones there?"

"There were six soldiers who fired three volleys over the grave, a bugler and a color sergeant. I think they call them color sergeants."

"But you all were the only mourners?"

"There was also a man from the CIA. A Mr. Undean."

"First name?"

"Gilbert."

Pouncy wrote the name down and said, "But that's all?"

"That's all."

"Your dad with the CIA?"

"You'll have to ask them."

"But he'd served in some branch of the service?"

"Not to my knowledge."

"Then how come they buried him in Arlington?"

"Miss Gelinet arranged it."

"How?"

"You'll have to ask the people at Arlington."

"How long'd you known her?"

"As long as I can remember."

"And Burns?"

"How long've I known him or how long has he known her?"

"Both."

"I can't remember when I didn't know Tinker Burns and I'm sure he knew Miss Gelinet all her life."

"Burns a good friend of your dad?"

"Yes."

"Was Gelinet sleeping with him?"

"Who? Burns?"

"Your dad."

"Two or three years ago she moved out to his farm near Berryville to help him write his autobiography. I don't know whether she was sleeping with him. I didn't ask; she didn't say."

"So after the funeral or whatever, the three of you go to lunch at, uh, Mac's Place. Then you leave for an appointment with your dad's lawyer. When you get back to Mac's Place, Gelinet's gone but Burns is still there. That right, Granny?"

"Yes."

"Then what?"

"Then I talked with Mr. McCorkle in his office."

"The owner?"

"One of them."

"When you came out of his office was Burns still in the restaurant?"

"Yes."

"Where'd you go then, Granny?"

"Mr. McCorkle's daughter gave me a ride here but on the way we stopped for coffee."

"What's her name?"

"Erika McCorkle."

"Where'd you have the coffee?"

"At the Odeon near Connecticut and R."

"How long you in there?"

"Fifteen, twenty minutes."

"And she dropped you off here?"

"Yes."

"How'd you get in?"

"I rang her apartment and somebody buzzed the front door, but didn't ask who I was. So I didn't go in."

"Made you suspicious, huh?"

"I didn't think Isabelle would buzz somebody in without

59

knowing who it was. I rang again and the same thing happened. But this time I went in."

"And did what?"

"Bought a *New York Times*."

"Okay, Granny. Now you're in the lobby and you've got yourself something to read on the way up in the elevator. You get to the fourth floor, go down the hall and knock on Gelinet's door. Then what?"

"There wasn't any answer so I tried the door. It was unlocked and I went in."

"Can we get to the blood on the carpet now?"

"Sure. Mr. Burns grabbed me from behind the moment I came through the door. I broke away, turned and whacked him on the nose before we recognized each other."

"Where'd you learn to roll a paper up all nice and tight like that?"

Haynes shrugged. "High school maybe."

"They teach it in arts and crafts? Never mind. So when you went up there with the *Times* all rolled up nice and tight, who were you expecting to hit?"

"Nobody. It was just in case."

"Just in case of what, Granny?"

"In case I might have to defend myself."

"Because nobody asked who you were over the intercom?"

"Right."

"So you and Burns had a little tussle and you gave him a bloody nose."

"Yes."

"Then what?"

"When his nose stopped bleeding we went into the bathroom and he showed me Miss Gelinet's body."

"Then?"

"Then we called the police."

"What's Burns do for a living?"

"He sells weapons."

"Where?"

"Paris."

"What'd he do before he did that?"

"He was a professional soldier."

"In whose army?"

"The American Army and after that the French Foreign Legion. There may have been other armies after the Legion, but you'll have to ask him."

"He an American citizen?"

"French."

"But he used to be American?"

"Yes."

"And you're an actor, that right, Granny?"

"Yes."

"And what'd you do before you got to be an actor?"

"I was a homicide detective."

The detachment left Detective-Sergeant Pouncy's face, shoved aside by sudden anger. "No call for smartass stuff. No call for that at all."

"I was with the LAPD for almost ten years, seven of them in homicide."

"You gotta know I'm gonna check it out."

"Go ahead."

"So how come you didn't lemme know right away from the start?"

"Because if I'd found some guy in a dead woman's apartment who right away wants me to know he's an ex–D.C. homicide cop, I probably wouldn't've let him loose till around midnight. If then."

"Figure he's dirty, huh?"

"It'd make me wonder."

"You really an actor?"

Haynes nodded.

"Been in anything I might've seen?"

"You watch TV?"

"Not unless she makes me."

61

"I was in a *Wiseguy,* a *Jake and the Fatman,* and I had two speaking roles in a couple of *Simon and Simons.*"

"That the one with the black cop called 'Downtown Brown'?"

"Yes."

"You ever know a real cop that'd tell a private one what year it was?"

"Never."

"Then how come they're always such asshole buddies on TV?"

"Because the private cop has to have a legitimate connection to law and order."

"Who says?"

"Hollywood ethics."

"What the fuck's Hollywood ethics?"

"Nobody knows," said Granville Haynes.

Ten

It wasn't until after he had used the dead Isabelle Gelinet's telephone to call the Los Angeles Police Department and speak to the irrepressible Sergeant Virgil Stroud in robbery and homicide that Detective-Sergeant Darius Pouncy was nearly convinced that Haynes and even Tinker Burns were probably what they claimed to be.

After an exchange of the usual amenities and the usual information about the weather (a high of 72 degrees and fair in Los Angeles; down to 41 degrees and looking like rain or snow in Washington), Pouncy asked, "You ever have a real slick article out there in homicide by the name of Granville Haynes?"

"Haynes . . . Haynes," said Sergeant Stroud. "Doesn't ring a bell."

"Claims he used to work for you people."

"And you need his home phone number, right?"

"What the fuck I want with his phone number?"

There was a brief silence until Stroud said, "Oh. You mean *Granny* Haynes. Sure. He used to work here. What's he up to?"

63

"Up to his ass in a homicide investigation, is what."

"Who bought it—somebody rich?"

"Not hardly."

"Reason I asked is because Granny's the one we liked to send when rich folks bought it. Real nice manners. Neat dresser. Spoke French, Italian and fair Spanish. Made some damn good cases, too. You're lucky you—"

Pouncy broke it off. "Hey. We're not looking to hire him. We just wanta check him out. Claims he used to be a homicide cop but now he's an actor."

"Ever see a low-budget slasher flick called *Thirteen Hangingtree Lane*?" Stroud asked. "Came out two, three years back and Granny goes down into the basement of this big old house. The one in Hangingtree Lane. And there's this fat sack of slime down there with an ax. Now, this is Granny's first feature speaking role. So just before this guy with a face like a four-cheese pizza takes Granny's head off with the ax, Granny gets to say, 'Listen! Please! I'm here to help you!' And then his head goes flying off and they cut to the corner of the basement and there's Granny's head, looking surprised as hell."

"Guess I missed it," Pouncy said. "How much you figure he got paid for doing all that?"

"Probably SAG minimum. Maybe four hundred bucks."

"What's SAG?"

"Screen Actors Guild."

"He was a cop then?"

"Sure."

"Out there you let cops be actors?"

"Lemme ask you something," Stroud said. "If you've gotta moonlight, which'd you rather be—an actor or a liquor store security guard in some low-rent neighborhood?" Without waiting for an answer, Sergeant Stroud chuckled his goodbye and broke the connection.

The driver of Tinker Burns's hired limousine had chosen Park Road as the best route to 16th Street. It was nearly 8

P.M. and they were somewhere in darkest Rock Creek Park when Burns ended the long silence in the back seat. "I'll take care of Isabelle's cremation and funeral and everything."

"They'll have to do the autopsy first," Haynes said.

"I mean after that."

"Will the cops call Madeleine?" Haynes asked. Madeleine was Madeleine Gelinet, mother of the dead Isabelle and former mistress of Tinker Burns.

"You think Sergeant Pouncy speaks French?"

"Maybe Madeleine's learned English."

"Never," Burns said. "I figured I'd go back to the hotel, have a couple of drinks and then call her."

"Does she know about Steady?"

"I don't think so."

"You can tell her about him, too."

Burns shifted uneasily in the seat, not quite squirming. "Maybe you'd rather call her?" he asked without hope.

"No thanks," Haynes said. "She still in Nice?"

"Where else? She'll never part with that house."

There was another silence that lasted until they turned south down 16th Street. It was then that Burns asked, "Who d'you think killed her?"

"No idea."

"Guess."

"Maybe a guy prowling for a TV set. Maybe the neighborhood rapist. Maybe even some weirdo who followed her home and got off on tying her up and drowning her in the bathtub."

"They said there weren't any signs of forced entry."

"Forced . . . entry," Haynes said, spacing the words as if to savor them. "Let's say he rings the bell from downstairs. Isabelle asks 'Who is it?' over the intercom and he says it's Federal Express. Well, Federal Express people are about as common as mailmen. I know guys in Century City who use Federal Express to send scripts from the tenth to the thirty-sixth floor by way of Memphis. So Isabelle buzzes him

65

up. He knocks at her door. She opens it on the chain and sees this guy with a clipboard and a Federal Express packet he's fished out of the trash can. She opens the door all the way and winds up dead in the bathtub." Haynes paused. "How'd you get in?"

"When I pulled up in the limo there was an old couple coming out who held the door for me. Isabelle's door was unlocked."

"A limo's almost as good as being from Federal Express. You don't expect a killer to take one to work. Although there were two guys in L.A. who used to hire limos whenever they decided to go stick up a bank."

"Know what I think?" Burns said.

"What?"

"I think it's got to do with that book she and Steady wrote."

"Must be some book."

Burns turned to give Haynes his coldest stare. "The difference between you and me, kid, is I've got a damn good idea of what Steady did over the years. How he did it and who to. Who paid him and how much. And last, but as sure as hell not least, who told him to go do it."

"What about lately, Tinker? Fifteen, ten, even five years ago is ancient history."

"You're forgetting it's a brand-new administration."

"No, it's not. It's a succession."

"But the guy who took the oath last Friday was DCI when certain people at Langley went after Steady back during the Ford administration. Jesus. It was like a vendetta. Let's all jump up and down on Steady Haynes. Then it stopped. All of a sudden. It was just like Steady gave the rug a jerk. Just a little one—know what I mean?"

"Thirteen or fourteen years ago is the Ice Age."

"Yeah, but what you've got now is the first Director of Central Intelligence ever to be President, which they don't seem to mention much anymore. So maybe Steady decided it was time to give the rug another jerk, harder this time, just to see what'd happen. So he checks into the Hay-Adams with Isabelle and tries to fix himself up with choice seats at the North trial. He's advertising, that's what he's doing, because you know damn well Steady's not gonna pop for the Hay-Adams when Isabelle's got a free-for-nothing pad up on Connecticut."

"Advertising what?" Haynes said.

"That he's got something to sell."

"His book?"

"What else?"

"And after he died, you think Isabelle decided to solo?"

"How the hell you think she got him buried at Arlington? Remember when I asked her if she'd blackmailed them into it? And she said 'of course.' I was kidding. She wasn't."

"Tell me something, Tinker. Do you think you're in Steady's book?"

"What the fuck kind of question is that?"

"The kind you should avoid answering," Haynes said.

Just before leaving Mac's Place, Haynes had called United Airlines to have the bag he had left in its care sent to the Willard. When the rented gray limousine dropped him at the hotel, after first depositing Tinker Burns at the Madison, Haynes was pleasantly astonished to discover the bag had been delivered.

A Latino bellhop was dispatched to collect it from the checkroom. Haynes used the time to inspect the restored lobby that boasted a concierge desk that resembled a flower petal built out of rich-looking yellow marble. There was also a long, long corridor or promenade that led off the main lobby and seemed to go on forever. A bellhop later told him it was called Peacock Alley and went all the way to F Street. Both it and the lobby boasted big comfortable-looking chairs, convenient tables and a near jungle of potted palms growing out of glazed Chinese pots.

It all looked like old expensive stuff or like new old stuff that was three times as expensive. Haynes thought a fifth of the lobby must have been dipped in gilt. There was an abundance, maybe even a wealth of intricate plaster moldings. Huge milky chandeliers of the half-globe variety hung down from thick bronze chains. Haynes started to count them and had reached number twelve when the bellhop returned with his bag.

In the elevator, the bellhop boasted that the mint julep had been introduced to Washington in the Willard bar by a certain Señor Henry Clay. Haynes said he hadn't known that.

After the bellhop was tipped and gone, Haynes discovered yet again that regardless of price a hotel room is primarily a box the bed comes in. His $145-a-night box also came with a bath, two phones, a radio, a TV set, a miniature refrigerator and a window with a view of the National Press Building across 14th Street where quite a few people, mostly men in shirt sleeves, still seemed to be working.

Haynes had just finished hanging up his other jacket and his other pair of pants when he heard the knock. After opening the door he found Gilbert Undean standing in the corridor, wearing a sheepish look and the same clothes he had worn to Steadfast Haynes's interment.

"Got a minute?" Undean said.

"Come in."

Undean entered the room and looked around curiously. "First time I've been up in one of these rooms in twenty-five years. I was out of the country when they closed the place in sixty-eight after downtown business went to hell." He nodded approvingly. "Pretty fancy. They claim Julia Ward Howe wrote 'The Battle Hymn of the Republic' here. Or in the Willard that was here way back then. But it's probably bullshit."

"I sometimes enjoy bullshit," Haynes said. "Care for a beer or something?"

"A beer'd be fine—if you're having one."

Haynes removed two cans of Heineken from the small

refrigerator, opened both and handed one to Undean, who took a long swallow, sighed and sat down in an armchair. Haynes chose the edge of the bed.

"They heard about Isabelle Gelinet," Undean said.

"They?"

"The agency."

"You must be their utility mourner."

"I'm not here to express condolences. I'm here because of that book Steady wrote."

"What about it?"

"They want to buy it."

"Why not just suppress it the way they did some others I can think of?"

"That's what I told 'em. They said they can't because, one, Steady's dead, and two, he never worked for them. At least they can't prove he ever did."

"How do they know about the book?"

"Gelinet. She used it to blackmail them into burying Steady at Arlington."

"That's all she asked for?" Haynes said. "No money?"

"Just a plot of hallowed ground," Undean said. "I'm quoting them. They thought they'd got off cheap."

"Have they read it?"

Undean drank two more swallows of beer, then shook his head. "Say they haven't."

"But they think Isabelle's murder and the book are somehow connected."

"They get paid to think like that. First I heard of the book was this afternoon right after they buried Steady. I told 'em to buy it and save themselves a lot of grief. They laughed it off."

"Why'd you tell them to buy it, Mr. Undean?"

"Because I knew Steady. Saw him operate and know some of the corners he cut, the lies he told, the deals he made, the promises he broke, the deaths he caused."

"He killed people?"

"The things he did and the lies he told caused people to die. And those who died put the fear of God in the ones who managed to stay alive. Their minds got changed. And maybe their politics. When you get right down to it, Steady was sort of a mental terrorist."

"My father, the mindfucker."

"And damned good at it, too."

"In Laos?"

"That's where I watched him work. Even hurrahed him on some. I've only heard about what he did in other places, but I believe eighty percent of what I've heard."

"What's the real reason they didn't try to buy the book after Isabelle told them about it?"

"No demand."

Haynes frowned. "I just lost my place."

"No demand for dog vomit," Undean said after a swallow of beer. "That's what they figured Steady's book'd be and why there'd be no demand for it. Even if it got published, nobody'd buy it. But when Gelinet got killed, the price of dog vomit shot up and now they figure there must be a big demand for it after all."

"Have they figured out where the demand's coming from?"

"They're still working on that."

"How bad do they want it?"

Undean shrugged. "Pretty bad."

"What's your lowball offer?"

"Thirty-five."

"And you can bump it to what?"

"Fifty."

"Cash?"

"Any way you want it."

"What happens to the book?"

"What book?"

"Will they read it before it goes into the shredder?"

"I doubt it. If they read it, it'd ruin their deniability. If nobody reads it, then nobody knows what's in it and they can deny all knowledge of its contents. Then it'd be just like it was never written."

"What if I read it before I sold it to them?"

"I'd advise you not to mention it."

"And fifty thousand is your best offer?"

"That's it," Undean said. "So what do I tell 'em?"

"Tell them I want a minimum of seven hundred and fifty thousand."

"They'll fall about laughing."

"When they're finished, tell them I know where I can put my hands on enough offshore development money to produce a feature film based on Steady's book. Tell them I'll also direct, write and play the lead. And finally, you can tell them the name of the film will be the same as the book, *Mercenary Calling*."

Undean smiled for the first time that night. "I'll also tell 'em you look just like him."

"One more thing, Mr. Undean."

Undean nodded, still smiling.

"Tell them I've already had an unsolicited offer of one hundred thousand for all rights to the manuscript but turned it down. So if they want to stay in the bidding, they'd better start thinking in terms of important money."

Undean's smile broadened until he looked almost delighted. "Know what else I can say? I can say you not only look and talk just like him, you also think just like him. Except faster. And right after I tell 'em that is when they'll start passing peach pits."

71

Eleven

Howard Mott, the criminal defense lawyer, ignored the flashing red light that meant his telephone was ringing. With his feet up on an ottoman and the rest of him sunk into a favorite armchair, Mott was listening to the final act of *Tosca* on a new compact disc that magically had recaptured the voice of Leontyne Price with Karajan conducting.

It was 9:47 P.M. and Mott had been lost in the opera since a dinner of roast pork tenderloin that a second cognac was helping him digest in his study-cum-music room on the second floor of the large old house on 35th Street Northwest in Cleveland Park. His household had been given firm instructions not to disturb him for any reason—his household consisting solely of his pregnant wife, the former Lydia Stallings.

The red telephone light stopped flashing, but stayed on, which meant that Lydia had taken the call. The light was still on a minute or so later when she entered and silently handed him the yellow three-by-five Post-it notepad she always used for messages. This message read: "G. Haynes on phone. I. Gelinet murdered. Needs advice & counsel."

Mott sighed and looked at his watch. There were at least fifteen or twenty minutes of Leontyne Price to come. He took a ballpoint pen from his shirt pocket and scrawled something on the yellow notepad. Lydia read it, borrowed the pen and wrote, "He be hungry?"

Mott quickly answered the written question with a firm headshake, hoping it would discourage her from preparing a meal that would feed everyone within walking distance. He blamed his wife's growing compulsion to feed the world on her pregnancy and the two years she had spent in the Peace Corps.

In the kitchen, Lydia Mott picked up the beige wall phone and said, "Mr. Haynes? Howie's worried that you may not have eaten and wonders if you could make it out here by ten or ten-fifteen? He'll be having some soup and sandwiches then and thought you might like to join him."

Haynes hung up the hotel room phone and memorized the 35th Street address he had written down. He put his hand back on the phone, hesitated, picked it up, tapped a number for an outside line, then tapped 411 and asked directory assistance for the number of Mac's Place.

Haynes recognized the faintly Teutonic tones of Herr Horst when a man's voice answered with, "Reservations." Haynes identified himself and asked to speak to Michael Padillo, adding that it was a personal call.

Thirty seconds later another voice said, "This is Michael Padillo."

"Granville Haynes. Sorry, but it's bad news."

"All right."

"Isabelle's dead. She was murdered sometime this afternoon in her apartment. Tinker Burns and I found her."

There was the usual silence. When he had first joined homicide, Haynes often suspected that such silences would never end or, at best, continue on and on into next week. But he soon discovered that they ended quickly, usually with a sob, a curse or an expression of disbelief. Sometimes with all three.

Padillo, however, ended his brief silence with the essential question: "Who killed her?"

"They don't know."

"They have any idea?"

"Not yet."

"What happened?"

"She was found in the bathtub, her head under water, her wrists and ankles wired with what looked like coat hangers. No other visible marks or abrasions."

"Drowned?"

"Maybe. An autopsy will tell."

There was another silence before Padillo said, "You've known her a long time, haven't you?"

"About as long as I can remember."

"Does this have anything to do with Steady?"

"It might."

"I want—well, I'd like to talk to you about it."

"All right."

"Where are you now?"

"The Willard."

"Can you come over here?"

"I have to see a lawyer first."

"Can you make it by midnight?"

"Probably."

"I'll be here," Padillo said.

The table was the one McCorkle and Padillo always reserved for themselves, the one near the swinging kitchen doors that everybody else shunned. It allowed them to keep an eye on both the help and the customers. It also allowed the chef to poke his head out occasionally to ask a question, register a complaint or merely satisfy himself that someone was really eating his cooking.

When the call for Padillo came, the three of them had almost finished a celebratory dinner in honor of Erika McCorkle's completion of her university studies. All celebration ended when Padillo returned to the table, sat down as if he had grown suddenly weary, pushed away his plate and said, "Isabelle's dead. Apparently murdered." He then repeated in a low voice everything he had been told about the death.

McCorkle was the first to speak, but only after he leaned back in his chair to study Padillo carefully. It was then that he sighed and said, "I'm sorry, Mike. There was always something splendid and unique about Isabelle. I'm going to miss her." He paused. "They have any idea of who did it?"

"No."

Erika McCorkle had turned pale. When she tried to speak, it came out as a croak. She cleared her throat, and this time it came out as a whisper. "In her—bathtub?"

Padillo nodded.

"Drowned?"

"Possibly."

Still whispering, she said, "Then it's all my fault."

"Why yours?" Padillo said. "And why all the whispering?"

She made no reply, letting the silence continue until she finally spoke again in a voice not much louder than her whisper. "Because I used to daydream about her drowning. But not in a bathtub. In the Anacostia."

McCorkle, an eyebrow raised, looked at Padillo, as if hoping for an explanation. But Padillo only shrugged. McCorkle turned back to his daughter and asked, "Why did you dream about her . . . drowning?"

"I told you. I was jealous."

"You didn't tell me," McCorkle said.

She frowned, staring at him. A moment later the frown

vanished and she said, "Right. It wasn't you. It was Granville Haynes I told. This afternoon."

"You told him you were jealous of Isabelle because of her and Steady?"

The frown returned. "Not of her and Steady." She looked at Padillo. "Of Isabelle and you."

Padillo stared at her as his right hand dipped automatically into his shirt pocket, seeking the cigarettes he had abandoned five years ago. "Christ, kid," he said. "Isabelle and I ended it when you were thirteen, maybe fourteen."

Although her expression seemed to be one of pity, there was only scorn in Erika McCorkle's voice when she said, "You have no idea, do you?"

"Of what?" Padillo said.

"Of what vicious daydreams a lovesick thirteen-year-old can have when the man she's in love with is fucking somebody else?"

Nodding calmly, Padillo said, "Go on."

"With what?"

"With why it's all your fault."

"Because I used to daydream about it and—and, oh God, I'm so sorry she's dead."

McCorkle leaned toward his daughter. "Erika, may I say something?" he asked in a gentle voice.

She nodded.

"This is the silliest goddamn conversation we've ever had."

It was as if he had struck her. First came the surprise, then the hurt and finally the anger. "You guys can't even remember what it was like being thirteen."

"Thank God," McCorkle said.

"It hurt."

"Everybody hurts at thirteen," Padillo said. "They hurt so much they later write books about it. The same book. Over and over. But you're a long way from thirteen."

"And you're suddenly more—" She stopped and began again. "I'm sorry. I guess the shock brought on the silly talk.

Poor Isabelle. When I was thirteen she was everything I wanted to be and now that she's dead I just can't accept it."

"You and Haynes talked about her?"

Erika nodded. "He told me how they used to go skinny-dipping when they were six or seven, around in there, and I told him how I'd daydreamed about her drowning in the Anacostia but he said there wasn't much chance of that because she was a damn fine swimmer and—aw, hell, Pop, can we go home now?"

"What a great idea," McCorkle said.

Twelve

It was the first time the Burma analyst, Gilbert Undean, had been to the house of the courtly Hamilton Keyes. The house was in the exorbitantly priced Kalorama Triangle whose isosceles tip points south, just touching Dupont Circle, with legs formed by Connecticut and Massachusetts and a base that rests on a slice of Rock Creek Park to the north.

Located on California Street between 23rd and 24th, the house had been bought by Keyes's rich wife, the former Muriel Lamphier, while he was in Tegucigalpa on agency business. Keyes had always hated surprises and was furious when told of the purchase upon his return. But because it was Muriel's money and because, from the first, they had agreed it was impossible and unnecessary to live on his government salary, Keyes said only that the house looked "terribly impressive," letting Muriel interpret that any way she liked.

She chose to interpret it as a compliment of sorts, but seemed less interested in the house itself than in how cunningly she had outwitted a K Street lawyer, who had been trying to buy it for an unnamed South American—a Colombian, she suspected—but dropped out of the bidding after she topped his final offer with one of $535,000.

Ten years later the same K Street lawyer, now representing a Japanese industrialist, offered the Keyeses four times their purchase price, which they turned down with what each confessed was a certain amount of smug satisfaction.

Gilbert Undean, a widower, lived in Reston, Virginia, and seldom ventured into the District unless it was unavoidable. Although he had made no definite appointment to see Keyes, Undean still felt he was running late, especially after he took Connecticut Avenue out to California Street only to discover he couldn't make a left turn—at least not there. After wandering around for fifteen minutes he finally got onto California and found the Keyeses' house.

It was of enormous size but austere design that made it resemble what a talented 6-year-old might draw if given a ruler. The giant three-story Georgian house was built of red brick with white trim and dark gray shutters that matched the slate of its dormered roof.

Softening the stern lines was a stand of fine old trees. Although it was now too dark to be certain, Undean would have been surprised if the trees weren't elms. He was very surprised when Muriel Keyes herself answered the doorbell. Undean had been expecting a maid and hoping for a butler.

She held out her hand, gave him a memorable smile and said, "Mr. Undean. How nice to see you again."

Her grip was firm, her hand was warm and she used the firm warm grip to guide him over the threshold and into a foyer with a marble floor, releasing him only after he was safely inside.

"Ham's in the library," she said with another one of her remarkable smiles.

"Not late, am I?" Undean asked, trying not to stare at the almost perfect face that featured a pair of soft warm gray eyes. The gray of her eyes complemented the natural frosting in her dark hair and almost matched the color of her cashmere sweater. It was the way she filled out the sweater that made Undean recall a tag of agency gossip, corridor stuff, that had Muriel Keyes, then Muriel Lamphier, taking a Hollywood screen test on a bet, but turning down a role they had offered her. Guessing that she was now 40 or maybe even 42, Undean found himself almost basking in her soft warm glow of utter confidence, which, he suspected, came from old money, prudently invested.

Muriel Keyes assured Undean that he wasn't at all late and led him down the nicely proportioned entry hall and into a living room stuffed with antiques. She glanced back, smiling again, as they crossed the living room and entered a smaller room that had a wall of books, most of them still in their shiny dust jackets.

"It's Mr. Undean, Ham," she said.

Hamilton Keyes rose from a desk that wasn't nearly so fine as the one in his office, thanked his wife with a smile, nodded at Undean and said, "You want something?"

"To drink, he means," Muriel Keyes said before Undean could misinterpret the question.

"No, thanks."

"It's been so nice to see you, Mr. Undean," she said, smiled again and left.

"I'm having a Scotch," Keyes said, moving to a silver tray that held bottles and glasses. "Sure you won't join me?"

"I'm sure," Undean said and took in the rest of the room while Keyes poured his drink. It was a long narrow room with the desk at one end. The desk faced away from French windows that overlooked a garden lit with low-wattage orange lamps. Against a wall was a brown leather couch that was too wide for two but not quite wide enough for three. A leather armchair matched the couch.

There were also a burled walnut coffee table, some reading lamps on more walnut tables, a few pictures and a fine oriental rug of some kind that covered at least a third of the gleaming quarter-sawn oak floor. With his drink now in hand, Keyes used it to motion Undean to the odd-size couch and chose the armchair for himself.

"How high'd you have to go?" Keyes asked, once they were seated.

"The limit. I went to fifty and Haynes turned it down. He says somebody else had already offered him a hundred thousand that he also turned down. He says he knows where he can raise some offshore development money—"

"He's being offered foreign money?"

"He just claims he knows where he can raise enough of it to produce a picture show based on Steady's memoirs that he'd also direct, write and star in—meaning he'd play Steady. That's about the only thing he said that made a lot of sense because he sure as hell looks like him."

"I believe I can safely classify that hundred-thousand-dollar offer as imaginary," Keyes said.

"Think he's lying, do you?"

"Don't you?"

Undean shrugged. "I'm just telling you what he said. His main point seemed to be that if you're serious about buying Steady's book and all the rights thereto, you'd better start the bidding with important money. He thought three quarters of a million would be just about important enough."

The amount didn't seem to faze Keyes, who asked, "But he gave no hint of who else is bidding for it?"

"Are we talking about that imaginary bidder again?"

"All right, Gilbert," Keyes said, making the words snap. "Perhaps there is a real bidder."

"He didn't hint because I don't think he knows."

Keyes leaned back in the armchair, looked up and seemed to inspect the off-white plaster ceiling carefully, as if for hairline cracks. "Let's stipulate for the sake of discussion," he said to the ceiling, "that the hundred-thousand offer is genuine. Next, let's ask ourselves who'd profit most from securing all rights to an unvarnished account of the life of

81

Steadfast Haynes, and whether this interested party would be foreign or domestic."

"I don't know squat about domestic," Undean said.

"Foreign then," said Keyes as he brought his eyes down from the ceiling. "After all, it is your bailiwick."

"If it's foreign money," Undean said, "then it's a good bet it comes from somewhere that Steady operated. That means the Middle East, Africa, Southeast Asia or Central America. Of those, I'd put my money on the Middle East, with the oil Arabs heading the roster and Israel close behind."

"And after them?"

"I'd eliminate Africa, except for Libya, who's showing signs of wanting to climb down off the top of our shit list."

"It's an oil Arab country anyway," Keyes said, then asked, "You're ruling out Central America?"

"Not much shock value left down there. Anything Steady might've done to them would only get yawned at now. Except for maybe the drug cartels. One of them might like to have Steady's book in reserve if there's ever any plea bargaining to be done."

"Southeast Asia?"

"Nobody. But move a little north and you've got a number one suspect. Japan."

"He never worked Japan."

"Doesn't matter. Let's say one of the countries I've mentioned wants something we don't want 'em to have. So Country X buys Steady's steamy memoirs for seven hundred and fifty thousand, maybe even a million, and locks it away. The time comes when Country X brings Steady's stuff out of the safe, dusts it off and offers to trade it for our yes, no or even our maybe, which could be worth billions to it."

"What a peculiar mind you have, Gilbert."

"Too much imagination. It's what kept me from going any higher than I did."

"What we're talking about, of course, is blackmail."

"Diplomacy's other name," Undean said. "But you started

paying blackmail the moment you agreed to bury Steady at Arlington. And with my usual hindsight, it's pretty obvious that Mlle Gelinet was just making a test run."

"She'd be back for money the next time?"

"And the time after that."

"But she, poor woman, is dead and now we must negotiate with Steady's son." A look of faint hope flickered across Keyes's face. "Is it possible he might've killed her?"

"Tinker Burns was with him. Maybe they both killed her."

"I really don't like being patronized, Gilbert."

"Just softening you up for some more free advice you don't want."

"Which is?"

"Walk away from it."

"Only this afternoon you were urging me to buy."

"That was this afternoon. If you'd've picked up the phone and bought all rights for twenty or thirty thousand, fine. But now you're probably dealing with folks who can call and raise every time. You really want to go dollar for dollar against the Saudis? Japan? The Medellín cartel?"

"There are alternatives, I suppose."

"Black-bag it, you mean."

Keyes frowned. "Really, Gilbert."

"I don't want to know. But there are a couple of things you should know about young Haynes." Undean rose and stared down at the still seated Keyes. "He looks like Steady. He smiles like Steady. He even walks and talks like Steady. But the kid is six times as smart as Steady ever was. And that's fairly goddamn bright, you gotta admit."

Hamilton Keyes rose, shaking his head in what seemed to be mild sorrow, much as if he had just been told of the death of a second cousin he had never met. "How unfortunate," he said, paused and added, "I noticed that when you were reeling off that list of various nationalities who might like to lay hands on Steady's manuscript, you steered away from one in particular."

"Which one?"

"The Americans."

"Like I told you, I never did understand those fuckers," said Gilbert Undean.

Thirteen

They ate in the kitchen of the large old three-story house on 35th Street Northwest. Haynes had a sandwich of thinly sliced cold roast pork on home-baked bread and a bowl of interesting navy bean soup that Lydia Mott said was her own improvement on the U.S. Senate's recipe. Haynes drank beer with the meal—his first food since the lunch with Tinker Burns and Isabelle Gelinet nine and a half hours earlier.

Howard Mott drank a bloody mary as he finished off the last slice of a lemon meringue pie. Lydia Mott ate nothing and lingered only long enough to accept Haynes's gracious and obviously sincere compliments on the soup and sandwich.

After she left, Mott swallowed the last bite of the pie, pushed his plate away and said, "You found Isabelle?"

"Tinker found her and showed her to me when I got there."

"Could he have killed her?"

"Maybe, if he knows how to drown somebody in a bathtub without getting all wet. I suppose he could've done it naked,

85

then put his clothes back on. Providing she really was drowned."

"What do the cops think?"

"Nothing they're willing to share with me."

After Haynes finished his sandwich, Mott said, "If you'd like dessert, Lydia baked some cookies."

"No, thanks."

"Then let's go upstairs."

Insisting that Haynes take the deep armchair with the ottoman, Mott sat in an old oak swivel chair that matched his equally old rolltop desk whose pigeonholes and slots were stuffed with letters, handwritten reminders, business cards, newspaper clippings, invitations to past and future events and an impressive number of bills. Haynes suspected that Mott remembered where he could instantly locate each item.

"Who was Isabelle's closest living relative?" Mott asked.

"Her mother. Madeleine Gelinet. She lives in Nice."

"Then she'll probably get Steady's farm in Berryville—or the proceeds from its sale."

"When?"

"After probate."

"She could use the money now."

"It's possible, of course, that Isabelle made out a will."

"Unmarried thirty-three-year-olds seldom make out wills," Haynes said.

"True."

"I was just wondering."

"About what?"

"Whether it would be okay for me to go up to the farm and look around. Inside the house."

Mott seemed to take the question under advisement for several seconds before he nodded gravely and said, "Steady's will specifies that you're to have your pick of his memorabilia—keepsakes, souvenirs, snapshots, family Bible and so forth, although I can't recall his mentioning a Bible."

"There isn't one."

Mott cocked his head to the left and gave Haynes an amused look. "I somehow get the feeling you're really not much interested in Steady's mementos."

"You're right. I'm not."

"What you're really hoping to find is a true copy of his memoirs tucked away someplace."

"Or even in plain sight."

"And I also suspect you think Isabelle's death is an indication, if not evidence, that such a copy might actually exist."

"That's occurred to me."

"Me, too," Mott said, nodded again, this time more to himself than to Haynes, swiveled around to face the desk, studied the pigeonholes for a moment, reached into one of them and took out a key that was attached by wire to a cardboard tag.

He swiveled around to toss Haynes the key. "It unlocks the front door," Mott said as he again turned back to his desk, picked up a ballpoint pen and began drawing something on a yellow legal pad. "I'll draw you a map of how to find the place after you get to Berryville."

Haynes looked at the tag that was wired to the key with a paper clip. Hand lettering on the tag read, "S. Haynes farm, front door." He decided to give Howard Mott an A-plus for efficiency.

Mott rose, went over to Haynes and handed him the sheet of ruled yellow paper. "Berryville has two traffic lights," he said. "When you get to the second one, turn south, go exactly one mile, turn west, go exactly another mile and you're there."

Haynes examined the map for a moment or two, looked up and said, "Maybe I'll take along a guide."

"You don't like my map?"

"A guide could also be a witness."

"To what?"

"To whatever might happen."

87

"You have a guide in mind?"

"Erika McCorkle."

"Ah."

"What's 'ah' mean?"

"It means you'll be taking along someone who knew Steady rather well, which might prove useful, and who is also attractive enough to make a pleasant drive even more pleasant." He paused. "That's what 'ah' means."

Haynes ignored the explanation and said, "I'd like to retain you as my attorney."

"I cost too much."

"This would be strictly on an 'in case' basis."

"In case you land in the shit."

"Exactly."

"That'd cost less but still too much. Go pillage some government agency for a few million, then give me a call."

"What kind of shape is Steady's seventy-six Cadillac convertible in?"

"You're changing the subject again," Mott said, his tone suddenly wary.

"Am I?"

"It's in perfect shape," Mott said. "Steady babied that car, even nurtured it."

"Where is it?"

"I had a mechanic in Falls Church go pick it up. He's the same one who's serviced it for the past seven years."

"What's it worth?"

"It's the last convertible Cadillac made—until they started making those fifty-thousand-dollar jobs in Italy nobody'll buy. I guess Steady's would bring at least ten or fifteen thousand. Maybe twenty."

"You ever ride in it?"

"Twice, and salivated both times."

"It's your retainer."

"You always strike at the most vulnerable spot?"

"Always."

Mott sighed. "Okay. You have yourself a lawyer. Anything else?"

"What's Mr. McCorkle's home number?"

Mott reeled it off from memory.

"May I use your phone?"

Mott nodded at the phone on his desk, then asked, "Want me to leave?"

"What for?" Haynes said as he rose, went to the desk, picked up the phone and tapped out the number. It rang three times before it was answered with a woman's hello.

"Erika?" Haynes said.

"Yes."

"Granville Haynes. Do you know the way to Berryville?"

Fourteen

After the taxi stopped in front of Mac's Place, Haynes paid off the driver, got out and held the door open for a fiftyish U.S. senator from one of the western states—either Idaho or Montana, he thought—who was accompanied by a pretty woman in her late twenties.

The senator read, classified and dismissed Haynes with a practiced glance and a nod of thanks. But the woman noticed him the way many women did—with a slight start, as if struck by the notion that he must be somebody important, famous or at least rich. But a second glance, which she now gave him, produced the usual counterconviction that Haynes, despite his looks, was nobody at all. And as always, the reassessment caused more relief than disappointment.

Haynes held the taxi door for them until they were inside, closed it carefully and, after a faint smile from the woman, entered the restaurant to keep his midnight appointment with Michael Padillo. Although now 11:58 P.M. in Washington and the rest of the eastern time zone, it was, as ever, twilight at Mac's Place.

This lighting, or lack of it, had been chosen by McCorkle

90

and Padillo long ago after a series of unscientific experiments had convinced them that midsummer twilight—at a certain moment not too long after sunset, but well before moonrise—was precisely what was needed to flatter the features of customers over 30, yet enable them to read the menu without striking a match. Customers under 30, McCorkle had argued, would regard the gloom as atmosphere, maybe even ambience.

Haynes counted four solitary males at the long bar, all of whom bore the stamp of practicing topers. At widely separated tables, two obviously married couples dawdled over coffee and dessert, as if dreading the prospect of home and bed. A pair of waiters, one old, the other young, stood talking quietly in their native tongue. Something the young waiter said made the old one yawn.

Herr Horst, his coat off, was making short work of a trout at the management table near the kitchen's swinging doors. He looked up from his supper, saw Haynes and pointed, thumb over shoulder, to the office in the rear, then returned to the trout.

When he reached the office door, Haynes knocked, waited for the "Come in" and entered to find Padillo, in shirt sleeves and loosened tie, seated at what Haynes thought was his side of the partners desk, a pot of coffee and two cups at his elbow. Padillo indicated the brown leather couch. Haynes sat down.

"Why would anyone kill her?" Padillo asked.

Haynes said, "Where'd you first meet Steady?"

"Coffee?" Padillo said.

Haynes shook his head.

Padillo poured himself a cup, sipped it, put the cup down, leaned back in the chair, put his feet on the desk and crossed them at the ankles, revealing muted argyle socks but no shoes. "I met him in Africa," Padillo said. "In the early sixties."

"Where in Africa?"

"What're we going to do—trade confidences?"

"It might be useful."

After thinking about it, Padillo said, "Then I'll go first and begin with Isabelle. Maybe I'll get to Steady later. Maybe not."

"Fine," Haynes said.

With his feet still on the desk, his hands and forearms relaxed on the arms of his chair, Padillo, staring at Haynes, began to speak in a voice so quiet and uninflected it was almost a monotone. Leaning forward a little to make certain he missed nothing, Haynes suspected Padillo must have used that same quiet voice to tell truths, half-truths and lies to other trained listeners, and found himself wondering who they were and what languages had been spoken.

"Nine years ago this month," Padillo said, "a twenty-four-year-old French woman walked in here and introduced herself as Isabelle Gelinet of Agence France-Presse. She said she'd been sent over from Paris to write fluff features on the presidential campaign and election. But she didn't want to write fluff and wondered whether I could help her with advice, tips, introductions, anything. Her sole personal reference was a letter from Tinker Burns to me."

"Not the most impeccable reference," Haynes said.

"But an interesting one."

"Where'd you first meet Tinker?" Haynes asked.

"In France."

"When?"

"March of forty-five."

"Was that after he parachuted in with the fifty thousand in gold that fell into the Loire and never quite made it to the Resistance?"

"One of Steady's taller tales, right?"

Haynes confirmed the guess with a nod and said, "They send you after Tinker?"

"Who?"

"The OSS."

"I had better things to do," Padillo said. "But in forty-six in Marseilles, I believe I did bump into Tinker again and mention that the Army's CID was getting warm, thus earning his eternal gratitude. On Tinker time, of course, eternity is about two and a half weeks."

"That must've been when he joined the Legion."

"About then," Padillo said. "But to get back to Isabelle. When she walked in here with nothing but Tinker's letter, it hit me that she might be more than just another kid reporter looking for the big break." He paused. "Although God knows this town's always had a surplus of them."

"L.A., too," Haynes said.

"So I introduced her to Karl Triller."

"Your bartender."

"And minority stockholder."

"The one who helped nurse Steady through his fourth divorce."

"The same," Padillo said. "For more than twenty years Karl has studied congressional antics. It's been a very thorough, very German study, and notice I said antics, not actions."

"I noticed."

"What began as a hobby turned into an informal clearinghouse of information."

"A gossip exchange."

Ignoring Haynes's clarification, Padillo said, "Karl gets quoted a lot by air and print reporters, although never by name. He's always a veteran Congress watcher, a well-informed source, or that grand old standby, the seasoned Washington observer. It was Karl who tipped Isabelle off to a couple of stories that she beat AP on and impressed her editors so much that, after the nineteen eighty conventions, they assigned her to the Bush campaign and, in the final month, to Reagan's."

"A couple of nice hops," Haynes said.

"So nice that soon after the election she began getting invitations. To dinners. Embassy receptions. Various balls.

Intimate gatherings of twelve in Spring Valley. Things like that. Sometimes she needed an escort; sometimes she didn't. When she did, she usually asked me, probably because I had a dinner jacket and knew how to tango."

Haynes grinned, which again caused Padillo to realize how closely the son resembled the dead father. "Anyway," Padillo said, "we lasted eighteen months, maybe twenty, and then came Steady."

"What'd he have to offer other than limitless charm?"

"New directions."

"Leading where?"

"To covert action fiascoes. Terrorism, theirs and ours. An assortment of foreign intrigue imbroglios. Homegrown money spies. Redefecting defectors. It was heady times and Isabelle began to wonder if it wasn't mostly because old Bill Casey was back."

"Back?"

"From his glory days in OSS."

"You knew him then?"

"In a way."

"And Isabelle?"

"Eventually, she did an unauthorized and very unflattering three-part profile on Casey," Padillo said. "She had a lot of help from Steady and a mixed bag of Casey watchers he'd rounded up for her. A few even let her quote them by name. She later sent me a copy of the piece. I think I still have it somewhere—a hell of a story. But twenty minutes after AF-P moved it, they sent out a kill. Isabelle got mad and quit, did some free-lancing for a while, then moved in with Steady at his farm either to write or help him write his memoirs—or so I gathered from what she said at lunch today."

After studying Padillo for almost fifteen seconds, Haynes said, "You haven't always run a saloon, have you?"

"I've always wanted to."

"What'd you do before you and McCorkle opened this one?"

"We ran one in Bonn."

"What happened to it?"

"They blew it up."

"Who're they?"

"McCorkle's always been convinced it was the CIA who supplied the bomb and the KGB who threw it." He smiled slightly. "But then McCorkle has a rather jaundiced view of world events."

Another silence was again ended by Haynes, talking at first to the floor, then to Padillo. "Isabelle was my oldest friend. We grew up almost next door in Nice. When Tinker came back from the Legion, Dien Bien Phu and all that, he rented a room in the house of a pregnant widow in Nice. Three months later, Isabelle was born. Tinker stayed on as Madeleine Gelinet's paying guest, lover and surrogate father to Isabelle. In nineteen fifty-nine my mother died. I was three. Steady and I moved from Paris to Nice and rented a house three doors up from Madeleine Gelinet. That's how Steady and I met Isabelle and Tinker."

"I've wondered," Padillo said.

"Not long after Steady married my stepmother number one, he and Tinker were off to the Congo—but on different sides. When Tinker came back, he started up his arms business and resumed his on-again, off-again affair with Isabelle's mother."

"Where'd he get the capital?" Padillo asked. "One day Tinker's an out-of-work mercenary, the next day he's a budding international arms dealer."

"He stole it. He and Steady. Want the details?"

"I don't think so," Padillo said. "When'd you last see Isabelle—before today?"

"Almost twenty years ago. It was just before Steady had me fly here to enroll in St. Alban's. By then, I was living in Italy with stepmother number two. As always, Steady sent cash. So I took a bus to Nice, saw Isabelle and caught a flight from Paris to Washington. But before I left Nice, Isabelle and I

95

swore our undying love, which expired six or seven months later. But we always wrote each other long letters at Christmas—until she moved in with Steady."

"Who stopped writing?"

"She did."

"I would've guessed you."

"Along with my old man's goofy smile, I also inherited a lot of his goofy laissez-faire attitudes."

Padillo took his feet down from the desk and slipped them into a pair of black loafers. As he bent down to tug the left shoe up over his heel, he said, "Is there really a book?"

"Steady's lawyer and your landlord handed me a manuscript this afternoon."

"You look at it?" Padillo said, once more leaning back in his chair.

Haynes nodded.

"A lot of people in this town would pray they're not in it."

"Think you're in it?"

"I hope so. It might give our lunch business a boost."

Haynes rose. "Like to see it?"

Padillo nodded. "Especially if it has an index."

"It doesn't, but McCorkle was kind enough to put it in your safe for me this afternoon."

Padillo examined Haynes thoughtfully. "The Willard has a much better safe."

"I'm sure it does."

"But the Willard also gives receipts and keeps records."

"Right again," Haynes said.

Padillo rose, went over to the old safe, spun the combination and tugged open the heavy door. From the safe he took the folded-over grocery sack and handed it to Haynes, who placed it on the partners desk. "Have a look," Haynes said.

Padillo studied him again, briefly this time, before turning to the desk and removing the brown-paper-wrapped package from the sack. He read the address label and asked, "Steady mailed it to himself?"

"He thought it would ensure the copyright's validity."

"Did it?"

"It was already valid."

Padillo slowly removed the wrapping paper and lifted the top from the Keebord box. He read the title page without expression, then the four lines by Housman and the dedication to the dead author's son. After reading the two sentences that composed Chapter One and also the entire book, Padillo quickly leafed through the rest of the blank pages, turned to Haynes and said, "Why'd you really want me to see this?"

"Because you were Isabelle's friend."

"Did this all begin as one of Steady's diddles?"

"I don't know."

"Is there a book somewhere?"

"I'm not sure, but everything you just read is copyrighted—except the Housman quote."

Padillo carefully put the top back on the box. "And what can you do with the copyright to a two-sentence book?"

"I can sell it."

"As is?"

"Possibly."

"Who to?"

"The highest bidder. Which is when I might need a little help."

Padillo nodded, but it was a noncommittal nod. "And who do you think the highest bidder will be?"

"Whoever killed Isabelle," Haynes said. "Or had her killed."

Fifteen

Erika McCorkle picked Haynes up in front of the Willard Hotel at exactly 7 A.M. that Saturday, each of them surprised at the other's promptness. After muttered good mornings, she handed him a plastic container of Roy Rogers coffee and sped them to Pennsylvania Avenue and M Street, then across Key Bridge and onto the George Washington Memorial Parkway in what Haynes suspected was record time, even for a Saturday morning.

After passing the road sign that beckoned passersby to CIA headquarters, Haynes ended the long silence with a question: "You usually eat breakfast?"

"Never. Do you?"

"No."

"You're not much on morning chatter either," she said.

"Turn on the radio."

She said it was broken.

Another silence began and lasted until she turned off to take the Old Georgetown Pike that dipped and curled its way through rolling Virginia countryside. They were now in a holdout exurbia of wintry browns and grays where a faded bumper sticker on an old Volvo station wagon begged for propertied recruits to enlist in a rearguard action against unnamed developers. Haynes guessed it was a skirmish the exurbanites had already lost.

In some of the deeper brush- and tree-protected gullies—or runs, which were what Haynes remembered arroyos were called in Virginia—he could see patches of dirty snow. And since the sky was overcast with dark wet-looking clouds, he asked Erika McCorkle if she had heard a weather forecast.

She glanced at him, frowning at his tweed jacket, gray slacks, blue tieless shirt and absent topcoat. "Fifty percent chance of snow—or can you remember what snow is?"

"I saw some two weeks ago."

"Where?"

"Big Bear."

"Where's that?"

"Up in the mountains a couple of hours east of L.A."

"You went skiing?"

"I did a commercial."

"*You* were in a TV commercial?"

"Right."

"What's a homicide cop doing in a TV commercial?"

"Selling mustard."

"That yellow hot-dog stuff?"

"Grey Poupon. And I'm no longer a homicide cop. I quit. Three weeks ago. Almost four."

"And now you're what—security consultant to the rich and famous?"

"An actor."

There was another silence that lasted long enough for the Cutlass to accelerate from 50 to 68 miles per hour. "An actor," she said. "Steady was an actor, which is probably why I believed everything he said—some of the time."

"You're doing seventy-three," Haynes said.

She slowed the car to 50. "Did it just happen?"

"You mean like cancer?"

"You know what I mean."

"A TV producer's fourteen-year-old daughter was killed and raped in that order. I nailed the guy, and the producer was so grateful he decided to make my dreams come true by offering me a one-line part in his cop series that was about to be cancelled."

"Was it your dream?"

"No. But he thought it was everyone's. So I did it. An agent caught the episode, called up and asked if I'd like to do more TV stuff. We had lunch and she said I might make a bare living at it because the camera was kind to me. But if I wanted to make a decent living, I'd have to go against the box." He paused. "She talks like that."

"What'd she mean?"

"That there're an awful lot of blond guys in Hollywood who want to play lifeguards and fighter pilots because they look like lifeguards and fighter pilots are supposed to look."

She glanced at him. "You could play a fighter pilot. An older one."

"I'd rather play a bank teller turned embezzler."

"You look too honest."

"Exactly her point."

"When'd you get the big break?" she said, slowing down for the red light at the intersection where the Old Georgetown Pike met the Leesburg Pike. "The one that let you quit the cops."

"About three weeks ago," he said.

"What's the part?"

"I get to play a working stiff who wins a million-dollar lottery."

She sniffed. "Not too original."

"No," Haynes said, "but I think I'll enjoy it."

* * *

By the time they reached the outskirts of Leesburg they were hungry and Erika McCorkle claimed to know an old diner, a real one, where the food was cheap, fast and good. But the old diner had been demolished to make way for a discount appliance store and they had to settle for a Denny's a little farther on.

Inside, Haynes pretended to listen to Erika McCorkle's diatribe against the destruction of places and things that composed her memories. She stopped only when the waitress came over, handed them menus and waited until they both ordered chicken fried steaks at 9:16 in the morning.

A little more than an hour later they reached Berryville, the Clarke County seat. Its four- or five-block-long Main Street offered two traffic lights, two banks, two restaurants (one open, one permanently closed), the usual antique shops and too many marginal-looking businesses. Haynes thought the closed restaurant must have been the place where Berryville's establishment once gathered for morning coffee.

After he asked Erika McCorkle to double-park, Haynes got out and bought a newspaper from a vending machine. The paper's masthead said it was an independent publication established four years after the Civil War and published every Thursday.

Back in the car, Haynes turned the page until he came to the obituaries. "He made it."

"Who?"

"Steady," Haynes said and began reading aloud. "'Steadfast Haynes, 57, of Route 1, Berryville, died Monday in Washington, D.C., where he was to have attended the inauguration.'

"Paragraph. 'Born in Philadelphia, Haynes served in the Korean conflict, later attending the University of Pennsylvania, where he was elected to Phi Beta Kappa. He subsequently

101

joined the U.S. State Department, serving in Africa, Central America, the Middle East and Asia. Mr. Haynes had lived in the Berryville area for the past several years.'

"Last paragraph. 'He is survived by his son Granville Haynes of Los Angeles, California. Interment was scheduled for Arlington National Cemetery.'"

As Haynes refolded the paper and placed it on the rear seat, Erika McCorkle pulled out into the traffic and said, "I didn't know he was Phi Beta Kappa."

"He wasn't. Turn left at the next light, go one mile, turn right and go another mile."

She glanced at the odometer, turned left on green and said, "But he did serve in all those places."

"I'm not sure 'serve' is the operative word, but he was there, although not for the State Department."

"The CIA, right?"

When Haynes only shrugged, she said, "That's what I figured," and, one mile later, turned the Cutlass onto a narrow county blacktop that ran straight as a knife past small farms of not much more than thirty or forty acres. Some of the farms boasted orchards. Others seemed to grow mostly alfalfa, now baled into fat rolls that would feed the dozens of horses who, standing behind barbed wire or split-rail fences, marked the car's passing with indifferent stares.

Exactly one mile from where they had turned off was a crooked, left-leaning oak post that supported a small box on whose side someone had painted "S. Haynes" in neat black letters. The mailbox was at the foot of a long drive that could have used another load or two of gravel.

The drive swept up a gentle slope to a six- or seven-room two-story house. Painted white, although not recently, the house was shielded by a stand or grove of winter-bare trees at least forty or fifty feet tall. To the left of the house was a large pasture of ten or fifteen acres. Behind the house was a sturdy-looking brown barn built of wood. A white board fence, in need of both paint and repair, marked the property lines.

Dead grass and weeds decorated the center of the long drive that ended in front of the house, where a big blue Ford pickup was hitched to a horse trailer.

"Whose truck and trailer?" Erika McCorkle asked.

"I don't know," Haynes said.

She drove slowly up the drive, which was at least seventy-five yards long, and parked behind the empty horse trailer. They got out and went up seven steps to a covered porch. As Haynes took from his pocket the front door key Howard Mott had given him, he noticed a large thermometer. Its reading was 31 degrees Fahrenheit.

Out of habit, Haynes tried the door before using the key. It was unlocked. He looked at Erika McCorkle, who shrugged. Haynes opened the door and they went in to find themselves in an entry hall. To the right was the living room. To the left, an old mirrored hatrack, possibly an antique. From it hung a duffle coat. Just ahead were stairs that led to the second floor.

Haynes called, "Anyone home?"

He was answered by a thumping sound that seemed to come from a closet built beneath the staircase. When they reached the closet door, Haynes tried the knob and found it locked. He knocked on the door and was again answered by the thumping noise.

"Pick the lock," Erika McCorkle said.

"With what?"

"A credit card."

He ignored her and inspected the door, which seemed to be a thick, solid one that had been hung by a craftsman who had left the usual three-quarters-of-an-inch clearance at the bottom.

He looked at Erika McCorkle and said, "Ever change a tire on that car of yours?"

"Sure."

"You know the thing that takes the nuts off the wheel?"

"The lug wrench."

"I could use it."

She was back with the lug wrench in less than two minutes. Haynes was relieved to see that one end of it formed a jimmy, useful for prying off hubcaps. He used the lug wrench to knock the pin out of the door's top hinge, then repeated the process on the lower one. After slipping the fingers of both hands beneath the bottom of the door, he gave it a tug and it came off its hinges.

A woman lay on her back in the closet among the rubber boots, old shoes and two pairs of ancient galoshes. She wore a blue knitted watch cap. Across her mouth was a two-inch-wide strip of industrial duct tape. She also wore an old zipped-up leather flight jacket and a pair of straight-leg blue jeans that were stuffed into expensive riding boots. The boots were taped together at the ankles. Her obviously bound hands were beneath her.

"Take the tape off her mouth while I go find something to cut her loose," Haynes said.

Erika McCorkle nodded and knelt beside the woman. Haynes turned and entered the living room that contained mismatched pieces of sixty-to-seventy-year-old furniture, much of it gathered around the fireplace. A pair of open sliding doors could divide the living room from the dining room, which had been converted into an office furnished with two battered metal desks and a pair of fairly new four-drawer metal file cabinets. There were also a couple of phones, one on each desk, an IBM Wheelwriter and a personal computer. A swinging door led from the dining room/office into the kitchen, where Haynes found a paring knife with a sharp blade.

He hurried back to the staircase closet. The tape had been removed from the woman's mouth and she now sat leaning against the closet wall, her feet still bound, her hands still behind her back. She stared up at Haynes and whispered, "My God."

Erika McCorkle said, "Mr. Haynes, may I present your former stepmother, Letitia Melon. Letty, this is Steady's son, Granville."

Sixteen

Although no great beauty, Letty Melon was a noticeably pretty woman in her early forties with short dark hair, eyes of such a deep blue that they verged on violet and the legatee of a Virginia drawl that she used to announce her immediate needs.

Her most pressing need, she said, was to pee. After that she would need a drink. "There's got to be a bottle around here someplace," she said. "If you all can't find any in the kitchen, look behind the books in the front room where he used to keep his emergency ration."

By the time she rejoined Haynes and Erika McCorkle in the kitchen, they had found a bottle of Scotch whisky in the bookshelves behind Shirer's *The Rise and Fall of the Third Reich* and Vidal's *Burr*. Erika had also found a jar of instant Yuban and a kettle. The kettle was just coming to a boil on the electric stove.

Letty Melon sat down at the pine kitchen table, reached for the bottle of Scotch and poured a measure into a glass. She drank it off in two swallows, sighed appreciatively, removed a package of Camels from her old flight jacket and lit one with a gold Zippo that Haynes knew to be a collector's item worth at least a thousand dollars. She inhaled deeply, blew the smoke out and said, "There were two of them."

Haynes nodded.

"They had sacks over their heads with eyeholes in them."

"Cloth or paper?"

"Paper. Brown paper. Grocery sacks."

"Which grocery?"

"Safeway."

Erika placed two cups of coffee on the table and said, "There's sugar but no milk or cream."

"I'll just sweeten mine with a drop of this," Letty Melon said and poured a taste of whisky into her cup. After sipping the Scotch and coffee, she said, "I knew they were here the moment I stepped through the door."

"How?" Haynes said.

"The place was warm. As warm as it is now. That meant somebody'd turned on the heat. So I did what you did. I called to see who was home. When nobody answered, I went from the living room into the dining room that looks like some kind of office now, and then on through the swinging door into the kitchen. And here they were. I started to yell, but one of them grabbed me and the other slapped that tape across my mouth. Then they taped my hands and feet and locked me into that little old stairway closet and, damn, I got mad."

Erika McCorkle sat down at the table with a cup of coffee. She offered the sugar bowl to Haynes, who put a spoonful of sugar into his cup, stirred it slowly and said, "What time was this?"

"A little after eight."

"You didn't see a car?" Haynes said.

"There wasn't any unless it was in the barn, where Steady keeps that old Cadillac of his."

"Was the front door locked?"

"It was locked."

107

"But you had a key?"

"Of course I had a key."

"They say anything?"

"Not a word."

"Were they tall, short, fat, skinny, what?"

"Tall."

"How were they dressed—other than the sacks?"

"Jeans. Running shoes. Down jackets, one brown, one blue. And gloves. They both wore gloves."

"What kind?"

"Driving gloves. You know the kind that're half leather and half knitted with open backs just below the fingers?"

Haynes nodded. "Did you hear them leave?"

"No."

"Where do you live?"

"Just outside Middleburg."

"That means you left there when—around seven?"

"Around in there."

"Why'd you want to get here so early?"

She smiled at him then, displaying some remarkably well cared for teeth. "That sounds like something Steady might've asked. Not what the hell were you doing here, but why'd you come so early? Well, the reason is I got worried about old Zip."

"Who's he?"

"Steady's nine-year-old hunter. A bay gelding. I didn't even think about Zip till late last night and then I almost couldn't sleep for worrying about whether Steady'd got somebody to look after him or even boarded him out somewhere."

She stopped talking and stared down into her cup, as if she felt the late Steadfast Haynes was due a second or two of silence. Erika McCorkle quickly ended the silence with a question. "He'd be in the barn if he's still here?"

Letty Melon looked up and nodded.

"I'll go look," Erika McCorkle said, rose, opened the

kitchen door, examined it briefly and turned back to Haynes. "They came in here," she said. "The door's been jimmied."

Haynes rose and went over to examine the gouged-out doorjamb. Erika left and Haynes returned to the kitchen table.

"Where'd you all meet?" Letty Melon asked.

"Her father introduced us."

"They at Steady's burial?"

"No."

"I heard it was at Arlington. I didn't go because, well, because Steady and I'd grown to detest each other in a fairly cordial sort of way."

Haynes nodded.

"Many people there?"

"Not many."

"Tinker Burns?"

"Yes."

"Isabelle?"

"She was there."

"And you. Anybody else?"

"One or two others."

"I suppose everybody tells you how much you look like him."

Haynes again nodded.

"When that closet door opened and I saw you—well, for a second there I thought it was Steady. Or maybe his ghost."

Haynes smiled slightly, drank the rest of his coffee and said, "What d'you think those two guys wanted?"

"Something to steal."

"That's a Rolex you're wearing. You lit your cigarette with a gold Zippo. They didn't take those. What about your purse?"

"I carry a wallet," she said, removed it from her right hip pocket and looked inside. "All my credit cards are still here along with about eighty dollars in cash."

109

"Want me to call the sheriff?"

She seemed to think about it as she replaced her wallet. After a couple of slow headshakes, she said, "I wasn't robbed and I wasn't really hurt—except for some bruised dignity. But I can get over that without any help from the sheriff." She looked around the kitchen, as if searching for any other major changes her ex-husband might have made. When she was done, she looked at Haynes and said, "He leave this place to you?"

"To Isabelle," Haynes said.

If he hadn't been watching for it, Haynes might not have noticed the slight tremor that barely rippled her shoulders. "Isabelle," she said, pouring another measure of whisky into her glass. She drank the whisky, put her cigarette out, lit another one and said, "I suppose she'll sell it."

"Isabelle's dead."

She stared at him, eyes wide, as a flush began at the base of her neck and rushed to her cheeks. "When?"

"Yesterday afternoon. In her apartment on Connecticut Avenue. Tinker Burns and I found her—more or less."

"Well, did you or didn't you?"

"Tinker found her and when I got there a few minutes later, he took me into the bathroom. Isabelle was lying in a tub of water with her wrists and ankles wired."

Haynes couldn't decide whether it was a delayed reaction to her own ordeal or the shock of Isabelle Gelinet's death that caused Letty Melon to tremble and then to shake. She was still shaking, although not nearly as much, when Erika McCorkle came through the kitchen door and said, without preamble, "There's a dead horse in the barn."

Zip, the 9-year-old bay gelding, apparently had gone down on his forelegs first because they were still tucked beneath him. His rear legs were splayed out to the side. His head rested on the fairly clean straw in his stall. The feed bin was half full and there was water in a wooden tub made from a large barrel that had been sawed in half. He had been shot once through the white blaze that formed a rough diamond between his eyes.

Letty Melon, no longer shaking, ran a gentle hand down his neck. She looked up and said, "He's still almost warm." She rose, glanced around the stall and said, "Poor old Zip."

"Did you hear the shot, Letty?" Erika McCorkle asked.

"No, but he could've been dead when I got here."

She took what seemed to be a long last look at the dead Zip, turned and walked to the center of the barn where four Dukakis posters had been arranged to catch a car's slight oil leak and prevent it from soaking into the barn's hard-packed dirt floor. Letty Melon stood for a moment, staring down at the Dukakis signs, then turned to Haynes and said, "Somebody pick up his old Cadillac?"

"His lawyer sent someone."

"It was a mistake."

"What?" Haynes said.

"My coming here. If I'd known about Isabelle, I wouldn't've come near the place. With both her and Steady dead, it makes me look like a ghoul." She paused, took a deep breath and said, "Look. I don't want to have anything more to do with Steady. Nothing at all ever again."

Haynes nodded.

"I want to go home now."

"Fine."

"And after I get there, I don't want any calls or visits from the Clarke County sheriff or his deputies."

Haynes again nodded.

"You going to talk to him—the sheriff?"

"I have to."

"But you won't mention me?"

"No."

"Or the guys with sacks over their heads?"

"If I don't tell the sheriff about you, I can't tell him about them."

"Well, what are you gonna tell him?"

Haynes turned to look at the dead Zip. "I'm going to ask him what to do with a dead horse."

Seventeen

Haynes got the number of the sheriff's office in Berryville from directory assistance. After the man who answered said he was Deputy Soullard, Haynes identified himself and reported the death of the horse.

The deputy put Haynes on hold until a stern baritone voice came on, announced that it belonged to Sheriff Jenkins Shipp-with-two-*p*'s and asked, "You Steady's boy?"—somehow turning the abrupt question into a warm greeting.

After Haynes replied yes, Sheriff Shipp asked, "What's your name again?"

"Granville Haynes."

"I'm sure sorry about your daddy, Granville, and I do mourn his passing."

"You're very kind."

"Now what's this about old Zip?"

Haynes said he had arrived at the farm to discover the horse had been shot and killed.

"Got a call from your daddy's lawyer in Washington about Zip last Thursday. Tell a lie, Friday. He's the one that told me

Steady was dead and gone. Lawyer by the name of Mott, I believe."

"Howard Mott."

"That's right, Howard. Said he was sending somebody out to pick up Steady's old Cadillac and wanted to know if I could think of anybody who'd go out there and take care of Zip till he made other arrangements. Right away I thought of the Dyson kid—lives just down the road from Steady. Mott said he'd pay the kid twenty bucks a day to water and feed Zip, clean out his stall and exercise him some." The sheriff paused. "And that's what the kid's been doing."

"When?" Haynes said.

"After school."

"If I drop the money off at your office, will you see that the Dyson boy gets it?"

"Yes, sir, I can do that. Be happy to."

"One other thing, Sheriff. What should I do with a dead horse?"

There was a pause. "Uh—Granville, you happen to know if old Zip was insured?"

"No idea."

There was another longer pause that made Haynes wonder how delicately the sheriff would put his next question.

"Well, sir," Shipp said, "Zip was a pretty fair old hunter and I reckon if he *was* insured, it'd be for at least fifteen hundred, maybe even a couple of thousand."

"That much?" Haynes said.

"At least."

"I'd almost pay that much to have him hauled off and buried."

"No need for that," Shipp said, sounding relieved and almost happy. "What I'll do is call up the Blue Ridge Hunt Club and they'll come fetch him and it won't cost you a cent because they'll chop old Zip up and feed him to the club dogs. Sort of recycle him, so to speak."

"I know my father would've approved."

114

"One other thing, Granville. Would you mind sticking around till a deputy drives out there and takes a look-see? Folks here do get upset when a horse is shot dead like that."

"I'll wait till he gets here," Haynes said.

After he and the sheriff said goodbye, Haynes hung up one of the two phones in the office that once had been the dining room. Erika McCorkle, seated in a squeaky swivel chair at the other desk, also recradled the extension phone, rose, went to the window, looked out and announced, "It's snowing."

Haynes joined her at the window to inspect the snowfall. They stared at it silently until she said, "I was sure you'd tell him about Letty and the two guys with sacks over their heads."

Still watching the snowfall, Haynes said, "It's really coming down."

"Why didn't you tell him?" she asked. "Because you never break a promise—or because you only make the kind you won't have to break?"

"I make and break them all the time," he said. "Especially the ones I make to myself."

"Well, I think it's awfully sweet that you didn't tell him."

Moments later, Haynes found himself wondering whether it was Erika McCorkle's mild flattery or mere impulse that had caused him to tell her about the missing memoirs. Whatever it had been, his normal caution prevented him from telling her about those who were anxious to buy them, sight unseen.

Erika seemed to ponder what he had told her before she asked, "So you think, or maybe just suspect, that somewhere, maybe even here, there's a true honest-to-God manuscript chock full of political dynamite and shocking revelations and other assorted hot stuff?"

"Right," Haynes said and watched a sudden thought streak across her face, which, he realized, would never be any good at dissembling.

115

"Then that's what those two guys were really after, wasn't it?" she said. "The ones who tied up Letty."

"That doesn't exactly follow."

"Sure it does," she said. "And the same two guys who shot Zip and tied up Letty must've threatened to drown Isabelle unless she told them where the manuscript was. But after she told them it was here at the farm, they drowned her anyway."

"You just set the new indoor record for intuitive leaps."

"I take it you're not buying."

"I might," Haynes said. "If everything checks out."

"What the hell's everything?"

"Let's start with Letty and why she was here."

"She was worried about Zip."

Haynes stared at her for a moment, turned, went back to the phone, picked it up and tapped out a long-distance number. When the phone began to ring, he said, "Get on the extension."

After Erika McCorkle lifted the extension phone to her ear, she heard it ring two times before a woman answered with, "Mott, James, Lovelandy and Nathan."

"Mr. Mott, please. This is Granville Haynes and it's important."

After a brief pause, Howard Mott came on the line with, "Nothing can be important on a Saturday morning."

"I'm at Steady's farm."

"So?"

"Did you call Sheriff Shipp and ask him to find somebody to take care of Steady's horse?"

"Sure," Mott said. "When I called to tell him Steady was dead and that I was sending a guy out to pick up the Cadillac, I also asked if he knew anybody who'd feed, water and exercise the horse for twenty bucks a day. He said he did."

"How'd you know about the horse?"

"Steady told me about—what'd he call him, Zip?—a year or so ago. But I forgot about him till Steady's ex-wife called me."

"When?"

"The morning after Steady died. She was worried about the horse. I told her I'd take care of it and to stop worrying. What's wrong?"

"Somebody shot the horse."

There was a brief silence until Mott said, "What d'you want me to do about it?"

"Nothing."

"Good," Howard Mott said and hung up.

Eighteen

They began the search upstairs, where they discovered three bedrooms, one bath, two old mirrored wardrobes and a lone closet. Haynes's inspection of the bathroom medicine cabinet revealed an empty bottle of St. Joseph aspirin, a new toothbrush still in its plastic package and somebody's diaphragm.

The smallest of the three bedrooms was meanly furnished with a thin mattress on a brass bed that was little more than a cot. An oval rag rug lay beside it on the pine floor that had been stained a dark brown. A chest of drawers, painted Chinese red, was empty. The other furniture consisted of a 1940s bridge lamp, a straight-backed wooden chair and an ancient wardrobe whose mirror was turning silver-gray. Haynes looked inside the wardrobe, found two wire coat hangers and decided he was in a guest room that had been deliberately furnished to discourage long stays.

They found little of interest in the next bedroom other than a short stack of explicit sex magazines in a bedside table drawer. The magazines featured photographs of pairs of naked women, fairly young, who groped and grabbed each other while apparently trying to decide whether to fix hamburgers or meat loaf for dinner.

Erika McCorkle flipped through one of the magazines and called it a sexual crutch. Haynes went through another issue more slowly and said nothing. As he put the magazines back into the table drawer, Erika McCorkle gave the room a further inspection and said, "I don't know why, but this doesn't look like Steady's room to me."

"Maybe it was Isabelle's."

Erika McCorkle nodded at the table that held the magazines. "Those were hers?"

"Maybe," Haynes said, went to the wardrobe and opened it, revealing some neatly hung dresses, blouses, pants, skirts and, below them, a half dozen pairs of women's shoes. He closed the wardrobe door, turned to Erika McCorkle and said, "This must've been her room unless Steady was into cross-dressing."

"And the magazines?"

He shrugged. "Maybe when Steady got the urge, he'd hurry down the hall, hop into bed and they'd lie there, flip through the magazines and get it on. But if you're really curious about which way Isabelle went, ask Padillo."

"Go to hell," she said and stalked out of the room.

Haynes caught up with her in the third and last bedroom, the only one with a closet. She was standing near the double bed, sniffing at something. "This was his room," she said. "You can still smell the cigarette smoke."

Haynes opened the two doors of the wide shallow closet. There were six blue shirts and six white shirts from Paul Stuart that had been bought in New York or Tokyo or, more likely, by mail order. The shirts were on hangers and looked as if they had been washed and ironed by loving hands.

A row of tweed jackets, all remarkably alike, took up another yard of closet space. The rest was occupied by a dozen pairs of gray and tan trousers, which were followed by

119

a dark blue suit, a windbreaker and a Burberry raincoat with raglan sleeves.

Haynes knew he was viewing a collection of the semi-uniforms his father had worn throughout his adult life, even in the hot countries. He remembered color photographs—mostly Polaroids—obviously taken in one tropical clime or other, where Steadfast Haynes's dress code had been either a blue or white long-sleeved oxford button-down shirt, but no tie, tan cotton pants and shoes that didn't have to be laced up. If it were only hot, the shirt sleeves might be rolled up two full turns; if sizzling, they might be rolled above the elbows.

"Steady's room," he agreed and shut the closet door.

Turning to give it all one final look, Erika McCorkle said, "Not much, is there? No watercolors on the walls or oriental rugs on the floor. No snapshots of you at seven or nine. No souvenir ashtrays from Djakarta or assegai spears from Africa."

"They didn't use assegais where he was and he travelled light."

"And alone?"

"Nearly always." Haynes gave the room his own final inspection. "This must be the only house he ever owned."

"What'd he do with his money?"

"Lived well, spent it on alimony and sent me to expensive schools."

"Which university?"

"Virginia."

"Huh," she said. "That's where I went."

Downstairs, they searched the kitchen first, Haynes using a kebab skewer he had come across to probe sacks, bags and cartons of staples, not at all sure of what he expected to find. He found nothing.

While Erika McCorkle searched the living room, Haynes put on the old duffle coat that hung from the hall hatrack and walked through the falling snow to the barn. He spent twenty minutes searching it, saving Zip's stall until last, but found nothing beneath the oats or under the straw or in the half barrel of water.

He finally knelt beside the dead horse and looked closely at the entry wound. There was no exit wound and Haynes guessed that the single round had been fired from either a revolver or semiautomatic handgun of 9mm caliber or less.

It was snowing even more as he walked back to the house, entered through the jimmied kitchen door, hung the duffle coat back on the hall hatrack and found Erika McCorkle in the dining room/office, standing beside the two gray steel filing cabinets.

She pulled out a top drawer and said, "Empty. All empty."

Haynes opened and closed a couple of the drawers, glanced around the room and indicated the personal computer that was next to the IBM Wheelwriter. "How friendly are you with computers?" he asked.

"Chummy," she said, sat down, switched it on, studied its keyboard and tapped out a demand for entry. The computer promptly requested a password. Erika first tried "Steady" without success, then several others with the same result. She looked up at Haynes and asked, "What was Steady's mother's maiden name?"

"Cobbett with two *b*'s and two *t*'s."

After she tried Cobbett, the computer lowered its drawbridge and moments later Steadfast Haynes's memoirs appeared on the screen, line by line.

"Stop and start over," Haynes said.

"Slower?" she asked, tapping the keys.

"Slower."

Once again the title page appeared, followed by the four lines of Housman, then the father's cryptic dedication to the son and, finally, page four and Chapter One, containing the two sentences that composed what Haynes had come to think of as the false manuscript:

"I have led an exceedingly interesting life and, looking back, have no regrets. Or almost none."

There was a short gap on the screen until one word began appearing in capital letters, filling the rest of the fourth page and all of the fifth, sixth and seventh with, "ENDIT ENDIT ENDIT ENDIT ENDIT ENDIT . . ."

"Shut it down," Haynes said.

After the screen went blank, Erika McCorkle said, "What's an endit?"

"Cablese. Steady used to sign off his cables with it when I was a kid: 'Arriving Tuesday Air France 1732 GMT meet me endit Steady.' Ten words exactly."

Erika McCorkle's face shone with what Haynes suspected was yet another revelation. "That's why the house is so damned neat. Those two guys with sacks over their heads knew just where to look. In the computer."

"Unless they weren't here to find but to plant something. Maybe a dead end."

"The endits?"

Haynes nodded, rose, went over to the computer and bent down to unplug it. "Let's put this in your car."

"Are you stealing or borrowing it?"

"Neither. I'm inheriting it. Howard Mott says Steady left me all of his keepsakes, souvenirs and memorabilia."

"There aren't any."

"Right, but should the question arise, Mott can argue that a man's personal computer is as much a part of his memorabilia as his diary."

"That's bullshit trying to be sophistry."

Haynes nodded agreeably. "So it is."

They were going down the slippery snow-covered front porch steps, carrying the computer, when the sedan silently emerged from behind the curtain of falling snow. The sedan, a large Ford with chains on its rear wheels, came to a stop and a lean man in his fifties got out. Staring at Haynes with blue eyes that looked as if they would stay well chilled, winter or summer, the man let his right hand stray toward the holstered revolver on his hip just before he used a hard baritone voice to say, "I sure as hell hope that's you, Granville."

It took five minutes under the shelter of the covered porch to convince Sheriff Jenkins Shipp that the son and heir of Steadfast Haynes was carting off the computer only because he hoped it would contain his dead father's last thoughts.

Finally, the sheriff nodded his narrow head in half-convinced agreement. The head was topped by an abused Stetson that once must have been pearl gray but was now the color of old city sidewalks. The sheriff's face seemed to be mostly cheekbones and chilly blue eyes, but there was also an assertive chin, an interesting nose and a thin-lipped mouth that would have looked cruel if it hadn't curled up at both ends.

"You're saying a computer's like a man's diary?" the sheriff asked, his skepticism still evident.

"Exactly," Erika McCorkle said.

He acknowledged her answer with a small neutral smile that said he didn't believe her, then studied Haynes for a moment or two before he posed another question. "Know why I don't ask you for any I.D., Granville?"

"Because I look so much like him."

"Spittin' image," Shipp said, gave Erika another small but more friendly smile and added, "Or is that spit *and* image, Miss McCorkle?"

"Authorities disagree," she said. "But in this case it's irrelevant because he sure as hell looks like Steady."

"Don't he though?" said Sheriff Shipp.

After he helped Haynes carry the computer to the Cutlass and put it in the trunk, the sheriff, now back on the porch, carefully wiped his boots on the doormat. Once inside the house, the first thing he said was, "How come that door's off its hinges?"

Haynes said it was because of the snow. He had left his topcoat in Washington and needed one to go to the barn. He thought there might be one in the closet but it was locked.

"And was there?" Shipp asked. "A coat?"

"Right behind you," Haynes said.

Shipp turned to eye the old duffle coat that hung from the hall coatrack. He touched the coat, as if to make sure it was damp, nodded, turned back to Haynes and said, "Want some help with the door?"

Once the door was back on its hinges, the sheriff, apparently musing aloud, said, "Wonder if I'd best take a look upstairs?"

"You think whoever shot Zip might've left some clues up there?" Erika asked.

"Never can tell," Shipp said, turned toward the stairs, then turned back. "How'd you all know his name was Zip?" Before either could answer, the sheriff said, "I didn't tell you, did I?"

"You must have," Haynes said.

Shipp frowned, as if recalling their telephone conversation. "Believe I did, at that," he said, headed again for the stairs and mounted the first two steps before he stopped and again turned back. "Aren't you all coming?"

"We'd only get in the way," Haynes said.

When the sheriff came back down the stairs five minutes later his tanned cheeks had turned dull red and Haynes knew Shipp had found the sex magazines. He also knew the sheriff would never mention them.

They trailed Shipp through the living room, the office/dining room and into the kitchen, where it was obvious that the sheriff made mental notes of the three coffee cups on the kitchen table, Letty Melon's whisky glass and also the three cigarette butts she had ground out in an ashtray.

As Shipp went through the kitchen door, heading for the

barn, he noticed the gouged-out doorjamb. "What happened?"

"When we went out to the barn that first time," Haynes said, "we locked ourselves out and had to use a lug wrench on it."

As he inspected the damage, Shipp asked, "Either of you happen to smoke?"

"Sometimes," Haynes said.

"Luckies?" the sheriff said hopefully.

Haynes recalled Letty Melon's gold Zippo and the pack of cigarettes she had taken from her flight jacket pocket. "Sorry," Haynes said. "Camels." His right hand dipped into his jacket pocket as if to make sure a pack was still there. "Want one?"

"Quit thirteen years ago," Shipp said and gave the ruined doorjamb another look. "Better get some boards and nail that sucker up."

"I plan to," Haynes said.

In the barn, Shipp knelt beside the dead Zip and, like Letty Melon, ran a commiserative hand down the dead animal's neck. "Talk to your daddy's insurance man yet, Granville?"

"I'm not going to file a claim."

Shipp rose. "Then I don't reckon you shot him."

The sheriff helped Haynes and Erika McCorkle carry some old boards, nails and a hammer from the barn to the house. But when Haynes, who couldn't recall the last time he had driven a nail, kept bending the first one he tried to hammer, Sheriff Shipp began to fidget. When he could no longer stand it, he said, "Lemme try."

Shipp nailed the boards over the back door in less than ten minutes, driving each nail home with no more than four blows of the hammer and sometimes only three. When done, he stepped back to admire his work and say, "That oughta hold her."

His audience thanked him, praised his skill and walked

him back to the Ford sedan, where Shipp gave Haynes, Erika and the farm one long last curious look. "You all planning to drive back to Washington today?"

Erika McCorkle, the driver, said they were.

The sheriff looked up at the falling snow. "That deputy I was gonna send out here went off the road, hit a tree and busted his left leg. And when I was driving out here the weatherman was talking blizzard. I was you, I'd find me a place to spend the night real quick. Maybe even right here."

"You don't think they'll be back?" Erika McCorkle asked.

"Who's they, Miss McCorkle?"

"He. They. Whoever killed Zip."

"Can't kill a horse twice," Sheriff Shipp said, touched the brim of his old gray Stetson, climbed into the Ford, started the engine and drove off into the snow.

Nineteen

At seven o'clock that same Saturday morning, Hamilton Keyes, the courtly CIA careerist, had received a wake-up call summoning him to Langley for an emergency meeting at nine. When he arrived at 8:45, another caller informed him the meeting had been postponed until noon.

Keyes's office phone rang again at 11:45 A.M., and yet a different caller told him, without apology or explanation, that the meeting wouldn't be held until three that afternoon, or possibly even four. It was then that Keyes recognized the nearby sound of the woodman's ax in the bureaucratic forest.

Just to make certain, Keyes made two brief phone calls and, once they were completed, began removing all personal effects from his 137-year-old rosewood desk and placing them in his own 105-year-old walnut wastebasket. With that done, he uncapped a fountain pen, wrote the date at the top of a sheet of personal stationery and began a letter of resignation.

The meeting finally took place at 4:07 P.M. just as the snow that had been falling on Berryville since before noon finally reached Washington and its suburbs. Keyes was confident that the forecast of six to seven inches of snow would not only shorten his meeting, but also ruin God knows how many carefully planned dinner parties, including the one his wife was giving.

The office Keyes entered was on the same floor as his own. But even though it was appreciably larger than his, it contained only a gray metal desk, a standard high-backed swivel chair, a telephone and a single visitor's chair, which was armless. Keyes immediately understood the sparse furnishings were meant to alert him that he had indeed been summoned to the den of bad news.

A man in his late forties sat behind the desk, a telephone pressed to his left ear. As the man listened impassively to whatever the voice on the phone had to say, he flicked his eyes from Keyes to the lone visitor's chair. Keyes took it as an invitation and sat down.

Although they had never met, Keyes knew the man's background, reputation and, of course, his name, C. Robert Pall. He also remembered that the C. stood for Clair; that Pall held a doctorate in economics from Chicago and had served three terms as a Republican congressman from Pennsylvania until being trounced in 1986. Before serving in Congress, Pall had taught at Stanford and the Wharton School; summered at a number of prosperous think tanks; written a couple of The-End-Is-Nigh books; and, less than two years ago, signed on with the Bush campaign as what Pall himself had called its "token troglodyte."

The man with the phone to his ear had one of those curiously sweet round faces in which almost everything pointed up—his nose, the corners of his mouth, the outer ends of the dark thickets that were his eyebrows—everything except his backsliding chin that was poorly camouflaged by a short patchy beard the color of ginger.

After nearly thirty seconds of listening, Pall finally spoke into the phone and ended the one-sided conversation with, "Sorry, Larry, but there's not one goddamn thing I can do about it." After putting the phone down, he smiled at Keyes without displaying any teeth and said, "You must be Hamilton Keyes. I'm Bob Pall, the FNG."

Although the acronym was hopelessly inappropriate and dated back at least twenty years to Vietnam and Laos, Keyes nodded politely and said, "The Fucking New Guy."

Pall enlarged the smile to reveal a top row of light gray teeth. "You wanta beat around the bush awhile or what?"

Keyes looked at his watch. "Not really. I presume the White House sent you out to do the deed?"

Pall stopped smiling and nodded, serious now, even grave. "We've got a whole lot of past-due bills, political stuff, and we need your slot and some others to pay 'em off with. Nothing personal. Fact is, everybody I've talked to says you do one hell of a job."

After acknowledging the compliment with a slight smile that vanished almost instantly, Keyes removed the sealed envelope that contained the letter he had written and placed it on the desk.

Frowning at the unexpected, Pall picked up the envelope, used a thumb to rip it open, fumbled a pair of glasses from his shirt pocket and read the letter with a glance. His frown disappeared. "Okay. Great. You're talking early retirement." He looked up from the letter. "But, hey, there's no big rush. Next week, the week after, that'll be soon enough."

"I see no reason to prolong things."

"What about the hand-over?"

"Everything my successor needs is in the files and he'll probably be ecstatic that I'm no longer underfoot."

Pall rose with a grin that displayed most of the light gray teeth. "After listening to sniffles all day from a bunch of crybabies, it's a treat to run across a grown-up." He held out his hand and added, "Anything else you'd like to mention?"

"I don't believe so," Keyes said, shook the offered hand, nodded a cordial goodbye, turned, headed for the door, then turned back. "There might be one thing not yet in the files."

"What?"

"The Steady Haynes manuscript."

Pall sat down slowly in the swivel chair and leaned back, his mouth now pursed, his small greenish eyes alert and wary. "Tell me," he said.

It took the still standing Hamilton Keyes not quite three minutes to give a thumbnail sketch of the late Steadfast Haynes and tell of Isabelle Gelinet's initial blackmail call; the burial at Arlington; Gelinet's death; and of his own and someone else's subsequent attempts to buy all rights to the Haynes manuscript from the dead man's son.

"Sit down, fella," Pall said.

Keyes resumed his seat in the armless chair.

"Okay," Pall said. "Once again, nice and slow, step by step, from the beginning."

Keyes led him through it again with a still precise but much more detailed summary that left Pall pink-faced, smoldering and reminding Keyes of some just-lit giant firecracker that might or might not go off.

After completing his second account, Keyes asked, "Any questions?"

"Questions?" Pall said, snapping the word in two. "Well, yeah, friend, I've got a couple or three. You offered this kid, Granville Haynes—"

"He's thirty-two and scarcely a kid."

"—this kid fifty K for his old man's memoirs, but he turns it down because he's already turned down a hundred K from God knows who and thinks he can raise enough foreign money to produce a flick about his old man's life with him playing the lead?"

When Keyes remained silent, Pall said, "Well?"

"Was that a question?"

"What the fuck did you think it was?"

"A rather pithy recapitulation."

"Is that what happened?"

"Essentially. Yes."

130

"Okay. You believe any or all of it?"

"Without evidence to the contrary, I don't disbelieve it."

"Let's go back to the French broad, what's her name, Gelinet? Was she killed over the Haynes manuscript?"

"I'm not positive," Keyes said, "but it seems sensible to assume she was, which is why I had that offer made to young Mr. Haynes."

"What were you going to use for money?"

"Discretionary funds."

"Who'd you clear it with?"

"Nobody."

"Why the hell not?"

"There was no need," Keyes said. "If our offer was turned down by Haynes the younger, as, in fact, it was, then we were dealing in imaginary money. In other words—"

Pall cut him off. "Okay, okay, I've got it."

Rage again surfaced in Pall's green eyes as he leaned forward, rested his arms on the desktop and clasped his hands together so tightly that they turned pale from lack of circulation. He also locked eyes with Keyes, who stared back calmly, taking note of Pall's barely suppressed rage and, just below it, something else, which Keyes quickly diagnosed as fear.

The stare-down was ended by Pall, who gave his watch a quick glance and asked a question. "It ever occur to you that somebody might be trying to run a shitty past us?"

"My very first thought."

"Then why'd you fold so quick and ask DOD to bury him at Arlington?"

"One, because I knew Steady well. Very well. And two, because I know a bargain when I see one. The blackmail price was cheap—a plot of land. The blackmail threat was grave because if Haynes's memoirs do exist, and if they reveal what he actually did, their publication could cause serious political embarrassment. Extremely serious. So that's why I folded and asked DOD to have the Army bury him

131

with a bugler blowing 'Taps' over his grave." Keyes paused. "If you don't like it, of course, you can always dig him up."

"We'll leave him lie for now," Pall said. "But let's go back to the mystery offer—the one for a hundred K."

"We have only young Haynes's word on that."

"You believe him?"

"I have no reason not to."

"Next question: who else wants to buy 'em and why?"

"There're two possibilities," Keyes said. "The prospective buyer could be someone—and by that I mean an individual, a group, even a country—who feels that publication of the memoirs would cause unacceptable repercussions. Or it could be someone who simply wants a club to beat the administration over the head with."

"The fucking Democrats maybe?"

"That hadn't occurred to me."

"I bet," Pall said, frowned and asked, "You claim Steadfast Haynes never worked for us officially and was always paid in either cash or gold, right?"

Keyes nodded.

"Well, if there's no record, why don't we just say we never heard of the son of a bitch?"

"Because I must assume that Steady had acquired proof to the contrary."

An almost wistful note crept into Pall's voice when he asked, "Isn't it possible that the Haynes stuff isn't nearly as bad as you think?"

Keyes conceded the point with a nod, then promptly obliterated his concession. "You can probably measure the damage it could cause by the one-hundred-thousand-dollar price somebody's apparently willing to pay for it. Then there's Steady's rather curious behavior just prior to his death."

"Curious how?"

"He reserved a room at the Hay-Adams for the next three

months and was all over town, calling in old markers to get himself a permanent seat at the North trial."

"Jesus," Pall said.

"Of course, it could've been mere advertising."

"For what?"

Keyes shrugged. "Who knows? Maybe his manuscript. Or he even may have been hinting that he knew something awfully juicy about North, Poindexter and company—or perhaps about other White House residents, past and present, whose names needn't be mentioned." Keyes paused. "Unless you want me to, of course."

Pall swivelled away from Keyes to stare at the top left corner of the room behind the desk. Still staring, he said, "The Haynes kid turned down your offer of fifty K and that other so-called offer of a hundred K. So what's his asking price?"

"I understand it to be seven hundred and fifty thousand."

Pall spun around to face Keyes. "Buy 'em."

"The memoirs?"

Pall nodded.

"With what?"

"With any currency he wants, in any bank he chooses."

"You'll arrange the money," Keyes said and succeeded in not making it a question.

Pall again nodded.

"But suppose," Keyes said, "just suppose that the memoirs turn out to be nothing more than a rehash of wicked deeds done long ago and very far away—in the Congo, for instance?"

"You believe that?"

"No, but it remains a possibility."

"Buy 'em," Pall said again. "Once they're bought, you get a ten percent finder's fee. Seventy-five thousand bucks, cash in hand."

Keyes sighed and looked away as if faintly embarrassed.

"This is extremely awkward, but I do feel I should mention that my wife is rather rich and awfully generous."

It took a moment or two for Pall to erase his surprised look and replace it with a knowing gray smile. "I get it. You want your old job back."

"Not really."

"Then what?"

"Ambassador."

First came a pained expression, then a sigh and, finally, the question. "Where?"

"I rather fancy the Caribbean."

"The Caribbean," Pall said, staring at Keyes with a mixture of wonder and dislike. "Okay. You've got it. But let me spell out what else you've got. And that's exactly one week to get ahold of the Haynes memoirs. If you've got 'em by then, we'll announce your nomination as ambassador to the democratic island republic of Rumandsun or some such."

Pall fell silent for a moment, leaned forward, bared most of the light gray teeth in a snarling smile and said, "But if you haven't got ahold of 'em by then, we'll leak it that you've been fired from the agency for gross incompetency or worse. Probably a lot worse." He paused to let the awful smile vanish. "Did I make all that clear?"

"Yes, I do believe you did," said Hamilton Keyes.

Twenty

Erika McCorkle gave up eighteen miles out of Berryville when she saw the Tall Pine Motel's blue Neon vacancy sign winking at her through the snowfall.

She and Granville Haynes had left his dead father's farm shortly before 5 P.M. It was now 6:07 P.M. and dark, but they had managed to drive only eighteen miles, their progress impeded first by the snow, which gave no sign of letting up, and then by four wrecks, the last a Chevrolet pickup that had spun out on a curve and flipped over, killing its 52-year-old driver and his 37-year-old girlfriend.

Haynes and Erika McCorkle reached this fourth accident just after state troopers had set out warning flares. Two patrol cars, bar lights flashing, aimed their headlights at the wreck. Haynes rolled down his window and talked to one of the troopers briefly while waiting for him to wave them on. When the trooper did, Haynes stared at the dark pool beneath the upside-down pickup and decided it was blood and not engine oil after all.

* * *

As the Cutlass slid to a stop on the packed snow in front of the Tall Pine Motel office, Erika McCorkle said, "See if you can get two rooms. If not, try for twin beds. But if all they have left is a double bed, we can work it out."

"There's nothing to work out," Haynes said.

"Like hell."

"If there's only one bed," he explained, "I'll sleep in it. You're welcome to join me, of course. But if you feel that's too intimate, there's either the floor or the bathtub."

"Just get the room, prince, before a two-man line forms with you at the end."

Haynes got out, brushed snow and ice off the car's Virginia license plate, memorized the number and entered the motel office. He came out five minutes later, carrying a paper sack full of something. Back in the car with the sack on his lap, he said, "We got the last room left—down at the end on your right."

"Twin beds?" she asked as she put the car into reverse and backed up.

"I didn't ask."

They drove to the room in silence. The Tall Pine Motel formed a curve that bowed back from the highway. There were eighteen units, nine on each side of the office. The motel was built of used brick and covered with a sharply pitched shake-shingle roof. Each unit had a window, a door and space for a single car. Haynes looked for the tall pine but couldn't find it and blamed his failure on the snow.

After she pulled to a stop in front of their room, Erika McCorkle ended the silence with a question: "What's in the sack?"

"Dinner," Haynes said. "Four Cokes, two Baby Ruths, four almond Hersheys and four packets of things that look like peanut butter between Ritz crackers."

"Those peanut butter things aren't bad," she said.

* * *

Erika McCorkle came out of the bathroom after a ten-minute shower, wearing her camel's-hair polo coat as a robe. Haynes sat near the double bed in one of the room's two chairs, watching a rerun of *The Scarecrow and Mrs. King*.

Erika McCorkle stood, watching the program and running a comb through her damp hair. When a commercial came on she said, "I never understood the premise of that show."

"James Bond meets Erma Bombeck."

"Let's eat," she said.

She traded him her Baby Ruth for one of his almond Hersheys because she said Baby Ruths always tasted like Ex-Lax. They divided the packets of peanut butter and Ritz crackers evenly, washing everything down with Coke. They ate and drank in silence, Haynes in his chair, Erika McCorkle now on the bed, leaning against its headboard.

After another commercial came on she said, "You watch TV a lot?"

"No. Do you?"

"I like disaster reruns. A president or a premier gets shot. A shuttle blows up. A crown prince falls off his horse. A cardinal checks into Betty Ford's. Why accept substitutes when you can watch the real thing?"

"You may have a point," Haynes said, leaned forward and switched off the set.

She finished the last of her Coke, carefully crushed the can, aimed it at the wastebasket, made the shot and said, "When you were a cop, did it ever happen to you—the real bad shit?"

"Once in a while, but with homicide I usually got the residue—the leavings."

"Ever shoot anyone?"

"No."

"Anyone ever shoot at you?"

"Twice."

"Did you like it—being a homicide detective?"

He thought about her question. "I got to be good at it and most people like doing what they're good at."

"You like acting?"

"Not yet, but it's a pleasant way to meet women."

She swung her bare feet off the bed and reached for the telephone. "I'd better call Pop and tell him not to worry." After she picked up the telephone, she looked back at Haynes as if to reassess his harmlessness.

He gave her his inherited smile and said, "You're safe."

"Too bad," she said and tapped out the long-distance number. After McCorkle came on the line, she told him they were snowed in at the Tall Pine Motel eighteen miles east of Berryville.

McCorkle wanted the motel phone number and address. After she read them to him, he asked when she'd be back. She said probably tomorrow morning. McCorkle said he had a message for Haynes and, after he told her what it was, she promised to deliver it, urged him not to fret and hung up.

Once more turning toward Haynes, she said, "Pop said Tinker Burns has been calling him every fifteen minutes to ask if anybody's heard from you. Pop says he would very much appreciate it if you'd get Tinker off his back. He's at the Madison."

"I know," Haynes said.

"But you aren't going to call him, are you?"

Haynes shook his head.

"What if it's important?"

"If it is, it's important to Tinker, not to me."

She rose from the bed and pulled down its covers. "I bet you let phones ring."

"Sometimes."

"The TV won't bother me if you want to turn it back on," she said, removed the polo coat and draped it over the back of the room's other chair. She was wearing only a brassiere and panties, which Haynes thought were probably less re-

138

vealing than the standard bikini. She slipped into the bed and drew the covers up to her chin.

"Good night, Mr. Haynes."

"Good night, Miss McCorkle."

He rose, switched off the room lights and sat back down. He continued to sit in the dark, recalling in detail everything he had seen and heard that day, especially his encounter with his former stepmother, Letty Melon. He had just reached the point where he had mistaken the pool of blood for engine oil when he heard Erika McCorkle stir and ask in a soft but wide-awake voice, "Aren't you ever coming to bed?"

"Right away," said Granville Haynes.

Twenty-one

In his fourth-floor room at the Madison Hotel, which offered an unspectacular view of 15th Street to the north, Tinker Burns listened, the phone to his right ear, the good one, as McCorkle, lying cheerfully, said that Erika had just called from a gas station between Berryville and Leesburg to tell him that because of the snow she and Granville Haynes wouldn't make it back to Washington until two or three in the morning.

"Well, thanks for letting me know," Burns said, put the phone down and turned to the pair of seated men whom he knew only by their work names of Mr. Schlitz and Mr. Pabst.

"Sorry for the interruption," Burns said, resumed his seat in a wingback chair and leaned forward enough to rest elbows on knees. After clasping his hands together, he spread a look of deep interest across his face, aiming the interest first at Schlitz, then at Pabst.

"Since you guys didn't get very far before the phone rang, I wonder if you'd back up and start from the beginning?"

Pabst looked at Schlitz. "Where'd I start?"

"With the horse."

"Right," Pabst said and nodded a head that seemed a shade less wide than his nineteen-inch neck. The rest of Pabst was also broad and thick, although not very tall. Probably five-eleven, Burns guessed, still using feet and inches to measure height despite his more than four decades of exposure to the metric system.

Pabst frowned as he tried to recall what he'd already said. The frown wrinkled a pale forehead below a shock of hair so blond it looked almost white. He wore the hair long—too long, Burns thought—as if to compensate for his nearly invisible eyebrows. Below the faint brows were eyes that seemed to be fading from pale sky blue into rain gray. They were set too close to a tiny nose that Burns suspected of having stopped growing when Pabst was 5 or 6 some thirty years ago.

"Yeah, the horse," Pabst said. "Well, we get there, like I already told you, about six in the morning when it's still dark, and park in the barn. Then this horse starts kicking up a fuss and screaming or whatever horses do—"

"They neigh," said Schlitz.

"Okay, he's neighing and kicking with his hind feet and when he gets tired of that he rears up and tries to use his front feet to duke it out with us. So the last time he goes up and comes down, I shoot him."

"Right between the eyes," Schlitz said with a strange wide smile. "Hell of a shot."

Although Schlitz, like Pabst, had a tree-trunk neck, he also had one of those reflexive all-purpose smiles that show too much gum and are used to express pleasure, rage, pain, hope, fear, mirth, approval and sometimes nothing at all.

Tinker Burns had seen such smiles in the Legion and knew that they often belonged to nut cases. He remembered two particular Legionnaires, both borderline sociopaths, who had died two days apart in terrible agony, each of them gut-shot, their all-purpose smiles firmly in place.

In addition to the smile, Schlitz came with popped brown

141

eyes that were divided by a nose that went straight, then left, then straight again. Above was a tangle of thick black curls frosted with gray, while down below, at the face's bottom, was a jutting chin that Burns thought you could hang your hat on.

"So you shot the horse, huh?" Burns said to Pabst.

"Yeah."

"That was dumb."

"He was about to wake up the whole fucking neighborhood."

"The nearest neighbor is half a klic down the road."

Schlitz smiled the all-purpose smile. "He's still dead, Mr. Burns."

"So he is," Burns said. "Go on."

"Well, after I shoot him," Pabst said, "we go in through the back door."

"Still dark out?"

"Yeah, and once we jimmy the door and get inside, we wait till it gets light because we don't wanta turn on any lamps or use a flash in case somebody driving by sees them. So after it gets light, we start looking—upstairs first, then downstairs. We'd just got started in the kitchen when we hear her."

"Hear her do what?" Burns said.

"Drive up," Schlitz said. "She makes a hell of a racket on the gravel. Slams her door, bangs her heels on the porch and then comes in."

"Through the front door, right?"

"She's got a key."

"Where were you two then?"

"Still in the kitchen," Schlitz said. "We hear her go in the dining room and walk around. Then she stops and doesn't make a sound for about a minute. After that she goes back outside, comes back in and walks right into the kitchen."

"And sees you two," Burns said.

"Yeah, but by then we got grocery bags over our heads," Schlitz said. "Pabst here grabs her and I slap some duct tape

142

across her mouth. Then we tape her wrists and ankles up good and stick her in a closet—the only place that's got a door we can lock. I still got the key."

Burns sighed. "Then what?"

"Me and Pabst leave."

"What'd she look like?" Burns said.

Pabst glanced at Schlitz and said, "Not bad, huh?"

Schlitz agreed with the all-purpose smile.

"Dark hair," Pabst said. "Good teeth. She's got on blue jeans and riding boots and a leather jacket. Pretty good muscle tone for somebody her age."

"How old was she?"

Again, Pabst looked at Schlitz. "Forty—around in there?"

"Forty-two at least," Schlitz said.

"You steal anything?" Burns asked.

Schlitz's smile appeared, vanished and reappeared. "What d'you mean, steal anything?"

"A TV set. Her watch. Even her purse. Anything to make it look like a burglary."

"You didn't say to steal anything," Schlitz said, still smiling. "You just told us to go in and try and find something."

Tinker Burns leaned back in the big chair, rested his arms on its arms, took a deep breath, let some of it out and said, "After you tied her up and locked her in the closet, then what'd you do?"

"We take off," Pabst said. "But we do it quiet. Schlitz sneaks down to the road first and signals when it's all clear. Then I drive out of the barn, coast down the drive, pick him up and leave without nobody seeing us."

"But before you did all that you searched her car, didn't you?" Burns said.

Schlitz, forgetting to smile, looked puzzled. "What the hell for?"

"You said she came into the house," Burns said. "Then she went into the dining room and stayed there for almost a minute, very quiet, then went back out to her car and came

143

back in again. It kind of hit me that maybe she knew where to look for what you guys didn't find. That maybe she found it and took it out to her car."

Schlitz, smiling again, shook his head from side to side three times. "Never happen, Mr. Burns."

"Why not?" Burns said, his voice almost gentle.

"Because she wasn't there for that."

All gentleness deserted Burns's voice. "How the fuck d'you know what she came for?"

"You weren't there, Mr. Burns," Pabst said. "And you didn't see it."

"See what?"

"The horse trailer hitched to her pickup," Schlitz said, his smile triumphant. "She wasn't there for what we were after. She was there for the horse."

"Right," Burns said. "Of course." He rose. "The horse." Reaching into the breast pocket of his gray suit, he withdrew a plain white No. 10 envelope and handed it to the still seated Schlitz, who looked inside, counted the forty $100 bills, smiled his satisfaction and rose. Pabst also got to his feet.

Still smiling, Schlitz stuffed the envelope into his right hip pocket and said, "You ever want us to handle anything else, Mr. Burns, you know how to get in touch."

"That I do," said Burns, went with them to the door, saw them out, locked the door and put on the chain. Back in the center of the room he took a slip of paper from his pants pocket. Printed on it in pencil were two names. Mr. Schlitz and Mr. Pabst. Below the names was a telephone number.

Tinker Burns looked around for an ashtray until he remembered he had checked into a nonsmoking room. He went into the bathroom, burned the slip of paper over the toilet, let the ashes fall into the bowl and flushed them away.

Again in the room, he sat down on the bed next to the telephone and took a small address book from a pocket. With the phone cradled between his right ear and shoulder, the address book held open in his right hand, Burns used his left hand to tap out an eleven-digit number.

After five rings it was answered by a woman's voice. Burns said, "Letty? Tinker Burns. I think maybe we oughta get together and have a little talk."

"Go fuck yourself, Tinker," Letitia Melon Haynes said and broke the connection.

Burns slowly hung up the phone, rose, stared down at it for a moment, then went to the desk and poured three fingers of Scotch into a glass. He added tap water in the bathroom. When he came out he crossed to the window, where he stood for a little more than thirty minutes, sipping his whisky and watching the snow fall on 15th Street at night.

Twenty-two

McCorkle broke up the drunken two-blow bar fight just before the third punch was thrown. He broke it up the way he usually did, by grabbing each man by an ear and holding him as far away as possible from his opponent.

Once he had them separated, McCorkle issued his standard injunction: "All right, gentlemen. I let go the ears when I see the car keys on the bar."

The keys to a Jaguar landed on the bar first, followed by those to a Mercedes. Karl Triller, the bartender, scooped them up and said, "You guys can pick 'em up anytime after noon tomorrow."

The two barroom fighters were both well regarded and highly paid K Street lobbyists in their mid-forties, who would have been prosperous, even wealthy, had it not been for their recent and very expensive divorces. For solace and comfort they had formed a two-man support group whose therapy consisted of drinking too much while reminiscing about the dimly remembered 1950s. For the past two months they had done much of their reminiscing in Mac's Place.

The shorter of the lobbyists, who looked the way everyone thought a senator should look, and who was often mistaken for one by tourists, stood five-ten and weighed 182 pounds, very little of it muscle. He peered up at McCorkle with the old spaniel eyes that were his trademark and asked, "This mean we're eighty-sixed?"

McCorkle turned with a sigh to Triller. "Let them nurse one more till their cab comes."

"When the snow failed to cease," said the taller lobbyist, drawling the words, "I fear we came down with a slight case of cabin fever."

At six-four, the other lobbyist was so lean and weathered that strangers often assumed he must be from somewhere west of Cheyenne where he was probably called Slim or Hoot or even Tex—until they learned he was from Connecticut and had been called Nipsy by childhood friends and classmates at Phillips Academy and Yale. It was what most people still called him, even on slight acquaintance.

"Do me a favor, Nipsy," McCorkle said. "The next time it snows, pick another cabin."

There had been seventeen dinner cancellations because of the snow, which, as usual, had caused as much havoc in Washington as it would have in Palm Beach. After checking with Herr Horst, who informed him of three more cancellations, McCorkle made a circuit of the dining room, nodding at regulars but avoiding Padillo, who was listening over braised veal to the woes of a former girlfriend and recent widow with money problems and a son at MIT.

McCorkle was wondering whether the check Padillo would write her would be for $2,000 or $3,000 when a woman's voice behind him asked, "Excuse me, sir, but do you work here?"

McCorkle turned to find himself confronted by a remarkably plain woman who wore tinted snow-wet glasses, no makeup, a knitted red cap and a long tan raincoat that years ago had lost its waterproofing. The coat ended just above her ankles, which were concealed by tan rubber boots. On her hands were knitted red gloves that matched her cap. The gloved hands clutched a package wrapped in heavy white paper and sealed with Scotch tape.

Guessing she was either an old 25 or a young 40, McCorkle replied that yes, as a matter of fact, he did work there.

"Then maybe you can help me," she said.

"How?"

"It's awfully complicated."

"Maybe you'd like to sit down?"

She looked around nervously and McCorkle could see her eyes moving behind the tinted glasses. He guessed that her eyes were blue—not bright blue or dark blue, but plain old blue. She said, "I really shouldn't because, well, I'm not dressed or anything and, you know, I wouldn't feel—"

"There's an office."

She brightened. "I'd feel a whole lot more comfortable in an office."

As he and the plain woman headed toward it, McCorkle noticed Padillo glance up. Once he and the woman were in the office and seated on opposite sides of the partners desk, McCorkle also noticed that she held the white package in her lap with her still gloved hands resting on top of it.

"You're Mr.—?"

"McCorkle."

"I'm Miss Skelton. Reba Skelton. I'm a professional typist and word processor and also do some calligraphy. You know. Invitations. Announcements. Things like that."

McCorkle nodded.

"About a month ago, maybe a little more, a Mr. Steadfast Haynes asked me to type a single copy of a manuscript he'd written. I charge a dollar fifty a page, but if they want carbons, I get fifty cents per carbon copy. Except hardly anybody ever asks for carbons nowadays because, you know,

148

it's just a whole lot simpler and cheaper to have Xerox copies made."

To keep up his end of the conversation, McCorkle said, "I suppose."

"Well, the manuscript Mr. Haynes gave me was an awful mess. Some of it was typed—and single-spaced at that. Some of it was written in pencil. Some in ink—or with a ballpoint anyway. And he used all kinds of paper. Legal pads. Hotel stationery. Some cheap yellow stuff. Even pages from school tablets. It wasn't, well, you know, *orderly*."

Because she seemed to expect a response, McCorkle gave her an understanding smile.

"So that's why I didn't get it done on time. Because it was so, well, you know, *messy*."

"When was it supposed to have been finished?"

"Eight days ago. He wanted it delivered to the Hay-Adams Hotel, but when I went there today, they told me he was dead."

"He died a week ago Thursday," McCorkle said.

"That's what the hotel people said. So when I asked them where I could find Isabelle Gelinet because, you know, she was with him when he delivered the thing—"

"Delivered it where?"

"To my place in Hyattsville. Here." She reached a gloved hand into the pocket of her raincoat, brought out a business card and handed it to McCorkle. It read: "Reba Skelton, Professional Typist, Word Processor & Calligrapher (Eleven Years Experience!), 4706 40th Ave., Hyattsville, MD, 20781." There was also a telephone number with a 301 area code and, below that, a last line that boasted: "FAST! ACCURATE! PROMPT!"

McCorkle dropped the card into a desk drawer and asked, "What'd the hotel say when you asked for Miss Gelinet?"

"Well, they went all, you know, funny. And then they told me she was dead and right after they told me that, they went all snotty and said if I wanted to know anything else about

149

her, I'd have to ask the police. So I left and went to a pay phone and called them."

"The police?"

"Yes."

"And?"

"Well, they pretended they didn't know anything about any Isabelle Gelinet and kept transferring my call from one person to another until finally they transferred me to a Sergeant Pouncy, who was colored—"

"How could you tell?"

"Well, you can just, you know, *tell*."

"I didn't know that," McCorkle said. "So what'd the sergeant say?"

He said the Gelinet woman was, let's see, the subject of an ongoing homicide investigation. And then he wanted to know who I was and why I wanted to talk to her and all that. And I, well, I just hung up on him."

"Good thinking," McCorkle said. "But why come here?"

"Because I'm looking for Mr. Haynes's son."

"Granville?"

"Yes. At least that's what he's called in the manuscript."

"I still don't understand why you'd expect to find him here."

"Well, after I hung up on that Sergeant Pouncy, I started thinking. So I called the Hay-Adams back and told them a fib. I told them I was Miss So-and-So with American Express and that we had some outstanding charges on Mr. Steadfast Haynes's account and wanted to know who was handling his estate. I was talking to the hotel accounting people this time, and they weren't nearly so snotty as those stuck-up things on the desk."

"When did you talk to the accounting people?"

"Today. Just before noon."

"What'd they tell you?"

"They told me to call his lawyer, Howard Mott. So I called his office right away, even if it is Saturday, but by then it was

150

beginning to snow and nobody answered. So I looked up his home number and called that, but he wasn't there. I did get to talk to Mrs. Mott and told her I was looking for Granville Haynes and she was very nice. She told me to try the Willard Hotel and, if young Mr. Haynes wasn't there, maybe somebody at Mac's Place might know where I could find him."

McCorkle leaned back in his chair and studied the woman in the red knitted cap. "You're quite a detective, Miss Skelton."

"What I am, Mr. McCorkle, is broke."

"You want me to give Granville a message?"

"No, what I'd like you to give him is this." She lifted the white package an inch or so off her lap.

"That's the typed manuscript?"

"Plus all the original stuff. And my bill's right on top where he can't miss it. Three hundred and eighty-two pages at a dollar fifty a page comes to five hundred and seventy-three dollars."

"Granville's out of town," McCorkle said. "But he'll probably be back later today."

"Will you see him then?"

"Maybe."

"Can you make sure he gets this?" Again she lifted the white package a few inches from her lap.

"Yes, I can do that," McCorkle said, anticipating the expression on Haynes's face when confronted with yet another true copy of Steady's memoirs.

"I'd hate to see it get lost or misplaced or anything," she said. "It's the only copy."

"I just happen to have a safe."

"Oh, wow! A safe would be great!" she said, obviously relieved. "Could you also give me a receipt?"

McCorkle nodded, rose and went to the old safe. "What'd you think of it?" he said, giving the combination a turn.

"Of what?"

"The manuscript."

151

"Oh, well, I thought it was awfully complicated. All those different countries and funny foreign names. I don't follow the news much anymore and—" She stopped when McCorkle tugged open the old safe's door.

"Please turn around, Mr. McCorkle," she said in a new voice that McCorkle found cold and hard and full of authority.

Instead of turning, he said, "1 know that voice. That's the one they always use when there's a gun in their hand."

"It's a thirty-two-caliber Sauer semiautomatic with a one-shot silencer," she said.

McCorkle slowly turned around and took in the small semiautomatic with its four-inch silencer. The gun was aimed at his chest, a fairly large target. She held it in a gloved right hand that showed no sign of a tremor. The sealed white package that had been on her lap was now on the partners desk.

"There's no money in the safe," he said. "Although you're welcome to look."

"But there is a brown paper sack in there. I want you to take it out and place it on the desk. I want you to do that now."

"Maybe I keep a gun in the safe."

"Maybe you do."

McCorkle faced the safe again and removed the brown paper sack that contained the mostly blank manuscript Howard Mott had given to Granville Haynes. McCorkle turned yet again, went slowly over to the desk and placed the sack on it.

"Now pick up the package I brought," she said.

"And after I pick it up?"

"You lock it in the safe."

"Sort of a trade, right?" McCorkle said and picked up the white package.

"Right."

"Now we take it to the safe," he said as he turned and went

152

back to the old Mosler. "Now we place it just inside." Slowly, almost tenderly, he put the package inside the safe. "Now we close the safe's big door." When that was done, he gave the combination a spin and asked, "So now what do we do?"

"You've locked a bomb in your safe," she said in the same matter-of-fact voice. "It's powerful enough to blow the safe door and do considerable damage to your office and anyone in it. But the bomb is easily disarmed. All you need to do is remove the package from the safe, unwrap it carefully and lift off the lid. It will then be disarmed. That should take you approximately three minutes. You may wish to look at your watch now because the bomb is timed to go off exactly"—she glanced at her own watch—"three minutes and twenty-two seconds from now."

McCorkle, still at the safe, his back still to her, looked at his watch and said, "Goodbye, Miss Skelton."

"Goodbye, Mr. McCorkle."

When Padillo looked up from his dinner and saw the woman hurrying across the dining room, carrying the brown paper sack, he murmured a quick excuse to the impoverished widow, rose and hurried after the woman with the sack.

Padillo came out of Mac's Place in time to see her climb into the driver's seat of a black Mercedes sedan that had tinted windows and a license plate whose numbers had been hidden by packed dirty snow. The Mercedes, its headlights off, rolled away silently and disappeared into the snowy night.

Padillo raced back into the restaurant. As he burst into the office, McCorkle was removing the last of the white wrapping paper from the package. Without looking up he said, "Get out of here."

"How much time's left?"

"None," McCorkle said and peeled off the last piece of white paper, revealing a cardboard box that once had held five hundred sheets of Southworth bond paper. Padillo dropped to the floor. McCorkle turned his head to the right, squeezed his eyes shut, bared his teeth in a snarling grimace and lifted off the box top. When nothing happened, he opened his eyes, looked down and said, "Okay. You can get up."

Padillo rose, went to the desk and stared down at the open box that contained half a red brick and a Big Ben alarm clock of Chinese manufacture that no longer ticked. The brickbat and the clock were nestled in a bed of the universally despised white plastic packing nodules.

Padillo lowered himself carefully into the chair that Reba Skelton had recently vacated. "Maybe she was just trying to scare you to death."

McCorkle made no reply until he had located his pack of Pall Mall cigarettes, two glasses and the bottle of Irish whiskey. After assembling them on the desk, he poured two drinks, handed one to Padillo, lit a cigarette, inhaled deeply, blew the smoke out and said, "Then she came goddamn close."

Twenty-three

Erika McCorkle left the engine running as she and Haynes kissed goodbye at 9:27 that Sunday morning under the amused gaze of the Willard Hotel doorman. After the kiss ended at 9:29, the unshaved Haynes opened the Cutlass door and had his right foot on the curb when he turned back with a smile that raised goose bumps on her forearms.

She replied with a bawd's grin that ratified the Treaty of the Tall Pine Motel where the question of sexual congress had been raised and settled. Once Haynes was out of the car, she sped off toward the U.S. Treasury Building that, shimmering in the snow-polished sunshine, looked as if it didn't owe a dime to anyone.

After she drove away, Haynes entered the hotel and was heading for the concierge's desk to check for messages when Detective-Sergeant Darius Pouncy rose from one of the lobby's huge high-backed chairs that apparently had been built with guests the height of Lincoln in mind.

Pouncy's dark blue vested suit was so well tailored it took at least fifteen pounds off his weight. A red and blue foulard tie used a half-Windsor knot to fill the collar of a beautifully ironed shirt that had never seen the inside of a commercial laundry. On his feet were plain black shoes with glossy toes.

With only a nod of greeting to Haynes, Pouncy turned to retrieve his dark gray Chesterfield topcoat from the back of the huge old-looking chair. Once he had the coat draped just so over his left arm, he turned back and said, "I was about to give up on you."

"I was snowbound," Haynes said.

"Where?"

"Twenty miles this side of Berryville."

"That's where they lived for a while, wasn't it? On a farm near Berryville. Your daddy and Miss Gelinet."

"Nobody ever called him my daddy, but that's where they lived. For a while."

"Find anything interesting?"

"A dead horse and a stepmother I'd never met. I think she may have come for the horse."

Pouncy nodded solemnly, as if Haynes had just said something profound, then glanced at his watch. Haynes was vaguely relieved to see that it was a gold-plated Seiko.

"It's nine thirty-three now," Pouncy said. "And I gotta carry my wife to church about ten-thirty, so I expect we just got time for coffee and a jelly doughnut or two."

"Sounds good," Haynes said.

The Willard's glittering Expresso Cafe was one of those glass, chrome and black-and-white-tile places with Neon accents that Haynes always avoided in Los Angeles. But its coffee was good and if the menu was devoid of jelly doughnuts, it did offer fresh strawberry tarts in January. Pouncy ordered two of them and coffee. Haynes settled for coffee.

After disposing of both tarts, Pouncy gave his mouth a couple of dainty wipes with a cloth napkin and announced: "The autopsy says she drowned."

"Was she conscious?"

"Probably. There wasn't any concussion. No scrapes or

bruises except where they wired her up. We found the gag they must've used to keep her quiet. It was in the trash. But no sign of opiate use and no alcohol to speak of."

"She had a glass of wine at lunch," Haynes said. "A vermouth."

"Well, using that lunch to measure by, the coroner figures she wasn't dead long when you and Burns showed up. So it looks like they wired her up, filled the tub and drowned her."

"They?"

"Not too easy for one person to wire somebody up with coat hangers. You gotta use two hands to straighten the things out. So if you don't bop your victim over the head first, how you gonna do it? Especially if the victim's young, fit and—" Pouncy paused. "I was gonna say: and don't wanta be drowned. But who the hell does? So I'm guessing it took two of 'em. At least two. Bathroom floor wasn't even wet. Mop was dry. No wet towels." He paused again. "She wasn't raped or sodomized."

"Anything missing?" Haynes asked.

"TV set, VCR and CD player are all still there. So's that nice new personal computer. Her watch was still on her wrist."

"That was a thirty-two-dollar Swatch."

Pouncy praised Haynes's memory with a tiny smile and said, "Don't know if she had any diamonds, gold, pearls or stuff like that because we didn't find any. But she did have a nice full-length mink and it's still hanging in her closet. So if it wasn't rape or robbery, it's gotta be something else and I figure there're two possibilities. One, somebody hated her to death. Or two, she wouldn't tell somebody something they wanted to know."

Pouncy finished his coffee, pushed the cup and saucer away, again used his napkin on his lips, leaned across the white marble-top table toward Haynes and said, "So that's why you and me're having strawberries and coffee at a quarter to ten of a Sunday morning."

157

"Because you've decided I might know what they thought Isabelle knew—providing there was a they."

Pouncy nodded.

"I saw Isabelle for the first time in almost twenty years at my old man's grave at Arlington. She said maybe fifteen or twenty words. Then she, Tinker Burns and I had lunch at Mac's Place, where she said maybe another fifty or seventy-five words. If that."

"Talked about a book, I believe."

"You've been busy."

"Talked about your daddy's autobiography. Memoirs."

"They were mentioned."

"She either wrote the thing or helped write it."

Haynes nodded.

"What kind of book you think it is?"

"The story of his life."

"Well, shit, I know that. I mean is it one of those red-hot exposé books? You know: Bill stole this. Tom stole that. But I didn't steal nothing."

"Some might think so."

"Even worry about it?"

"Possibly."

"Maybe even try to hush it up? Put a lid on it?"

"Who d'you have in mind?"

Pouncy shrugged. "The CIA. Who else?"

"Then ask them."

"Your daddy worked for them, didn't he?"

"A lot of people say he did, but you'll have to ask the people out at Langley."

"Already have," Pouncy said. "At least, I got somebody to ask for me. Somebody with a little more clout than I got since mine's right down there next to zero. Know what they told him, this deacon of mine with all the clout? Told him they got no trace of any Steadfast Haynes ever working for them."

"I'm not surprised," Haynes said.

"Not surprised at what? That they didn't have any trace of him? Or that they'd lie about it?"

"Take your pick," Haynes said.

After Sergeant Pouncy left to take his wife to church, Haynes checked with the concierge and found that he had eight messages. Six of them were from Mr. Burns. The other two were from Mr. McCorkle, who had called at 8:42 A.M., and Mr. Padillo, who had called at a quarter past nine.

Up in his room, Haynes called Tinker Burns first at the Madison Hotel and listened to the phone in room 427 ring nineteen times before the hotel operator suggested that Mr. Burns must not be in his room. Haynes agreed, thanked her, broke the connection and called McCorkle.

When his daughter answered the call, Haynes said, "Your dad left a message for me to call him. Is he apoplectic?"

"Apologetic," she said.

"Why?"

"I'd better let him tell you."

Although she obviously had covered the mouthpiece with her hands, Haynes could still hear the yell. "Pop. It's Granville."

There was the sound of an extension phone being picked up, followed by McCorkle's voice. "Granville?"

"Yes."

McCorkle was silent for a few seconds until he sighed and said, "Okay, Erika, hang it up."

Once his daughter did so, McCorkle said, "I've got rotten news."

"How rotten?"

"I was stuck up last night by a false frump with a dummy bomb and a silenced Sauer thirty-two." He paused, sighed again and said, "She got Steady's manuscript. I'm very sorry."

There was a long pause that Haynes finally ended with, "A silenced Sauer is what a pro would use. But the dummy bomb's a new touch. I'd like to hear about it after you answer one question."

"What?"

"Was anyone hurt?"

"Only my pride."

"Then you must've done everything exactly right."

"Padillo doesn't think so."

"She take both of you?"

"Just me. But Padillo's even more burned than I am. He saw her heading out the front door, carrying that grocery bag the manuscript's in. He thinks he should've stopped her."

"I think he's lucky he didn't try."

"We'd like to get together," McCorkle said. "The three of us."

"That must be what he called about," Haynes said. "When?"

"Noon today?"

"At the restaurant?"

"His place," McCorkle said and recited an address. "It's a small town house in Foggy Bottom. The best way to get there is—"

"I'll let the cabdriver find it," Haynes said.

"Just one other thing," McCorkle said. "I want to thank you for looking after Erika last night. I was worried about her being out in that blizzard."

"It was my pleasure."

"Yes," McCorkle said. "I imagine it was."

Twenty-four

The nine-hour blizzard had dumped eleven inches of snow on Reston, Virginia, the carefully planned new town that was no longer new and had been built twenty-four years ago not far from Dulles International Airport and—depending on the traffic—within reasonable commuting distance from the District line.

Reston's eleven inches of snow would lie undisturbed for a day or so before it was either melted by the sun or, less likely, shoveled and plowed away by removal crews. Meanwhile, Reston residents could ice-skate on Lake Anne, the thirty-two-acre artificial pond that had been named for the daughter of the town's visionary founder, who, pressed for cash, had sold out to Gulf Oil, which in turn had been swallowed by Chevron.

Whenever this much snow fell, some Restonites got out their skis to test weak ankles on gentle slopes. Others hauled out the $65 Flexible Flyers they had ordered by phone from the Hammacher Schlemmer catalogue during bouts of nostalgia, and went coasting down the steepest slopes they could find.

One skier, well bundled up against the cold in sweater, ski pants, ski mask, dark glasses and knitted cap, glided expertly down the center of the sloping Waterview Cluster Drive and came to a neat stop in front of 12430, a three-story town house that was almost at the end of the cul-de-sac.

The town house, one of the first built on the shores of the artificial lake, featured a small wooden dock, a loggia, two bedrooms, two baths, two fireplaces and an outside steel spiral staircase that went from the dock up to a second-floor balcony. When new in 1965, the town house had sold for $32,500 with 10 percent down. Its mirror twin, three doors up, had sold a month ago for $225,000.

After leaning the skis against the house, the skier rang the door chimes. The door was opened two minutes later by Gilbert Undean, the 67-year-old Burma expert, who had had to walk down two flights of stairs from his third-floor office-study, where, dressed in an old blue flannel shirt, khaki pants and fleece-lined slippers, he had been reading a gloomy editorial in the Sunday *Washington Post*.

"I think you'd better let me in," the skier said.

Undean, staring down at the small silenced semiautomatic pistol in the skier's right hand, nodded and backed away. The skier entered, closed the door and used the gun to indicate the stairs. Undean started up them with the skier close behind.

On the second floor, they made a quick tour of the living room, dining alcove and kitchen before climbing the second flight of stairs to the third floor, where they inspected the master bedroom that had a view of the lake.

They then went down a short hall to the smaller bedroom that Undean thought of as his office. Except for the space taken up by two closet doors and a window that overlooked the street, the walls of the smaller room were covered from floor to ceiling by crowded bookshelves.

Again using the pistol to issue instructions, the skier waved Undean into a swivel chair behind an old golden oak flat-top desk. Once Undean was seated, the skier opened the closet door to reveal a pair of gray metal filing cabinets but no clothing. The rest of the closet was taken up by back copies of the *New York Times* that were piled in two 5-foot-high stacks.

A wingback brown leather chair was the only inviting piece of furniture in the room. A brass floor lamp was positioned just so on the left-hand side of the chair. The skier, still wearing ski mask, gloves, dark glasses and knitted cap, sat down in the chair, aiming the pistol at Undean with both hands.

"You don't seem surprised," the skier said.

Undean shrugged. "You really going to do it?"

The skier nodded.

"There oughta be some way we could work it out."

"Don't beg."

"Well, what the fuck," Undean said. "I'd've been dead soon anyway."

The silenced semiautomatic coughed almost apologetically. A small dark hole appeared in the lower left quadrant of Undean's forehead. He rocked back, slumped forward and since there was nothing to prevent it, toppled out of the swivel chair onto the floor.

Tinker Burns sat behind the wheel of the rented Jeep Wagoneer, trying to decide whether he could make it through the two- and three-foot snowdrifts that blocked Waterview Cluster Drive. Burns had hoped to find pioneer tire tracks made by braver drivers and was disappointed that there weren't any.

He did see footprints in the snow. But they only led from front doors to parked cars whose owners apparently had come out to brush snow off windshields before ducking back inside. Burns also noticed that someone had skied toward the bottom of the Waterview Cluster cul-de-sac, but he couldn't quite make out where the ski tracks ended.

With little faith in the Wagoneer's snow tires and four-wheel drive, and even less in his snow-driving ability, Burns got out of the station wagon and stepped into seventeen inches of drifted snow that came up over the tops of the rubber boots he had bought that morning at a Peoples Drugstore.

Having spent much of his adult life in hot countries, Burns detested snow, which he equated with famine, flood, plague, earthquakes and other natural disasters. As he slogged down the slope, cursing the white stuff, he noticed someone in a skiing outfit come out of a town house that was almost at the end of the cul-de-sac. After shouldering a pair of skis, the skier began plodding up the slope.

Burns noticed that the skier wasn't very tall, no more than five-nine or -ten, if that, and was so masked and bundled up that the only distinguishing features were the lack of them. When they were almost abreast, Burns smiled and asked, "Know which house Mr. Undean lives in?"

The skier replied with a headshake and trudged on. Burns growled, "Thanks a lot, friend," and resumed his inspection of the house numbers. When he found the one he was looking for, 12430, he realized it was the house the skier had just left. It was then that Burns, ever wary, almost turned and went back to his Wagoneer.

But because he had driven for nearly two hours on unfamiliar, snow-slick highways, most of them with only two lanes open to crawling traffic, Burns decided he should at least ring the doorbell to see who answered it. He rang it six times at ten-second intervals. When there was no response, he tried the doorknob. It turned and Tinker Burns went inside.

Through a glass door that led to the loggia he could see a fireplace, a redwood picnic table, the attached dock and, beyond that, the frozen lake. Burns stamped the snow off his boots onto the pebble-studded concrete floor, making as much noise as possible. But when no voice called down, demanding to know "Who's there?", Burns shouted up the staircase, "Hey, Undean! Anybody home?"

The answering silence increased Burns's wariness. As he climbed the two flights of stairs, his wariness also mounted and, by the time he reached the third-floor landing, it had turned into trepidation. Panting slightly from the climb, Burns entered the master bedroom, found nothing, left it, walked slowly down the short hall and into the book-lined office-study, where he found Gilbert Undean dead on the floor.

After squatting down to make sure Undean was really dead, Burns rose and looked at his watch. It was exactly noon. He picked up the telephone on the oak desk, called the Willard Hotel and asked for Granville Haynes. Burns let the hotel room phone ring eight times before he broke the connection and called Mac's Place. There the call was answered on the first ring by Karl Triller, the bartender, who said, "We're not open yet."

"Karl? Tinker Burns. I—"

Interrupting, Triller said, "Hold it a second, Tinker."

Burns could hear Triller's slightly muffled voice talking to someone. "Okay, here're the car keys. When I get off the phone you guys get one bloody mary each but that's the absolute limit."

Burns heard some kind of protest, also muffled, which he couldn't make out. And then came Triller's normal voice. "Yeah, Tinker?"

"I need to find Granny Haynes because it's an emergency and I don't need any of your usual dumb questions."

"What kind of emergency?"

"The bad-jam kind, asshole."

There was a long pause—which anyone but Burns might have taken for a hurt silence—before Triller said, "Try Padillo," recited a telephone number and hung up.

Burns tapped out the number which Padillo answered on

the second ring with a neutral hello. "It's me, Tinker. And I need to talk to Granny Haynes."

"Why all the hard breathing?" Padillo said.

"I'm standing next to a dead body."

"I'll put him on."

Burns heard an extension phone being picked up just as Haynes came on the line with a question. "Whose dead body?"

"Gilbert Undean's. One neat shot to the head. Small caliber. In his house out in Reston."

"You shot him or found him?"

"Found him."

"What were you doing at Undean's?"

"I was going to talk to him about Steady's book."

"Why would Undean know anything about it?"

"You saying he didn't?"

"I'm not saying anything, Tinker. It's your dead body. Your second one in three days."

"Okay, right, it's mine and I'm calling you because I may need a lawyer and thought maybe I oughta get what's his name that Steady had."

"Howard Mott."

"Yeah. Mott."

"No chance of walking away from it?"

"I already made three calls on Undean's phone."

"You're fucked then."

"I already know that, Granny. Now gimme Mott's number."

Haynes recited Mott's home number only once and Burns said, "Now lemme talk to Padillo."

"You're out in Reston?" said Padillo when he came back on the line.

"Right."

"Okay. That's Fairfax County. Dial 911 and tell whoever answers your name, the address and that you've found a dead body. Then hang up and call your lawyer. In fact, you'd better call him first."

"Christ, you're making it sound like I got something to worry about."

"Tinker, the D.C. and Fairfax County cops are going to climb all over anybody who finds two dead bodies in three days. So keep your mouth shut until your lawyer gets there."

"You don't think I oughta tell them how I saw the hitter coming out of the dead guy's house wearing a ski mask, dark glasses and carrying a pair of skis over one shoulder?"

There was a long silence until Padillo said very softly, "I really wish you hadn't told me that."

Burns chuckled. "That's what I figured you'd wish."

Twenty-five

Seated in leather armchairs before three blazing pine logs that occasionally spat and hissed at the fire screen, McCorkle and Padillo resembled nothing so much as a pair of senior club members listening with mild interest to a younger member's account of the so-so polo match he had just witnessed.

What they were actually listening to was Granville Haynes's theory of how his dead father and the equally dead Isabelle Gelinet had conspired to sell Steadfast Haynes's nonexistent memoirs for large sums.

"Sums?" McCorkle said.

"Steady would've figured out how to sell them more than once."

"And Isabelle?" Padillo said.

"If she and Steady were working a con, and if Isabelle decided to solo on after he died, she could've made some basic mistake. Steady was always very cautious, very secretive, and he might not've told her what step two was. So it could be that Isabelle skipped from step one to step three, missed step two, tripped, fell and drowned."

Padillo rose, looked at his watch, saw it was 12:32 P.M. and asked, "Who wants a drink?"

Both Haynes and McCorkle asked for Scotch and water. Padillo turned and headed for the small dining room that was really an extension of the living room. To the left of the dining room was the kitchen and, beyond that, the tiny snow-covered backyard. The yard was divided between a ten-by-twelve-foot garden, in which Padillo grew roses and basil, and a one-car alley garage, in which he kept his 1972 Mercedes 280 SL coupe.

His small white brick Foggy Bottom row house sat on a thirty-foot lot and would have had a flat front were it not for a bay window that McCorkle said made it look seven months pregnant. The house had two bedrooms and a bath upstairs. Downstairs were the living and dining rooms, kitchen, a half-bath and another flight of stairs that led down to the full basement, where there was a regulation Brunswick snooker table, at least sixty years old.

The snooker table had come with the house and nobody remembered how it had made it down the stairs and into the basement that also contained the furnace and a washer and dryer. The basement was a place Padillo tried not to visit more than three or four times a year.

He had bought the house the day Richard Nixon resigned and furnished it the following Saturday morning by walking through an upscale furniture store out on Wisconsin Avenue and pointing to floor samples that could be delivered that same afternoon. He had wound up with a lot of leather, tweed, teak and pine stuff that McCorkle told him made the downstairs look like a psychiatrist's waiting room. Padillo had replied that that was exactly how he wanted it to look.

The only memorable pieces in the house were the dining room's refectory table, reportedly four hundred years old, and the intricately carved mahogany sideboard that Padillo used as a bar. A young candy heiress, now more than twenty years dead, had given him the refectory table as a birthday

169

present. He had bought the sideboard from a former first secretary at the Finnish embassy who needed the money to pay off some poker debts.

Padillo returned with the drinks, carrying two in his left hand and one in his right. He served McCorkle first, then Haynes and said, "What makes you so sure Steady's memoirs don't exist?"

"You saw the so-called manuscript I left in your safe?"

Padillo nodded as he sat back down in the leather chair, but McCorkle said, "I never saw it."

"Three hundred and eighty-odd mostly blank pages," Padillo said.

"That should miff the lady with the Sauer," McCorkle said.

Haynes said, "Let's come back to her."

McCorkle shrugged. "No hurry."

After tasting his drink, Haynes said, "When Erika and I reached Steady's farm yesterday, his ex-wife was there. The fourth and last one. Letitia Melon. You two know her?"

"We know Letty," Padillo said.

"But not well," McCorkle added.

"She was locked in a hall closet under the stairs, bound and gagged."

"She hurt?" Padillo asked.

"No."

"Who'd she say did it?"

"Two guys with grocery sacks over their heads. She said they were already in the house when she got there."

McCorkle asked, "Why was she there?"

"Because of Steady's horse. She claimed she was worried nobody was looking after it."

"Why do I get the impression you don't believe her?" Padillo said.

"Because after she left I called Howard Mott. He told me Letty'd called him right after Steady died to remind him of the horse. Mott told her not to worry, that he'd take care of it, and he did."

"Where's the horse now?" McCorkle said.

"Dead."

"How?"

"Shot. Either by Letty or the guys with sacks over their heads."

"Why would she shoot him?"

"Why would they?"

Padillo said, "Then what?"

"I reported the dead horse to the sheriff, who seemed to be a member of Steady's fan club. Then Erika and I searched the house, looking for a true manuscript."

"You told her what you were looking for?" McCorkle asked.

"Why not?"

McCorkle frowned first, then shrugged and said, "Go on."

"Erika discovered a new version of the manuscript in Steady's computer. This new version reads just like the one I left in your safe except for one thing. Instead of three hundred and eighty-odd blank pages, this one has line after line and page after page filled with just one word: endit— spelled e-n-d-i-t. I think of it as the long version of the false manuscript. The woman with the Sauer got the short version." He smiled slightly at McCorkle. "It would be awfully neat if she were Letty Melon in disguise."

"It wasn't Letty," McCorkle said.

"Tell me about her—whoever she was."

"I didn't see her hair," McCorkle said, "because she wore a red knit cap pulled down almost to her eyebrows. I didn't see her hands because she wore red knit gloves. I didn't see her feet because she wore rubber boots. I can't tell you much about her build because she wore a man's old London Fog raincoat, probably with a zip-out liner. I know it was old because the waterproofing was gone—maybe dry-cleaned away. That leaves her face. She wore yellow-tinted glasses and her eyes were a blue that could've come from contacts. She had a regular nose, mouth, chin and no makeup. She

171

had two voices. One was her flibbertigibbet voice. Her other voice was the convincer—uninflected, exact, experienced. It and the Sauer made me do exactly what she said I should do."

"No scars, moles or tattoos?" Haynes said.

"No, but she did have nice skin," McCorkle said. "Very few lines and no wrinkles—although she could've rubbed her face with Preparation H just before she came through the door. That can tighten things up for an hour or two."

"She had two walks," Padillo said. "One was shy and one was bold. She used the shy walk when she came in—a pigeon-toed shuffle, almost clumsy. On the way out: long strides, graceful, even athletic."

"How old was she?" Haynes asked.

"More than thirty," McCorkle said. "Less than fifty."

Haynes finished his drink and turned away from McCorkle to put it down on a side table. Still turned away, he asked, "How'd she know the manuscript was in your safe?"

McCorkle winked at Padillo and said, "That's been bothering me. It's been bothering me so much that when I woke up this morning the first thing I asked myself was: who knew I'd put the thing in my safe?"

"I knew," Haynes said. "You knew." He indicated Padillo with a nod. "And so did he."

"Did Mott know?" Padillo asked.

"He knew I had the manuscript. He didn't know it was in your safe."

"Remember when I got out of the cab Friday afternoon and mistook you for Steady?" McCorkle said. "You were headed for Howard Mott's office empty-handed."

Haynes nodded.

"The next time I saw you was at the bar—just you, me, Tinker Burns and Karl. And by then you were carrying that folded-over grocery bag."

Haynes again nodded.

"But when you left with Erika, you weren't carrying

anything. A fairly observant person might've noticed this and concluded you'd left the grocery bag with me for safekeeping." McCorkle paused to sip his drink. "Safekeeping suggests a locked box of some kind. Maybe even a safe."

"Someone had a tail on him," Padillo said.

"Maybe," Haynes said. "I wasn't in Howard Mott's office more than ten minutes before he got a call. By then he'd handed me all those blank pages. The call was from a lawyer, some ex-senator who wants to buy all rights to Steady's memoirs for an anonymous client. He offered one hundred thousand. On my instructions, Mott told him I wanted five hundred thousand because I claim to know where I can raise enough offshore money to turn Steady's life into a film I'd write, direct and star in. Mott may even have told him I was going to produce it."

"What'd the ex-senator say?" McCorkle asked.

"He moaned and groused, then said he'd have to consult his client and get back to Mott on Monday. Tomorrow."

"Any other offers?" Padillo said.

"One."

"Who from?"

"After Isabelle was killed," Haynes said, "and after I'd talked to the cops and was up in my room at the Willard, a guy from the CIA dropped by and offered me fifty thousand."

"Sight unseen?" McCorkle said.

"Nobody seems to want to read the thing," Haynes said. "They just want to bury it. I told the CIA guy about the hundred thousand I'd just turned down, then gave him the same crap about turning the memoirs into a feature and finished by telling him my new asking price was seven hundred and fifty thousand."

"What'd he say when he recovered?"

"He seemed pleased—in a strange kind of way."

"Heard from him since?" Padillo said.

173

"Indirectly," Haynes said. "He's the dead body Tinker Burns discovered out in Reston. Gilbert Undean."

McCorkle leaned back in his chair and gazed up at the ceiling. Padillo rose and stood, staring at the fire. Finally, he turned to Haynes and said, "Steady left you a mess, didn't he?"

"He led a messy life."

"Our lady of the silenced Sauer," McCorkle said, still gazing at the ceiling. "I keep wondering just how pissed off she was as she leafed through those three hundred and eighty-odd blank pages."

"If she is pissed off," Haynes said, "she's pissed off at you guys, not at me. She might even suspect you two of pulling a switch. She might even suspect that you know where the true manuscript is."

"I think," Padillo said to McCorkle, "that we've just been invited to the dance."

"Summoned is more like it," McCorkle said. "I wonder if it'll be fast or slow and if I can remember the steps."

"You might still manage a waltz," Padillo said. "If it's not too brisk."

"You've already accepted, right?"

Padillo nodded and said, "Isabelle," as if the dead woman's name explained everything.

McCorkle took a moody swallow of his drink, the last swallow, placed the glass on a table and turned to Haynes. "What d'you plan to do—auction the memoirs off, or at least pretend to?"

"Only the rights to them."

"What if the bidders demand a quick peek?"

"Each bidder is already convinced of what's in them," Haynes said. "If they weren't convinced, they wouldn't be bidding." He smiled then, that charming smile he had inherited from his dead father. "But the important thing now is to convince the bidders that the true manuscript is guarded by a pair of dragons."

174

"He means us," Padillo said.

"Then he means a pair of old dragons with dull claws, missing teeth and not too much fire left in their bellies."

Haynes smiled his inherited smile again and said, "You could even let it be known around town that for a slice of the gross you've agreed to handle—what's the best thing to call it, the security?—on a very fat but very murky deal."

"I suppose we could drop a discreet word here and there," Padillo said, looking at McCorkle, who frowned, as if trying to think of ears a discreet word could be dropped into. A moment later the frown disappeared and he smiled contentedly.

"I believe this is called setting out the bait," Padillo said.

Haynes nodded. "If the prospective buyer or buyers believe they can steal what otherwise they'd have to pay a great deal of money for, I think they'll try to steal it."

"Especially," McCorkle said, "if they're convinced that only the Alzheimer boys will be guarding it."

"It might be better," Haynes said, "if they hear that I'm guarding the true manuscript and that you two're guarding me."

"How easy or hard do you want us to make it for them?" Padillo said.

"Medium hard."

"And after they get past us—then what?"

"Well, then I suppose I'll have to make some kind of citizen's arrest, won't I?" said Granville Haynes.

Twenty-six

It was shortly before 1:45 P.M. that Sunday when the Salvadoran maid appeared on the south-facing glassed-in sun porch where Hamilton and Muriel Keyes were just finishing a lunch of ham salad, with custard still to follow. The maid was carrying a beige telephone, which she plugged into a jack, while informing Keyes in Spanish that a functionary from his bureau was determined to speak with him, even if it meant violating the meal.

Keyes thanked the maid and waited until she disappeared into the house before he picked up the phone and greeted his caller with, "Now what?" After listening without expression for two minutes, Keyes said, "I'm leaving now," broke the connection and put the phone down beside his scarcely tasted glass of white wine.

"Well?" Muriel Keyes said.

"It's Undean. Gilbert Undean."

She frowned and said, "Whatever does he want now?"

Keyes stared at his wife with the unseeing expression of someone who is thinking hard about other things. "Nothing. He's been shot."

She bit her lower lip as if in minor penance for the snippiness of her last question. "I'm sorry. Suicide?"

"No," Keyes said as he rose and looked at his watch. "I should be back by five or five-thirty."

"Please be careful. I almost spun out twice in McLean this morning."

"How was she? You never said."

"Dilly?" Muriel Keyes shrugged. "Well, Dilly's depressed and Dilly's despondent. Maybe even suicidal. She's finally realized he isn't coming back this time."

"Can't blame him," Keyes said. "But I wish he would so you could resign as her chief hand-holder."

"Poor Dilly," she said. "And poor Mr. Undean. Did he have a family?"

"No."

"He lived alone?"

"In Reston."

"How very sad."

It was the 43-year-old sheriff of Fairfax County himself who briefed Hamilton Keyes in a small conference room in the Reston Library. A three-man team of CIA specialists was still prowling through Undean's house, hunting for possibly classified material and ignoring the gibes of the county homicide investigators.

Keyes and the sheriff sat at the six-foot-long conference table, the sheriff at one end, Keyes at the other. The sheriff wore a dark blue suit, white shirt and a red and blue tie. Keyes suspected him of having attended church that morning. Keyes, who hadn't attended church in twenty years, wore what he often wore on Sundays: a gray tweed jacket, a very old and frayed pink shirt with a button-down collar, gray wide-wale corduroy pants, rather new, and a pair of gleaming fifteen-year-old cordovan loafers that had been resoled three times. The sheriff had given the pink shirt a dubious glance.

177

"You want it from the beginning, I expect," the sheriff said, producing a long notebook that Keyes thought resembled those used by newspaper reporters.

"If you would, please."

After placing the notebook on the table, the sheriff removed his gold-rimmed glasses, held them up to the ceiling's fluorescent lights for a cleanliness inspection and resettled them over gentle brown eyes that Keyes thought were possibly a disguise.

The glasses rested on jug-handle ears and a born-to-pry nose. The ears were partially camouflaged by a mass of auburn hair that had been shaped by an artist. Below the glasses and nose was a wide thick-lipped mouth, curiously pale, that reigned over a smallish chin. From six feet away, Keyes thought he caught a faint whiff of Canoe after-shave.

The sheriff opened the notebook, studied it for a few moments, frowning, and then used a bass drone to describe how a male Caucasian, identifying himself as Tinker Burns, had used 911 to report the death of Gilbert Undean, 67. After two deputies arrived at the house of the deceased, they determined that Mr. Undean was indeed dead, apparently from a single gunshot wound in the forehead. A quick search revealed no weapon, virtually ruling out suicide.

Mr. Burns refused to give the investigating deputies any information other than his name, age (66) and place of permanent residence (Paris, France) until he talked with his lawyer. The lawyer arrived fifty-seven minutes later and conferred with his client. Mr. Burns then agreed to make a statement.

"Who's the lawyer?" Keyes asked.

"Howard Mott himself."

"Well, now."

Again consulting his notebook, the sheriff said Mr. Burns claimed to have met the deceased for the first time two days before at the funeral of a mutual friend, a certain Steadfast Haynes. This morning, on impulse, Mr. Burns decided to

178

visit the deceased to reminisce about their friend. When Mr. Burns reached Reston, he hesitated to drive down the steeply sloping street to Mr. Undean's house because of the deep snow. Instead, he had walked. It was while walking to the deceased's house that Mr. Burns saw someone come out of it, shoulder a pair of skis and start up the street toward him.

As the sheriff paused to turn a page, Keyes said, "Then what?"

"Mr. Burns asked the person with the skis which house was Mr. Undean's. But the person replied with a headshake and continued up the street."

"Person?" said Keyes.

"Mr. Burns claims he couldn't tell if it was a man or a woman because the person was wearing sunglasses, ski mask, knitted cap, parka, ski pants, gloves and, of course, ski boots."

"Tall, short, what?"

"Medium."

Keyes sighed and gave the sheriff a go-ahead nod. Resuming his report, the sheriff said Tinker Burns rang the deceased's doorbell repeatedly. When there was no response, Mr. Burns tried the door, found it unlocked and entered the house, discovering the victim's body on the third floor in a small bedroom converted into a study. Upon questioning, Mr. Burns admitted making five calls from the dead man's telephone. These calls were confirmed by the telephone company. The first call was to the Willard Hotel. The second and third calls were to numbers in the District of Columbia. The fourth call was to 911 and the final call was to the home of the lawyer, Howard Mott, also in the District.

"Who got the second and third calls?" Keyes asked.

Again, the notes were consulted. "The second call was to an establishment called Mac's Place and the third was to a Mr. Michael Padillo," the sheriff said, rhyming Padillo with Brillo. "Know him?"

"I believe he owns half of Mac's Place," Keyes said. "A saloon."

The sheriff made a careful note of that before disclosing that a subsequent investigation turned up two observant housewives who independently confirmed what Burns had said about encountering the ski person.

"The neighborhood watch and ward society?" Keyes said.

"What?"

"Nothing," Keyes said. "Where's Burns now?"

"We let him walk."

"You check him out with D.C. homicide?"

The sheriff, not taking his eyes off Keyes, closed his notebook and carefully stored it away in a breast pocket. "Should I?"

"Merely a suggestion," said Keyes and went on to outline how the Federal government trusted that Fairfax County would handle the body of Gilbert Undean, his effects and any publicity concerning his death.

In a Wendy's on the Leesburg Pike, Howard Mott sipped coffee and reading upside down, watched Tinker Burns write a check for 2,000 pounds on a Knightsbridge branch of Barclays' Bank in London.

"I prefer dollars," Mott said.

Burns finished signing Tinker to the check and looked up. "Why the fuck didn't you say so? Cash okay?" He reached into a pants pocket of his gray suit and brought out an impressive roll of hundred-dollar bills.

"Cash is definitely not okay," Mott said. "I'll take the pounds instead."

"What's wrong with cash?" Burns asked as he added his surname to the check.

"Cash is becoming virtually illegal in this country," Mott said. "Dope has tainted cash and inflation has debased it. A one-hundred-dollar bill is now worth what three tens were fifteen years ago, but nobody likes to accept hundreds

180

because it's claimed that ninety percent of them bear a faint residue of cocaine. That may well be bullshit, of course. But it may also be true, especially when you consider that our five percent of the world's population snorts, smokes or injects eighty percent of the world's dope."

Burns grinned, tore out the check and handed it to Mott. "Sounds like the IRS is auditing your ass."

Mott folded the check and stuck it into his shirt pocket. "The cost of a continuous IRS audit is factored into the fees we charge our clients, who, for the most part, are alleged embezzlers, con men, mountebanks, swindlers and malefactors of great and medium wealth. My firm's task is to keep them out of jail or, failing that, secure them the most lenient sentences possible. Grateful clients often wish to pay in cash. But we insist upon certified checks drawn on reputable domestic banks."

Burns's grin grew wider. "What's my uncertified check for two thousand quid buy me?"

"Bought, not buy," Mott said. "It bought you temporary release from the clutches of the Fairfax County sheriff, who'll be anxious to ask you a few hundred more questions once he finds out you discovered the body of Isabelle Gelinet."

"When that happens, I want you representing me."

"I'm awfully expensive."

"And I'm kind of rich. It's a perfect match."

"There could be a conflict of interest."

"Who with?"

"I already represent Granville Haynes."

"What's representing Granny got to do with representing me?"

"You can answer that far better than I."

Tinker Burns again produced his checkbook. "Would a five-thousand-quid retainer clear up that conflict-of-interest question?"

Mott shook his head. "Tell you what. When the sheriff

hauls you in again, give me a ring and we'll try to work something out."

"That a guarantee?"

"A guarantee suggests a refund," Mott said. "We'll call it a promise."

Outside the Wendy's, Mott was unlocking the door of his wife's Volvo sedan when Tinker Burns, the door of his rented Jeep Wagoneer already open, turned and said, "What's the best way to Middleburg?"

Mott turned around slowly to stare at Burns for several seconds. "You don't want to go to Middleburg."

"Why not?"

"The snow."

"I got four-wheel drive and snow tires. Besides, a lot of it's melted by now."

Mott examined Burns for another five seconds before giving directions. "Straight out the Pike till you get to Leesburg. Then south on U.S. Fifteen till you hit U.S. Fifty. West on Fifty for seven or eight miles and you'll be in Middleburg."

"Thanks," Burns said, got in the Wagoneer, started its engine and drove off as directed.

After watching him leave, Mott went back into the Wendy's and located the pay phone next to the men's toilet. He briefly considered the ethics of his decision, then looked up a name and phone number in his pocket address book and used a phone company credit card to place a long-distance call to Letty Melon, the former Mrs. Steadfast Haynes, at her 360-acre horse farm near Middleburg, Virginia.

Twenty-seven

At a little past 5 P.M. that Sunday, Hamilton Keyes stood at the large window of his library, staring out at the snow-blanketed garden and wondering what it would be like to go outside and build a twilight snowman. Finding it to be a mild temptation, easily resisted, he instead took a long swallow of his iced vodka and, without turning, made an announcement.

"After I resigned yesterday they offered to make me an ambassador."

Muriel Keyes was sitting on the odd-size leather couch, wearing gray slacks, white Reeboks, a turtleneck of black silk and holding a Scotch and water. The announcement made her slosh a little of her drink onto a burled-walnut parsons table.

Using a paper napkin to mop up the spilled water and alcohol, she said, "You resigned?"

Keyes turned from the window. "I believe we've arrived at one of our ghastly need-to-know times."

"Yes," she said. "I do believe we have."

"There's a catch, of course," Keyes said as he crossed the

room and sat down. They now sat exactly as he and Gilbert Undean had sat on the previous Friday evening: Keyes in the leather armchair and his wife in Undean's spot on the couch.

Keyes had another quick swallow of his drink, then made an exploratory pass over his bald head with the palm of his left hand and said, "The catch goes by the name of Steadfast Haynes."

"Who died."

"But who, before dying, managed to finish his memoirs, entitled *Mercenary Calling*."

She began a smile that ended as a laugh that was almost a giggle. "He didn't—call them that?"

"Afraid so."

"What a juicy read they must be."

"More than juicy, I'd say. Steady probably told everything he suspected, which is enormous, and all he knew, which is alarming."

She nodded gravely and studied her husband for a moment. "From what you've said, I assume you haven't read them yet."

"All I did was dispatch Gilbert Undean to buy all rights from Steady's son."

She nodded again, this time as if at some nagging question. "Which is why Mr. Undean came calling Friday night."

"Yes."

"I don't remember his name," she said. "The son's."

"Granville."

"He must be fully grown now. Didn't Steady always keep him parked somewhere—or warehoused? What is he now— twenty-three or -four?"

"Thirty-two."

"Good Lord. He was here for the services, of course. Have you talked to him?"

"No. I merely instructed Undean to offer him fifty thousand dollars for all rights to his father's memoirs. The offer was rejected."

184

"Do the memoirs have anything to do with Mr. Undean's death?"

"I really don't know."

"How did you find out they existed? Did Steady try to sell them to you? It sounds so very like him."

"His live-in companion called just after he died. She said that unless he was buried at Arlington with standard military honors, the memoirs would be sent to some New York literary agent. It was blackmail, of course, but the price was cheap, so I paid."

"She was French, I believe. Isabelle Gelinet."

Keyes nodded.

"She came to see me a few years ago when she was doing a story for Agence France-Presse. Something silly about the wives of spies. My answers nearly bored her to tears.

"And the story never ran."

"Are her death and Undean's connected?"

"If I were to guess, I'd say probably."

"I'm sorry."

"How many friends would you say Steady had?" he asked.

"I'd say dozens. Perhaps even hundreds."

"There were only four at the Arlington services. Four, including Undean, who'd known him only in Laos."

"You didn't go?"

"I sent Undean."

"You should've gone, Ham."

"Perhaps it's just as well I didn't. Of the four who were at Arlington, two have been killed. Murdered."

She shivered slightly. "Leaving only the son and who else?"

"Tinker Burns. An ex-mercenary turned small-time arms dealer. He's an old friend of Steady's. Perhaps his oldest."

Muriel Keyes put her drink down and stared at her husband. "Tell me about your resignation and the offer to make you ambassador."

"That royal summons I received yesterday morning?"

She nodded.

185

"It was from a White House hatchet man. A new boy. They need a few slots to pay off some political debts—to the far right, I'd guess, but I could very well be wrong. Anyway, it seems my job will do nicely. So I resigned before the chop landed, but then, at the last moment, maybe on impulse—"

"You never did anything in your life on impulse."

Keyes smiled. "At the last moment, I told the White House hatchet wallah all about the memoirs of Steadfast Haynes. He turned quite green. That done, he ordered me to buy the memoirs and hang the cost."

"He would seem to be a real player."

"He wants to be, but lacks finesse. He even offered me ten percent of the memoirs' price."

Muriel Keyes giggled again.

"Somehow sensing his faux pas, he then offered me my old job back. I made him a counterproposal."

"Ambassador," she said.

Keyes nodded, smiling and looking quite pleased.

"How much does young Haynes want for Steady's memoirs?" she said.

"Seven hundred and fifty thousand."

"Then it's really quite simple, isn't it? You buy the memoirs. Young Haynes gets three quarters of a million. The White House sleeps nights. And you become ambassador."

"It would be that simple," Keyes said, "were it not for the mystery man."

She giggled for the third time. "A mystery man. Dear God."

"He's the one responsible for the bidding escalation."

"When do you make your new offer to—Granville, isn't it?"

"Tonight. Whenever he gets back to his hotel room."

"What if the mystery man tops your bid?" she asked. "Will the White House raise back?"

"I doubt it. They'd probably fall back on damage control instead. And I can forget about being ambassador."

"Was a particular posting mentioned?"

186

"The Caribbean."

"Better than Chad."

"Much."

Muriel Keyes rose, went over to her husband's chair, sat on its broad arm and absently began to massage his neck with one hand. "If the mystery man tops your bid of seven hundred and fifty thousand, he'll probably go to eight hundred, right?"

"Probably."

"I think we can afford to increase the White House bid with a personal contribution of, say, two hundred and fifty thousand."

He turned to stare up at her with a look that was part wonder and part admiration. "Making it a preemptive one million."

"Yes."

"I see no reason to mention your generosity to the White House."

"Why would you?" she said. "After all, they have no real need to know."

Tinker Burns found Letitia Melon's house just before dark. It was a huge 201-year-old fieldstone place, three stories high, with a pair of newer two-story wings that were 143 and 96 years old respectively. The old house sat on the crest of a rise a quarter of a mile from the county blacktop. It was surrounded by tall pines whose branches were bowed under their burdens of snow and ice. A narrow concrete drive, only 44 years old and clear of snow, ran from the county blacktop up to the house. At the top of the drive was a small green John Deere tractor that Burns assumed had done the snow-plowing.

He turned the Jeep Wagoneer into the drive, stopped and studied the house and the snow-covered roof of the long low horse barn which could be seen just beyond the crest of the rise. Burns looked for signs of life but found none. The last of the sun's rays were turning the stonework of the house into old gold but Burns ignored the pretty-picture effect and instead examined the six chimneys for smoke. There wasn't any.

He drove up to the house and parked in front of its entrance on jigsaw slabs of black slate. Once out of the station wagon, he scanned the windows for chinks of light. Finding none, he went back to the station wagon and blew its horn five times. Somewhere, close by, a dog barked. Thus encouraged, Burns mounted the six steps and rang the doorbell. He rang it six times before trying the big brass knob only to find the door locked. Burns stubbornly jammed his right thumb against the doorbell and hammered the door itself with his left fist.

He was still ringing and hammering away when a woman's voice from behind him said, "Get the fuck off my property, Tinker."

Twenty-eight

Without turning, Tinker Burns stuck cold bare hands into his topcoat pockets and said, "How you doing, Letty?"

"Get off my property. Now."

"We've gotta talk."

"No, we don't."

"Mind if I turn around?"

"You have to turn around to get off my property."

Burns turned slowly to his left and, when all the way around, smiled at Letty Melon and the pump shotgun she was aiming at his chest.

"You look cold, Letty. Have a long wait?"

"Go, Tinker. Now."

"I figured Howard Mott'd let you know I was coming. That's why I didn't call myself."

"You've got ten seconds to get in your car."

"Look. You know you're not gonna shoot me and I know I'm not gonna leave till we talk. Now, we could stand out here all night freezing our butts off, but that's sort of dumb. So why not go inside where it's nice and warm and have a taste and a talk? After that, I'll be on my way. I even brought a jug of Turkey along. You still drink Turkey, Letty?"

Letty Melon said nothing. She wore a buttoned-up shearling coat and had tied a gray cashmere scarf over her head. The rest of her outfit consisted of blue jeans, boots and the pump shotgun. She raised the shotgun with her left hand, letting its barrel rest on her left shoulder. Her right hand dug a key out of her jeans pocket. She moved around Burns, went up to the front door, unlocked it and went inside. Burns turned and followed.

They sat in front of an enormous fireplace where four oak logs blazed. They held tumblers half full of 101-proof Wild Turkey bourbon whiskey, the good stuff, undiluted by either ice or water. After a sip of whiskey, Letty Melon lit an unfiltered Camel. Tinker Burns swallowed a third of his drink and looked around the fifty-foot-long living room with obvious appreciation.

"I never got invited here," he said. "I got invited to that little place over by, what's its name, Berryville, a couple of times when you and Steady were still married, but never here."

"We couldn't stand each other's friends," she said. "I invited mine here; he invited his there. I reckon we couldn't stand them because his friends were mostly women and mine were mostly men."

"Well, that's how it goes sometimes."

"What's really on your mind, Tinker?"

"That fire," he said. "We come in here and it's all dark and kind of cold, but you turn on a gas jet, put a match to it, throw on some logs, and a couple of minutes later we got ourselves a real nice fire going. Now, some people'd claim that's no way to build a fire—that you oughta do it with kindling and—"

"Is this some kind of allegory?" she said.

Burns tried to look hurt and almost succeeded. "I was just trying to edge into it."

"Don't edge. Jump."

Tinker Burns sipped his bourbon, stared at the fire and said, "Ever know a spook name of Undean? Gilbert Undean?"

"No. Why?"

"He died."

"So?"

"He was one of the mourners at Steady's burial at Arlington. There were only four of us there. Steady's kid, me, Undean and Isabelle. Steady was buried Friday. Isabelle was killed the same day. Undean got killed this morning."

Letty Melon drank more bourbon, inhaled smoke, blew it out and said, "I heard about Isabelle."

"I found her body. I also found Undean's—about noon today. Maybe a little after."

"What'd you do?"

"I called the cops. What else?"

"Where'd he live?"

"Reston."

"So you zipped straight out here. What the hell for? I told you last night we've got nothing to talk about."

Burns took another mouthful of bourbon, rolled this one around on his tongue, swallowed and sighed his appreciation. "Did you know Steady'd written his memoirs—him and Isabelle?"

"I know he'd threatened to for years."

"Well, he finally did."

"Have you read them?"

"No."

"Who has?"

"Maybe Granny. Maybe not."

"You ask him?"

"No."

"How come?"

"Lemme tell you how I got into this thing," Burns said, finished his bourbon, put the glass down and leaned toward Letty Melon with the confident and faintly conspiratorial air of a man who'd spent much of his adult life selling dubious wares to suspicious customers.

"I really don't want to know, Tinker."

He ignored her and said, "About nine or ten days ago, right before Steady died, I get this call from a guy I once did some business with. I'm in Paris and he's in, well, it doesn't matter where he is. He tells me he's heard Steady's written his memoirs. Now, this guy knew Steady in Zaire when it was still the Congo. They later cut up a few touches together in Southeast Asia and Central America. Know what I mean?"

"Not really."

"Did stuff they maybe shouldn't've. Stuff that there's no statute of limitations on."

"Shitty stuff," she said. "Steady's specialty."

"Yeah, all right. Shitty stuff. But since then this guy's moved uptown. And now whenever the world's about to end, he gets calls from CNN or maybe from that kid with the speech impediment on NBC and they want him to give 'em the exact time and date of Armageddon and a rundown on the aftermath in fifteen seconds or less."

"He's in government then," she said.

"No. He's not in government, but he makes a lot of money advising governments."

"I see. One of those."

"Yeah. Right. One of those. So he calls me and says he's heard about Steady's book and since I'm an old asshole buddy of Steady's, he's wondering if I can get a peek at the thing and see if Steady's mentioned those touches they cut up together years ago. He also says he just happens to know where I can unload some twenty-year-old left-behind Vietnam ordnance I got rusting away down in Marseilles on a certain party with an end-use certificate who'll pay in Swiss francs. So I tell this guy, sure, I'll try and look into it. But before I get around to it, I get this call in Paris from Isabelle, who's at the Hay-Adams, telling me Steady's lying there dead in the bed. Okay so far?"

"So far."

"Well, I fly over for the burial. And what gets me is that Steady knew hundreds and hundreds of people, but nobody shows up at Arlington except me, Granny, Isabelle and this old semi-retired spook, Gilbert Undean. So Isabelle, Granny and me have lunch and Isabelle starts talking about how she'd helped Steady write his memoirs. But I can't talk to her in front of Granny and Padillo—"

"You ate at Mac's Place," Letty Melon said. "How sweet. I think Steady practically lived there for a time after we split."

Burns ignored the interruption. "Anyway, an hour or two later I go in this limo I rented out to Isabelle's apartment to see if I can talk her into letting me read the thing. Steady's book. I go up to her floor, knock on her door, no answer. So I try the door and it opens. I go in and find her stark naked in the bathtub, wrists and ankles wired, drowned. Probably."

Letty Melon looked away from Burns and toward the far end of the big room. "How was the Undean guy killed?"

"Shot."

She turned back to him. "You also found him, right?"

Burns nodded. "Looks kinda funny, doesn't it?"

"Very."

"I can't help how it looks. All I can do is keep nosing around, trying to find out who's got Steady's book."

"Maybe I should get up and poke the fire, Tinker. Isn't that what people in movies do when they're about to deliver the bad news?"

Burns thought about it. "Yeah, I guess I've seen a lot of fire-poking in movies. You got some bad news, Letty?"

Instead of answering his question, she said, "Right after

193

Steady died, the next day, in fact, I got a call from one of our few mutual friends who told me Steady'd been quietly spreading the word around Washington that he'd written his memoirs. So I asked this mutual friend, a rather silly little bitch, 'Why tell me?' She said she just thought I might be curious about how Steady'd treated me in his book. I told her I didn't give a damn and hung up."

"But you gave a real big damn, right?"

"Sure I did. Mostly because he was such a liar."

"He could dream 'em up all right," Burns said with obvious admiration.

"The day after his burial," she said, "I drove out to our—well, his place near Berryville. I still had a key. I went in and found a manuscript in the dining room. He and his girlfriend had turned it into an office of sorts. The manuscript was in a typewriter-paper box. I only read the title page, 'Mercenary Calling,' then his name and a line at the bottom about the copyright. I put the lid back on the box and took it out to my truck. After that I came back in and went into the kitchen to fix a cup of coffee. A couple of guys with paper sacks over their heads jumped me, tied me up, gagged me and locked me in a little dark closet where I'd still be if Erika McCorkle and Granville hadn't shown up."

"The McCorkle kid was with Granny, huh?" Burns said, sounding interested. "You were lucky."

"You wouldn't know anything about the two guys who jumped me, would you, Tinker?"

"No, ma'am."

"Maybe who hired them?"

"What makes you think somebody hired 'em?"

"Because they didn't steal anything."

Burns considered her logic, gave it a grudging nod of agreement and said, "You still got it?"

"The manuscript? Of course."

Burns edged forward, his excitement partially concealed

by an earnest expression. "Letty, I'd really appreciate it if I could just look through it real quick."

"See whether your friend is mentioned?"

"Right. It won't take long."

Letty Melon smiled for the first time. "No, it probably won't."

She rose and began walking toward a wall of books at the room's far end. Burns rose and followed. In front of the books was a black walnut library table. On it was a white Keebord stationery box. Letty Melon indicated the box and said, "Help yourself."

Burns stared at the box, picked it up gently, gave it a little shake, put it down and carefully removed its lid. He bent over slightly to read the title page, then lifted out all 386 pages and placed them almost reverently on the table. After turning the title page facedown on the table, he read the Housman lines, turned them facedown, read the dedication to Granville Haynes, put it facedown on top of the other pages and began reading Chapter One. He read its two lines, stopped, read them again and slowly turned his head to glare at a now grinning Letty Melon.

Burns opened his mouth, as if to say something, changed his mind and, his face now turning a dangerous red, flipped quickly through the remaining blank pages. It was then that he straightened, turned and bellowed his question: "Where the fuck is it, Letty?"

"You're looking at it, Tinker, just as I found it. A fake manuscript. If you want it, it's all yours."

Tinker Burns turned back to the four-inch-high stack of mostly blank pages and, after arranging them neatly, put them back in the box and replaced the lid. He picked up the box, cradled it against his chest and looked around the room, as if trying to remember where he'd left his coat.

"I'll talk to Granny," he said, more to himself than to Letty Melon. "He's gotta know where it is."

"What if there isn't any book?" she said. "What if it's Steady's farewell hoax? His last lie?"

He stared at her long enough for his face to resume its normal tanned and weathered look. "Then a couple of people died for nothing, didn't they?"

Twenty-nine

Granville Haynes, propped up in bed on pillows and wearing only Jockey shorts, looked up from a *New York Times* feature about Hollywood agents to watch a nude Erika McCorkle stroll out of the bathroom, cross to the wheeled room-service table and pop a cold French-fried potato into her mouth. From there she went to the closet to slip on a long white terry-cloth robe that the Willard Hotel gently warned guests they would be billed for if they stole it.

While tying the robe's belt, she said, "That was the best seventeen-dollar-plus-tip cheeseburger I ever ate."

A mildly bawdy response occurred to Haynes but before he could utter it the phone rang. He picked it up, said hello and heard a pleasant baritone voice ask, "Mr. Haynes?"

"Yes."

"I'm replacing Gilbert Undean."

"Not in the morgue, I trust."

There was a hesitation, not quite long enough to be considered a pause, before the baritone said, "Then you've heard?"

"I've heard."

197

"On the radio?"

"I haven't listened to a radio recently."

"Perhaps from Mr. Padillo then? Or even from Mr. Mott, who, I understand, is now representing Tinker Burns."

"Since you're dropping names, why not drop yours?"

"Not over the phone," the baritone said. "I was hoping you'd come down to the lobby and join me for a drink."

"We can drink up here."

"You're asking me up?"

"I'm not asking you to do anything, Ace. But if we talk, we talk up here in front of a witness."

"Out of the question."

"Too bad," Haynes said and hung up.

Erika McCorkle said, "Who the hell was that?"

Haynes shook his head and held up a warning hand. The telephone rang a moment later. He answered it with, "Well?"

"Who's your witness?" the baritone asked.

"Think of her as my fiancée," Haynes said, causing Erika McCorkle to chuckle.

"Her name?"

"Introductions aren't necessary. You know who I am but I don't know who you are. That gives you the advantage."

"A very slight one."

"Take what you can get."

There was another hesitation that this time lasted long enough to qualify as a pause. "Five minutes?"

"Make it ten," Haynes said and broke the connection.

Erika McCorkle returned to the room-service table, picked up another French fry, bit off half of it, chewed thoughtfully, swallowed and asked, "Who were you on the phone just then?"

"Hardcase Haynes of Homicide."

"A bit overdone, wasn't it?"

Haynes smiled. "Think so?"

She frowned. "Unless that wasn't acting."

A silence grew as she waited for his response. When he

made none she untied the robe's belt and said, "I'll get dressed."

"Don't," Haynes said as he rose from the bed, picked up his shirt and began putting it on.

Erika McCorkle slowly retied the robe's belt as she watched him button the shirt and pull on his pants. When he sat down and reached for a sock, she said, "You're setting the scene, right? The remains of a room-service meal. The half-drunk drinks. The rumpled bed. And the unmistakable reek of sex on a Sunday afternoon."

"I want an edge," Haynes said.

"And where do you want me—recumbent on the bed, showing a little thigh, a glimpse of tit?"

Haynes now had one sock on, changed his mind, stripped it off and stuck both bare feet into his loafers. "I want you on the bed, well wrapped in the robe and doing the *Times* Sunday crossword puzzle. With a ballpoint."

Her grim expression vanished, replaced by her sunshine smile. "Blasé and bored, right?"

"Exactly," Haynes said, rose, found the crossword puzzle and handed it to her along with a ballpoint pen. She rearranged the pillows, settled cross-legged onto the bed, tucked the robe carefully around her, glanced at the puzzle, then looked up at Haynes and asked, "What does whoever he is want?"

"He wants to offer me a lot of money."

"For Steady's memoirs?"

Haynes nodded.

"Will you take it?"

"I don't know."

"When will you know?"

"Maybe tomorrow—or the next day."

She gave him a sudden smile that Haynes thought was full of childlike anticipation—her can't-wait smile.

"God, this is interesting," said Erika McCorkle.

199

* * *

Exactly ten minutes after Haynes had hung up the telephone, there was a soft knock at the door. He opened it to admit the courtly Hamilton Keyes, carrying a gabardine topcoat and still wearing his old tweed jacket, corduroy pants, pink shirt and ancient loafers.

Once inside, Keyes's glance flickered past Erika McCorkle to inventory the room itself, noting the wheeled table, the female clothing draped carelessly over a wingback chair, the bucket of melting ice, the half-full glasses and the two empty miniature bottles of vodka and Scotch. Done with his survey, he turned to Haynes and said, "I'm Hamilton Keyes. I knew your father."

After a nod from Haynes that was mere acknowledgment and nothing more, Keyes turned to Erika McCorkle, who still sat cross-legged on the bed, obviously engrossed in her puzzle. "I also know your father slightly, Miss McCorkle."

"How nice," she said without looking up.

"Have a chair," Haynes said, wondering how Hamilton Keyes had managed to identify Erika so quickly.

The courtly man chose the chair draped with female clothing. He picked it up, a piece at a time, placed it on top of the mini-refrigerator, sat down, topcoat in his lap, and said, "As I mentioned, I also know Michael Padillo."

Haynes was now leaning his rear against the sill of the window that overlooked 14th Street. "Who else?"

"Quite a few people across the street in the National Press Building—many of whom, I'm afraid, keep binoculars in their desk drawers."

Realizing he had just been given a polite, if oblique, reply to his unasked question about how Erika McCorkle had been so quickly identified, Haynes abandoned the windowsill, drew the curtains, crossed to the writing desk and leaned against that.

"Tell me," he said. "Are you the guy who can say yes or no?"

"I am, providing you're the guy who has something to sell."

"Steady left his memoirs to me in his will. The copyright to them anyhow."

"Have you read the manuscript?"

"Some of it."

"And do you still think it might make a motion picture?"

"All-American boy—Steady, of course—turns badass mercenary agent. That's one film they won't have to clutter up with a lot of boring cold-war spy crap."

"But surely not yet another dreary motion picture with no hero?"

"There'll be a hero: Steady's kid, the overeducated, ex-L.A. homicide cop who backtracks Steady's life while hunting down whoever killed his old man's two best friends. And if Steady and Undean weren't really all that friendly, well, we can fudge it a little."

"I presume you'd play both Steady and yourself?"

"My catapult to stardom."

"Well, I must say you do resemble him—in more than one respect." Keyes looked away and rested his eyes on Erika McCorkle. He was still looking at her when he said, "How much?"

"The same price I quoted Undean," said Haynes. "Seven hundred and fifty thousand."

"A very respectable sum," Keyes said, now looking at Haynes.

"For a very hot property. It's so hot that Steady wasn't three hours in his grave before somebody was offering me a hundred thousand for it."

"Which you rejected?"

"Yes."

"And demanded how much instead?"

"Half a million."

"And what was the reaction to your counterproposal?"

"They said they'd get back to me tomorrow."

"They?"

"They."

"And if *they* do offer you five hundred thousand?"

"I'll tell them I've since been offered seven hundred and fifty thousand," said Haynes with the charming smile that made him so resemble his dead father. "I have been offered seven fifty, haven't I, Mr. Keyes?"

"Yes. Providing I have last refusal."

"The right to top any bid, whatever it is?"

Keyes nodded.

"Okay," Haynes said. "You have it."

"What precisely am I buying?" Keyes asked. "And please be specific."

"World rights to everything. No exclusions. Full copyright. Which means nobody can legally use a word of it without your permission."

"How many Xerox copies are floating around?"

"No idea."

"Who'll conduct the bidding?"

"Howard Mott, Steady's lawyer and now mine."

"How?"

"By phone, I suppose."

"Oh," Keyes said, sounding less than pleased.

"You want everybody in the same room?"

"I'd have no objection."

"They might."

"Very well, by phone then," Keyes said. "What about payment?"

"What d'you suggest?"

"It can be deposited in any currency you choose in virtually any bank in the world."

"The IRS wouldn't like that, so make it a certified U.S. dollars check."

"Then you intend to pay taxes on it," Keyes said.

"Disappointed?"

"Not in the least. It means we'll be getting some of it back." Keyes rose and handed Haynes a card. "Please ask Mr. Mott to call me at my home number once the bidding arrangements are completed."

"Okay."

Keyes went to the door, turned back and, nodding farewell to each in turn, said, "Mr. Haynes. Miss McCorkle."

Erika McCorkle looked up from her crossword puzzle. "What's a five-letter word for blackguard that begins with a *k*?"

"I tried 'knave' this morning," said Hamilton Keyes. "And it worked quite nicely." He opened the door and left, closing it softly behind him.

Thirty

Rumor insisted that it all began on a gloomy Bay of Pigs Sunday afternoon in 1961 when two depressed mid-level CIA careerists left the Old Executive Office Building next to the White House and, desperate for drink, wandered by chance into a dingy bar-cafe hard by the now demolished Roger Smith Hotel at 18th and Pennsylvania.

Once inside, the careerists were pleasantly surprised to discover they could buy coffee cups of Scotch whisky in direct violation of the District of Columbia's since-repealed Sunday prohibition law. It was shortly after this discovery that members of the capital's intelligence and freebooter community made the scofflaw bar their unofficial rendezvous. They continued to drink, if not eat, there for nearly fourteen years until that day in 1975 when the last helicopter lifted off the roof of the U.S. embassy in Saigon.

The next day, as if compelled by some migratory instinct, they abandoned the bar back of the Roger Smith and trekked a few blocks farther west out Pennsylvania Avenue to another gin mill not quite opposite the now vanished Circle Theatre. And it was here, in what was always called "the new joint," that five years later they held their notorious eighteen-hour-long postmortem on the botched U.S. hostage rescue mission that had ended with death and, some claimed, dishonor in a Persian desert.

It turned out to be less of a postmortem than a verbal brawl that began around noon and was still raging at 5:57 the next morning when Metropolitan Police, summoned by shouts, yells, oaths and the sound of breaking glass, arrived, closed the new joint down and sent everyone home in taxis.

A week after the disastrous postmortem session, they migrated yet again, this time far, far out Wisconsin Avenue, almost to the Maryland state line, where scouts had discovered a nearly bankrupt Thai restaurant called Pong's Palace that was located in a strip mall and offered the four prime requisites: a valid liquor license, few customers, bad food and ample parking. Two weeks later, by silent acclamation, Pong's Palace was elected to serve as the third unofficial sub-rosa watering hole.

The dark green seventeen-year-old Mercedes 280 SL turned into a parking space three doors up from Pong's and came to a stop in front of Naughty Marietta's XXX Video Shoppe. After the car's engine was cut and its lights switched off, the driver's door opened and Michael Padillo got out. McCorkle emerged from the passenger side a moment later. When they reached the entrance to Pong's Palace, Padillo went in first.

When he opened the Palace in 1978, Pong had devoted most of its interior to a dining area, leaving only enough space for a small bar with a few stools where customers could have a drink while waiting for their tables.

But there had never been any waiting because there had never been any customers except for a few neighborhood ancients who didn't much care what they ate as long as it was cheap and filling. Pong was seriously considering bankruptcy when the first of the scouts arrived.

The scouts were a clutch of white-haired OSS relics from the Second World War and the cold one that was its substitute. They were quickly followed by the assessors. These were prosperous-looking, gray-haired ex-Kennedy operatives, who still seemed to come in only two models, hearty or smooth.

After the assessors made their favorable report, the others descended on Pong's. The largest contingent was composed of ex-CIA types (most of them dumped by Jimmy Carter) who, if pressed, admitted they still might be willing to do a little of this or a little of that. Right behind them came the new bunch—survivors of the longest war—whose thousand-yard stares had then been reduced by a third or even by half, and who kept asking everyone whether the jungles of Central America could really be all that fucking different from those of Southeast Asia.

Two months after what Pong and his wife always referred to as the invasion of *les anciens espions,* the Palace's books were in the black. Pong quickly transformed the large dining area into a large drinking area; installed a much longer bar and fired his chef, replacing him with a microwave oven and a steady supply of almost edible frozen pizzas. He also hired his wife's three pretty cousins to serve as barmaids. The cousins spoke little English but it didn't seem to matter because many of *les anciens espions* spoke a semblance of French and a few even knew some Thai.

McCorkle and Padillo didn't have to wait for their eyes to adjust inside Pong's Palace, where the dominant colors were firecracker red and grass green and where it was always afternoon bright. As usual, most of the customers were intelligence types, past and present. There were also some mercenary hangers-on, hustling their suspect services. Unacknowledged accomplices were represented by an assortment of co-opted reporters and ambitious congressional committee staff members.

At the rear of the Palace two tables had been pushed together to accommodate seven men who sat, three to a side, with the seventh man at the far end, his back to the wall. The seventh man was a fortyish big-shouldered redhead whose bright pink skin and green eyes almost allowed him to blend in with Pong's color scheme. The redhead now looked up, saw McCorkle and Padillo, and invited them over with a grin and a beckoning wave.

The noise in Pong's was that of a cocktail party that had lasted ninety minutes too long. Padillo raised his voice to make himself heard. "We might as well start with Warnock."

McCorkle agreed with a nod and a near shout. "I'll pay the courtesy call." He crossed to the bar and smiled at the small man who presided behind the cash register near the entrance. "How's business, Billy?"

"It sucks. And yours?"

"Also."

Billy Pong's grin was gleeful. "We both a couple of fancy-pantsy liars, huh, Mac?"

Matching Pong's grin, McCorkle said, "Still following Padillo's advice—all cash, no plastic or checks?"

"What's a check?" said Pong.

After McCorkle rejoined Padillo, they made their way past serious and even devout drinkers, some of them occasional customers at Mac's Place. A few looked up to shoot quick baleful glances at Padillo.

McCorkle had seen these same baleful glares on other occasions although Padillo apparently hadn't noticed—or pretended he hadn't. The glares came from men in their late fifties and early sixties who had known Padillo in the old days and now glared at him with envy, malice and even outrage.

McCorkle interpreted the glares as accusations that charged Padillo with having stolen the secret of eternal middle age—if not of youth itself—and since he obviously

207

wasn't going to share his secret with anyone, the glares said he should be arrested, tried, convicted and maybe even hanged. McCorkle always thought of them as the Dorian Gray glares and noticed with some regret that none ever came his way.

When they reached the pushed-together tables, Harry Warnock, the redheaded man, stood up with yet another grin and a few happy nods of welcome. He then scowled at the six still seated men and said, "Move down, you lot, and give the new lads a place to sit."

The six men, each of them either big or enormous, and all of them in their thirties or early forties, made the move without complaint. Padillo took the chair on Harry Warnock's right; McCorkle on his left. One of the pretty cousins hurried over to take the order. Padillo stirred the air with a forefinger, signalling another round for all, and then whispered something in French that made the cousin laugh.

After she left, Warnock said with an Irish lilt that came and went like the tide, "What'd you say to the lass, Michael? I could use a giggle myself."

"I told her that because I had to drive my father here home, I'd like some chilled Evian water in a martini glass."

Warnock stared at McCorkle. "Has he gone teetotal on us, Mac?"

"No, but he has been getting notional."

"Well, since it's himself who's buying, I'd best make introductions. Okay, lads, the generous one's Mike and the other's Mac. Now, starting on my left and going clockwise is Mr. Stroh, Mr. Ranier, Mr. Jax, Mr. Pabst, Mr. Schlitz and, lemme think now, Mr. Coors."

"Why didn't you just number them, Harry?" McCorkle said.

"Because I'm not at all sure they can count to six."

The six big men grinned and elbowed each other in appreciation of their leader's wit. A couple of them were still grinning when the pretty cousin returned and served the new round of drinks. Padillo gave her three $20 bills and waved away the change.

When she was gone, Warnock picked up Padillo's glass, sniffed its contents and announced, "Pure gin."

Padillo picked up the drink Warnock had put down, tasted it and said, "She must've made a mistake. Either that or I lied."

McCorkle smiled reassuringly at Warnock. "As I said, Harry, he's getting a little notional."

"I'll not be playing any of your mind-fucking games this night, Michael Padillo. So let's get to what really brings the pair of you out to the far edge of town on this cold and miserable Sunday."

"My wife's in Frankfurt," McCorkle said.

"Ah, well, then, had I known she was there and you were here, I'd've been there."

"That's very thoughtful of you," McCorkle said.

Padillo sipped a little more of his gin and said, "How's business, Harry? Are the terrorists taking Sunday nights off these days?"

Warnock sighed. "Business isn't what it was, Michael, and that's a fact. I blame some of the fall-off on the drop in oil prices which made a lot of my Arab clients cut back on security. But I blame most of it on Gorbachev himself and all that sweetness-and-light preaching of his. Jesus, it was but three, four years ago we had Libyan hit squads, sneaking across the borders up in Canada or down in Mexico, heading for the White House itself. My business shot up forty-two percent in that month alone." He sighed again. "We'll not be seeing the likes of those good times again."

"The cold war's over then?" McCorkle asked.

"Course it is. It's just that the old dears who'd counted on apprenticing their sons and grandsons to the military-industrial trade are too stubborn to admit it—and who can blame 'em, say I?"

"Heard about Steady Haynes?" Padillo asked.

"I hear he died broke and the government had to bury him."

"He left a little something," Padillo said.

"Debts?"

"His memoirs."

Warnock yawned. "I'll wait for the paperback."

"Remember Isabelle Gelinet?" Padillo said. "I sent her to you when she was still with AF-P and researching a story on old Bill Casey. She said you were helpful."

"What about Isabelle?"

"She helped Steady write his memoirs."

"She's also dead," Warnock said. "Somebody drowned her in her bath and before you ask me how I know what wasn't in the papers, I'll tell you it was Tinker Burns who found her and 'twas him who told me."

"Tinker in the market for some protection?" Padillo asked.

"Old Tinker and I go back a few miles, we do," Warnock said. "He made a nice bit of money off me, as well you know."

"Off the IRA," Padillo said.

"'Twas one and the same."

"Then."

Warnock shrugged. "That's right. Then."

McCorkle said, "After you defected from the IRA—"

"I never defected," Warnock said. "I deserted."

"Right. After you deserted and went into business, I seem to remember you sent out a rather fancy announcement."

"All it said was that Warnock and Associates were a new security consultant firm, specializing in antiterrorism."

"Wasn't there a line at the bottom in italics about 'Twenty Years Experience with the IRA'?"

"The best fucking credentials I could have," Warnock said.

"What I've always been curious about," McCorkle said, "is who were the associates in Warnock and Associates back then? One day, Harry, you're a room-and-a-half office on the wrong side of Fourteenth Street and three weeks later you're half a floor at Nineteenth and M. Who furnished the clout? Bill Casey? The National Security Council. The Saudis?"

"If you're looking to hire me, Mr. McCorkle, sir, I've got many a fine reference you'll be able to examine once a fee is agreed upon."

"We *are* in the market for some security stuff," McCorkle said.

"Is it your place you want swept then?"

"We're concerned about Steady's kid," Padillo said. "Except he's no kid. Thirty-two or -three. Around in there. Steady left him the copyright to the memoirs. And the kid, Granville, has decided to sell them to a private collector instead of trying to get them published. He's asked us to sort of look after him until the memoirs are sold."

Warnock gave his six associates a warning stare. "You're not hearing a word of this, are you?"

Mr. Coors said, "No, sir. Not a word."

Looking first at McCorkle, then at Padillo, Warnock said, "The kid wants you to baby-sit him?"

"To mind how he goes," Padillo said.

"A bit of money involved, is there?"

"Three quarters of a million," McCorkle said. "At least. Maybe more."

The surprise that raced across Warnock's wide pink face quickly changed into shock and then into anger. "What the fuck did Steady know that's worth that?" he demanded. "He was never in on the real shit. He was always farting about in Africa or the Middle East or Central America—or out there in Southeast Slopeland doing his truth-juggling act. So what shocking revelations does old Steady have to tell? The CIA ran drugs, did it? Well, who the fuck cares? That they did in the Congo's Lumumba, or had him done, along with maybe three or four dozen others over the years? So what? That they've kept a prime minister, a premier, a king or two and God knows how many other despots and satraps on their payroll? Who gives a shit? Christ, this country of yours lets some half-baked light-colonel run it's so-called foreign policy out of the White House annex and when he's caught, you turn him into a fucking hero. So why'd anyone give a good goddamn about the memoirs of a nobody called Steady Haynes? And what could old Steady possibly invent half as dirty as what's really happened? And who the fuck'll pay three quarters of a million for it?"

Warnock glared up at the ceiling, as if the answer might be written there. He then brought his glare down to aim it first at McCorkle, then Padillo. "It just doesn't parse."

In a very quiet voice Padillo said, "What do you care whether it parses or not?"

Cocking his head to the left, Warnock leaned back in his chair to study Padillo. The examination went on long enough for the bright red in his face to vanish, replaced by its normal pink. "Well, now, Michael, you struck a nerve, you did. And you're right, of course. All I care about is how much you're willing to pay me."

"Your going rate," McCorkle said. "Less the usual professional discount."

"No discounts to the trade," Warnock said, still staring at Padillo.

"I had to try," McCorkle said.

"So who's the package to be, Michael? Steady's kid, what's his name, Granville?"

"McCorkle and I are the package," Padillo said. "If anybody comes for Granville, they'll have to go through us. But McCorkle's gone soft and I've lost a step, so to get to us, Harry, they'll have to go through you."

Utter skepticism spread across Warnock's face and crept into his tone. "When'll you know for certain that it's on?"

"Tomorrow," McCorkle said. "Tuesday at the latest."

"Who's the opposition?"

"We don't know."

"Foreign or domestic?"

"We don't know that either," Padillo said. "Does it matter?"

Warnock smiled. "Would I be telling you if it did, Michael?"

Thirty-one

The trunk lid of the Mercedes coupe was open and one of the thieves, bent over, was rummaging around inside. The other thief, half in, half out of the open passenger door, was rifling the glove compartment. Padillo automatically noticed the slit in his car's convertible top and berated himself for not having switched to the steel top on November 1.

He waited as McCorkle, ducking low, slipped around the rear of four parked cars and came up behind the thief at the open trunk. McCorkle glanced back, got a nod from Padillo, took three long quick steps and slammed the trunk lid down on the thief's back. The thief yelled. He yelled a second time when McCorkle raised the trunk lid and slammed it down again. There was a third yell when McCorkle, using the rear bumper as a stepping-stool, sat on the trunk lid, all 221 pounds of him.

At the first yell, the thief rifling the glove compartment had backed hastily out of the car's open right-hand door and turned, only to run his right cheek just below the eye into the point of a Swiss Army knife's longest blade. The thief crossed his eyes, trying to see what kind of knife it was, but gave up when Padillo used the knife point to turn him around until he faced the car.

"Hands on the roof, feet spread, just like always," Padillo said.

When the thief hesitated, Padillo touched the knife point to the back of the man's neck. "If you try anything brave or dumb, the knife'll go in exactly four centimeters and, unless I miss, you'll be a vegetable. If I miss, you'll be dead."

The thief leaned against the car, moved his feet back and spread them apart. Padillo searched him quickly and found a .25-caliber Beretta semiautomatic in an ankle holster. As Padillo rose, the thief in the trunk yelled something that may have been a plea. McCorkle replied by bouncing up and down once on the trunk lid.

Padillo closed the Swiss Army knife and returned it to his pocket. He then touched the muzzle of the Beretta to the back of the leaning thief's neck and said, "Now turn around and tell him what I've got."

The leaning thief turned and called, "He's got my piece, Marv!"

"Lemme out!" Marv yelled.

McCorkle jumped down from the trunk, raised its lid, put a lock on Marv's right arm, pulled him out of the trunk and marched him over to Padillo. Tears rolled down Marv's cheeks toward a fixed smile that displayed a great deal of gum.

"Big bastards, aren't they?" McCorkle said.

Padillo looked at the man with the apparently perpetual smile. "You're Mr. Schlitz, right? And your partner here's Mr. Pabst."

Schlitz's tears had stopped but the smile was still in place as he nodded. Mr. Pabst wiped his tiny nose with the back of an immense hand.

"Something funny?" McCorkle asked the smiling Schlitz.

215

Schlitz shook his head but the smile didn't go away. Pabst said, "He can't help it. It's a nervous thing."

"Reflex," Schlitz explained, still smiling. "A nervous reflex."

"What did Harry Warnock say to look for in my car?" Padillo asked.

Pabst shook his head and said, "You're not gonna shoot us."

"What you mean is I'm not going to kill you," Padillo said. "But try this on: a citizen comes out of a bar and finds two thieves stealing his car. The citizen takes a pistol away from one of the thieves and shoots him in the knee. The other thief comes down with a sudden case of good sense and surrenders. Think the cops will like that?"

"They'll love it," McCorkle said. "But how do you decide whose knee?"

"Flip a coin and let them call it."

"And the one who loses the call loses the kneecap," said McCorkle, nodding judiciously. "It's only fair."

"Harry didn't send us," Pabst said.

"No?" Padillo said. "Who did?"

"Nobody."

"Flip the coin," Padillo said to McCorkle.

"We heard you talking about the book," Schlitz said, hurrying to get the words out. "The memoirs." His smile was back after disappearing momentarily when he closed his lips to say the *b*'s and the *m*'s.

"Why'd you think the memoirs would be in my car?"

"The way you were talking in there," Schlitz said. "You were talking real money, three quarters of a mill or more, so we figured you'd keep the thing close by."

"How'd you know this was my car?"

"When you and him were in the head, we asked Pong what kind of cars you guys drive. He said he didn't know about your partner here, but you always drove a real old dark green Mercedes coupe. It wasn't hard to spot."

"And what were you going to do with the manuscript?" McCorkle asked.

Pabst shrugged. "Sell it back to you."

"For how much?"

"We hadn't got that far."

His disbelief obvious, Padillo said, "And you thought all this up in the five minutes it took us to pee and tell Billy Pong goodbye?"

"If you get an idea, you gotta go with it," Schlitz said.

McCorkle reached Schlitz with a single step. "I'd better pop this liar back in the trunk while you kneecap the other one."

The words came tumbling out of Pabst's mouth, tripping over themselves. "Tinker Burns," he said. "We were gonna take the thing to Tinker Burns."

Padillo looked first at McCorkle, who raised an eyebrow that managed to express doubt, surprise and even a little disappointment. Padillo looked back at Pabst. "From the beginning," he said and glanced at his watch. "We've got all night."

It didn't take all night. It took only fourteen minutes for Pabst and Schlitz, sometimes interrupting and contradicting each other, to describe how Tinker Burns had hired them through Harry Warnock for a vague one-shot that might involve a little breaking and entering.

After first complaining about how little they had been paid, $2,000 apiece, they described how they had shot Steadfast Haynes's horse, broken into his farmhouse, searched it and bound and gagged "some woman" who walked in on them. But they vehemently denied—despite repeated questions from Padillo and threats from McCorkle—that they had found any trace of the Haynes manuscript.

"What'd Tinker say when you told him all this?" McCorkle said.

"He was sort of pissed off," Pabst said.

"If you think he was pissed off, imagine what Harry Warnock's going to be when I tell him I caught you burgling my car." Padillo paused. "And why."

Schlitz's eyes darted quickly away to his left. Pabst stared down at the parking lot asphalt.

"Harry's mean," McCorkle said, making it sound as if he were musing aloud. "And he also knows all those IRA interrogation techniques. The nasty stuff. The first thing he'll probably ask you is whether you're really working for him or for Tinker Burns. And no matter what you tell him, he'll have to make sure you're not lying."

Pabst, still staring at the asphalt, muttered, "Harry don't have to know."

"Sorry?" Padillo said.

Pabst looked up. "I said Harry won't know if you don't tell him."

"Why wouldn't I tell him? You sliced my car top. But Harry won't pay for it unless I tell him what you two did and why."

"Maybe we could work it out," Schlitz said with a broad smile utterly lacking in confidence.

"How?"

"I mean if you guys need something done, well, maybe we could do it and that'd sort of pay for your car top and then Harry wouldn't have to know about this."

Padillo studied Schlitz for a moment before asking, "Does Tinker Burns worry either of you?"

"Nope," Pabst said. It was a quick answer and McCorkle thought it was probably far too quick.

"Then you wouldn't mind lying to him, would you?" Padillo said.

After a cautious nod, Pabst said, "Go on."

"We want you to call Tinker at his hotel," Padillo said. "If he's not there, leave a message. The message will say only that you've learned that McCorkle and Padillo have the Haynes manuscript. That's all. But if Tinker himself answers the phone, tell him you were at Pong's with Harry Warnock and the lads and heard talk that McCorkle and I have the Haynes manuscript. When Tinker asks for details, tell him that's all you know. Absolutely all."

It was Schlitz who repeated a reasonably close version of the instructions and asked, "When d'you want us to call him?"

"Now," Padillo said.

"I'll use your car phone."

"I don't have a car phone."

Not bothering to conceal his astonishment, Schlitz said, "Jesus, everybody's got a—"

"I don't," Padillo said.

"He doesn't have a fax machine either," McCorkle said.

"Well," Schlitz said, "I guess we can use the phone in my car."

After McCorkle knocked on the hotel room door, it was opened by his daughter, who apparently wore nothing other than a man's white oxford shirt and it rather loosely buttoned.

"They have house phones in the lobby," she said.

"We can wait out here till you get—"

McCorkle was interrupted by Granville Haynes's voice from behind the partially open door. "Who is it?"

"It's Pop and the old guy who rides shotgun."

"Then ask them in."

"You're invited," she said, walked away from the half-open door and disappeared into the bathroom.

McCorkle entered the room, followed by an amused-looking Padillo. Once inside, McCorkle turned slowly, nodding at Haynes, who wore pants, shirt and loafers, but no socks. McCorkle continued his slow turn, noting the room-service cart, the empty and half-empty glasses, the discarded copies of the Sunday *Washington Post* and *New York Times*, the rumpled bed and, finally, Padillo's amused expression.

"What's so funny?" McCorkle said.

"Outraged fathers are always funny."

219

"Who says I'm outraged?"

"Your choleric flush."

"Care for a drink?" Haynes said.

McCorkle turned to stare at him. "Care? No. Need? Yes."

"Scotch, vodka, beer, what?"

"Scotch."

"Mr. Padillo?"

"Nothing, thanks."

"You may need one after you hear about our threatening phone call."

"Who from?"

"Since Erika took the call, I'll let her tell it."

After the drinks were poured and served, Erika McCorkle came out of the bathroom, wearing pants and over them the man's white shirt, now buttoned except for the collar button and the one just below it. She went to the mini-refrigerator, removed a can of beer, popped it open and drank thirstily. She then turned to her father and said, "Okay. Let's have it."

McCorkle took another look around the room. "I suppose this is as good a way as any to spend a long Sunday afternoon. Your mother and I used to spend them like this in Bonn a hundred years ago. Usually out at her place in Tannenbusch. She lived in a one-room studio on the top floor of a *Hochhaus* with a view of the Rhine and the Drachenfels. Padillo always opened up on Sundays, so I'd drop by Fredl's around noon with a bottle of wine or two and a couple of steaks. People still ate steak then. Fredl would read the papers, all six or seven of them, and after that we'd talk and fool around, then eat, and talk and maybe even fool around some more. Around six or seven I'd drive out to Godesberg to take over from Padillo. Sometimes she'd come with me."

"She came with you most of the time," Padillo said.

McCorkle nodded. "I guess she did."

"You two weren't married then?" Erika asked.

"Not even engaged."

"How old was she?"

"Fredl? Twenty-four, twenty-five."

"And you?"

McCorkle looked at Haynes, who was leaning against the windowsill again and wearing what seemed to be a look of polite sympathy. "Thirty-two, thirty-three," McCorkle said. "Around in there."

"This was the late fifties?"

"The late, late fifties."

"You and Mutti never talk about it, do you?"

"Not much."

"He's not talking about it now," Padillo said.

"Then what's he saying?"

"For Christsake, Gurgles," Padillo said.

"Don't call me that."

"Gurgles?" Haynes asked.

"When she was learning to talk," Padillo said, "she couldn't quite handle Erika McCorkle and it came out Erigga McGurgle. I called her Gurgles until she turned six and made me stop."

"That still doesn't explain what Pop was saying."

Padillo shrugged. "Ask him."

She turned to McCorkle. "Well, what was it—a roundabout invitation to join the grown-ups?"

"Who wants that?"

"What then?"

"I think it was a promise," McCorkle said.

"What kind of promise?"

"That next time I'll use the house phone."

Wearing her sunshine smile, she hurried over to McCorkle, went up on tiptoe, kissed him and, still smiling, turned to Granville Haynes and said, "You can tell we're a very demonstrative family."

"If the demonstration's over, maybe you should tell the family about the threatening phone call."

She turned automatically to Padillo, as if he were the usual receiver of bad news. "Mr. Tinker Burns called," she said. "About twenty or thirty minutes before you got here. He was looking for you and Pop. After I told him we didn't know where you were, he asked—no, he told me to give you a message. I asked him to hold on while I got something to write with. But he said I wouldn't need anything because his message was short and simple."

"And was it?" Padillo said. "Short and simple?"

She nodded. "Mr. Burns told me to tell you that unless you let him look at Steady's manuscript, he's going to break your fucking necks. Or have it done."

Thirty-two

The four of them traded information for the next twenty minutes. Haynes and Erika went first with their account of Hamilton Keyes's offer of $750,000 for all rights to the still unfound, unread memoirs of Steadfast Haynes. McCorkle and Padillo then described events leading up to their encounter outside Pong's Palace with Mr. Schlitz and Mr. Pabst.

After that they went back over everything—poking at this, recalling that and speculating about other just-remembered bits and pieces, most of them inconsequential, until they suddenly stopped when it became apparent they were getting nowhere. A silence began and lasted nearly two minutes before it was ended by Granville Haynes.

"Since Tinker's obviously got his own deal going," Haynes said, "I think I'll drop by his hotel around two-thirty or three tomorrow morning and ask him what it is."

"He won't tell you," Padillo said.

"His lies might tell me something."

"Gestapo stuff," Erika said.

It wasn't much of a smile that Haynes gave her. "Tonight

the knock on the door, tomorrow the national I.D. card. Where will it all end?"

"You tell me, sunshine."

"Don't worry about Tinker's civil rights or liberties," Mc-Corkle told Haynes. "If you go knocking on his door in the small hours, he won't open it unless it's to tell you to buzz off."

"Maybe he still thinks there's such a thing as the right to privacy," Erika said.

"Privacy vanished with the arrival of the driver's license, the Social Security number and the credit card," Haynes said.

"What about the right to be left alone?" she said.

"It no longer exists—if it ever did."

"And you think that's just wonderful, don't you?"

"You haven't a clue to what I think," Haynes said.

"I think I'll go home," McCorkle said before his daughter could either reply or explode. He rose, looked at her and asked, "Coming?"

"You bet," she said.

The four of them stood silently just inside the Willard lobby, waiting for Erika's aging Cutlass to be brought around from the hotel garage. She stared at Pennsylvania Avenue through the glass door, ignoring the three men. They in turn ignored her silent rage.

When her car arrived, Haynes said, "I'll call you tomorrow."

"Why?" she said and pushed through the glass door.

McCorkle gave Haynes a small baffled smile and hurried after his ride home.

Padillo watched them go, turned to Haynes and asked, "Hungry?"

Haynes had to think about it. "Yes."

"Let's eat then."

By 9 P.M. there were only a dozen or so diners left in Mac's Place. The bar, however, was lined with drinkers, quietly stoking up for the Monday to come. Padillo chose a booth instead of his regular table near the kitchen. He and Haynes were just settling into it when Herr Horst slow-marched over to announce that Tinker Burns had been in twice, demanding to see either Padillo or McCorkle.

"Sober?" Padillo asked.

"Sober-mean."

"Any message?"

"I believe he intends to do you both grave bodily harm."

Padillo nodded, as if at old news, and asked, "What's good tonight?"

"The duck," Herr Horst said. "With wild rice and an exceptionally tasty cucumber and limestone lettuce salad."

Padillo looked at Haynes. "You like duck?"

"Duck's fine."

"An aperitif, Mr. Haynes?" Herr Horst asked.

"A vermouth, please."

Herr Horst looked inquiringly at Padillo, who said he'd like a sherry.

After the drinks were served and Haynes took his first sip of vermouth, he said, "Hamilton Keyes says he knows you."

"He drops by now and then."

"For conversation or food?"

"He likes to talk about wine, but never about his job or his wife."

"What's wrong with his wife?"

"Nothing—except that when I knew her a long time ago she was still Muriel Lamphier."

"Lamphier as in Crown-Lamphier?"

Padillo nodded.

"What's a long time ago?"

"Seventeen, eighteen years back."

"What happened?"

"Why?"

Haynes smiled his inherited smile. "Just routine."

"You seem a hell of a lot more routinely interested in Mrs. Keyes than Mr. Keyes."

"I'm interested in money. It makes me curious. I'm especially curious about a guy who walks into my hotel room and in front of a witness offers me three quarters of a million for all rights to some memoirs that he hasn't read and probably don't even exist. He claims he's offering me government money. Now I hear he's married to the Lamphier in Crown-Lamphier, which used to make a third or maybe half of this country's glass, but diversified into electronics, paper, solvents and, for all I know, catfish farming. The former Muriel Lamphier is major money. Keyes married it. You dated it. And my first question is did she and Steady ever have something going?"

Padillo shook his head. "The only connection I know of between her and Steady is that her husband was Steady's last handler at the agency—or as much of a handler as Steady ever put up with."

"How do you know that?"

Padillo was silent for a moment, trying to remember. "Isabelle told me."

Haynes finished his vermouth and said, "Mind talking about it?"

"About Muriel and me?"

Haynes nodded.

Padillo hesitated, then said, "Well, why not? Back then she was twenty-four or twenty-five and I was in my forties. It only lasted a few months. She was a little too rich and a little too wild. The rich I might've handled but the wild was just so much bother. After it ended she went out to Los Angeles and fell in with what used to be called the wrong crowd. I think they all had something to do with films."

"Did she want to act?"

"She had the looks, God knows. But I don't think she really knew what she wanted. Then something happened in L.A. I don't know what. Maybe she just got bored. So she came back

226

here and went with the agency." Padillo paused. "To her it was probably just something to do."

"She have any qualifications?"

"Looks, brains, connections, sixty or seventy million dollars, good French, fair German and a degree in medieval history. You might say she and the agency made a tight fit."

A waiter came over to serve the salad. Padillo asked Haynes whether he wanted his salad now or later. Haynes said now was fine.

"Twenty years ago," Padillo said, "about fifty percent of our dinner customers ate their salads last. Now only ten percent do."

"When I first got to L.A., some places were serving frozen forks with the salad."

"Why?"

"I never asked."

They ate in silence until Haynes finished, put down his fork and said, "What'd she do at the CIA?"

"She was a field hand in operations, which is where she met Keyes. He then seemed headed for one of the top slots, maybe even deputy director, but now he's one of the might-have-beens. Karl the bartender keeps up with all this stuff and blames Keyes's fall or decline on his bald head. It's Karl's theory that if two male candidates for anything have the same qualifications, the one with the most hair wins."

"I've heard dumber theories," Haynes said. "But not many."

"Anyway, Muriel quit the agency in late seventy-four and married Keyes in seventy-five."

"She wasn't with it very long then, was she?"

"A couple of years at most."

"Ever see her around?"

"The last time was four or five years ago at a Spanish embassy party. The ambassador's sister and I were attempting a modified flamenco. Muriel came over to compliment us. After the ambassador's sister drifted away, Muriel and I had a long chat about the weather."

"She went from wild to tame?"

"So Isabelle said."

"How would she know?"

"Remember Isabelle's AF-P story that got killed?" Padillo said. "The one on Casey?"

Haynes nodded.

"While she was working on it, she decided she needed a sidebar on agency wives. Somebody suggested Muriel Keyes. After a lot of trying, Isabelle finally set up an interview and came away with forty-five taped minutes of what she called demure merde."

The duck arrived and was served with more precision than flourish by Herr Horst himself. He waited until Haynes tasted it, looked up and pronounced it marvelous. Herr Horst, smiling contentedly, turned and marched slowly away.

"You told me you still had a copy of the story Isabelle wrote," Haynes said, cutting himself another bite of duck.

"In the office."

"Can I see it?"

"It's in French."

"I think I can handle that."

"Sorry," Padillo said. "I wasn't thinking."

Herr Horst reappeared, carrying a telephone. He plugged it into a jack and placed it beside Haynes's plate. "It's Mr. Mott," Herr Horst said.

Haynes picked up the phone and said, "Yes, Howard?"

"The ex-senator just called me," Howard Mott said. "His client wants to postpone the bidding for two days. Until Wednesday."

"Why?"

"The senator says that's none of our business, but if we still want to *do* some business, we'd better agree to the postponement. I told him I'd have to check with my client."

Haynes said, "Call him back and tell him I've got a new firm offer of seven hundred and fifty thousand."

"I don't lie well enough to convince him of that."

"You don't have to. The CIA made the offer in person this afternoon in front of a witness."

"What witness?"

"Erika McCorkle."

"Ah."

"What's 'ah' mean this time?"

"It means I'll call the senator back and agree to the postponement—providing, of course, that he agrees the bidding will begin at seven hundred and fifty thousand."

"What d'you think he'll do?"

"I think that this Wednesday the senator will offer you eight hundred thousand dollars," Mott said. "The real question, of course, is what will you do?"

"See whether the CIA raises, what else?"

Thirty-three

Back in his room at the Willard Hotel, Haynes counted the rings of the phone call he was making. Halfway through the sixth ring, Howard Mott answered with a gruff hello.

After Haynes identified himself, Mott said, "Now what?"

"Suppose I wanted to find out—"

"Why don't we just skip the 'suppose'?" Mott said.

"All right. I want to find out where some CIA people worked in nineteen seventy-three and seventy-four."

"Ask the agency."

"They'd just tell me to fuck off."

"Sound advice."

Haynes said nothing, letting the silence build until Mott said, "You're serious."

"Very."

There was another silence, briefer this time, before Mott said, "I can give you a number to call."

"What about a name?"

"There's no name. Just some rigamarole."

Haynes sighed. "Okay."

"Go to a pay phone and call the number I'm going to give you. You'll reach an answering machine that'll repeat the number you've just dialed. At the sound of the beep, you say, 'Warren Oates,' read off your pay phone's number and hang up. Got it?"

"Warren Oates," Haynes said.

"Two minutes after you hang up, the pay phone will ring. Pick up just after the first ring and, instead of saying hello, say—hold on a second—"

"I say, 'Hold on a second'?"

"No, goddamnit, you don't say that. I'll tell you what to say in a moment."

In the brief silence that followed, Haynes pictured Howard Mott rummaging in the pigeonholes of his old rolltop oak desk, searching for the secret password.

Mott came back on the phone with a question. "What's the date—the twenty-ninth?"

"Right."

"Okay. New Hampshire is alphabetically the twenty-ninth state. So you say, 'Concord.'"

"Which is its capital."

"State capitals are the code of the month."

"State capitals and dead actors," Haynes said. "Then what?"

"Then you'll have thirty seconds to explain what you want."

"Who are these nuts?" Haynes asked.

This time it was Mott who sighed. "You don't want to know, Granville, and they don't want to know who you are. Think of them as misguided do-gooders. Very expensive misguided do-gooders."

"Okay," Haynes said. "What's the number I call?"

Mott spoke the number slowly, then repeated it even more slowly and hung up without saying goodbye. Haynes put down the hotel room phone, took the elevator to the lobby, got two dollars in quarters from the cashier, went to a pay phone, dropped in fifty cents, which he knew to be too much, and tapped out the number Mott had given him.

After two rings a man's recorded voice murmured the number Haynes had just dialed. At the beep, Haynes said, "Warren Oates," read off the number of his pay phone and hung up.

Two minutes later the pay phone rang. Immediately after the first ring, Haynes picked it up and said, "Concord."

A woman's voice said, "You got thirty seconds."

"I want to know where and exactly when four CIA employees were stationed in nineteen seventy-three and seventy-four. Their names are Hamilton Keyes, Steadfast Haynes, Muriel Lamphier and Gilbert Undean."

"Spell 'em," said the woman's voice.

After Haynes spelled them, she said, "We can work a whole lot faster if you know if they were stateside or overseas."

"Overseas. Maybe Laos."

"Okay. No sweat. What's the time now?"

Haynes looked at his watch. "Eleven thirty-three."

"Bring three thousand in fifties and twenties—"

"Where the hell am I going to get that at this hour?"

"That's your problem. Yes or no?"

"Yes."

"Three thousand in a sealed envelope. Connecticut and Woodley Road. Northeast corner. Second streetlight north. There'll be a big old yellow brick at its base. What you want'll be under the brick. Leave the money envelope in its place. Got it?"

"What time?"

"Two-eleven A.M. exactly. If you don't leave the money, I guarantee it'll get messy."

She hung up. Haynes pressed down on the pay phone hook, released it, dropped in another fifty cents and tapped out a different number. The voice that answered said, "Mac's Place. We're closed."

Haynes recognized the voice of Karl Triller, the head bartender. "This is Granville Haynes. Padillo still around?"

"Hold on," Triller said.

A few moments later, Padillo came on the line with, "You need something, right?"

"I need to cash a check for three thousand in twenties and fifties. Can you handle it?"

"If you hurry."

"I'll be there in ten minutes," Haynes said.

Seated on his side of the partners desk, Padillo counted $3,000 into three $1,000 piles as Haynes watched. After looking up and getting a nod from Haynes, Padillo took a plain No. 10 envelope from a desk drawer, placed the $3,000 inside and handed it to Haynes unsealed. Without recounting the money, Haynes ran his tongue over the envelope's flap and sealed it.

Padillo put Haynes's check and a thin leftover sheaf of tens, twenties, fifties and hundreds into a steel cash box, closed its lid, rose and put the box in the old safe.

"You didn't lock it," Haynes said.

"The cash box? We lost the key. But then we decided if a thief opens the safe, a cash box won't present any problem."

After closing the old safe's door and giving the combination a couple of spins, Padillo turned to Haynes and said, "Need a lift?"

"I can get a cab."

"I think you need a lift."

"I don't want to keep you up."

"I don't sleep much anymore."

Haynes smiled. "Well, maybe I could use a lift at that."

At 1:17 A.M., Padillo dropped Haynes off at Connecticut Avenue and Calvert Street, then continued out Connecticut for five blocks before he turned around, drove back down the same broad street and parked on its west side only thirty yards up and across from the streetlight where money would be swapped for information.

At 2:03 A.M., a dark blue Ford panel van stopped in front of the streetlight. Padillo couldn't tell whether the driver was a man or a woman. But when the driver didn't stir from behind the wheel, Padillo assumed someone in the van's rear was making use of the sliding door. Counting by thousands, Padillo timed the transaction at less than thirty seconds because he had just reached 28,000 when the Ford van pulled away.

At 2:09 A.M., Haynes came into view, walking north along the east sidewalk of Connecticut Avenue. By 2:11 A.M., Haynes had reached the designated streetlight. He knelt down, as if to tie a shoelace, rose, turned around and walked south, retracing his steps.

The blue van reappeared twenty seconds later. Again, the driver didn't stir from behind the wheel. Counting once more by thousands, Padillo had reached 16,000 when the van sped away from the curb and north on Connecticut.

Padillo waited four minutes, then started his aging Mercedes coupe's engine and drove south. He stopped at the stone lion at the south end and west side of Taft Bridge. Haynes opened the passenger door and got in.

"Where to?" Padillo asked.

"The Madison."

"It was a blue Ford van," Padillo said as he drove away. "It was too dark to read the license plate and I couldn't tell whether the driver was a man or a woman, but whoever it was never left the wheel. So there had to be at least two of them."

"You have a map light?" Haynes asked.

Padillo switched it on.

Haynes held a plain three-by-five-inch card to the light. The card contained four lines of typing. Haynes read them aloud:

"'Hamilton Keyes, Saigon, South Vietnam, 8-3-72 to 6-1-74.

"'Muriel Lamphier, Vientiane, Laos, 10-2-73 to 4-15-74.

"'Gilbert Undean, Vientiane, Laos, 2-13-68 to 5-1-74.

"'Steadfast Haynes, no official trace, repeat, no official trace.'"

"You spent three thousand for that?" Padillo said.

"Right."

"Why?"

"That's what I'm going to ask Tinker—among other things."

"Want me to help you ask him?"

"No need."

"I think I will anyway," Padillo said.

Thirty-four

P adillo, leaning on the counter, stared thoughtfully at the Madison Hotel front desk clerk and managed to make a quiet suggestion sound like a death threat. "Why not call him, tell him we're here and see what he says?"

The clerk swallowed, nodded, picked up a phone, tapped out a room number and listened to the rings. After what Granville Haynes guessed was the fourth ring, the clerk said, "This is Edwards at the desk, Mr. Burns. Sorry for the disturbance, but a Mr. Padillo and a Mr. Haynes insist on seeing you."

Pressing the phone tightly against his ear, as if to muffle the shouts and curses, the clerk closed his eyes and began nodding almost rhythmically. He finally stopped nodding, opened his eyes and said, "I understand perfectly, Mr. Burns."

After replacing the phone, the clerk looked first at Haynes, then at Padillo and said, "He says come up at your own risk."

Tinker Burns opened the door of his room, stepped back and silently watched Haynes enter, followed by Padillo. Haynes looked around the room, as if comparing it to his own at the Willard. After crossing to the bathroom, he switched on its light, gave it a quick inspection, switched the light off, turned, walked past Burns again, still ignoring him, picked out a chair and sat down. Padillo chose a chair on the opposite side of the room.

Tinker Burns inspected the seated Padillo first, then Haynes. He nodded, as if at the answer to some troublesome question, tightened the belt of his white terry-cloth hotel bathrobe, went on huge bare feet to the small refrigerator, took out a can of beer, opened it, drank deeply, belched loudly and sat down on the bed.

"Let's hear it, Tinker," said Haynes.

"You just did," Burns said, and belched again. "But now you've got me repeating myself."

Padillo rose, went to the refrigerator and removed two miniatures of Scotch whisky. He located a pair of glasses and used them to pour two drinks. He gave one drink to Haynes and returned to his own chair with the other. Once seated, Padillo tasted the whisky, looked at Burns and said, "I called Letty Melon just before we got here. She was still up."

"Still up and still smashed, right?"

"Not too bad," Padillo said.

"Bet you told her how I hired those two dummies who tied her up and all. Schlitz called and told me you and McCorkle've got Steady's manuscript. But that didn't make any sense because you guys wouldn't tell those two morons even if you did have it, which you don't."

"Herr Horst said you came looking for me," Padillo said. "Twice."

"I was just pissed off enough to wanta find out what you and McCorkle were up to." Burns paused, drank more beer and said, "I finally figured out you were up to nothing."

"Letty was awfully talkative," Padillo said. "But she got even more so after I told her that Schlitz and Pabst were working for you."

"Told you about that fake manuscript, did she?" Burns said.

Padillo answered with a nod. "But then she began telling me about that phone call you got in Paris just before Steady died. And that's when I turned her over to Granville."

"I didn't believe her," Haynes said. "At first."

"Don't blame you."

"It was a crazy story, Tinker, all about an old friend of yours who's now some big shot and wants a peek at Steady's memoirs just to see whether he's mentioned. Letty says that if you can swing that for him, this same very important somebody will provide you with access to an end-use certificate that'll let you dump all that left-behind Vietnam ordnance you've got rusting away in those Marseilles warehouses."

"Letty remembers pretty good," Burns said. "Even when she's deep in the sauce."

"I believed some of what she told me," Haynes said. "I believed the part about your getting a call in Paris before Steady died. But I don't believe it was from anyone you knew."

"I don't give much of a shit what you believe, Granny."

"I think the call was from somebody who wants to read Steady's memoirs—maybe even buy them. I think you got the call because you'd known Steady forever and this same somebody thought you could arrange it somehow. I think you told this somebody you'd give it a try. But before you could, Steady died on you. I think this same somebody is still willing to pay you a lot of money for either the memoirs or just a peek at them. So you flew over here for the burial to see what could be salvaged. I also think that's why you went to see Isabelle at her apartment."

Haynes paused, as if to make sure he hadn't forgotten

238

anything. "There's something else. I think, Tinker. No, I'm convinced of it. I'm convinced that if you hadn't smelled money, there'd've only been three of us at Arlington: Isabelle, Undean and me."

Burns rubbed his chin with a big hand as he studied Haynes. The palm of his hand made a slight rasping sound as it scraped across bone-white bristles.

"Know something, Granny?" Burns said. "I didn't think anybody young as you could be so fucking sanctimonious. Steady was dead. D-e-a-d. You must know what dead is. Christ, you were in the trade. Steady never expected me to show up for his funeral any more'n I'd expect him to show up for mine. But I went anyhow and why I did's none of your fucking business."

"How much did he offer you, Tinker?" Padillo said. "This somebody who called you in Paris?"

"Did somebody call me?" Burns said.

Haynes leaned forward, elbows resting on knees, both hands holding his barely tasted drink. His face suddenly seemed to acquire harsher planes and darker shadows. His stare grew bleak and his voice made each word sound like a slap.

"Butt out, Tinker," Haynes said. "They're my memoirs now. Steady left them to me in his will. I'm going to auction them off Wednesday. The bidding will start at three quarters of a million. But if you keep messing around, you'll just fuck things up. So go back to Paris, Tinker. Go home and forget about the memoirs."

Burns's old tan couldn't quite conceal the dark red flush that raced up his neck and spread to his cheeks and ears. "Who the hell're you to tell me what to do? About anything? Especially Steady. I knew him better and liked him more'n you ever did. But you waltz in here at three in the morning like God's last messenger, and who the fuck d'you bring with you? Why, it's Señor Death himself, that's who." Burns jerked a thumb at Padillo. "What d'you really know about this guy, Granny?"

"A family friend," Haynes said.

Burns grunted. "Some fucking family. Some fucking friend."

"Tell him, Tinker," Padillo said. "It might lower your blood pressure."

Burns jumped to his feet and stretched one arm out full length to aim an accusatory finger at Padillo. Haynes thought Burns's blazing eyes, quivering forefinger, bare feet and long white robe made him look rather biblical—like some ancient prophet with too much time in the wilderness.

"Know who they used to send when they needed somebody fixed?" Burns demanded. "They sent him. That's who. Michael Padillo, the assassin's assassin. How many did you fix over the years, Mike? Fifty? A hundred? Two hundred?"

Padillo smiled. "Counting the war?"

Burns opened his mouth to say or shout something. But before he could, Haynes said, "Just answer one question, Tinker. How well do you know the former Muriel Lamphier who's now Mrs. Hamilton Keyes?"

It was then that Burns warned them to get the fuck out before he called the hotel security people.

In the elevator, Haynes asked, "What was all that assassin stuff?"

"History."

"Real or invented?"

"You don't want to know."

"The hell I don't."

"Ask McCorkle."

"Does he know?"

"He knows."

"Will he tell me?"

"I have no idea."

"What about Erika?"

"I think she suspects."

"Should I ask her?"

"You can ask anyone you want to."

"Will she tell me?"

"I don't think so," Padillo said.

Padillo gave the Madison's drowsy doorman twenty dollars to let them park the old Mercedes coupe in front of the hotel's 15th Street entrance, where the big glass doors allowed them to watch the bank of pay telephones near the elevators. After they waited five minutes, Padillo said, "Maybe he used his room phone after all."

"And leave a record of the phone number on his bill?" Haynes said. "Tinker's way too cagey for that. Let's give him another ten minutes."

After two minutes of silence, Padillo said, "That was a nice performance you gave."

Haynes smiled at the praise. "You mean the way I let my paranoia peep shyly forth?"

Padillo nodded. "You must've drawn on your time with the L.A. cops. I say that because half the cops I ever met were paranoid."

"Half the cops," Haynes said, "and all the actors."

Thirty seconds later Tinker Burns came out of one of the two elevators they could see from the car and headed for the pay phones. Burns had dressed quickly and was wearing only a shirt, pants, shoes, but no socks. As he neared the pay phones, he hesitated, looked around, made a quick tour of the virtually empty lobby, then went back to the phones and dropped coins into one of them.

With Padillo's powerful binoculars now up to his eyes and the long-memorized three-across-and-four-down Touch-Tone phone pattern firmly in mind, Haynes read off the seven numbers that Burns tapped as Padillo jotted them down on the back of an envelope.

"Four. Six. Five. Nine. One. Nine. One."

241

"You're sure?" Padillo said.

"Christ, no."

"Good. I'd be a little edgy if you were."

They watched Burns talk and listen for two minutes and thirteen seconds by Padillo's watch. Burns then hung up and reentered the same, still waiting elevator. As its doors closed, Padillo said, "Any ideas?"

"About how we find out who belongs to 465–9191?"

Padillo nodded, started the engine and pulled away from the curb.

"Tonight?" Haynes asked.

"Why not?"

"I'm open to suggestions."

Padillo glanced at him. "Are you much of a mimic?"

"Try me."

"Do Tinker Burns."

Haynes closed his eyes, breathed deeply two times, opened his eyes, deepened his voice, gave it a rough edge and bellowed, "Okay! That's it! Now get the fuck outta here before I call security!"

Padillo smiled. "Perfect."

They made the call from Padillo's Foggy Bottom house. Haynes made it from the wall phone in the kitchen with Padillo on the living room extension.

After Haynes tapped out the 465–9191 number, it rang four and a half times before it was answered by a man's sleepy mumbled hello.

"Tinker Burns again," Haynes said. "There's one more thing I forgot to tell you."

"Mr. Burns, this is twice tonight that you've robbed me of sleep," said the voice that once again reminded Haynes of soothing syrup. "I assure you we can discuss it, whatever it is, when we meet tomorrow morning. And now, sir, good night."

The connection was broken. Haynes put the wall phone

back on its hook and went into the living room. Padillo turned from the extension and said, "Well?"

"One, he's a lawyer. Two, he's an ex-U.S. senator. Three, he's the guy who's been talking to Howard Mott about buying all rights to the memoirs for some anonymous client. And four, he's obviously from way down south."

"Near Mobile," Padillo said.

"Is that a guess or do you know him?"

"We've met," Padillo said.

Thirty-five

The one-term senator from Alabama practiced law in a three-story building that sat on a small triangle of land where Connecticut Avenue met 19th Street just north of Dupont Circle.

The building had once offered fine apartments, including one that a former Speaker of the House of Representatives, now dead, had lived in for years. It was still an article of faith in Washington that its weird taxicab zones had been redrawn to make sure the Speaker would pay the absolute minimum fare for his rides to and from the Capitol.

Tinker Burns paid off his own taxi, got out and examined the yellow brick building that time and smog were turning light tan. He hoped the senator hadn't chosen the building for its quaintness. Burns despised and mistrusted anything that hinted of quaint.

The senator had made his law office look as much like his Senate office as possible. There were the same dark blue leather chairs and couches, the same massive desk and, on one wall, the same rather good watercolors of Mobile Bay. The other walls were covered by either bookshelves or the

244

eighty-seven black-and-white photographs of the senator and eight-seven of his oldest and dearest friends, past and present. Some of the past friends had died and others had quickly—too quickly, some said—drifted away after the senator lost his bid for reelection in 1986.

But the photographs remained on display, offering informal portraits of the senator with three living former U.S. Presidents, one prince, six premiers, one chancellor, two prime ministers, twenty-one U.S. senators, thirteen U.S. representatives, nine state governors, three secretaries of state, five directors of Central Intelligence, one ex-President-for-Life and a five-year-old blue tick hound who was now curled up fast asleep on one of the leather couches.

The senator was on the telephone when his secretary ushered Tinker Burns into the paneled office. Burns was greeted with a warm smile and a beckoning hand that waved him silently into the most comfortable leather armchair.

Once assured that Burns was safely seated, the senator went back to his listening. He did it with his eyes closed. When open, the eyes were a remarkable blue that reminded one former Senate colleague, no admirer, of twin Neon periods.

The rest of the face was lean, maybe even skinny, with scooped-out cheeks, sharp nose, thin gray lips and a chin that came to a point. The face was topped by lank gray hair that was inexpertly cut by his wife every three weeks. The kitchen haircut and the shabby suits he wore helped foster the senator's chosen image—that of a sly rustic. At 23 and just out of law school, he had nicknamed himself Rube. Now 53, he still liked to be called that by close friends.

The senator stopped listening, opened his eyes and spoke into the phone. "I respect that, Frank, but we've still got a long way to go before we get to the well. Lemme call you back later today . . . Yes, sir, I'll surely do that . . . G'bye."

The senator put the phone back into its nook on the

console and rose, right hand extended. "Mr. Burns. Sorry to be so rude."

Burns half rose, gave the offered hand a quick shake and sat back down, confining his greeting to, "How you doing?"

"Not too sure," the senator said, resuming his seat. "Not too sure at all. I was kind of hoping you could let me know."

"I'm going to tell you what I think, Senator, and then I'm going to tell you what I know."

"Logic would dictate the other way around but you just go right ahead."

"I think Steady and Isabelle never wrote any memoirs, never intended to write any and that the whole thing's been a shuck from start to finish."

The senator stuck out his lower lip and nodded judiciously. "Early this morning—very early, I might add—you called to tell me you'd met with Letitia Melon, the former Mrs. Steadfast Haynes, and that she'd given you something 'important,' I believe you said."

"Yeah. She gave me a copy of Steady's manuscript that turned out to be three hundred and eighty-something mostly blank pages."

"And from this you reason there is not now, nor has there ever been, a true manuscript?"

"I knew Steady a long, long time and I knew Isabelle all her life. What I'm pretty sure they did was hole up at Steady's farm and map the whole thing out."

"The shuck—not the manuscript?"

"Yeah. Then right before the inauguration, they check into the Hay-Adams and start spreading the word around town that Steady's just finished his red-hot memoirs and needs a permanent seat at the North trial because it's gonna provide him with the epilogue for his book. Now lemme ask you this: was Steady really trying to end his book, or was he trying to scare the shit out of somebody?"

"An interesting question."

"I say he was trying to scare the shit out of somebody," Burns said. "Your client."

"We will not discuss my client, Mr. Burns."

"Okay. Fine. Then let's discuss Steady's kid and his backup, the grim reaper, who came pounding on my door at three o'clock this morning just like they were the Gestapo or the fucking FBI making a house call."

"The grim reaper?"

"Michael Padillo. Know him?"

"We've met."

"I imagine you have," Burns said, paused and then continued. "Anyway, they barge in and start their rain dance that's supposed to make me wet my drawers. And I've gotta admit, it's not bad. Padillo can just sit there, saying nothing, and make you believe he's gonna bite your nose off. And Granny, well, he's the big bass drum, the talker, the one who tells you to get outta town. Mr. Deadly Do-right. But he also made damn sure he told me how he's gonna auction off his old man's memoirs and that the bidding's gonna start at three quarters of a mill and climb on up from there. And it's just about then that he says the two magic names."

"What magic names?"

"Muriel Lamphier and Hamilton Keyes."

Tinker Burns liked the way he had tossed in the two names right there at the end. He leaned back in the blue leather chair to study the senator, who had just shuttered his Neon eyes again and was arranging his thin mouth into the faintest of smiles.

A moment later, the eyes opened and the smile, if it had been a smile, went away and the senator said, "Lamphier, I believe you said, and Keyes."

"Mr. and Mrs. Hamilton Keyes. He's a top spook out at Langley. She's rich."

"How were the names mentioned?" the senator said. "I mean, in what context?"

"They came up all of a sudden. Granny wanted to know

247

how well I knew Muriel Lamphier, who's also Mrs. Hamilton Keyes. So I told 'em to get the fuck outta my room before I called security."

"And they went without argument?"

"Like lambs."

"Then what?"

"Then I went down to the lobby and called you from a pay phone and said—well, you know what I said."

"That you were having second thoughts."

"Yeah."

The senator leaned back in his Chief Justice swivel chair and again gave the almost invisible smile permission to play around his thin lips for a second or two. "Are we now going to share these second thoughts of yours, Mr. Burns?"

"I can't decide."

"Why not?"

"Because I'm a businessman, Senator. The kind who believes that market forces should set the price of everything. If there's a strong demand, raise your price. If demand's weak, drop it. And never, never give anything away."

"Not even a sample?"

"Well, maybe a sample."

"You're very generous."

"No, I'm not," Burns said, paused, frowned, nodded to himself and said, "I got a lot of friends who used to fly for Air America."

"When it was a CIA proprietary venture."

"Yeah, then. Hell, some of my friends even used to fly for Chennault and Chancre Jack in China. But they're all pushing eighty now and not too right in the head. But I'm talking about ex-Air America pilots who're a lot younger'n that and used to fly out of Laos. Out of a place called Long Tieng, otherwise known as Spook Heaven. Ever hear of it?"

The senator only nodded.

"Well, I figured you would've since you were on one of those intelligence oversight committees. Anyway, these not-so-young-anymore Air America guys I know still like to drink and bullshit and they sort of look up to me because I was at Dien Bien Phu with the Legion and all, and they still think that was pretty hot shit. Okay?"

The senator nodded again.

"If I remember right," Burns said, "the CIA went into Laos back in sixty-one but by sixty-three it was already a backwater operation—what old Dean Rusk called the wart on the hog or something like that. But there was still lots of dope. Lots of booze. Lots of flying. And just one hell of a lot of spooks. Okay?"

"Still with you, Mr. Burns."

"Good. So now it's nineteen eighty or eighty-one and I'm in Bangkok doing a little business when I bump into some of these ex-Air America hotshots I know who never went home. It was in some bar, Spiffy's, I think, and they were all reminiscing about Laos in the good old days. For them, that's just before the end in seventy-four when everything fell apart and you guys bugged out."

"In May and June of nineteen seventy-four, I believe," the senator said.

"That's what I said. So we're sitting around in Spiffy's and they're talking about all the weird and wonderful characters they'd known in Laos. But none of the names meant much to me till somebody mentions Steady Haynes."

"Favorably?"

"Oh, yeah. Sure. It was all about how Steady saved the neck of some young spook who made a real bad mistake. Tragic's what they called it. And how Steady flip-flopped it to make it look like something else altogether. The young spook's name was Lamphier and the reason I remember it now is because I asked them if that was Lamphier like in Crown-Lamphier glass and they said yes. And because they also said the spook was a she instead of a he."

Burns stopped talking and began to smile.

"That's my taste?" the senator said.

"That's it."

"Mr. Burns, when I retained you for a not inconsiderable fee in Paris just before Steadfast Haynes died so unexpectedly, all I asked of you was to exploit your friendship with Mr. Haynes and Miss Gelinet—"

Burns interrupted, his impatience obvious. "And talk 'em into giving me a peek at the memoirs."

"Exactly. But you couldn't for obvious reasons—Mr. Haynes's death and then Miss Gelinet's. But now you seem to be going off on some tangent that I find alarming. Most alarming."

"Sorry you feel that way, Senator."

"No, you aren't. But tell me this, and please think carefully before you do. Are you sure it was Granville Haynes and not Michael Padillo who first brought up Muriel Lamphier's name?"

"Positive."

"Then that suggests the memoirs really do exist and that young Haynes has read them."

"Or that it's what Granny wants you to think, Senator. You know, if I was Granny, I'd do just what he's doing and try to jack up the price by hinting at how much I know. That's what I'd do, if I was Granny. Now, if I was you, I'd call his bluff and tell him I need to read before I buy."

"Don't think I haven't thought of that," the senator said.

"Then why don't you?"

"If I did, he'd simply threaten to send them to a publisher. And to prevent him from doing that, I'd again have to increase my bid."

"Just can't afford to take the chance, huh?" Burns said.

"No."

"Then it doesn't much matter if the memoirs are real or make-believe because you're still going to buy the rights for your client—whoever she is."

"Goddamnit, Mr. Burns, I will not discuss my client with you."

"Okay. Fine. We won't discuss her."

The senator took a deep breath and said, "But I think we had better discuss just what it is you have to sell."

"Silence."

"And how much does silence cost?"

"Not as much as you think," said Tinker Burns.

Thirty-six

McCorkle sat in an immense wingback chair and watched Harry Warnock, the IRA deserter turned security consultant, work the lobby of the Willard Hotel. It was nearly 10 A.M. and McCorkle had been watching Warnock for an hour.

Wearing a neat dark blue suit and carrying a gray herringbone topcoat over his left arm, Warnock scanned each face as it came through the hotel entrance. McCorkle imagined a classification system inside Warnock's head that stamped each face with yes, no or maybe. So far, there had been only no's, except for one maybe. But when the maybe, a noticeably jumpy man in his mid-thirties, hurried over to a woman in her late sixties, kissed her cheek and called her "Mommy," Warnock had turned away, looking a bit disappointed.

It was a few minutes after 10 A.M. when Warnock wandered over and stood beside McCorkle's chair, looking not at him but at the hotel entrance. "I go off in ten minutes," Warnock said.

"Who relieves you?" McCorkle asked.

"Mr. Coors. Remember him?"

"The big guy?"

"They're all big," Warnock said. "But he's the one with the hint of human intelligence."

"Now I remember him," McCorkle said. "What happens if Granville Haynes leaves the hotel?"

"I've got a two-man team outside—aw, shit."

McCorkle looked where Warnock was looking. The doors of one of the elevators had just opened and a man was hurrying across the lobby toward the Pennsylvania Avenue exit.

The hurrying man wore a dark gray suit, blue tie, white shirt and black wing tips. He was of average height, five-nine or -ten; average weight, around 155 pounds; and had fairly short hair the color of wet sand. He also had two small ears, two light gray eyes, a snub nose, an unremarkable mouth and appeared to be in his mid- to late forties.

Harry Warnock turned away from McCorkle, stepped into the path of the hurrying man and said, "Hey, Purchase."

The man called Purchase didn't change expression or break stride. He was still twenty feet away from Warnock when his right hand darted across his stomach at belt level, vanished beneath his unbuttoned suitcoat in a cross-draw and reappeared a second later, holding a semiautomatic pistol. Still moving toward the exit, Purchase fired at Warnock. The round struck Warnock's left side and knocked him halfway around.

Purchase broke into a trot that carried him past the still seated McCorkle. Without weighing the possible consequences, McCorkle stuck out his long right leg and tripped Purchase, who went into an awkward, stumbling fall. If he had dropped the pistol, he could have broken the fall with both hands. But he didn't drop it and wound up sprawled on the marble floor, his right hand still clutching the gun.

McCorkle, now on his feet, slammed one heel down on the gun hand. Purchase grunted and released the pistol. Mc-

Corkle kicked it away, turned back and kicked Purchase in the face. The kick made Purchase grunt again.

McCorkle hurried toward Warnock, who, down on his knees, was pressing his left side with his left hand just below the rib cage. His right hand held a revolver that McCorkle thought might be a five-shot Smith & Wesson.

McCorkle was ten feet away when Warnock roared, "Behind you, damnit!"

McCorkle spun around. Purchase was in a seated position and bleeding from his mouth and nose. His knees were up, as was his right pants leg, which revealed a black ribbed sock and an empty ankle holster. Purchase used both hands to aim a very small semiautomatic at McCorkle. Automatically classifying the small gun as a .22 caliber, McCorkle made a desperate side-hop to his right, alarmed and dismayed by the way the gun followed him, as if it were just waiting for him to land.

Purchase's left eye disappeared with a bang. McCorkle, at the end of his hop and suffering from terror-induced detachment, tried to decide whether he had heard the gunshot before or after the left eye disappeared. He was still trying to decide when Purchase seemed to melt onto the marble floor of the lobby where he lay, dead or dying, in a small puddle of urine and blood.

Then the shouts began. One man cursed monotonously. A woman decided to scream. A pair of hotel security men, guns drawn, rushed up to the still kneeling Warnock, who snarled something that made them put away their guns, help him to his feet and into a chair. A few gawkers, mostly men, slowly circled the dead Purchase, staring down at him with morbid fascination.

Once seated in the chair, Warnock grimaced, looked around, located McCorkle and nodded toward the elevators. McCorkle hurried into one of them and, as its doors closed, lit a Pall Mall cigarette with hands that he suspected might never stop trembling.

* * *

McCorkle pounded on the door of Granville Haynes's room until a man's muffled voice demanded, "Who is it?"

"McCorkle."

"You alone?"

"Christ, yes."

"Prove it."

"Open the door."

"Not yet."

"Then how the hell do I prove it?"

"Turn around and put your hands on your head," Haynes said through the door. "After I open up, back in. If there's a problem with you, he'll have to go through you to get to me."

"The problem's down in the lobby—dead."

There was a long silence before Haynes said, "We'll still do it my way."

McCorkle turned so that his back was to the room's door. He held his cigarette between his lips and clasped his hands on top of his head. He heard the door open and Haynes say, "Back in."

McCorkle backed in, hands still on his head. He lowered them and took the cigarette out of his mouth as Haynes closed the door, shot all of its bolts and fastened the chain lock. Haynes wore only boxer shorts. McCorkle thought his stomach was too flat.

Haynes turned, noticed McCorkle's cigarette and said, "This is a nonsmoking room."

McCorkle nodded politely and blew smoke at the ceiling.

Haynes said, "I had a visitor."

"Tell me about him."

"He came with a small bolt cutter for the door chain and a pass-card—one of those electronic gizmos you can stick in the slot to open any door in the hotel. You can buy them the way you used to buy passkeys, but they're a lot more expensive."

"What kept him out?" McCorkle said.

"Acting."

"Acting?"

"He was working on the chain with the bolt cutter when I started playing two parts—myself and Tinker Burns. Tinker and I talked about what we'd do to the son of a bitch once we got him inside."

Suddenly, an uncanny duplicate of Burns's voice came out of Haynes's mouth. "You hold him, Granny, and I'll reach down his throat and yank his gizzard out." Haynes paused and resumed speaking in his normal voice. "The guy left and I thought he might've stuck a piece in your face and made you come back with him. But you say he's dead."

"Shot dead," McCorkle said and headed for the room's small refrigerator. He removed a miniature bottle of Scotch whisky, poured its contents into a glass and drank half of it.

"Who was he?" Haynes asked.

"Harry Warnock called him Purchase."

"And who's Warnock?"

"The guy Padillo and I hired to look after us while we mind you till the auction's over."

"How'd it play out?"

"Purchase shot Warnock in the side. Then Warnock killed him."

"Where were you?"

"After he shot Warnock, Purchase made a dash for the front entrance. I tripped him, stomped his gun hand and kicked his piece away."

"Then turned your back on him, right?"

McCorkle nodded. "To see about Warnock."

"Dumb move," Haynes said. "You should've kicked his face in first."

"I thought I had."

"What were you doing in the lobby?"

"Making sure Harry was on the job."

"He's an ex-cop?"

"Ex-IRA. The Kuwaitis are said to dote on him."

"But he got shot."

"Right."

"And let this guy Purchase make it up to my room."

"When Harry gets better, maybe he'll send you a nice little note of apology."

"How hurt is he?"

"That's what I have to find out," McCorkle said. "But there's no need to drag you into it." He reached into a pants pocket, brought out a key case, removed a key and handed it to Haynes. "Know where I live?"

Haynes nodded.

"The key'll get you in. You'd better get dressed, get out of here and find a cab not too close by. Once you're inside my apartment, go down the hall to the last bedroom on the left. In the chiffonier, third drawer down underneath some sweaters, you'll find a Chief's Special."

"Loaded?"

McCorkle looked at Haynes curiously. "Of course."

"Handy, too," Haynes said. "Third drawer down underneath the sweaters."

"Forget it then."

"I'll think about it," Haynes said. "Will Erika be there?"

"Probably."

"What do I tell her?"

"Tell her you're sorry."

"For what?"

"For all your faults," McCorkle said.

Thirty-seven

Darius Pouncy, the homicide detective-sergeant, didn't get around to McCorkle until after the body of the man identified as Horace Purchase was removed from the lobby of the Willard Hotel. By then it was 11:33 A.M. and Pouncy, after announcing he was hungry, invited McCorkle to join him for what the detective promised to be "a little light lunch."

In the hotel's glittering Expresso Cafe, Pouncy ordered a large bowl of lentil soup and what turned out to be an enormous ham sandwich. McCorkle confined himself to a Beck's beer and a cup of the soup, which he found to be quite good.

Pouncy apparently didn't like to let conversation interfere with his food. He ate silently and quickly with precise movements and frequent, even delicate use of his napkin. McCorkle thought the detective had the best table manners he had seen in years. When Pouncy finished his ham sandwich, he called the waitress over, ordered a cappuccino for dessert and urged McCorkle to join him. McCorkle said he would have another bottle of Beck's instead.

After the cappuccino came, Pouncy took a sip, leaned back in the booth and examined McCorkle. "Mac's Place, huh?"

McCorkle nodded.

"Ate there a couple of times. Had us some real fine rack of lamb for two and, the second time, a hell of a roasted rolled pork."

"I hope you'll come again."

Pouncy nodded, as if he would have to think about it, and sipped his cappuccino. After putting the cup down, he said, "Understand you tripped him, stomped his hand, kicked his piece away, then kicked his face in. That right?"

"Yes."

"You know who he was?"

"I knew he'd just shot Mr. Warnock."

"But you didn't know who Purchase was?"

"No."

"But Warnock knew."

"He called him by name."

"What'd he say exactly—Warnock?"

"He said, 'Hey, Purchase.'"

"And that's when Purchase shot him, trotted by you, and you tripped him?" Not waiting for an answer, Pouncy examined McCorkle curiously and asked, "Aren't you getting on up there in years to be pulling damn fool stunts like that?"

"Want me to promise never to do it again?"

Pouncy smiled. "Warnock works for you, right?"

"Not quite. My partner and I retained his firm to provide security for a friend of ours."

"Granville Haynes?"

"Yes."

"Granville doesn't seem to be up in his room," Pouncy said. "You think Warnock might've been keeping an eye on an empty nest?"

"I think Mr. Haynes may have decided to go somewhere more secure."

"Where'd that be?"

259

McCorkle shrugged.

"Moving your shoulders up and down like that could mean, 'I don't know,' 'Who cares?' or 'None of your beeswax.' Which?"

"It means he could've gone to see his lawyer, a friend or to another hotel."

"But you're pretty sure Granville was the target Purchase wanted to hit?"

"I assume so."

"Lemme tell you a little about Horse Purchase and who he really was. Horse started killing folks for a living when he was nineteen years old. But it was all legal then because he was with Special Forces in Vietnam. When Horse got killed here today he was forty-five. He went to Vietnam in sixty-three and stayed on till sixty-nine. After he came home and got out of the Army, he went into the killing business as an independent contractor."

"Who hired him?"

"Folks that could afford it. The street says he charged fifty thousand a job and tried to do at least two a year. He got half up front and the rest on completion. They say he never had a dissatisfied customer and I'd say you're awful lucky to be alive, Mr. McCorkle."

"You're probably right."

Pouncy finished his cappuccino, sighed his appreciation and said, "Ever know a Mr. Gilbert Undean?"

"No."

"What about Isabelle Gelinet?"

"I knew Isabelle."

"Tinker Burns?"

"I know Tinker."

"Seen him recently?"

"Not since Friday, but my partner had a phone call from him Sunday. Yesterday."

"Then he's probably still alive," Pouncy said. "Reason I say that is because Mr. Undean and Miss Gelinet were both

260

murdered and Tinker Burns discovered their bodies. Now, there were only four mourners—I reckon they were mourners—at the burial of Steadfast Haynes on Friday and here it is Monday and half of 'em are already dead. What I'm getting at, Mr. McCorkle, is that I sure hope I don't get another call from Tinker Burns telling me he's just stumbled across the body of Granville Haynes."

"I hope not either," McCorkle said.

"If you see Mr. Burns, you mind telling him he oughta call me?" Pouncy paused. "Might even put it a little stronger than that."

"You try his hotel?"

"Been trying all morning. He's not there."

"If I see him, I'll tell him," McCorkle said. "Is that it?"

"Just about," Pouncy said and looked at his watch. "I got a few more questions but they're not gonna take much more'n thirty or forty-five minutes."

McCorkle leaned back in the booth, took out his cigarettes, lit one and said, "Maybe I'll have some cappuccino after all."

When Granville Haynes slipped out of the Willard Hotel through its rear F Street exit, he was surprised to find the temperature had shot up into the mid-fifties. The mild weather, along with its accompanying sunshine, convinced Haynes that he should walk to McCorkle's apartment, which he remembered was in either the 2200 or 2300 block of Connecticut Avenue.

Haynes's route took him past the Treasury Building and the White House and the Old Executive Office Building to Seventeenth Street where he turned north. By the time he reached the Mayflower Hotel it had clouded over and the temperature had dropped into the mid-forties. Long accustomed to southern California's weather, Haynes decided his choices were to take a cab, buy a coat or freeze to death.

Haynes spotted a Burberry shop at the intersection of Connecticut and Rhode Island. Inside, he asked to see a topcoat. The saleswoman said she thought he would look marvelous in a trench coat. Haynes said he would prefer something a little less dashing. She showed him a lamb's-wool topcoat with raglan sleeves. The lightweight wool had a pattern of small brown and beige houndstooth checks. Haynes tried the coat on without asking its price, looked at himself briefly in a mirror, said he would wear it and handed her an American Express card.

He walked the rest of the way to McCorkle's old gray stone apartment building on the west side of Connecticut Avenue. He reached the building at about the same time Darius Pouncy began asking McCorkle the first of the "few more questions" that would continue for another twenty-six minutes.

Haynes examined the key McCorkle had given him and noticed it was one of the tricky Swiss kind that had "pimples and craters" rather than teeth, and which couldn't be duplicated, at least not in the United States. Haynes wasn't sure about Switzerland.

McCorkle had said his apartment number was 405. Haynes reached it after a ride up on an obviously new Otis elevator. He knocked on the door. When there was still no answer after he knocked a second and third time, he used the Swiss key to let himself in.

He entered a small foyer with a parquet floor and a wall table that might have been a very good imitation Sheraton. On the table was a large cut-glass bowl full of M&M candy. Hanging above the table and illuminated by a single light were two oil paintings. The first was a rainy-day scene of a cozy-looking European bar-cafe with a small red neon sign that spelled out "Mac's Place." The second painting was a rainy-day scene of the same bar-cafe after it had been destroyed by either a bomb, a fire or both.

Haynes breakfasted on four of the M&Ms as he studied the two pictures, deciding that they must have been painted from photographs. The M&Ms, he discovered, were of the chocolate-covered peanut variety.

Popping another M&M into his mouth, Haynes went down the long hall, heading for the last bedroom on the left. It was a fairly large room, at least twelve by eighteen feet, with parquet floors, an oriental rug and a huge double bed that had been hastily made up. The room also contained a dressing table, the promised chiffonier and, placed in front of the casement windows, two disparate but comfortable-looking armchairs, each with its own table and reading lamp.

One of the chairs was of an elegant Scandinavian design and looked particularly inviting. Piled on the table beside it were books dealing with American politics and economics, plus four recent autobiographies of former White House aides who had left the Reagan administration under clouds of varying density.

The other chair, an old and battered leather wingback affair of impressive dimensions, seemed vaguely familiar until Haynes realized it was very much like the chair in his Ocean Park apartment—the one in which he could sit and stare at the monster pale yellow house across the street.

On a table beside the leather chair were four books without dust jackets. Haynes picked them up, one by one, and saw they were library books, four days overdue. They consisted of an early Vonnegut, an H. Allen Smith, a Mark Twain diatribe against Mary Baker Eddy and Doughty's *Travels in Arabia Deserta*, a book that Haynes had never finished.

He replaced the books, crossed to the chiffonier and opened the third drawer down. Under what seemed to be five layers of cashmere sweaters, he found the short-barreled Smith & Wesson Chief's Special. It was the airweight aluminum frame model loaded with .38 Special cartridges. Haynes knew the pistol to be fairly accurate within six or seven feet.

He closed the chiffonier drawer and was about to slip the revolver into one of his new topcoat's pockets when the sleepy voice behind him asked, "What the hell're you doing here?"

Haynes turned to find a tousled, barefoot Erika McCorkle, wearing a flaming red silk robe that looked like a Japanese kimono.

"Borrowing this," he said and displayed the revolver before dropping it into the topcoat pocket.

"Bought yourself a new coat, I see," she said.

"You just get up?"

"What was wrong with Steady's old duffle coat?"

"I decided to walk."

"From the hotel?"

Haynes nodded.

"And?"

"Halfway here it turned cold so I bought a coat."

"That's a Burberry," she said. "I can tell."

Haynes held the coat open and looked at the inside breast label for the first time. "So it is."

"You want some coffee?" she said.

"When did you get to sleep last night?"

"Four. Five. Around in there."

"Why so late?"

"I need coffee," she said, turned and left the room.

The kitchen was larger than Haynes had expected and filled with intimidating German appliances that looked expensive. There was even a breakfast nook, which measured the age of the apartment and its building as surely as tree rings. To Haynes, breakfast nooks belonged to a prehistoric age of nuclear families with four or five members who sat down to breakfasts of juice, cereal, eggs, bacon and toast. Haynes thought such families to be as nearly extinct as breakfast nooks. None of the families he knew ever ate sit-down breakfasts together. Or lunch or dinner for that matter.

It took the German coffeemaker ninety seconds to produce a pint or so of coffee. Erika poured it into a pair of

Meissen cups, serving Haynes first and then herself. They sipped in silence until she said, "How'd you get in—Pop give you his key?"

Haynes nodded.

"Why?"

"There was some trouble at the hotel."

"Is Pop all right?"

"He's fine."

"What kind of trouble?"

Haynes told her exactly what McCorkle had told him but left out Horace Purchase's attempt to break into the hotel room. Erika listened intently, ignoring the coffee and not taking her eyes from his face. When he finished, she leaned back against the benchlike seat and said, "This guy Purchase was after you?"

"I'm not sure. Possibly."

"Pop shouldn't try that kind of stuff without Mike."

"He seems to have done okay."

"He could've been killed."

"But he wasn't," Haynes said, drank the rest of his coffee, then asked, "Tell me about Padillo."

"Tell you what about him?"

"Who he is and who he was."

"Ask him."

Haynes smiled what he hoped was his best smile. She quickly looked away, as if to avoid it. "Was what he used to do really all that rotten?" Haynes said.

She was frowning when she looked at him again. "I can't decide."

"About Padillo?"

"About you. Sometimes you remind me of Mike, some-times of Pop. But you really aren't like either of them. And maybe that's why I didn't sleep much last night."

"I'm sorry."

"For what?"

265

"That you didn't sleep much last night although I don't understand why."

"You're fishing."

"I wasn't aware of it."

"Okay. Here it is. I've decided I don't want to care about you too much. But that's not something I can switch on and off. And that's why I didn't get much sleep last night."

"I'm sorry."

"What're you sorry for this time?"

"For all my faults," Haynes said.

The wall telephone in the kitchen rang. Erika reached up and back, brought it down to her left ear and said hello. She listened, said, "Hold on," and handed the phone to Haynes. "It's Padillo."

After Haynes said hello, Padillo said, "You'd better stay where you are till I get there."

"Why?"

"Tinker Burns. They found him shot dead in Rock Creek Park."

Thirty-eight

Even dead, Tinker Burns wore his dove-gray Borsalino homburg at a slightly rakish angle. He sat on a wooden picnic bench, facing out, his back propped against the edge of the tabletop. There were two small black holes in the left lapel of his double-breasted gray suit—the one with the faint chalk stripe.

A civilian Metropolitan Police Department photographer squatted in front of the dead man for a close-up of the bullet holes. Burns's topcoat was folded neatly on the bench beside him. His hands lay palms-up in his lap. His eyes were closed; his mouth slightly open. His lined face had lost little, if any, of its old tropical tan.

The picnic area, only yards from Rock Creek itself, had been cordoned off by yellow crime scene tape. Plainclothes detectives and technicians poked about, muttering to each other. Uniformed police directed traffic on the park's asphalt roadway, hurrying the motorized gawkers along. Some walkers and joggers stood behind the yellow tape, waiting to see what happened next.

Darius Pouncy, with McCorkle in tow, arrived shortly

before the ambulance and just after an assistant coroner. Pouncy left McCorkle behind the yellow tape, ducked under it, went over to Tinker Burns and stared down at him for almost a minute. He then talked to the assistant coroner briefly; listened to what two senior detectives had to say; asked a few questions and walked back to McCorkle, who was still on the other side of the yellow tape.

"Looks like he got shot twice," Pouncy said. "Closeup."

"Who found him?"

"A couple of kids," Pouncy said, again looking at the dead Tinker Burns. He turned back to McCorkle with a bleak look and added, "Black kids. Fourteen and fifteen. Dropouts. Wallet was still in his inside breast pocket. Seven hundred dollars in it." Pouncy looked down at the ground, then up at McCorkle. "I figure the kids took a hundred apiece. Maybe more. Maybe less."

"Tinker won't care," McCorkle said.

Pouncy nodded glumly.

"How d'you read it?" McCorkle said.

"You mean how'd he get here?"

"That's a good place to start."

"I don't know," Pouncy said. "Cab most likely. Sun must've been out then because he took his topcoat off and folded it up all nice and neat. Sat there on the bench, face up to the sun maybe, waiting for whoever he was gonna meet. Party drives up in a car, gets out, goes over, says, 'Nice day,' does the business, does it twice in fact, gets back in the car and goes home or maybe into some bar for a little bracer."

"And Tinker just lets it happen?" McCorkle said.

Pouncy jabbed his finger into McCorkle's chest. "Take about that long to do it. Two seconds. Three tops."

"If it was somebody Tinker knew."

"Didn't have to be somebody he knew. Just had to be somebody he was expecting."

"You think this same somebody killed Isabelle and Undean."

"That a question?" Pouncy said. "Sure as hell didn't sound like a question."

"Let's make it one."

"Then, yeah, I think it's the same somebody. But thinking it's not proving it. All I got for sure is this: there were four people out at Arlington on Friday and by Monday three of 'em are homicide cases. The last one left of the four is the son of the guy they buried Friday. And the only reason he's still alive is because Horse Purchase fucked up somehow." Pouncy turned to watch Tinker Burns being zipped into a bodybag. "Got any notion of where Granville is?"

"Probably at my place," McCorkle said.

Pouncy turned back quickly. "Thought you said he might be at another hotel or with his lawyer or a friend."

"He's with my daughter. She's the friend."

"She watching out for him?" Pouncy asked, not bothering to soften the sarcasm.

"My partner's on the way."

"The Mr. Padillo you called from the Willard?"

McCorkle nodded.

"He know how to do?"

"He knows."

"Course, it's not like Granville's exactly helpless—him being an ex-homicide cop out there in L.A. and all."

"Far from helpless."

"Young, too. Younger'n your partner, I expect."

"Much."

"What'd your partner say when you called and told him Tinker Burns was dead?"

"He said, 'That's too bad.'"

Hamilton Keyes, the future ambassador, was behind the desk in his library when he heard the faint hum of the electric motor that raised the garage door. Glancing at his watch, he saw it was 1:16 P.M.

Muriel Keyes entered the library minutes later and sank into a chair with an exasperated sigh.

"That was a short lunch," Keyes said.

"She cancelled at the last moment," Muriel Keyes said. "Can you imagine? I spent the entire morning—well, an hour or two anyway—out at Neiman's, then drove all the way to the Hill to that awful restaurant she likes and got there at exactly twelve-thirty. She calls at twelve thirty-five. 'Sorry, sweetie, but the congressman has to go to New York and I'm driving him to catch the shuttle. It's my only chance to talk with him.'"

It was a perfect imitation and Keyes smiled.

"Goddamn all amateur lobbyists," Muriel Keyes said.

"You must be hungry."

"Not very. Did you go out?"

"For a while. When I got back there was a message from Senator Mushmouth."

"And?"

"He's talked to young Haynes's lawyer, Howard Mott— d'you know him?"

"I know his wife and her sister. His wife was Lydia Stallings and her sister, Joanna, is married to Neal Hineline at State."

"The noted thinker and car wax heir," Keyes said.

"He is a bit dim, isn't he? But Joanna's nice. I haven't seen Lydia Mott in years."

"Well, her husband wants to hold the—what? the auction?—in the senator's office. I told Mott it would be okay."

"Who cares where it's held as long as you get it over with?" she said.

"It'll start at ten Wednesday morning and I see no reason why it should last more than an hour, if that."

"Who'll be there?"

"The senator, of course. Howard Mott. Young Haynes. And I."

"Really? I thought it was to be only Haynes and the lawyers."

"It was, but I suspect Howard Mott decided he wanted to be a bit closer to the source of the Federal money."

"Who can blame him?" she said. "Is he a good lawyer?"

"He's a superb criminal defense attorney. One of the best."

"Well, let's hope we never need him."

"Why would we?" Keyes said.

His wife rose with a smile. "Who knows?" She began to say something else, changed her mind and asked, "How does a bacon and egg sandwich sound?"

"Tempting," said Hamilton Keyes.

After an hour the repetition began, as it usually does, and Howard Mott decided he had heard enough—or at least everything that was pertinent. He turned to Granville Haynes and said, "Go bury yourself somewhere until ten o'clock Wednesday morning."

The five of them were gathered in McCorkle's living room. Padillo had been there for nearly two hours. Mott for an hour and fifteen minutes. McCorkle had been the last to arrive, dropped off an hour before by Darius Pouncy with a stern reminder that the detective still wanted to talk to Granville Haynes.

Mott sat in one of the four cane-backed chairs that looked as if they should be drawn up to a bridge table, which they sometimes were. Erika McCorkle and Haynes sat side by side on a couch that wore a faded chintz slipcover. McCorkle was on the bench in front of the Steinway baby grand that his wife, Fredl, played beautifully and he played rather badly by ear. His best, if not his favorite, piece remained "Smoke Gets in Your Eyes."

The living room faced south and east. The east windows overlooked Connecticut Avenue. The south windows provided a view of the building next door. It was a large and pleasant room that offered what once had been a wood-burning fireplace. Six years ago, McCorkle had substituted gas logs for real ones. His stated reason had been that gas logs cut down on pollution. His true reason was that real logs were just too much bother.

The two McCorkles, Padillo and Mott stared at Haynes, waiting to see how he would respond to the suggestion that he go bury himself somewhere.

"A motel would be best," Haynes said.

"Consider Maryland," Mott said. "Or even West Virginia out near Harpers Ferry."

Haynes nodded his agreement and said, "I'll have to rent a car."

"Better you borrow one," McCorkle said.

Erika turned to Haynes. "You can have mine."

"Too many people know about you and Granville," Padillo said.

"Know what?" she snapped.

Padillo smiled and made a small defensive gesture with both palms. "That you've been hauling him around in your car—that's all."

Mott cleared his throat and said, "I think I have a solution." He took out his wallet, found a card and used a pen to write something on it. When finished, he rose, went over to Haynes and handed him the card.

"It's the garage in Falls Church where Steady's old Cadillac is," Mott said. "I'll call the owner and tell him somebody's picking it up."

Padillo liked the idea. "Take a cab out there," he urged Haynes. "You have any cash?"

"A few hundred."

Padillo took out a wallet, looked inside, then handed Haynes a sheaf of tens and twenties. "Here's a couple of hundred more." He looked at McCorkle, who was already examining the contents of his own billfold. "How much've you got?" Padillo asked.

"Three hundred," McCorkle said, rose and handed the bills to Haynes.

Mott took a small roll from a pants pocket, removed five $100 bills and gave them to Haynes. "A contribution from Tinker Burns."

Haynes grinned his father's grin. "Tinker pay you his retainer in cash?"

"He tried to."

"You know the routine," Padillo said.

Haynes nodded as he put the money away in a pants pocket. "Cash in advance. Use a phony name to register. I've always liked 'Clarkson' because it's not too common and not too rare. On the registration form, give the car's make but shift the model year up or down a year or two. Invent a license number. If they ask for a driver's license, walk."

"I'll go with you," Erika said. "That way you can register as Mr. and Mrs. Geoffrey Clarkson."

There was a brief silence before Haynes said, "I like the name," and turned to look at McCorkle. Padillo and Mott also looked at him. Erika didn't.

McCorkle was busy removing the childproof wrapping from a piece of Nicorette gum. Haynes noticed it was taking him much longer than usual. McCorkle finally got the piece out, popped it into his mouth and gave it seven or eight ruminative chews as he studied the ceiling.

He then looked at his daughter, whose back was still to him, and said, "That's not such a bad idea, Erika."

Thirty-nine

The private room on the third floor of Sibley Hospital in far northwest Washington was guarded by Mr. Pabst and Mr. Schlitz. When Pabst noticed Padillo and McCorkle coming out of an elevator, he nudged Schlitz, and the two big men rose from folding metal chairs to plant themselves in front of the room's door.

"No visitors," Pabst warned when McCorkle and Padillo were close enough to hear him.

The would-be visitors came to a stop. Padillo stared at Pabst for several seconds, then said, "Tell him we're here."

"I just told you. No visitors."

"Tell him," said Padillo, somehow managing to turn the two softly spoken words into pure menace.

Pabst studied the fire extinguisher to Padillo's right. "If he don't wanta see you, you don't go in."

Padillo, still staring at Pabst, said nothing. McCorkle gave Schlitz a friendly grin and a nod, which weren't returned. Pabst shot a furtive glance at Padillo, then darted into the hospital room and came out less than fifteen seconds later to announce: "Harry says it's okay."

Inside the room, McCorkle and Padillo found Harry Warnock lying in bed on his back. An intravenous drip solution had been inserted into a vein in his left arm.

McCorkle said, "You look like hell."

"But far better than Horse Purchase," Warnock said. "The fucker nicked my liver and the quacks say I best lay off the booze for a few months. And 'tis this sad news that's causing me to look so dismal."

"Sad news indeed," McCorkle said.

Warnock turned his head to look at Padillo, who had moved around to the other side of the bed. "You should've seen him, Michael."

"Who?"

"McCorkle."

"I heard."

"One had to be there. Especially when he took his high hop to the right. I thought he'd never come down. A regular fucking Nureyev, he was." Warnock paused, looked back at McCorkle and said, "How's the client?"

"Fine."

"All safe and sound?"

McCorkle nodded.

"I fucked up," Warnock said. "I didn't figure on the likes of Purchase and when he came through those elevator doors, he surprised the shit out of me. I thought he might be working a twofer—you *and* the client. All I could do was make him notice me first." He paused, took a deep breath, winced, let it out slowly and said, "If I'd even suspected it was Purchase who'd be coming, I'd've been up in the room with two helpers and the client locked in the bath." He looked at Padillo again. "Did Horse make a move on him?"

Padillo said he had.

"What made him miss?"

"The client," Padillo said. "He's something of a mimic."

Warnock grinned. "Voices, right? Two voices talking behind the hotel room door. By God, I like that."

275

"Tell us about Purchase, Harry," Padillo said.

"You never heard of him?"

"Never."

"I'd call that passing strange, Michael, except you've been out of it for years—or so they say."

"They're right."

"Well, young Horse Purchase joined the Army at eighteen in nineteen sixty-three and after they measured his I.Q., which was way up there, and noticed his fine eyesight, reflexes and coordination, they shipped him off to Special Forces—poor Mr. Kennedy's pet outfit. Horse did six years, most of it in Vietnam, and enjoyed his work. He enjoyed it so much the Army thought it'd best get rid of him. And that it did in sixty-nine. Horse never married. Never drank. Never did dope. But he had his trade and his trade was his life so he decided to hire himself out."

"Who to, Harry?" Padillo asked.

"Well, he sure as shit didn't run any ad in *Soldier of Fortune*, did he? But the word got around as it always does and he was choosy. Horse'd only work for those who could come up with twenty-five thousand cash."

"I heard fifty," McCorkle said.

"That was later. Twenty years ago when Horse was just starting out, twenty-five thousand was worth what seventy-five is today."

"You can hire a semi-pro in this town or Baltimore for two thousand," Padillo said. "If it's toward the end of the month and the rent's due, the price drops to seventeen fifty. New York's about the same, although I heard it's slightly higher west of the Rockies."

"And for those prices it's careless work you'll be getting, too," Warnock said. "Horse was a pro, a dedicated craftsman, and 'tis very, very lucky I am to be alive today."

McCorkle looked concerned. "Does it hurt much when your Irish starts hemorrhaging like that, Harry?"

Warnock grinned up at him, then looked at Padillo. "So it's

who hired Horse that you want to know, is it? Well, you should be asking yourself this, Michael: who can lay out fifty or seventy-five thousand cash for the services the late Horse Purchase was so willing and even anxious to provide?"

"Major dope dealers," Padillo said.

"To be sure. But who else?"

"The rich—private or corporate."

"And three?"

"Governments."

"Ah!"

"How'd you know Purchase, Harry?" McCorkle said.

"We met but once—late in my former life."

"Your IRA days," Padillo said.

Warnock ignored him and went on talking to McCorkle. "He and I once held some exploratory talks that went nowhere."

"Why not?"

"Because Horse felt the risk too great and the reward too small. But we parted amicably."

"You mentioned governments, Harry," Padillo said.

"*You* mentioned them, Michael. Not I."

"Which governments?"

"How would I be knowing a wicked thing like that?"

"It's your stock-in-trade."

"Well, far be it from me to spread rumors—even about the likes of such a shit as Horse Purchase, God rest his soul. But I have heard a whisper or two about how he once did bits of piecework for the lads out at Langley." Warnock paused to paint a coat of piety across his face. "But I don't believe that for a minute, do you, Michael?"

"Not even for a second," Padillo said.

Dark's Garage in Falls Church, Virginia, had a sign inside that read: "Foreign & Domestic, The Older the Better. Ledell Dark, Prop." Erika McCorkle read the sign aloud with obvious approval. As she read, Granville Haynes looked around the long narrow garage and noticed a Packard from the 1940s, an Avanti, a 1948 Buick Roadmaster, an ancient Citroën sedan (the getaway model), a Humber Super Snipe and a TR-3 that looked almost new.

The Cadillac that Steadfast Haynes had bequeathed to his son was being driven from the rear of the garage at a stately 2 mph by Ledell Dark, Prop. It was a 1976 Eldorado convertible, the last one made, with a glossy black finish, a black canvas top that looked new, black leather seats and what Haynes guessed to be a thousand pounds of glittering chrome. It also looked a block long.

It came to a slow stop the way a large boat might. Ledell Dark got out and removed the 6-foot-long, 2½-foot-wide strip of reddish paper, ripped from a butcher's roll, that had protected the driver's seat. After discarding the paper, Dark stripped off his immaculate white cotton gardening gloves and stuffed them into a pocket.

A contented-looking man in his forties, Dark wore a studious, almost pedantic air and a pair of white coveralls with "The Older the Better" stitched across the back in red letters. He had the build of the average man in his forties who shuns exercise. There was a slight stoop. A bit of a paunch. And a face that Haynes classified as American-mild—except for the blazing green eyes that could only belong to a fanatic.

The green eyes were now half closed and the head was slightly tilted as Dark listened to the idling Cadillac engine. He smiled and nodded approvingly, then walked over to Erika and Haynes. "Know what I'd do if she was mine?" he asked. "I'd buy her a set of gangster whites."

When Erika looked puzzled, Dark explained, "Big wide white sidewall tires like they had in the thirties and forties— but mostly the thirties."

"You're saying it needs new tires?"

"Well, it's not exactly a matter of need," Dark said, "although those four've got a few too many miles on 'em. It's more a case of, well, you know—"

"Esthetics," Haynes suggested as he opened the Cadillac passenger door for Erika.

"Yeah, right," Dark said. "Esthetics."

Once Erika was inside, Haynes closed the door and said, "I'll tell Mr. Mott."

"You also oughta tell him that some guy wandered in here late last Saturday, took one look and offered me twenty thousand cash for the Caddie. That means he'll go twenty-five. You can always tell how high they'll go by how much they slobber. I call it the drool factor." Dark paused. "I got his name and number if you want it."

"Okay," Haynes agreed.

"Said his name was Horace Purchase."

Haynes turned quickly toward the TR-3 to hide the surprise that he suspected was rearranging his face. Still staring at the old Triumph roadster, he said, "Purchase wants to purchase it, huh?"

Dark grinned, obviously amused. "Know something? That's exactly how I remembered his name. Purchase wants to purchase it."

Haynes turned back and said, "These old cars must be worth a lot of money."

"That Packard behind you?" Dark said.

Haynes again turned to look.

"That's a nineteen forty convertible with a Darrin body and a frame-off restoration. Probably fetch a hundred, maybe even a hundred and twenty thousand."

"Then you must have one hell of a security problem."

"But I also got me a state-of-the-art security system," Dark said with a proud smile that a frown suddenly erased. "When that Purchase fella was here, he wanted that old Caddie so bad I thought he might bang me over the head and drive off in it. So I sort of discouraged him."

"How?" Haynes asked.

Dark stuck two fingers in his mouth and whistled. Haynes heard them coming a second or two later, their claws clicking on the concrete floor, their growls punctuated by angry barks. He turned to find three Rottweilers racing toward him, fangs bared and eyes blazing. Haynes also found there was no time to run or hide and just barely enough to wonder how much it would hurt.

Dark whistled again. The dogs stopped abruptly, skidding a little, then sat down on their haunches. One of them yawned and scratched his right ear with a hind foot. The other two seemed to grin at Haynes.

"Three of them," he said.

"They fight over who's boss. Keeps 'em mean. With two, you get buddies. With three, rivals."

"What did Purchase do when you whistled them up?"

"He sort of froze just like you did. Just like everybody does. Still want his phone number?"

"I don't," Haynes said. "But Mr. Mott might."

Forty

By 5:32 P.M. that Monday they had checked into the Bellevue Motel in Bethesda, Maryland, as Mr. and Mrs. Jeff T. Clarkson. The room was $58 a night and the motel owner demanded a $100 deposit after Haynes announced he would pay cash. The owner wasn't in the least interested in either the make of Haynes's car or its license number. Nor did he ask to see a driver's license or other identification.

The pink and teal Bellevue Motel was built in the shape of a two-story U. The view it offered was that of the McDonald's across the street. Haynes's room was at the bottom of the U and as he nosed the Cadillac into the vacant parking space, he felt, then heard, the right front wheel run over and crush a glass bottle. He and Erika got out to inspect what damage, if any, a broken 750-milliliter Smirnoff vodka bottle had done to the tire. Apparently none, they decided.

Erika went into the room first after Haynes unlocked the door. He followed, carrying her canvas overnight bag that looked like something a stonemason might carry his tools in. After dumping the bag onto one of the twin beds, Haynes sat down on the other one, picked up the telephone and made a call to Sheriff Jenkins Shipp in Berryville, Virginia.

"That you, Granville?" the sheriff said, once a deputy had transferred the call to him.

"Yes, sir."

"What can I do you for?"

"I'm calling about that car my father left me."

"Steady's big old Cadillac?"

"Right. Did the man who came to pick it up check with you first?"

"That fella Dark? He like to talk my arm off." Sheriff Shipp paused to let a small measure of concern creep into his tone. "He was supposed to pick it up, wasn't he? Least, that's what Mr. Mott called and told me."

"That's right, he was," Haynes said. "But I'm wondering whether anyone ever said anything about wanting to buy it?"

"You fixin' to sell it?"

"Maybe."

"You know, Granville, a fella did drop by last week and say he was interested in buying it. Wasn't more'n a day or two after Dark came and got it. I told him to call Mr. Mott or go talk to Dark. Even gave him the address of Dark's garage in Falls Church. Tell the truth, I think this fella was more'n just interested. I think he was in love with that car."

"He give you his name?"

"If he did, I forgot it."

"Was his name Purchase by any chance?"

There was a long silence until the sheriff said, "Granville?"

"Yes."

"Just what the fuck're you up to? We may be way out here in the boonies but when somebody with the name of Purchase gets himself killed during a shoot-out in the lobby of the Willard Hotel, the name sort of sticks in the mind—know what I mean?"

"Probably a different Purchase," Haynes said.

"I'm afraid I lied to you, Granville. The man who wanted

to buy Steady's car—his name was Horace Purchase. The man who got killed in the Willard—his name was also Horace Purchase, or so CNN claims. Soon as I heard his name mentioned on the TV I got on the phone and called Washington homicide. They put me onto a real smart colored fella—Detective-Sergeant Pouncy—and him and me got to talking and it turns out he's just dying to have a word with you."

"I'll call him," Haynes said.

"Might be a good idea because soon as we hang up I'm gonna call and tell him I just talked to you." Shipp paused yet again. "Or I could have him call you if you'll gimme the number you're calling from."

Haynes made up a number. Shipp repeated it, sounding dubious, and said, "Just a couple of more things, Granville. First of all, I'm sorry I had to lie to you about not remembering that fella Purchase's name. And second, they came out early yesterday and got old Zip and I expect he's doggie dinner by now."

"Thanks very much, Sheriff," Haynes said, ended the call and turned to look up at Erika, who was standing between the two beds. "You get most of that?"

"Your lies anyway."

"Here's the rest: Purchase found out the car was at Dark's from the sheriff. The sheriff found out who Purchase was from CNN. He then talked to Sergeant Pouncy, who wants to talk to me more than ever."

"Why don't you call him?"

"When I have something to say, I will," Haynes said, rose and started toward the door, patting the right pocket of his topcoat as if to make certain McCorkle's pistol was still there.

Erika picked up her coat from the bed and asked, "Where're we going?"

"To stash the car someplace. Maybe at Howard Mott's."

"Why there?"

"So I can take it apart."

"Steady wouldn't have hidden the manuscript in his car."

"You might think that. And I might think that. But Horace Purchase sure as hell didn't. And I'm fairly sure that whoever hired Purchase has by now talked to Ledell Dark, Prop. And Mr. Dark has probably told him all about my interest in Purchase and even what your overnight bag looks like. And I'd also bet that right now somebody is checking motel registers by phone and in person, asking about an attractive young couple in an old black Cadillac convertible—not exactly the world's most anonymous car."

"The manuscript could be in a safety-deposit box—or buried on Steady's farm eight paces north of the sour apple tree."

Haynes stared at her. "You're convinced there is no manuscript, aren't you?"

"Yes."

"Pretend there is. Just pretend. If you pretend that, then you know where the manuscript isn't. You know it's not in Steady's farmhouse and wasn't in the hotel room where he died. You know it wasn't in Isabelle's apartment and that Undean didn't have it and neither did Tinker Burns."

"Explain why I know all that."

"Because the CIA and Mr. Anonymous, whoever he is, are still anxious to buy it."

"What about all those fake manuscripts?" she said. "What the hell were they for if not to pull some kind of rip-off?"

"How should I know?" Haynes said. "Sure. It could've been a dodge of some sort—a con. Even a false trail. Or maybe Steady'd decided he wasn't going to split fifty-fifty with Isabelle after all. You've got to remember that Steady wasn't expecting to die. And that manuscript, if there is one—or even if there isn't—was to be his annuity. His fuck-you money. And he could've decided it would fetch just enough for one but not nearly enough for two. So he hid the real manuscript where nobody would look and then salted the obvious hiding places with fake ones."

"Maybe we shouldn't be looking for a manuscript after all," she said. "Maybe we should be looking for a hotel claim check clipped to the sun visor. Or microfilm that was tossed into the glove compartment. Or maybe—"

"You going to put that coat on or not?"

She looked down at the polo coat she was still holding, slipped into it quickly and said, "Let's go."

Haynes went out the motel room door first, stopped, stared and said, "Well, shit."

The exterior light above the room's door shined directly down onto the Cadillac's flat front tire. The left one. Erika glanced at it and said, "No big problem."

"Not if there's a spare."

They hurried to the rear of the car, where Haynes unlocked the trunk lid. There was a spare. He also found the jack and the lug wrench. He handed the wrench to Erika and said, "You can start on the lugs while I get the spare out."

She nodded and went back to the flat tire. Haynes watched as she knelt, used the chisel end of the lug wrench to pop the hubcap off with one deft blow and started loosening the wheel nuts.

Haynes unscrewed the big butterfly nut that anchored the spare. With the aid of the trunk's interior light, he noticed that the spare's tread apparently had never touched the ground. After wrestling the heavy wheel out of its well, he stopped, balancing it on the lip of the trunk, and stared down into the wheel well at the thick, slightly curved manila envelope that the never-used spare tire had been resting on.

When Erika McCorkle returned from her mission to McDonald's, bearing two Big Macs, two large fries and two large coffees, she found Granville Haynes still sitting on the edge of one of the twin beds, still wearing his topcoat and still staring at the unopened manila envelope that lay on the opposite bed. The .38 Chief's Special in his right hand was still pointed at nothing in particular.

"I thought you'd be starting Chapter Three by now," she said, placing the food on the desk.

"I didn't open it."

"Why not?"

"I wanted a witness."

"Now that you have one, what do we do first—eat or open it?"

"Let's open it," he said, put the revolver back in his topcoat pocket and reached for the twelve-by-fourteen-inch envelope. After weighing the envelope and its contents by hefting it in the palm of his right hand, Haynes said, "Around three hundred and seventy-five pages."

"How d'you know?"

"Because it weighs about three times as much as a screenplay for a feature and they usually run one hundred and twenty to one hundred and thirty pages."

"Open it, for God's sake."

Haynes used a forefinger to rip the envelope's flap. He removed a 2½-inch-thick manuscript, quickly flipped through it and looked up at Erika. "No blank pages," he said.

"I noticed."

He turned to the last page. "Three hundred and seventy-four."

"You were close."

"So I was."

"How d'you want to work it?" she asked.

"Work what?"

"Do we eat first, read first or do both at the same time?"

"Let's eat first," he said. "Then I'll start reading and hand you each page when I'm done."

"You read fast?"

"Very."

"Good," she said. "So do I."

Forty-one

At 8:32 P.M. that Monday, just as Granville Haynes and Erika McCorkle reached page 102 of *Mercenary Calling* by the late Steadfast Haynes, a procession of invisible dignitaries was being led by Herr Horst through the twilight at Mac's Place.

After the stately, if imaginary, procession came to a halt, Herr Horst gave two newly arrived diners one of his whip-lash nods and said, "Mr. and Mrs. Pouncy. How nice. I don't believe we've had the pleasure of your company since June of last year. June fourteenth, I think it was."

A flattered Detective-Sergeant Darius Pouncy used gruff-ness to conceal pleasure. "Didn't make a reservation."

Herr Horst smiled. "We've just had a cancellation. Will a booth be satisfactory?"

"Yeah, that'll do."

"Please," Herr Horst said and led them slowly across the dining room that was unusually crowded for a Monday night. At the booth, a choice one, Herr Horst helped the Pouncys out of their coats, which he deposited in the waiting arms of a busboy. As he handed them menus, Herr Horst complimented Mrs. Pouncy on her dress, causing her to beam, and asked whether they would care for something from the bar.

Pouncy quickly ordered an extra-dry martini straight up, but not quickly enough to avoid his wife's disapproving glare. She asked for a lime-flavored Perrier, if such were available. Herr Horst assured her it was.

At the bar, Herr Horst handed the drinks order to a waiter, picked up the bar phone and tapped two numbers. When McCorkle answered, Herr Horst said, "Sergeant and Mrs. Pouncy. No reservation. I gave them the number three booth."

"Comp their drinks and take their orders yourself," McCorkle said. "He likes his food, by the way."

"I know," Herr Horst said a little stiffly. "And if he should ask for you?"

"I'm available."

"And Padillo?"

"Also."

"Very good," Herr Horst said, ending the call.

After a thoughtful and detailed discussion of the menu with Herr Horst, Sergeant Pouncy ordered grilled squab on a nest of green beans for himself and fettucine with strips of Norwegian salmon, tomatoes and blanched garlic for Mrs. Pouncy. By the time the food was selected, Mrs. Pouncy and Herr Horst were such friends that he even convinced her to have a glass of wine with her fettucine. Sergeant Pouncy announced that he didn't usually drink wine either, but maybe Herr Horst could recommend a glass of something to go with the squab. Herr Horst said he was confident that he could.

By 9:36 P.M. the Pouncys had finished their dinner, turned down dessert and were waiting for their coffee. In the Bellevue Motel, Erika McCorkle and Granville Haynes had just reached page 233 of *Mercenary Calling*. Neither had spoken for almost two hours except when Haynes occasionally said, "Here," when he handed her a new page.

McCorkle and the Pouncys' coffee arrived together. After being introduced to Mrs. Pouncy, McCorkle agreed to join them for an espresso. He found Ozella Pouncy to be an unusually handsome woman still a few years shy of 40. She wore a beige silk dress that complemented her olive-brown skin, whose shade, McCorkle thought, was almost that of true sepia. He noticed that she also had enormous gentle-looking eyes and a wide, surprisingly stern mouth. McCorkle decided that if she wasn't exactly formidable, she was at least stalwart and obviously her husband's self-appointed protector, although he couldn't help but wonder why she thought Pouncy needed one.

After the espresso arrived, Pouncy said, "That was one of the ten best meals I've had in a year."

"Then I'm not only pleased but flattered," McCorkle said.

"If you hadn't dropped by, I was fixing to ask for you."

"Any special reason?"

"That partner of yours around?"

McCorkle nodded. "Somewhere."

"Then maybe you oughta invite him to join us because what I've gotta say concerns the two of you and he might as well hear it firsthand."

When McCorkle hesitated, Pouncy said, "Don't worry about Ozella here. I tell her everything." He gave his wife a fond look. "Well, damn near everything. Helps keep my head on straight."

"I can imagine," McCorkle said, called a waiter over and asked him to relay an invitation to Padillo.

By the time Padillo arrived, McCorkle had learned that Ozella Pouncy taught music and art in a District junior high school, was an assistant choir director at her church and that there were two Pouncy children, Graham, 15, and Amelia, 12.

Once the introductions were made, Padillo sat down next to Sergeant Pouncy. When Ozella Pouncy asked if he would like some coffee, Padillo smiled and said he had already reached his limit for the evening.

Pouncy leaned forward, rested his elbows on the table and dropped his voice into a conspiratorial murmur. "I could've called you guys with what I'm gonna say, but I figured they might've tapped your phones by now."

He ended the statement with a glance at Padillo. If Pouncy was expecting a reaction, all he received was a polite nod. Pouncy nodded back thoughtfully and turned to McCorkle. "We closed the file on Horace Purchase early this evening. In fact, it was just after I dropped you off at your house with a message for Granville Haynes. He ever get my message?"

"He got it," McCorkle said.

"Haven't heard from him."

"He has a lot on his mind."

"Who closed the file on Purchase?" Padillo asked.

"Maybe you oughta be asking why, not who."

"All right. Why?"

"Because we were told to."

"Who told you?"

"The mayor told the chief and the chief told the captain who told the lieutenant who told me. I didn't have nobody left to tell so I started closing it out. You'll have to guess who told the mayor because juicy stuff like that never quite dribbles down to my level."

"What're you closing it out as?" McCorkle asked.

"Either self-defense or justifiable homicide," Pouncy said. "They were still arguing about it when I got up and left."

"It was both," McCorkle said.

"Well, you were there and I wasn't so I won't argue. Besides, we got plenty of eyewitnesses who back you up. But that ain't the point."

"What is?" Padillo said.

"The point is that they're not gonna go after who hired

290

Horse Purchase." Pouncy paused, frowned and said, "And that's why I got so pissed off, excuse me, sugar."

Mrs. Pouncy gave him a reluctant nod of absolution.

"They just say no?" Padillo asked.

"They don't ever come out and give you a flat no on something like that," Pouncy said. "They say it'd be inappropriate or maybe counterproductive or even—and this was a new one on me—nugatory." Pouncy's smile was bitter. "Nuga-to-ry. Shit."

Before Pouncy could apologize to his wife again, McCorkle said, "So you're dropping Purchase altogether?"

"Done dropped him right alongside of who hired him. Of course, that still leaves me with Gelinet, Undean and old Tinker Burns—except Undean's outta my jurisdiction, although me and the Fairfax County sheriff're trading back and forth on what we got, which ain't much. But those three are a kind of natural progression. Gelinet, one; Undean, two; Burns, three—and four could be Granville Haynes. Course, I'm not too worried about Granville because he was in homicide out in L.A. and knows how to do. But I thought somebody oughta tell him we're nugatorizing Horse Purchase and mention that whoever hired Horse is still on the loose. That means—well, Granville can figure out what it means for himself."

"We'll tell him when he checks in," Padillo said.

"When you reckon that's gonna be?"

"We don't know."

"Bet I know."

"Okay. When?" Padillo said.

"When it's too damn late. That's when."

Haynes watched Erika McCorkle read the final page of his father's memoirs and place it on the upside-down manuscript that was next to her on the bed. She sighed, leaned back into the four pillows she had piled against the bed's headboard, locked her hands behind her head and stared at the motel room's ceiling.

She was still staring at it a minute later when Haynes began speaking in a clipped, mannered voice whose intonation and timbre bore an uncanny resemblance to that of his dead father:

"Had it not been for certain operations I conducted at the behest of the Central Intelligence Agency in Africa, the Middle East, Central America and, to a certain extent, in Southeast Asia, at least five—and possibly six—third world countries would still be laboring beneath the yokes of their Marxist-oriented governments." Haynes paused dramatically. "My only failure was in Southeast Asia. And that was a failure of nerve. But it was America's nerve that failed—not mine."

Erika brought her gaze down from the ceiling, her hands from behind her head, and clapped softly three times.

Haynes grinned. "A fair summation?"

"Fair but broad," she said. "I've never read such crap."

"Maybe not such well-written crap anyway. No dull moments. Lots of action and lots of gossip. A bit of potted and easily digested history. And you get yanked from one adventure to another so fast you barely have time to wonder what happens next. Isabelle did a great job. She even made it sound like Steady when he'd had two or three belts and was feeling expansive."

"You're still sure she wrote it?"

Haynes nodded. "I think Steady gave her the blueprints and the specifications and she put it together. Didn't you notice the wire service urgency? Short punchy sentences with no more than two of them to a paragraph. All villains clearly defined, labelled and outnumbering our paramount hero—Steady, of course—by ten to one. But what's especially clever is the way the CIA comes across as a bumbling, if benevolent, think tank staffed by nice tweedy chaps who smoke pipes and twinkle a lot. Twenty thousand Allen Dulleses guarding the Republic night and day. Wonderful."

"That the Dulles they named the airport after?" she asked.

"That was John Foster, his brother and also secretary of state under Eisenhower. Allen was Director of Central Intelligence."

"Now I remember."

"Sure you do."

"Well, it's no steamy exposé, is it?"

"No."

"Then how could the CIA object?"

"They couldn't. That's the point."

"Of what?"

"Of Steady's very long, very elaborate joke."

"You sound relieved."

"Wouldn't you be if you discovered your father was a prankster instead of a blackmailer?"

"Not if his pranks got three people killed."

"Four—counting Horace Purchase."

"Okay. Four. But if Steady's memoirs are some kind of never-ending practical joke, wouldn't a lot of his satisfaction have come from making sure the CIA knew the joke was on them?"

"Sure. It would've come from that. And from the money. Don't ever forget the money."

"The money turns him into a con artist instead of a prankster."

"Still better than a blackmailer."

"So when was the CIA supposed to find out they were the butt of a joke?"

"After they paid Steady the money not to publish. And after they read the manuscript that he'd sent them to make sure they knew what they'd paid to suppress."

"And learned they'd been had."

Haynes looked thoughtful and, for the first time, a little

sad. "He must've had it all planned out—everything except the part about his death."

"His and the others," she said, sat up and swung her feet to the floor. "Okay. Now what?"

"Now we go see Howard Mott, stash the car with him and figure out some way to get what Steady wanted."

"The last laugh—or the money?"

Haynes grinned his inherited grin. "I don't know yet," he said. "Maybe both."

Forty-two

The first shot sounded like a stout stick being snapped in two. Haynes classified the weapon as a .22-caliber rifle and guessed the shooter to be at least fifty yards away because he heard the shot an instant after the round buried itself in the motel room door.

Haynes spun away from the door he had just closed and tackled Erika McCorkle from the rear, dumping her onto the walk in front of the old Cadillac's grille. She lost her canvas overnight bag and it skidded beneath the car.

Still half lying on her, Haynes turned his head to stare up at the bullet hole just as another round smacked into the room's door three inches to the left of the first one. The sound of the snapped-in-two stick again came a split second later.

A third shot took out the light above the motel room door. It was as if the shooter needed to prove that the first two rounds hadn't been misses, but marksmanship. Haynes slipped McCorkle's borrowed revolver from his topcoat pocket, crawled off Erika and wormed his way to the left side of the car where he peered around the front tire—the one that had replaced the flat.

As Haynes peered around the tire toward the top of the motel's U, he glimpsed a dark blue or black sedan speeding off into the night. Haynes rose, stuck the revolver back into his topcoat and helped Erika to her feet. Her mouth was open as she tried to suck great gobs of air into her lungs.

"You hyperventilating?"

She shook her head and kept on gasping.

"I can go get that sack the food came in and you can breathe into that."

She shook her head again, even more vigorously, and said still gasping, "Nobody—ever shot—at me—before."

"The shooter's gone," he said.

"You sure?"

Haynes nodded. "He wasn't shooting at us. He was shooting at the door and the light. He hit both."

"Oh, shit, I've never been so scared."

"You were supposed to be. How is it now?"

"I'm still shaking."

"I mean your breathing."

"It's okay."

"Then let's go see Mott."

"And where the hell can we go after that?"

"How do you feel about Baltimore?" Haynes said.

After retrieving Erika's canvas bag from beneath the car, they drove slowly toward the exit. Some half-clad motel guests were peeking out of partially open doors, as if trying to decide whether what they had heard were gunshots or backfires. The motel's owner, shivering outside in his shirt sleeves, gave the old Cadillac an uninterested glance before ducking back into the warmth of the motel office. Haynes estimated that his $100 cash deposit would cover the room and also the cost of damage to the door and the light fixture.

"How'd we get found so fast?" Erika asked just after Haynes turned onto Wisconsin Avenue and headed south.

"No idea."

"I thought you were a detective."

"I was."

"Well, suppose somebody like us came to somebody like you and said, 'Hey, we were trying to hide out from the bad guys but they found us and took a few shots at us. So what d'you think we should do now?'"

"I'm still a cop?"

"You're still a cop."

"Then I'd probably say, 'How d'you folks feel about Baltimore?'"

Since there was no polite way to refuse the freshly baked apple pie that Lydia Mott pressed on them, Haynes and Erika each had a piece, plus a cup of coffee, and then followed Howard Mott in his pyjamas and bathrobe up the stairs and into the study-cum-music room.

Once they were seated, Haynes gave Mott a concise report on the incident at the Bellevue Motel. After Haynes finished, Mott asked his first question. "How long were you there?"

"Five or six hours."

"Any idea of how you were found so quickly?"

"None—except whoever came looking must've had help."

Mott pushed back the left sleeve of his enormous blue-and-white-striped bathrobe to look at his watch. "You checked into the motel when—around six?"

"Closer to five-thirty."

"So the shooter found you by eleven—approximately."

"It could've been a lot earlier."

"Why?"

"Because whoever it was waited for us to come out of the motel room and we were in there for at least five hours."

"I went out once to get some food," Erika said.

Mott looked at her and asked, "When was that?"

"Not long after we got there." .

Haynes leaned forward suddenly, betraying his impatience. "The question is still, how did he find us and where does a shooter go for help? Not to the D.C. cops or the FBI—and who the hell else has enough bodies to check every motel in the Washington area?"

Mott smiled slightly. "Those weren't questions. They were the introduction to a theory."

"Or an approach from a different angle," Haynes said. "Answer me this: who saw and even touched Steady's old Cadillac other than Erika, myself and Ledell Dark, master mechanic?"

"Horace Purchase," Erika said.

Mott asked, "He was actually close enough to touch it?"

"Dark claims he was close enough to drool on it."

"And that means close enough to slap on a sender," Haynes said.

"An electronic transmitter," Mott said.

Haynes nodded.

"But why would Purchase be so interested in Steady's car?"

"It was the last place left."

Mott frowned. "To do what?"

"To look for the manuscript."

"Please, God, don't let him tell me there really is a manuscript."

"Yes, Howard, there really is a manuscript."

"You've actually seen it, touched it, maybe even read it?"

Haynes nodded.

"Me, too," Erika said.

Mott sighed. "All right, let's deal with the car and its sender first, then come back to the manuscript. Okay?"

Haynes again nodded.

"Apparently Purchase was hired to kill you and he also may have been given the additional and earlier assignment of locating and, I presume, buying the Cadillac."

298

"Dark claims Purchase offered him twenty thousand cash," Erika said.

Mott gave his right earlobe a thoughtful tug. "So when Purchase inspected the car, he had the opportunity to attach the electronic device." Without waiting for comment, Mott continued, still tugging at his earlobe. "But all that happened before anyone could've known you two would pick up the car. In fact, the idea didn't occur to me until a few seconds before I suggested it at McCorkle's. Therefore—and I'm getting a little weary from leaping to all these conclusions— someone was monitoring the car electronically when you picked it up. The someone obviously wasn't poor Purchase because he was dead. But whoever it was used the sender's signal to track you to the motel."

"Sounds about right," Haynes said.

"Have you attempted to find the gizmo?" Mott asked.

"No."

"Then that expert marksman may even now be lurking outside my house."

"Want to run him off?" Haynes asked. "Just dial 911 and tell the cops you've got burglars. After they notice your Cleveland Park address, they'll be here in three minutes flat. Maybe two."

Mott ignored the suggestions. "When you searched the car for the manuscript, why didn't you find the sender?"

"Goddamnit, Howard, I told you we didn't search the car."

"We didn't have to," Erika explained. "We had a flat and by pure dumb luck discovered Steady'd hidden his manuscript underneath the spare tire."

"But you do intend to look for it?" Mott said.

"When we leave here, I'll run the car up a lift in some all-night gas station and find the thing in less than ten minutes."

"And the sharpshooter?"

"Fuck him," Haynes said.

Mott nodded slowly. "That's not bravado, is it?"

"Hardly. He wants me scared, not dead. Otherwise I'd be dead at the Bellevue Motel. Now, can we get on with it?"

"All right, let's," Mott said, paused briefly and asked, "You've each read Steady's manuscript; what's your assessment?"

Haynes said, "It's a snappy adventure tale about how a rather picaresque Steadfast Haynes almost single-handedly saves a long string of tottering democracies—except for a few out in Southeast Asia whose loss isn't really his fault."

"Snappy?" Mott said.

"It moves right along," Erika said.

"And how is the CIA portrayed?"

"If not with reverence, at least with benevolent contempt."

"Nothing offensive, libelous or a threat to national security—whatever that is?"

"Nothing," Haynes said and gave Erika a go-ahead glance. She opened the canvas bag that rested on her lap, removed the manuscript and handed it to Mott.

After leafing through it quickly, as if to make sure he hadn't been handed yet another collection of blank pages, Mott looked at Haynes and asked, "Innocuous, you say?"

"Totally."

Mott placed the manuscript on the table beside his chair, clasped his hands across his stomach and stared up at the twelve-foot-high ceiling. "So Steady passes the word around town that he's written a killer exposé of the CIA. But because the agency can't prove he ever really worked for it, there's no way it can legally suppress publication. Fair enough so far?" he said, bringing his gaze down from the ceiling to rest it first on Erika, then on Haynes. They nodded.

"However," Mott continued, "Steady's convinced that eventually the agency'll make him an offer, which, after all the dickering's done, he'll accept and sign over all rights to Langley. And with that done and the money safely banked, he'll furnish them with a copy of the manuscript, whether they ask for it or not, just to make sure they fully understand what dopes they've been."

"His last laugh," Erika said.

"Except Steady died," said Mott.

"So did three others," Haynes said. "Or four, counting Purchase, who also helped spoil the joke."

"Somebody," Mott said, "is goddamned afraid of what Steady knew and of what he might've written. This same somebody is so afraid that he or she or even they were willing to kill Isabelle Gelinet, Gilbert Undean and Tinker Burns. Of these three, I think only Burns suspected he was in danger." Mott stopped to stare at Haynes, then nodded to himself and said, "I also think Tinker may have left the cause of his suspicion to you."

"What d'you mean 'left'?" Haynes said.

Mott rose, went to his old rolltop desk and picked up a Federal Express envelope. "This arrived late this afternoon," he said. "It's from Tinker. It was sent yesterday morning around eleven—which means it had to go all the way down to the Federal Express hub in Memphis, then back up to Washington."

"Did he send it to you or to me?"

"To me," Mott said. "But inside the Fed Ex packet was a large manila envelope. Printed across it was a somewhat melodramatic message: 'To Be Opened Only in the Event of My Death.' And underneath that was Tinker's signature. Well, since Tinker was indeed dead, I opened it. Inside was a small envelope addressed to you."

Mott went over to Haynes and handed him the smaller manila envelope. Haynes stared at the envelope. His name had been printed on it with a ballpoint pen. Down and a little to the right in big block letters was the one word PERSONAL, which had been underlined three times.

Haynes ripped open the envelope and removed three sheets of paper of different size and weight. One was a sheet of guest stationery from the Madison Hotel. The others were a carbon copy of a two-page, single-spaced memorandum, dated the previous Saturday and written by Gilbert Undean. The intended recipient was "File."

"May I make a suggestion?" Mott said.

"Sure."

"Read it to yourself first and then decide whether it's necessary—or even wise—for us or anyone to know what it says."

"Okay," Haynes agreed.

He read the note from Tinker Burns first. Then he read Gilbert Undean's memo to file. As Haynes read the memo, all expression left his face and it grew perfectly still except for his eyes, which danced from line to line. When he finished the memo, he looked up and Mott noticed that Haynes's eyes were no longer dancing. They now looked as old and still as death and just as implacable.

"I think you two should hear Tinker's note to me," Haynes said in a curiously formal tone as he looked first at Erika, then at Mott. Before either of them could reply, he began to read aloud:

"'Dear Granny: Here's a carbon of a memo that Gilbert Undean wrote to his personal file and I found underneath his desk blotter out in Reston after I'd called the cops to tell them he was dead. I thought I could make a few bucks with it but since you're reading this, I guess I made a mistake. The Big One. Ha. Ha. Anyway, do what you want to with it but play it smarter than I did and remember it's a carbon and that somebody has got the original. If you need help, you can figure out from the memo who to ask. So long. Tinker.'"

A long silence followed. Mott finally ended it by clearing his throat and saying, "I don't think Erika and I should hear any more. In fact, we may've heard too much already."

"Okay," Haynes said.

"I want to ask one question," she said.

Haynes nodded.

"When he said you'd know who to ask for help, who did he mean?"

"Padillo," Haynes said. "Who else?"

Forty-three

I t was easier to find the sender than an open service station after midnight. But Haynes finally found one far out on Georgia Avenue, almost to Silver Spring, where the old Cadillac made a hit with the two young black attendants and a gaggle of equally young kibitzers, who offered a steady stream of advice, if not assistance.

Haynes pulled into the full-service bay and got out. He almost had to shout to make himself heard over the extra-loud boombox rap. After he asked one of the attendants to fill it up, check under the hood and make sure the tires were okay, Haynes began his search for the sender by running an exploratory palm beneath the fenders. When the attendant, who now had the hood up, asked in a near shout what he was looking for, Haynes shouted back, "Rattles."

He found the sender stuck up underneath the left rear fender. It was the ZC-II model, made in Singapore, and much favored by DEA agents—at least by the several Haynes had met in Los Angeles. Back behind the wheel of the Cadillac, he showed the transmitter to Erika, who examined it curiously. "This the stick-on magnet?" she said, touching its smooth, dark gray side.

"Right."

"What'll you do with it?"

"Send it on its way."

"How?"

"That cab in the self-service bay?"

She looked and nodded.

"Let's go ask how much the fare is to Dulles. You do the asking."

They got out of the Cadillac and started toward the middle-aged cabdriver who was putting 87 octane into his two-year-old Chevrolet Caprice sedan. Erika went first. Haynes followed, using a white handkerchief to wipe fender grime from his hands.

"Excuse me," Erika said to the driver.

He nodded at her, neither friendly nor unfriendly. Haynes dropped the handkerchief and knelt to retrieve it. The driver gave him a glance, then looked back at Erika.

"I need to go to Dulles to meet someone coming in on a Lufthansa flight from Frankfurt, and I was wondering how much the fare is?"

Still kneeling, Haynes pressed the sender up against the taxi's frame just as the driver said, "This time of night I can't go out there for less'n sixty."

Haynes rose as Erika smiled ruefully and said, "That's what I was afraid of. Sorry."

"So 'm I, lady."

She turned to Haynes. "Sixty."

"Jesus," Haynes said.

They went back to the Cadillac. Erika got in while Haynes handed a twenty to the attendant, who wanted to know the year of the Cadillac's manufacture.

"Seventy-six," said Haynes.

"True slick," said the attendant and handed Haynes his change.

* * *

Looking frequently into his rearview mirror, Haynes turned either west or south every few blocks until he found himself on Nebraska Avenue Northwest, nearing Connecticut Avenue. He turned south on Connecticut and stayed on it. They rode in silence until they reached Calvert Street and were halfway across Taft Bridge. It was then that Erika spoke.

"If you came this way because you're thinking of dropping me off at Pop's, forget it."

"You'll be safer there."

"If I wanted safe, prince, I'd've taken one look at you and passed."

"You like getting shot at?"

"No, but it's a lot more interesting than looking for a job." She paused. "You want to know what I really like?"

"What?"

"I like eating seventeen-dollar room-service cheeseburgers at the Willard and matching smarts with smooth numbers such as the elegant Mr. Hamilton Keyes and shrewd shitkickers like Sheriff Shipp-with-two-*p*'s, who's probably twice as bright as most of the guys I ever met. I like checking into out-of-the-way motels and dining on Hershey bars and Ritz crackers. I like Lydia's Mott's full-belly policy and Howie Mott's brains and Pop's studied forbearance and Padillo's panther walk. I like watching you switch from Mr. Manners to Hardcase Haynes of Homicide and back again. But most of all, I like us in bed."

She paused and added, "You just passed my house."

"I know."

"Are we turning around?"

Haynes shook his head.

"Where're we going—Baltimore?"

"To the Willard."

"What happened to Baltimore?"

"To hell with Baltimore," Haynes said.

* * *

Haynes inserted the plastic card-key into the slot and opened the door to his room at the Willard. He stepped back out of habit to let Erika enter first, but changed his mind and held out a cautionary right hand. He slipped the hand into the pocket of his topcoat and wrapped it around the butt of McCorkle's revolver. Then he went in.

There was one light on and it came from a lamp that illuminated the easy chair occupied by Hamilton Keyes, who rose gracefully and said, "I'd almost given you up."

"Sorry we're late," Haynes said.

Keyes parried the thrust with a small polite smile and said, "Good evening, Miss McCorkle."

"I think evening's long gone," she said.

Keyes nodded his agreement and turned back to Haynes. "I apologize for my intrusion, but something's come up. If I could've reached anything other than Howard Mott's answering machine, I wouldn't have bothered you."

"Before you ask him what's come up," Erika said, "ask him how he got in."

"Hotel security let him in," Haynes said. "After he gave them a brief lecture on how the nation trembles for my safety."

"I was rather convincing," Keyes said as he sat back down. "And they were rather anxious not to have another dead body littering their hotel."

Haynes turned and went to the refrigerator. He opened it and went down on one knee to inventory its contents. "Drink, Mr. Keyes?"

"Thank you, no."

"Erika?"

"A beer would be good."

Haynes removed two Heinekens and poured them into a pair of glasses. He handed one to Erika, who was now seated in an easy chair and separated from Keyes by the lamp. Holding his own glass in his left hand, Haynes sat on the bed, facing Keyes. He slipped his right hand back down into the topcoat's pocket and asked, "What came up?"

Keyes tugged at the vest of his gray worsted suit that had a tiny herringbone weave. He wore a gold watch chain across the vest, but no Phi Beta Kappa key. Haynes assumed the key was lying forgotten in some top bureau drawer.

After the vest was to his liking, Keyes said, "One might say the level of anxiety came up. Or rose. We'd like to advance the meeting to ten tomorrow morning instead of ten Wednesday morning."

"Who had the anxiety attack?"

"My betters."

"What about the money?"

"That's been arranged."

"So everything remains the same—except the date?"

"Precisely."

"Then it's okay with me," Haynes said. "But I may have to drive out to Mott's and pound on his door to let him know about the new time."

"Perhaps you could call him early tomorrow morning."

"I'll think about it," Haynes said.

"Then I'll disturb you no longer," Keyes said, rose and picked up the navy-blue cashmere topcoat he had draped over the back of his chair. It was not quite a bow that he gave Erika. "Miss McCorkle."

"Mr. Keyes."

Keyes went to the door, opened it, turned once more and said, "Again, my apologies," and was gone.

There was a brief silence until Erika said, "So what d'you think, chief?"

"He knows how to make an exit," Haynes said, put his beer down on a table, picked up the bedside phone and tapped out a number.

Herr Horst answered with his usual, "Reservations."

"This is Granville Haynes. Is Padillo still there?"

"One moment, please."

After Padillo came on, Haynes said, "I have a problem."

"Can it be solved over the phone?"

"No."

"Then you'd better get over here."

It took twenty minutes for Haynes, seated on the leather couch in the office at Mac's Place, to tell Padillo about finding the true manuscript; target practice at the Bellevue Motel; the bugged Cadillac and the late night visit from Hamilton Keyes.

Padillo responded with his eyes, using them to signal interest, approval, surprise or simply, "Get on with it." He sat slumped low in the high-backed chair with his feet up on the partners desk, his shoes off and his hands locked behind his head. Haynes noticed that his socks were again argyle, but this time they offered shades of brown that ranged from chocolate to taupe.

"You say you and Erika read it—Steady's book?" Padillo said after Haynes stopped talking.

Haynes nodded.

"How was it?"

"It goes very quickly, once your disbelief is hanging by the neck."

"Then Isabelle must've furnished the quick and Steady the embellishment."

"If the CIA wanted to," Haynes said, "it could safely issue the thing as the world's longest press release."

"They haven't read it yet?"

"Not that I know of."

"But they're still going to bid for it tomorrow, unread or not?"

"Yes."

"And you're going to take their money?"

"Right again."

"Then what's your problem?"

"This," Haynes said, reached into a breast pocket and brought out the envelope that contained the note from

Tinker Burns and the memo by Gilbert Undean to his files. He handed the envelope to Padillo.

"Read the note from Tinker first," Haynes said.

Padillo nodded and, stockinged feet still up on the desk, read the note. When finished he shook his head sadly and began the memo from Undean.

After the first paragraph, Padillo's feet dropped to the floor and he sat up in his chair. He placed the memo on top of the desk and bent over it, elbows on the desk, head in his hands, his concentration total.

When finished, he looked up at Haynes and asked, "Anyone else read this?"

"Just you and I and Tinker Burns."

"And whoever has the original."

"I'd almost forgotten about the original."

Padillo tapped the memo. "Now I understand your problem. Tomorrow you have to be in two places at the same time."

"Exactly."

"And you want me to be at the other place."

"You and McCorkle."

Padillo grimaced slightly, as if at some seldom-felt tinge of regret or even a pang of self-reproach. "I should've told McCorkle."

"You knew?"

"Not when she came in. She fooled me with her frumpy outfit and that shuffling walk. But when she came out of the office, she was in a hurry, forgot her shuffle and shifted into her long athletic stride that's hard to forget once you've seen it. And that's when I knew it was Muriel Keyes."

"But you didn't know about the fake bomb then?"

"Not then."

"And you haven't told McCorkle it was Mrs. Keyes?"

"No. I haven't told him."

"Why not?"

"I'm not sure. Maybe because he wasn't hurt—except for

some injured pride. Or because of my secretive nature. Or because of Muriel and me a long time ago. Or maybe I was waiting for the other shoe to drop."

"It just dropped."

"So it did," Padillo said and again tapped the Undean memo. "This suggests that Mrs. Hamilton Keyes walked in here with a fake bomb and out with an equally fake manuscript to save her husband's career and her neck."

"You believe that?"

"I don't know," said Padillo. "But why not let McCorkle ask her tomorrow?"

Forty-four

At 3:21 A.M. that Tuesday, Granville Haynes left Howard Mott's house on 35th Street Northwest and drove back to the Willard in twenty-four minutes. At eight minutes to four he entered his room to find Erika McCorkle propped up in bed, reading a paperback novel that had on its cover a huge Nazi swastika formed out of human bones.

"Who's winning?" Haynes asked as he stripped off his topcoat and jacket and hung them in the closet.

"The Krauts—but it's only nineteen forty."

Haynes removed two sheets of stapled-together paper from his jacket's inside breast pocket and crossed to the bed. "More ancient history," he said as he handed them over.

Erika put her book down and accepted the stapled papers without glancing at them. "You look tired," she said.

"I am."

"Come to bed."

"I'll take a shower while you read it."

She looked at the first sheet. "The notorious Undean

memo. I thought Howie Mott said nobody but you should read it."

"He changed his mind," Haynes said. "Padillo's read it. And by now so has your dad. Mott is probably reading it for the fourth or fifth time."

Erika read the memo's first line, muttered, "My God," and, without looking up, said, "Go take your shower."

When Haynes came out of the shower ten minutes later, wearing a hotel robe, he found Erika still propped up in bed against the pillows, staring at the far wall, the memo now in her lap. She had locked her hands behind her head, which thrust her breasts out against the thin fabric of the thigh-length T-shirt that was her nightgown. Silk-screened across the front of the T-shirt was the line "This Space Available."

She stopped staring at the wall to stare at Haynes. "Have you told the cops yet—Detective-Sergeant what's his name?"

"Darius Pouncy. No."

"Why not?"

"Because a lot of the memo's conjecture and there's no proof that Undean wrote it. Maybe Tinker wrote it."

"Couldn't they compare the typing with Undean's type-writer? The FBI's always doing that kind of stuff."

"Maybe Tinker wrote it on Undean's typewriter."

"You really think she killed Isabelle and stuck a pistol in Pop's face?"

"I believe she stuck a pistol in McCorkle's face," Haynes said.

"Why d'you believe that and not the other?"

"Because somebody recognized her leaving Mac's Place."

"Who did?"

"It doesn't matter," he said, turned, went to the small refrigerator and took out a small can with a label that claimed it contained pink grapefruit juice from Texas. He held the can up for Erika to see and said, "Want some?"

"No."

Haynes opened the can and drank. "Tell me what it said."

She frowned. "What d'you mean?"

"Build a case for me. Pretend you're a lawyer."

She reached for the memo.

"No," Haynes said. "From memory."

"I don't understand what you want."

"That's a two-page single-spaced memo. I don't think Undean just sat down and batted it out. I think it was very carefully composed and went through maybe three or four drafts before all the holes were plugged."

"I'll have to tell it my own way then."

"Fine."

She took a deep breath. "Okay. It's Laos, early nineteen seventy-four. March. They were all in Vientiane, the capital. Steady. Muriel Lamphier, later to become Muriel Keyes, and Undean. Muriel's a young CIA—what—operative?"

"You're telling it," Haynes said.

"Okay. She's an operative, junior grade, with some kind of embassy cover job. Steady's doing his usual propaganda stuff and Undean's analyzing whatever he analyzes. Then somebody—and it's not clear from the memo who—suspects that a young American married couple, Mr. and Mrs. Fred—uh—Nimes aren't really doing church-sponsored relief work, but are actually homegrown antiwar lefties who're spying for the opposition, the Pathet Lao. Well, what to do?

"The solution somebody comes up with is to send in a femme fatale. So they send in Muriel to seduce Fred, feed him some false stuff and see if it's passed on. Well, Muriel gets Fred in the sack all right, apparently on more than one occasion. But one afternoon when they're rolling around in bed, Mrs. Nimes comes home unexpectedly. Her name's Angie—for Angela.

"What happens next is what the memo calls a 'domestic altercation.' Angie picks up a bottle and cracks it over Fred's head. Fred slams Angie up alongside the head. Angie produces a gun and shoots Fred dead. She then turns the gun on Muriel. But Muriel doesn't want to die and the two

314

ladies wrestle for the gun. It goes off and Angie takes a bullet in the face and dies.

"Muriel gets dressed, well, I guess she got dressed, the memo doesn't say, and bolts out of the house, almost petrified. But she has enough sense to find Steady. He goes to the Nimes house and has a look. Then he goes to see the CIA's pet Laotian general and offers him two hundred thousand U.S. dollars to put the fix in. The general agrees but wants cash in advance. Okay?"

"You're doing fine," Haynes said.

"Steady confides in Undean that he needs two hundred thousand for a special ultra-secret operation. But Undean isn't buying, probably with good reason, and insists on knowing the details. Steady tells him. Undean suggests that Steady get word to Hamilton Keyes in Saigon. Steady does and Keyes flies to Vientiane with the money. Steady hands it over to the general. I think all this took about a day. Meanwhile, the tropics are going to work on the bodies of Mr. and Mrs. Nimes.

"Well, once the pet general has the cash in hand, he orders six 14- and 15-year-old Laotian soldiers to burn down the Nimes house that night. They do and at dawn the kid soldiers are arrested, tried, convicted and shot for having raped Mrs. Nimes, killed Mr. Nimes, who tried to defend her, and then, to cover it all up, burned down the Nimes house.

"The two Nimes bodies, what's left of them, are gathered up, boxed and buried. Steady writes letters to their respective parents, lamenting the young folks' death and praising them for having done the Lord's work. Meanwhile, Hamilton Keyes instructs Undean to run an exhaustive check on the Nimeses' background. Undean does and discovers they weren't secret agents for another foreign power after all, but merely a couple of left-leaning, run-of-the-mill do-gooders. Undean doesn't make a written report of his findings, but does make separate verbal ones to Keyes and Steady.

"Keyes decides the best thing to do is arrange for their pet general to receive a special commendation and forget the whole thing—except for the beautiful Muriel Lamphier, whom he consoles, woos and, once they're both back in the States, weds. And that's the terrible secret of Mrs. Hamilton Keyes, née Lamphier." Erika paused, then asked, "Does that sound like some of your late daddy's handiwork?"

"Exactly," Haynes said.

"Okay," she said, "now we—what do they call it in Hollyweird?—we cut to—"

"Dissolve would be better," Haynes said.

"Okay, we dissolve to Washington some fifteen years later—make it almost sixteen. Steadfast Haynes is spreading word around town that he's just finished his searing memoirs. The word reaches Mrs. Hamilton Keyes. She contacts her lawyer, a distinguished former U.S. senator from the great state of Alabama, and instructs him to buy up the memoirs and hang the cost. But before negotiations can begin, Steady dies. The lawyer quickly contacts the son and heir's new lawyer, Mr. Howard Mott, and makes an offer of one hundred thousand dollars for the memoirs, sight unseen. But the son and heir, that's you, demurs and asks for half a million bucks. All this money talk happened the same day Steady was buried at Arlington.

"Well, that same afternoon, Mrs. Hamilton Keyes—or so Gilbert Undean suspects—goes calling on Mlle Isabelle Gelinet and demands to know where the manuscript is." Erika paused and frowned. "Why would Muriel do that?"

"Maybe she panicked," Haynes said.

Erika shook her head and said, "Anyway, Isabelle refuses to divulge—another Undean word—where the manuscript is and Muriel—you want me to go into all that? There's a whole lot of gruesome detail."

"No need," Haynes said.

"Undean suggests that regardless of whether or not Isabelle revealed where the manuscript was, Muriel couldn't let

316

her live because Isabelle knew her festering Laotian secret. That festering phrase is mine, not Undean's. So Isabelle dies and you and Tinker Burns discover her body. As soon as Hamilton Keyes learns of Isabelle's death, he summons Undean and instructs him to offer up to fifty thousand for the memoirs. Undean then goes into a lot of self-justification about how, earlier that same day, he had urged Keyes to buy the memoirs from you and how Keyes pooh-poohed the idea. Anyway, Undean finds you and offers the fifty thousand and you turn it down. Undean then reports to Keyes about how you'd also turned down the one hundred thousand from the senator and are now asking five hundred thousand because you think you can make a film out of Steady's life. Undean then counsels Keyes to walk away from the deal. And that's the end of the Undean memo."

"You did very well," Haynes said.

"I have a good memory."

"What was left out?" Haynes asked. "By Undean?"

"Well, he couldn't tell how Muriel killed him."

"Well, no," Haynes said. "But what else?"

"There's almost no mention of Tinker Burns and none of Horace Purchase."

"Undean wouldn't have known about Purchase and must've assumed that Tinker found Isabelle's body by accident."

"Maybe," she said.

"What's your overall impression?"

"It all seems to be aimed at giving Muriel Keyes sufficient motive. If she can't buy or destroy the memoirs, she can at least do away with the remaining witnesses to the Laotian mess. With Steady gone, the only witnesses left are Undean, her husband and—since she wrote the memoirs—Isabelle."

"Why do you think Tinker was killed?"

"I guess he was trying to blackmail her with the Undean memo."

"A logical guess."

317

"Why did you ask me to make that . . . that recitation?" she asked. "Your real reason?"

"The memo's too smooth—too logical. Too neat. I wanted to see how it would sound if it came out disjointed."

Erika's eyes went wide. "You bastard! You know who killed them all—Isabelle and Undean and Tinker Burns."

"No, I don't."

"You know something. I can tell."

"The only thing I know for a fact is that Gilbert Undean didn't write that memo."

Forty-five

McCorkle shifted his position again, trying to accommodate his long legs to Padillo's 280 SL. After failing to cross them for the third time, he said, "You ever think of buying something a little more sedate and comfortable—maybe a Volvo stationwagon?"

Padillo ignored the question and said, "He should've left by now."

"It's only a little after nine and the meeting's not till ten."

"Keyes isn't one to arrive last at any meeting," Padillo said. "Especially this one."

They were parked on California Street two houses east of the Georgian one that belonged to Hamilton and Muriel Keyes. They assumed that when Keyes left he would probably head west—away from them—then south. Otherwise, he would have to cope with California Street when it suddenly turned one-way.

"He's in there, sipping his second cup of coffee out of a gold-rimmed Haviland cup," McCorkle said. "And we're trapped in this clapped-out roadster with a slit top that lets in wind with a chill factor of fifteen degrees. And what have we got to drink? Cold Roy Rogers coffee in plastic cups."

"Howard Johnson coffee," Padillo said.

"I haven't had a cup of Ho-Jo coffee in twenty years and, by my troth, it hasn't improved any."

"I'd almost forgotten," Padillo said.

"What?"

"What a sunbeam you are in the morning."

"Mind if I smoke?"

"Open the window."

"It's thirty-three degrees."

"And life is a series of hard choices."

"I'll chew instead," McCorkle said and produced a packet of Nicorette gum.

"Here he comes."

"So he does," McCorkle said, putting away the Nicorette.

The automatic overhead door of the Keyeses' three-car garage was nearly all the way up. A moment later a dark blue Buick sedan, with Keyes at the wheel, backed out onto the turnaround slab. Keyes then drove down the driveway and turned west, away from Padillo's coupe.

"Which car does she drive?" McCorkle asked as the garage door came back down.

"The Mercedes sedan."

"How do you know?"

"I saw it."

"When—the night you forgot to tell me who she was?"

"I didn't forget," Padillo said, started the engine and drove less than seventy-five yards before turning into the Keyes driveway. He stopped his car a foot away from the overhead door, blocking it nicely. He and McCorkle got out, walked to the front door and pushed a bell that rang some chimes. A moment later the door was opened by the Salvadoran maid.

Padillo snapped out a sentence in rapid Spanish that was much too fast for McCorkle. The only words he got were "la Señora" and "los Señores Padillo y McCorkle." But the maid understood perfectly, especially the imperious tone, which caused her to duck her head, open the door wider and invite them inside to wait while she informed la Señora.

"The help must've loved you back at the old hacienda, *mi jefe*," McCorkle said.

"It was a verbal shortcut."

"Which scared the hell out of her."

"She heard worse in El Salvador."

"How do you know where she's from?"

Before Padillo could reply, the maid returned, still scurrying and bobbing a little, to announce that la Señora would join them presently in the room of reception.

Padillo gave her his most charming smile, thanked her graciously and inquired if her longing for San Salvador remained acute. She replied that it had lessened a little in recent months. Padillo said he hoped she would soon be able to return for a visit in safety. She thanked him and said he was very kind.

By then they were in the living room that was filled with antiques. The maid left and Padillo and McCorkle sat on what seemed to be the two sturdiest chairs. A few minutes later Muriel Keyes entered, wearing fawn slacks, sandals, a silk blouse the color of bitter chocolate and a nervous smile.

Padillo rose quickly, McCorkle more slowly. Muriel Keyes chose to ignore McCorkle, except for a brief glance, and smiled at Padillo. "Michael, how nice."

"Muriel."

After she offered him her cheek to brush with his lips, he said, "I think you met my partner, Mr. McCorkle, when you were playing Reba Skelton, noted calligrapher."

"Fast! Accurate! Prompt!" McCorkle said.

"Is that why you're here?" she asked Padillo.

"Not really."

She turned to McCorkle and said, "I apologize, Mr. McCorkle. It was very stupid of me."

"You were really very good," he said.

"But obviously not good enough." She looked at Padillo. "What gave it away?"

"You shuffled in but loped out. That Lamphier lope, once seen, is hard to forget."

"I was so damned frightened."

"Not as much as I was," McCorkle said.

"Please sit down," she said. "Could I offer you some coffee? It's probably still too early for a drink."

"Coffee'll be fine, Muriel," Padillo said as he sat down. "Especially since we're going to be here a while."

"Oh?" she said, going to the near wall to press an ivory button.

"There's something we'd like you to read," McCorkle said as he resumed his seat.

"Read? Read what?"

Before either of them could reply, the maid, who must've been hovering just outside the living room door, entered to find out what she would be asked to fetch or carry. Muriel Keyes, using serviceable, if halting, Spanish, asked for coffee and rolls.

When the maid left, Muriel Keyes turned back to McCorkle and said, "You said you wanted me to read something?"

Padillo said, "A memo from the late Gilbert Undean." He paused. "You did know him, didn't you?"

"A long time ago."

"Seen him recently?"

"Yes. He came to see my husband last—Friday, I think. Rather late."

McCorkle and Padillo said nothing. After the silence had gone on for thirty seconds, she said, "Why would Mr. Undean send you a memorandum, Michael?"

"He didn't send it to me."

"Then who did?"

"Tinker Burns sent it—indirectly. Tinker's the one your lawyer hired in Paris to do some work for you here."

"What kind of work was that?"

"Find out whether Steady Haynes had mentioned you in his memoirs. You're still interested in the memoirs, aren't you?"

"Not nearly as much as I was. I think that particular—what should I call it—problem?—"

"Problem's good," McCorkle said.

"I think that particular problem's been resolved."

"Sorry, Muriel," Padillo said. "It's just beginning."

Granville Haynes, driving the old Cadillac, was nearing McCorkle's Connecticut Avenue apartment building at 9:45 A.M. when Erika said, "I'll be your slave for a year if you can work me into that meeting."

Haynes smiled. "I would if I could."

"But I'll get a full play-by-play later?"

"Everything."

"God, that'll be interesting," she said and leaned over to kiss him goodbye just as he stopped in front of the old gray building's no-standing zone. The car behind honked immediately.

"Stick by the phone," he said as she got out and turned to give the honker the finger, which produced yet another honk. Just as she closed the door, Haynes raised his voice to say, "And keep your doors locked." She nodded that she understood and hurried toward the building.

Haynes continued down Connecticut, went around Dupont Circle and found a parking place in front of 1633 Connecticut next door to where the razed Junkanoo nightclub had once stood.

He dropped some coins into the meter, looked at his watch and saw that he had five minutes. He pulled the collar of his new topcoat up around his chin, stuck his hands down into its pockets and rediscovered McCorkle's pistol. It felt cold to the touch and he saw no need to wrap his right hand around its butt.

323

Although he was exactly on time, Haynes was the last to arrive at the 10 A.M. meeting in the former senator's office. Haynes thought the place had the leathery smell of a shoe store—or the way shoe stores smelled before they started selling so many athletic shoes.

Haynes shook hands with Hamilton Keyes first because it seemed to be part of some business ritual. He even shook hands with Howard Mott, who introduced him to the former senator. The senator had retained his professional politician's quick-release handshake.

Haynes sat down in one of the three leather armchairs in front of the ornate desk. He sat next to Mott, who separated him from Hamilton Keyes. The senator, presiding from behind the desk, smiled a brief smile of commerce and said, "Well, gentlemen, I think we can begin."

When no one objected, he continued. "We will entertain offers this morning for the copyright to a written work by the late Steadfast Haynes, entitled *Mercenary Calling*, said copyright being the property of Mr. Haynes's son, Granville, who is the sole owner."

He looked around for confirmation and received a nod from Howard Mott. "Papers for the consummation of the sale have been drawn up by Mr. Mott, who is Mr. Haynes's attorney. I have examined them and find them to be in order. Any questions?"

There weren't any. The senator nodded again and said, "There are two parties who plan to tender offers for the copyright. One is Mr. Keyes, representing Write-Away, Incorporated, of Miami, Florida. The other is a client of mine who wishes to remain anonymous."

Haynes decided to nod. So did Hamilton Keyes.

"Very well. Since Mr. Keyes is present he is entitled to make the first offer."

"Seven hundred and fifty thousand," Keyes said.

"Seven hundred and fifty thousand dollars," the senator

said. "I will now telephone the only other bidder to see whether Mr. Keyes's bid will be topped."

The senator pushed a single button on his telephone console. He listened just long enough for a phone to ring once somewhere before he said, "Seven hundred and fifty." There had been no faint click of a phone call being answered, nor of a voice saying hello. The senator listened for a moment to what seemed to be a silent voice, looked up at Keyes and said, "Eight hundred thousand dollars is bid."

Haynes smiled. Hamilton Keyes cleared his throat and said, "One million."

The senator spoke into the phone. "One million has been bid." He listened for a few seconds, nodded to the unseen caller and said, "I understand. Thank you."

The senator slowly put the phone down, looked at Keyes and said, "Yours is the high bid, Mr. Keyes. Congratulations."

Keyes nodded and Haynes said, "Where do I sign?"

Howard Mott produced five bound photocopied legal documents from his briefcase, placed them on the desk, offered Haynes a ballpoint pen and said, "Sign each document at the blue X on each last page."

Haynes quickly signed his name five times and said, "When do I get my money?"

Hamilton Keyes withdrew a plain white No. 10 envelope from the breast pocket of his dark blue double-breasted suit and handed the unsealed envelope to the senator. The senator opened it and took out five checks, three of them gray, two of them green.

"I have here five cashier's checks for two hundred thousand dollars apiece. Two of the checks are drawn on the Riggs National Bank and three on American Security."

He put the checks back in the envelope and handed it to Howard Mott, who looked at each check briefly, then passed them on to Haynes. Using the pen Mott had lent him, Haynes endorsed the checks and handed them back to Mott.

"Here you go, Howard. I'll tell you what to do with them

later." Haynes rose and shook his head a little regretfully. "Well, gentlemen, it would've made a hell of a picture."

He smiled at the senator, winked at Keyes, turned and left the room.

There was a long silence until the senator said, "I think that boy might've at least said, 'Much obliged,' or 'Kiss my ass.'"

"You would think so, wouldn't you?" said Howard Mott.

Forty-six

Haynes stood at a bank of three phones across the street from the faded tan brick building where the senator had his law offices and where the bachelor Speaker of the House of Representatives had long ago had an apartment. Haynes was turned around, facing the building, a phone to his ear, listening to Erika McCorkle relay a phoned-in report from Michael Padillo.

"It was *her* money?" Haynes said.

"Hers, not the spooks," Erika said.

"Does Padillo believe it?"

"He's ninety-nine percent convinced."

"He's coming out now," Haynes said, hung up the phone and jaywalked across the street, catching up with Hamilton Keyes, who had stopped at the corner for a red light. Guessing that Keyes hated to be touched, Haynes grabbed his left elbow, ready to give its prime nerve an almost crippling squeeze—even through the dark blue cashmere topcoat.

"Let's talk," Haynes growled.

A startled Hamilton Keyes quickly recovered and, without turning, said, "About what?"

"Your wife and the three people she killed."

That made Keyes turn and stare at Haynes. Haynes offered some clearly audible breathing through a slightly open mouth and also a noticeable collection of spittle in the mouth's left corner.

"You're really quite mad, aren't you?" Keyes said.

"If you mean angry, pissed off and enraged, you fucking-A right I'm mad. Two of the three people she killed were friends of mine—my oldest friends. You got a car?"

Keyes tore his elbow loose from Haynes's grasp, rubbed it and said, "Up the street."

"Let's go take us a ride and have us a talk then. Topic A will be the Undean memo."

Keyes cocked his head to examine Haynes almost sympathetically. "You don't even know you're raving, do you?"

Haynes raised a forefinger to his lips. "Shhh. They'll hear us."

When they reached Keyes's dark blue Buick sedan, Haynes stared at it for fifteen seconds, not moving, not even breathing.

"I've seen this fucking car before," he said and walked slowly all the way around it, pausing to kick two of the tires. He then whirled on Keyes and said, "This is the fucking car she shot at me from."

"She?"

"Your heiress wife. Muriel Lamphier Keyes."

"Shot at you, did she?"

"Last night at the Bellevue Motel out in Bethesda where nobody knew I was, except Muriel. She used a twenty-two rifle, probably loaded with longs. Could've wiped me out if she'd wanted to. Hell of a good shot."

"You saw her?"

"I saw this same exact car take off like a scalded snake right after she shot at me. Now I'm about to be taken for a ride in it. You might like coincidences, but I hate 'em." Haynes sounded even less happy when he asked, "This really your car?"

Keyes quickly unlocked the passenger door, as if to prove ownership. Haynes got in. After Keyes was behind the wheel, Haynes said, "Muriel borrowed your car last night, right? Sure she did. Probably scooted over in the seat, rolled down this very same window, used the sill for a rest—maybe even had herself a scope—squeezed off three rounds, bang, bang, bang, and missed me by inches on purpose."

Keyes started the engine and said, "I haven't the slightest idea of what you're talking about."

"Stick up for her then. I don't blame you."

With a sigh, Keyes asked, "Where to?"

"Straight out Connecticut to the District line. Makes a nice drive and ought to give us plenty of time to talk."

"About the Undean memo," Keyes said, pulling away from the curb. "Whatever that is."

Haynes said nothing for nearly two minutes, then snarled his question. "Where the fuck was she Sunday morning right after the big snow?"

"It's none of your fucking business, but she was with an old friend in McLean."

Haynes's expression turned sly, his voice insinuating. "Muriel a pretty fair skier?"

"She didn't go skiing in McLean."

"No, but she skied right up to old Gilbert Undean's front door in Reston, didn't she? All masked and goggled and bundled up so nobody could tell if she was male, female or in between. Undean let her in. Can't really blame him for that since she was pointing her piece at him. They go up the stairs to his office. Maybe they talk a little; maybe they don't. Or maybe they reminisce about old times in Vientiane when Muriel got caught fucking some woman's husband, and how the woman got mad and shot him and then fought Muriel for

329

the gun, but Muriel won and shot the woman dead. All that was in the Undean memo."

"Really," Keyes said.

"This is all old stuff to you, isn't it, Ham? In the memo it says you were the guy who brought the money from Saigon to Vientiane that paid off the slope general who covered the whole mess up. What a nasty piece of shit he must've been. But it wasn't a total loss because that's when you met Muriel, right?"

"That's when I met her," Keyes said, stopping for a light at Connecticut and Columbia Road.

"Can't be too hard to fall for a beauty who's got sixty million bucks in the bank. Most guys wouldn't have any trouble at all—even if Muriel is kinda weird. Take old Gilbert Undean. He was still covering up for her after all these years."

"Covering up what?" Keyes said, sounding a bit interested for the first time.

"In his memo Undean claims the two-hundred-thousand-dollar payoff to the slope general was spook money. But it wasn't. It was Muriel's. Of course, that's no flash to you since you were the bag man who toted it to Vientiane."

Keyes frowned, looking almost puzzled. "You're claiming the two hundred thousand wasn't agency money?"

"Hey! I said something he didn't already know. Lemme ask you this: where'd you pick up all that cash in Saigon? At a bank? The embassy?"

"It was delivered to me."

"Who by?"

"You don't ask."

"White man?"

"Yes."

"You sign for it?"

"Never."

"Well, there you go. It wasn't agency money. It was Muriel's. You wanta know what really happened?"

Keyes shrugged.

"I didn't hear that, Ham."

"I'll listen."

"Okay. Here's the no-shit story. After Steady makes his deal for the cover-up with the general, he tells Muriel she's gotta come up with two hundred K—all cash. Now, Muriel could've asked the spooks for it. And maybe they'd've come up with it and maybe they wouldn't have. But she'd've had to tell 'em all about what a wife-killer she was and once they heard that, they'd've bounced her back home and out of the agency, right?"

"Perhaps."

"Well, two hundred K's no problem to Muriel," Haynes said, recalling the information Erika McCorkle had relayed to him from Padillo. "But the slope general is an all-cash kind of guy, and there's no way Muriel can lay hands on that much cash in twelve hours or whatever time she's got. But Steady knows how."

"He would," Keyes said.

"Steady knows some three-for-two black-market guys in Saigon who'll front Muriel the two hundred K if she'll pay back three hundred K in a week or ten days. Well, what's a hundred thou in vigorish to somebody like Muriel? So she says, swell, let's do it."

"I doubt that she said 'swell,' but go on."

"Okay. She and Steady've got the money all lined up. But now they've gotta figure out how to get it from Saigon to Vientiane fast. Very fast. And that's where you come in, Ham."

"Steady's choice. I suppose I should be flattered."

"You were first pick because Steady figured that when you heard the Lamphier name, bells would go off. Cash register bells. You know the kind in old-timey cash registers that rang when you—"

331

"You're wearing it out," Keyes said.

Haynes smiled not only at his cash register metaphor but also at the irritation it had caused Keyes. "Bet it was love at first sight. You and Muriel."

"Hardly," Keyes said. "Are you sure Undean didn't know it was Muriel's money?"

"Absolutely positive. The only ones who knew were Muriel and Steady—plus the three-for-two guys in Saigon."

"But you said none of this was in Undean's memo."

"You calling me a liar, Ham?" Haynes said, trying to turn the question into a softly spoken death threat and not at all displeased with the result.

"Merely curious," Keyes said.

"I accept your apology."

"I made none."

"But the thought was there and I shouldn't blame you for asking dumb questions. If I was married to somebody who'd knocked off three people, I'd sure as hell want to learn everything about her I could."

"Please answer my question," Keyes said.

"Okay. I found out about the money stuff in Steady's memoirs."

"You read them?"

"What else would I do—lick it off the page?"

"When?"

"Right after I found them yesterday—or was it the day before? But lemme tell you one thing about the memoirs and it's just what I said in the senator's office. They'd make just one hell of a picture."

"May I ask where you found the manuscript?"

"Sure. In Steady's car. He had this old Caddie ragtop that he left me in his will and I've been driving it around. Well, it had a flat and when I changed it, there was the manuscript in a nice safe nest under the spare. And you wanta know something else about Muriel—about her and the old Caddie?"

Keyes nodded once as if he no longer trusted himself to speak.

"Muriel tried to buy the Caddie on the Q.T. because she figured the manuscript might be in it. She didn't try herself, of course. What she did was hire some pro hitter, a guy called Horace Purchase, to buy it. Ever hear of him?"

"I think I saw his name in the *Post*," Keyes said.

"Well, it looks like Purchase had three goals or assignments or targets—whatever. Number one was to switch my lights off and he damn near did it at the Willard. Number two: try and buy Steady's old Caddie. Well, he couldn't manage that, but he did do number three."

Haynes shut up and waited for Keyes to ask what number three was. Instead, Keyes asked, "You're quite sure Muriel hired him?"

"Who else would?"

Keyes shrugged and asked, "What was the third objective? Of the Purchase person, I mean."

"It was kind of a fallback thing. If he couldn't buy the Caddie, he oughta try and plant a sender on it. You know, an electronic transmitter."

"And did he?"

"How the fuck d'you think Muriel found and shot at me out there at the Bellevue Motel where nobody knew I was?" Haynes chuckled. "Funny thing happened to that sender though."

"What?"

"I found it and slapped it right up against the frame of some taxicab." He chuckled again. "Must've driven whoever was tracking me nuts following that cab all over town and out to Dulles and everywhere." This time Haynes giggled, hoping it would suggest neurosis.

He apparently succeeded because Keyes asked, "Are you all right?"

"Sure I'm all right. Why wouldn't I be all right?"

Keyes ignored the question to ask one of his own. "You still have a copy of the Undean memo?"

"Not of the original. What I got is a copy of the carbon and what you wanta know is how'd I get it, right?"

Keyes only nodded, not taking his eyes from the road.

"I figure Muriel found the original memo right after she shot old man Undean. But she missed the carbon. Now, who should waltz into Undean's house two minutes later but Tinker Burns himself, the born snoop. Tinker finds the carbon under Undean's desk blotter right after he calls the cops, which leaves him with nothing to do but snoop around till they get there. Now you gotta understand this. If the cops'd found that carbon it'd've been, So long, Muriel. I mean that memo really nails her. Motive. Opportunity. All that good shit. But when Tinker reads it, all he smells is money. And since he's on her payroll anyway, he knows just which buttons to push."

"On her payroll?" Keyes said, not trying to conceal his surprise.

"Well, maybe he was just on retainer. The senator'd hired him in Paris because Muriel'd heard rumors about Steady's manuscript. And since Tinker was tight with both Steady *and* Isabelle, it seemed possible that they might let him peek at the memoirs and see if Muriel was mentioned or not. And, if so, how? You know, bad or good?"

"And is she mentioned?" Keyes asked.

"What's that got to do with Tinker Burns?" Haynes said. "Let's stick to him. Okay?"

"For now," Keyes said.

"Before Tinker can even get started on seeing about the memoirs, Steady dies on him. But because he's already been paid, Tinker flies over for the funeral and then starts snooping around, but finds fuck all—except for Isabelle's body—until he stumbles across the Undean memo. Well, that memo is money in the bank to Tinker. The first thing he does is pay the senator a visit and put the arm on him. The senator reports all this to Muriel, who says she'll take care of it. She and Tinker agree on Rock Creek Park as the payoff site. But there's no payoff and it's goodbye, Tinker."

"You really think my wife killed Tinker Burns?"

"She'd already done two. What's one more? Besides, who else would've killed him?"

"Muggers," Keyes said. "Old enemies."

Haynes gave him a pitying look. "Since when do muggers or even old enemies leave six or seven hundred bucks in the victim's wallet?"

"I'm surprised that Burns wasn't more suspicious."

"He was suspicious, all right," Haynes said. "How the hell do you think I got a Xerox copy of the Undean carbon? Tinker Fed-Exed it to Howard Mott in an envelope marked, 'Don't Open Unless I'm Dead' or something like that. And inside that envelope was a smaller one addressed to me and marked personal, and in it was the Undean memo."

"So what're you going to do with it?" Keyes asked, suddenly brisk and businesslike.

"That's exactly what I need to talk to you about. I could give it to a certain homicide cop I know, a guy named Pouncy, and he could probably nail Muriel with it because he's pretty smart and probably a damn good digger. I even thought that you and me oughta go talk to Muriel—maybe try and talk her into giving herself up."

"Muriel wouldn't agree to that," Keyes said.

"No? Well, she's sure gotta pay somehow for what she did. I mean, you can't murder three people and expect to get away with it. What the fuck kind of civilization would that be?"

Keyes sighed. "I have the feeling we're talking about money now."

"Did I mention money? Even once?"

"How much?" Keyes made his question sound old and tired.

"Well, for a million I guess I could forget all about Muriel Keyes and the Undean memo."

"A million in the morning and another million in the afternoon," Keyes said. "This must be one of your more profitable days."

"It could be," Haynes said. "Except for one thing."

"What?"

"There's something in that Undean memo that still itches me."

"What itches you, Mr. Haynes?"

"Call me Granny. Well, it's when Undean writes about how Isabelle bought it. He goes into a lot of gruesome detail. But Isabelle got killed Friday afternoon and the *Post* only ran a couple of short graphs on it Saturday. You know: Woman Slain, Cops Investigate. When did you hear about it?"

"I think it came in late Friday afternoon on one of the wire services. Maybe UPI."

"But would UPI give out her address and apartment number and the fact that her wrists and ankles were tied with coat-hanger wire? Or the fact that she'd been gagged? That's the one that really bothers me. The gag. Because she sure didn't have one in her mouth when Tinker and I found her. So how the hell could Undean write on Saturday that she'd been gagged when the cops didn't even know it until two P.M. Saturday when they found the gag in the trash and ran tests on it." Haynes paused, stared at Keyes and said, "You must've figured out what it means, Ham."

"Sorry."

"Well, shit, it means Undean didn't write the memo, that's what."

"Then who did?"

"The killer, that's who."

"Muriel?"

"You know something, I just changed my mind about Muriel. Here's how I figure it now. If you wanta forge something with a typewriter, you gotta be careful. So I think whoever forged the memo used Undean's office typewriter at Langley—probably used it while Undean was down at the Willard offering me fifty thou for Steady's manuscript. I think the forger made an original and a carbon, then destroyed the original. And after the forger got through killing Undean Sunday, the carbon was slipped under the old guy's desk blotter where the cops'd be sure to find it—if Tinker Burns hadn't found it first. And like I said, that memo nailed Muriel for Isabelle's murder plus all that mess in Laos. So why would she write it, much less leave it for the cops to find?"

"Finally, a good question," Keyes said.

"So maybe Muriel didn't kill anybody. Wonder why I didn't think of that before? But if I'm finally thinking straight, then you're the only one who could've forged that memo on Undean's typewriter out at Langley. So I guess you killed him. And if you knew about that gag in Isabelle's mouth, you must've stuffed it there, right? Either you or old Horse Purchase, who must've held her while you straightened out the coat hangers. Or was it the other way around? Never mind. And when poor old Tinker tried to blackmail you, what happened to him is kind of obvious. Jesus, Ham, you're a real menace."

"And you're certifiable," Keyes said as he reached down as if to adjust his seat either forward or backward.

The McCorkle Chief's Special appeared in Haynes's right hand. "Bring it up by the barrel, Mr. Keyes. Very, very slowly, if you don't mind."

Keyes froze in his slightly bent-over position, peering at the traffic ahead, his eyes barely above the top of the steering wheel. Finally, Keyes's left hand came into view, its thumb and three fingers holding a small .25-caliber Beretta semi-automatic by the barrel.

Haynes switched his revolver to his left hand and poked its muzzle into Keyes's right ear. Haynes's right hand reached for the Beretta. Once he had it, he slipped it into his topcoat's right-hand pocket, then removed the revolver from Keyes's ear.

"Mr. Keyes, I suggest we go around the block very slowly, then back down Connecticut and over to your house, where we'll have a talk with Mrs. Keyes."

"About money?"

"Possibly."

"Who were you?" Keyes said as he turned right off Connecticut to circle the block.

"When?"

"During the last twenty-five or thirty minutes?"

"Well, that was old Hardcase Haynes of Homicide."

"I didn't much like him."

"I've now reverted to what a friend has called my Mr. Manners role."

"I don't like him either," said Hamilton Keyes.

Forty-seven

Trailed by Haynes, Hamilton Keyes entered his living room at 11:28 A.M. to find McCorkle and Padillo seated side by side on a couch, eating liverwurst-on-rye sandwiches and drinking pale ale.

Muriel Keyes sat across from them in an easy chair, a glass of what looked like Scotch and very little water in her right hand, a cigarette in her left.

Hamilton Keyes stopped to glare first at Padillo, then at McCorkle. Haynes didn't stop and kept moving until he could press the revolver in his topcoat's right pocket against Keyes's back. Keyes ignored the pressure, turned to his wife and asked, "Why are they here?"

She smiled at him reassuringly. "They're trying to keep me out of jail, darling."

"What a pleasant way to say they're blackmailing us."

McCorkle looked at Haynes and said, "How much are we asking?"

"I mentioned a million," Haynes said.

McCorkle nodded contentedly. "Not a bad morning's work."

Padillo put down his glass, rose and went over to Keyes. "Can you understand me, Hamilton?"

"I can understand you perfectly, despite having·been subjected to the ravings of this loony who's now poking his gun into my back."

"He means me," Haynes said.

Padillo studied Keyes. "Okay. If you can understand me, let's go somewhere private and I'll explain just how deep the shit you're standing in really is."

"I think I might be better at that than you, Michael," Muriel Keyes said.

"All right. Fine."

"Come on, darling," she said. "We'll go in the library and talk."

Keyes sighed and looked around the nicely furnished room, as if estimating the damage his guests had done. "Well, why not?" he said, turned and headed toward the library. She followed him in, closed the door and turned the key in a sturdy-sounding lock.

Padillo turned to Haynes, who still stood in the center of the living room, his hands in his topcoat pockets. "How'd it go?"

Haynes shrugged. "He's tough."

"If you want to know somebody else tough," McCorkle said, "spend an hour or two with Muriel Keyes."

"Think there's a case?" Padillo said.

"With a lot of work, they might get him indicted," Haynes said. "But I'd lay six to five against conviction. Anyway, I think he's decided to go nuts." He glanced around the room and asked, "Any chance of a drink?"

Padillo went over to press the ivory-colored wall button. The Salvadoran maid materialized and Padillo asked if she could provide their new guest with a double measure of Scotch whisky. She said it would be her pleasure.

Haynes, his topcoat now draped over a chair, had nearly finished his whisky when he heard the library door being unlocked. Muriel Keyes came out and turned back to lock the door from the living room side. When she turned again she was aiming a Sauer semiautomatic at the living room in general.

"I know that gun from somewhere," McCorkle said.

She moved slightly so that the Sauer was aimed at him. "Hamilton wants five minutes or so to collect his thoughts," she said. "I think he should have the time." She turned yet again until she was aiming the Sauer at Padillo. "Then you can go in, Michael, and explain how deep the shit really is."

Haynes glanced at his watch and thought about edging toward the topcoat with its armory of two pistols. Instead, he leaned back in his chair and closed his eyes. McCorkle sipped his ale. Padillo kept his eyes on Muriel Keyes.

It seemed like a long five minutes, especially after another fifteen seconds were tacked on at the end. It was then, exactly fifteen seconds after the five minutes were up, that they heard the muffled gunshot in the library. Muriel Keyes walked over to a table and placed the Sauer on it.

"You can all go in now," she said.

McCorkle didn't move. Padillo kept staring at Muriel Keyes. Then Granville Haynes opened his eyes, looked at her and asked, "Why'd you bid against yourself? That was you on the phone with the senator, wasn't it—the mystery bidder?"

She nodded. "I was trying to help buy him an ambassadorship. Somewhere in the Caribbean. He thought he might enjoy it."

Haynes rose, moved over to the library door, unlocked it and went in. He came out less than a minute later and said, "Through the roof of his mouth and out the top of his head. He used a forty-five Colt. It's messy."

"What'd you say to him, Muriel?" Padillo asked.

"I told him I had cut off all his money but he didn't seem to believe me."

"Must've changed his mind," McCorkle said.

Padillo looked at Haynes. "He leave a note?"

Haynes shook his head.

Padillo switched his gaze back to Muriel Keyes. "Then you have a lot to be grateful for, Muriel. If he'd written the right note, you could be halfway to jail."

She seemed honestly puzzled. "I wonder why he didn't?"

When no one answered her question she turned and went into the library to make sure, McCorkle later claimed, that Hamilton Keyes was really dead.

Two days later, at 3:14 P.M. Thursday, Howard Mott received a call from Granville Haynes, who said he was phoning from Dulles International.

"It's about that million dollars, Howie."

"I was wondering whether it had slipped your mind."

"How much will taxes and your fee take—forty, forty-five percent?"

"Forget my fee. After all, I have my storied Cadillac. But state and Federal taxes'll take about forty percent, maybe a little more."

"Find a small liberal nondenominational freshwater college and set up a scholarship fund with whatever's left."

"Could be some rather nice tax relief for you in that."

"That occurred to me," Haynes said.

"What do you want to call it?"

"The Steadfast Haynes Scholarship Fund for Propaganda Analysis."

"You're making me cry," Howard Mott said.

On Friday, which was exactly a week to the day after they had buried Steadfast Haynes at Arlington, McCorkle waited outside customs and immigration at Dulles International. The flight from Frankfurt was an hour late and he had been waiting for almost ninety minutes.

He finally saw her, the tall woman with the helmet of gold-gray hair that looked almost like platinum. Then her

342

enormous eyes found him, as did her smile, which he suspected he couldn't live without.

She hurried toward him, carrying only the large shoulder bag she always carried, which was her sole luggage no matter how long or far the journey. McCorkle found himself trotting toward her. They kissed, hugged, then kissed again.

It was after the last kiss that Fredl McCorkle looked around and asked, "Where's Erika?"

"Out of town."

"Where's out of town?"

"California."

"Where in California exactly?"

"Los Angeles."

"Doing what?"

"Visiting a friend."

"Does the friend have a name?"

"Granville Haynes."

"Would this Granville Haynes be any relation to Steadfast Haynes and, please God, let him say no."

"His son."

"When's Erika coming home? Next week?"

"I don't think so."

"Next month?"

"I'm not sure."

"What happened, McCorkle?"

"Well," he said, "that's a long and rather curious story."